GET READY

"I can show you what's registered," Varda says, "and some of what's unregistered, through unofficial channels."

Which means, at some level, that Varda is not entirely official—has been cut free of the standard security protocols that control what an IA has access to and what is off limits. Maybe that's what was going on during the trip to Tiresias, why the IA has been less of a *boca* lately, more withdrawn and circumspect.

"How long have you been able to do this?" Rigo asks.

"Do what?"

"You know. Stream things you're not supposed to without getting caught. That sort of thing."

No answer.

"Varda?"

"Not now," the IA says. "I'll wash up my act later."

The walled garde͏‌‌   s.
Rigo finds himself s   el
room.

"What's going o   d
by the sudden shift

"They're coming for you," Varda says. "Get ready."

CLADE

MARK BUDZ

BANTAM BOOKS

CLADE
A Bantam Book / December 2003

Published by Bantam Dell
A Division of Random House, Inc.
New York, New York

ISBN-13: 978-0-553-58658-9

ISBN-10: 0-553-58658-0

Manufactured in the United States of America
Published simultaneously in Canada

OPM 10 9 8 7 6 5 4 3 2

For Marina,
rose of my heart

What can we gain by sailing to the moon if we are not able to cross the abyss that separates us from ourselves?

—Thomas Merton

1

TIRESIAS

ONE

It's late, almost dusk, when Rigo finally gets off work, grabs a quick bite to eat at Salmon Ella's, and catches the Bay to Bay shuttle from Monterey to visit his ailing mother in San Jose.

The air in the train is full of sniffers, strings of broad-spectrum glycoproteins that are the molecular equivalent of flypaper. Rigo imagines he can feel them infiltrating his clothes, probing his asshole, prying underneath his fingernails for illegal moleculars. As a countermeasure, he's taken precautions. A few minutes before boarding, he dosed himself with antisense blockers, sticky proteins that will attach to the sniffers and cripple them as effectively as two dogs locked in a frenzied coupling.

Rigo finds an empty seat near the back of his pod and hunches against the window, a narrow ribbon of

plastic bordered by a retail outlet for Armani bodyware on one side and a display case for Japanese bento
meals on the other. The train is carrying commuters,
starched suits and students taking classes at UCSC's
Fort Ord extension. A few stare out the tinted bubble
plastic, mesmerized by the blur of passing scenery, the
fiery sunset that has turned the peeling bark of the eucalyptus trees into reddish tinder. Others browse the
display case windows of various in-pod stores. But
most of the passengers are interfaced with their information agents, sending and receiving e-mail, tuned to
music, news, or digital video downloads. For the most
part, people keep to themselves, hidden behind the cellophane eyescreens of their wraparounds and shades,
talking only to their IAs or to themselves over the soft
insect buzz of flitcams.

It makes for a quiet trip.

At Blossom Hill Road, the pod detaches from the
train and Rigo's in terra cognita. Stepping from the
pod, into the dissonant jungle of scents and sounds
where he grew up is like slipping into a pair of ill-
fitting clothes he's outgrown. The fabric of his well-
being pinches uncomfortably at the seams.

He doesn't belong here. Not like Beto, who never
left. But for some reason, he can't seem to break free.
Something is always dragging him back. It's as if
there's no escape from the place, or who he was.

Rigo checks the time. Six-fifteen.

The neighborhood is just beginning to rouse itself
from catlike slumber. *Tígueres* are beginning to prowl
their territories, looking for customers. In another
few hours the streets of the barrio will be raging. Rigo
can feel the energy building up, like ozone, the air get-

ting ready to crackle, filled with the wild spray of photons.

Sweat breaks out under his arms. His neck feels clammy.

Place hasn't changed much since he was a kid. Sure, new buildings have grown in, like weeds, to replace those that have been torn down—but many of the stores, aps, and residential houses are no different. Some have undergone cosmetic changes, retrofits for solar panels, humidity collectors, photovoltaic windows, and piezoelectric siding, to make them more energy efficient and ecologically sound. Chihuahua Noodles is still on the corner next to OD, the Online Discount store, The Steak Out, and w@ng's tattune parlor. But there are a lot more restaurants and stores that cater only to clade-specific clientele. He passes a dance salon that exudes a floral aroma that makes his eyes water; his skin itches as he approaches the open doorway of a wine-tasting club. The watery eyes and itch warn him to steer clear, advise him in no uncertain terms that he's persona non grata.

Rigo hurries on, rubs his arms through his sprayon shirt. Breathes in the dusty-olive smell of circuitrees, the roasted almond aroma of umbrella palms and other gengineered flora developed after the ecocaust. In addition to preventing total climactic collapse, public-domain ecotecture generates heat and electricity, purifies water, filters air, blocks UV rays, and provides a variety of other civic services, including waste disposal and bioremediation. Of course, a lot of private-domain ecotecture has been added over the years, creating a real laissez-faire biosystem that's nearly as diverse as the one it replaced.

The *tígueres* eye him warily, yet keep their distance. They spec he's not one of them but seem to know that he belongs here, is part of the ghetto community. It's as if he's still scented with his past. They can smell it on him, and recognize the odor as their own. Out of habit, his face hardens, his lips press tight, his eyes steel, and his jaw muscles bunch. As long as he keeps to himself, doesn't make direct eye contact, they won't be tempted to challenge him.

"Rigo?" his information agent says. The cochlear whisper is a nagging high-pitched whine marinated in a nondescript Asian accent mined from the mediasphere.

"What is it?" he asks, annoyed. As luck would have it, he ended up with a neurotic older sister for an IA. Varda.

"What are you trying to conceal on your person?" the nosy hyperware asks.

"None of your business."

"It's illegal." A stray molecule must have slipped into his bloodstream, shown up in a routine biomed readout.

"I'm trying to help my mother," he explains in his defense.

"Well, this is hardly the best way to do it. You could end up in jail. What kind of help is that?" For some reason the hypervigilant Varda believes it's its job to look after him. Keep him out of trouble.

"I know what I'm doing," he says.

"Famous last words. If you're not careful, you're going to end up pregnant without a paddle."

Varda's penchant for malapropisms, disfigured metaphors, and leaps of illogic is well-intentioned and endearing, but not always helpful.

"We can discuss this later," he says.

"So you're just going to ignore me," the IA says. "Like always."

As Rigo crosses the street to his mother's aplex, dodging hydrogen fuel cell motorcycles and electric two-seaters, he hears the playful melody of steel drums, bright as sunlight reflecting off waves. The pan player is busking on a corner, half a block down. He's wearing colorful badris shorts, a black leather jacket, and sandals. Instead of hair he's got a dreadlock tangle of Guatemalan beads.

The carbonated music lightens his mood. Each metallic note, pure and carefree, bubbles irreverently inside him, fizzing like laughter against the hollow shell he's built to protect himself. The reverberations shiver through him, break down the rigid pattern of atoms that comprise his attitude. Climbing the stairs to his mother's second floor ap, he feels a momentary buoyancy. A giddy zero-g suspension that leaves him mildly disoriented. Not quite himself.

At the landing, halfway up, he turns the corner and bumps into a skinny *tíguere*. Rigo blinks, takes a step back just as the *tíguere*'s right hand flicks toward him, quick as the tongue of a snake.

Rigo raises both hands, palms out. "*Oye, ese.* Easy."

The man squints at him. "Rigo?" The diamond blade, only a few hundred atoms thick and nearly invisible, wavers a moment before slithering out of view.

Pattern recognition kicks in: hollow cheeks, black close-set eyes, a mustache that resembles ripe refrigerator mold, and a gemstone-encrusted scalp. The gemstones threw him for a loop. Pink coral, opals, jade, sapphires. A real flaunt job. Rigo thought he was dealing with some upper-clade fuck, slumming in the barrio.

"Chuy." Rigo lowers his hands, feels his bowels uncoil. The dome of gems looks for all the world like the business end of a rhinestone-studded condom.

Well, Chuy always was a *pendejo*. As a *tiguerito*, back when they were both in grade and middle school, Chuy worked as an escort for slum-hounds, upper-clade clients looking to buy or sell black market goods in the barrio. He provided protection, guided them to where they needed to conduct business. Odds are he's performing the same service, but for a somewhat more eccentric patronage, judging by his coiffure.

The *tíguere* sniffs, wipes his nose. "*Que carajo quieres?* What are you doing here?"

"Visiting my moms." Rigo resists the urge to ask what Chuy's doing around his mother's ap building.

"Been a long time since I seen you." Chuy's eyes are all jittery. They roll loose in his sockets like one of those outdated, liquid-filled compasses that's always shifting direction.

"Been busy," Rigo says. "So. How's tricks these days?"

Chuy's slitted gaze, rock hard, settles on him for a moment. "You know. A little of this, little of that." He jukes his shoulders from side to side and grins, baring stiletto teeth. "What about you? Still sucking up? Kissing ass?"

Rigo stiffens. "That's harsh, man."

"Naw. It's a fact. You got out and sold out." Chuy grinds his teeth and breathes out. Rigo catches a whiff of burnt vanilla. The scent turns his knees to rubber, threatens to loosen his bladder.

"I'm surprised you're willing to show your face around here," Chuy says. He grabs his crotch and gives it a squeeze. "You got more *cojones* than I gave you credit for."

Rigo squirms, fighting the urge to wet his pants. "What're you talkin' about?"

"I guess *la gente de primera* figured they'd get an ex homeboy to check up on the lower classes. No sense riskin' their own ass. Not when they got a *lambioso* to do the job for them."

"Fuck you."

Chuy puckers his lips, makes a kissing sound.

Rigo takes a half step back from the badass pherion Chuy's putting out. The artificial hormone is getting seriously uncomfortable. If he hangs around much longer, things could get embarrassing.

Chuy thrusts out his chin. "My advice to you, *ese*, is to get your ass out of here while you can." He pushes past Rigo. "*Sola vaya.*"

Good riddance. And not a moment too soon. As soon as Chuy rounds the corner, Rigo bolts up the stairs, taking them two at a time. At the second-floor balcony, he pauses to suck in a few deep breaths and regain control of his urinary tract. Fucking Chuy.

"If you keep this up," Varda says, still in nag mode, "you're going to make love with the fishes."

"Sleep," he says, correcting the IA.

"Are you tired?"

Rigo shakes his head. Why does he bother?

From where he's standing he can see the lights of Silicon Valley, high-intensity halogen and xenon that metastasize north toward San Francisco, the Golden Gate Bridge and beyond. In the middle of all this, barricaded behind a hodgepodge of dikes, Los Altos, Menlo Park, and Redwood City raise their geek-chic hauteur over the submerged sections of Cupertino, Mountain View, and Palo Alto. Beneath custom ecotecture of powder-puff dandelion trees, most of Silicon Valley's condos, aplexes, stores, and bars form a data Eden that Rigo will never access. SV has some of the most advanced pherion encryption, decryption, and antipher defenses around. Homegrown pharmware that even the politicorps can't decode.

He's known *tígueres* who tried to crash some of the more exotic SM parlors, ones offering somatic recordings of kinky sex with sheep, horses, and a variety of undomesticated animals. The *tígueres* didn't stay long. Came back nauseous, covered with rashes. Some—those who had to be physically removed after succumbing to pherion poisoning—suffered lingering nerve damage, minor paralysis they wear proudly as a badge of courage. These *tígueres* are respected by some, but derided by others. They're easy to spot on the streets—poor motherfuckers crippled by defiance, bitter that they have nothing else to show for their bravado.

The wages of spite, his mother would say.

Rigo was always too cautious to put himself at risk. *Un niño pijo*, an elitist snob, according to Beto, who still has a spasm in the corner of one eye and chides Rigo good-naturedly but mercilessly about his *aspirations.* As with a lot of brothers, there's a hidden undercurrent, an unspoken subtext that's meant to accuse and shame him—as if Rigo's committed a crime by wanting to better himself.

Is that why he's agreed to deliver the pharm-bred meds to their mother? To prove to Beto that he has the balls? Or is it because he knows that Mama will never accept the drug if she knows it's from Beto? That Rigo's the only one who has a chance of getting her to take them?

Rigo presses a fingertip to the iDNA button on the ap's door, sees the little pad turn green in recognition. Instead of having her IA unlock the door, his mother insists on answering it herself. She's old-fashioned that way. Never mind that he has to stand there for five minutes while she struggles across the room. From her point of view, it would be impolite not to invite him in personally. Rigo listens to her labored breath through the door—a shallow palpitating wheeze that makes him dizzy. He gets oxygen deficient just listening to her. From the sound of things she could be climbing Everest. Finally, about six dead bolts click and the door swings open.

"*Mijo,*" she gasps, managing to affect both surprise and delight. "It's good to see you." Caged by recalcitrant ribs, her lungs refuse to fully inflate. Her jaws barely move, slurring the words.

"How's it going, Mama?"

"I've been watching DVDs all day. My feet are a little numb from sitting, but not too bad."

The wallscreen opposite the couch is tuned to an ancient black-and-white movie. Stark grainy images animate the glass, like shadows moving behind a curtain. She wasn't even alive when this stuff was filmed. But for some reason she's addicted. There's something atavistic about the personas that comforts her, smoothes away the rough-edged complexity of the present.

"Let me help you, Mama."

He takes one of her hands. It's warm, dry, and gnarled. Her knuckles are the size of peach pits, her fingers stiff as dried roots. It hurts to touch them. The sagging wrinkled skin of her arm is loose as an elephant's. She's wearing a red cotton print dress, sleeveless, that exposes her misshapen elbows and gnomish knees.

Late-onset fibrodysplasia ossificans progressiva. FOP. The disease has begun to turn her tendons and muscles into bone, solder her skeleton into a single, rigid piece. Ribbons, plates, and stalactites of bone are forming inside her. In a couple of months, when her joints fuse completely, she'll be a statue, something birds can perch on in a park. The condition is painful to look at. He thought it would get easier to deal with each visit. But it hasn't. It's worse than ever.

Well, this time he can offer more than sympathy.

She winces as he guides her across the living room, gritting her teeth with pain, effort, or both.

"Let go," she says, disengaging her hand and shooing him away. "I'm fine."

Tottering heavily for a moment she steadies herself, attains a precarious balance, as if the tidal pull of the moon is enough to disturb the delicate play of forces at work in her joints. A bead of sweat forms on one temple, releasing the smell of the lavender soap and rose-scented shampoo. Her breath smells of raw cloves, which she chews to combat halitosis.

Uncertain if it's okay to let go, Rigo hovers beside her, one hand on her arm, ready to catch her if she falls. In response, her black eyes flash, bright as Apache teardrops in sunlight. She tucks a few strands of woolen gray hair into the long braid that trails down her neck, frayed as a horse's tail at the end, and then hobbles toward the kitchen.

Rigo follows her. Memories dust the beige lichen walls, peeling bioluminescent strips, and age-yellowed windows. It feels like he's walking through a museum. Pictures of him and Beto hang on the walls, side by side with the Virgin Mary and several crucifixes. There's a little shrine on a table against one wall, decorated with flowers, pictures of the saints, and half-melted candles. The tapers look sad and weepy, hardened tears puddled on the doilies at their bases. The worn furniture is polished, the threadbare rug dirt-free. Through the sliding glass door at the far end of the room, plants are visible on the little railed balcony. A hanging garden of herbs, flowers, and vegetables.

"I saw Chuy," Rigo tells her, by way of conversation. "He was leaving just as I got here."

"Lucky you."

"Any idea what he was doing here?"

She shakes her head. "Who cares?" Not even an ounce of curiosity in her recalcitrant bones. "I was just about to fix dinner." She opens the refrigerator and starts laying vegetables on the counter. "Kung pao chicken. Your favorite."

He hadn't planned to stay. He'd planned to swing by, drop off the meds, and then hang with Anthea for the rest of the night. But now he feels guilty, like he doesn't have a choice.

"Okay." He forces a smile. "But only if you let me give you a hand."

When the chicken is cooked and the vegetables are steaming away in the wok, Rigo excuses himself. In the bathroom he instructs Varda to send a message to Anthea, telling her he'll be late—he's at his mother's—and apologizing, saying how sorry he is. Hopefully, Anthea will understand. Won't be too upset.

Just as he finishes taking a leak, Rigo gets a call from Beto. Great, the last thing he needs. Rigo fumbles on his pair of wraparound shades.

"How's Mama?" Beto asks, his face blossoming on the wraparound windows of the shades. "She going to take the meds I gave you?"

Rigo frowns at the image of his older half-brother. Unlike Rigo—who's a light-skinned *guero*—Beto's a pure, stringy-muscled *moreno* with more hair on his upper lip than his head. His eyes are a jaundiced, predatory yellow.

"I haven't given them to her yet," Rigo says. His flitcam hovers in front of him, bitmapping his image.

"What the hell you waiting for?"

"The right moment." With Mama, timing is everything. "You know how she is. Can't rush her into nothing."

"Yeah." Beto sniffs. "It's a miracle we were ever conceived."

"Don't worry," Rigo says. "I got it all figured out, how I'm going to play it."

Beto rubs his jaw, distracted. "Listen," he says. "I need to see you later tonight. As soon as you're done visiting Mama."

"What about?"

"We can discuss it later." Cagey.

Rigo furrows his brow, hoping to conceal his reluctance. "I don't know, bro. I'm pretty busy."

A muscle under Beto's left eye jerks. The tic yanks the lower lid to one side, as if he's been snagged by a fish hook. "You're as bad as Mama, you know that?" Beto says with what feels like only half-feigned derision. "Always got to sweet-talk your ass to get you to do anything."

"All right." Rigo gnaws his lip. This is a mistake, no doubt, but for some reason he can't stop himself. Can't say no. "Where?"

Beto squirts him the coordinates. "Like to see you by eight, bro. No later."

Rigo shakes his head. It's already six. No way Mama is going to let him leave in a half hour so he can pod down. "Eight-thirty," he says.

Beto nods. "No later, bro. I'm countin' on you. Don't be late."

His image fades, leaving behind a residue of unease that settles over Rigo like radioactive fallout. Back in the kitchen, his mother has set the table, and the air is saturated with the mouth-watering aroma of sesame oil, peanuts, and spicy red peppers.

*   *   *

After dinner, when the dishes are washed, they head back to the living room and sit together on the couch.

"How are you doing, Mama? Seriously."

"The stairs are a pain," she admits. "It takes a long time, and I'm tired afterward. Stiff as a board."

She's tried to swap aps with tenants on the first floor, change up buildings even, without luck. One of these days she's going to fall. It's inevitable.

"Why do you have to climb them at all?" he says. "You can get someone to pick up stuff at the store for you. The priest can come here to give you communion, listen to your confession."

"Going to church and the market is the only exercise I get. It's not that far—only three blocks. I can do three blocks."

She's always been a saint that way, torturing herself when she doesn't have to—as if suffering is the one way to cleanse herself, demonstrate her love for God.

"Pain is like fire," she once told him. "It burns away the sins of the flesh, purifies the soul."

Maybe she believes that if she suffers enough, God will take pity on her, decide to turn her into a miracle. Rigo has never understood that kind of devotion and self-sacrifice. It's incomprehensible to him, no different from the voices a schizophrenic hears. All he can do is bite his tongue and let her do what she wants. For him there are no miracles in the world, only reprieves.

"I hope you're right," he says.

"Just 'cause you got a decent job don't mean you

know what's what any more than I do. You just think you do."

Rigo takes out the small plastic bottle from one of his shirt pockets and hands it to her. The drug is a black-market generic cooked up by the pharm Beto rustles for. Supposedly, it's an alternative to the legal FDA-approved medication she doesn't have health coverage for and can't afford to buy on what social security and disability pays. She worked forty years without ever going on the welfare roll, raised two kids, and now she can't even get benefits.

"What's this?" She holds the bottle up, inspecting it like a crow examining road kill.

"Herbal supplement," Rigo says. "It's supposed to help reduce inflammation. I picked it up at The Food Chain." The Food Chain is a conglomerate of natural food stores that sell certified organic produce, vitamins and herbs. Rigo removed the original capsules from the bottle and replaced them with the tablets supplied by Beto.

She turns her head, fixes him with one bird-bright eye. "I never heard about this stuff. How do you know it's safe?"

"It's off the shelf, Mama. It wouldn't be over-the-counter if it wasn't safe."

"Hah! The Food and Drug rubber stamps whatever the politicorps tell it to."

"At least give it a try," he says, reasonably. "If it doesn't work, you're no worse off than you are now."

"I don't know."

"It's up to you," he says, shrugging.

She opens the bottle, pries off the tamper-proof seal he has meticulously glued back on, and sniffs the meds. Outside, through the living room window, the neighborhood is lit up. Glare from store signs and streetlights paints the walls, washes the ceiling through the panes of crinkly cellulose. Neon condensation drips from the canopy of palms, trailing phosphor streaks against the sky.

After a moment his mother sighs, shakes out a tab and washes it down with a glass of water sitting on the coffee table. She sets the glass down and settles back into the couch, looking suddenly tired and defeated, resigned to her condition.

"When are you going to see a doctor?" He's lost count of how many times he's asked her this. Often enough to be a ritual. If he doesn't pester her she feels neglected.

"I can't afford to see a doctor." Her usual excuse. She pats him on the leg. "What I really need is to get out of here. I've been thinking of applying for relocation to a subclade. One that offers medical."

"That's crazy." Most subclades are politicorp subsidized. Normally relocs are trained for a specific job in the sponsor corporation, then shuttled off to an environmental reclamation project or agrifactory in some drought-ravaged region of the world. The housing is flimsy prefabs, the food surplus stock. The good thing is the use of pherions is strictly controlled, limited to those approved by the politicorp for the emotional well-being of the community. There are no clades, no pherion-induced social order or economic stratification. Everyone gets along, more or less.

The problem is, no subclade will take his mother in her present condition. She's a liability, an economic invalid.

"I'm thinking of a church-sponsored one," she says. "Or a nonprofit that does charity work."

"What?" Rigo says. "You want to be a missionary? Live in some wasteland like the Mekong desert or the Texas-Louisiana dust belt?"

"I don't know what else to do," she says.

Rigo knows what he should do. He should offer to put her up. Take care of her. Make her feel useful. But he can't. The words won't come. He only has a one-bedroom ap. He'll end up sleeping on the couch.

That's not the real reason, though. The real reason is that it will be no different than growing up in the same ap with her. She'll infiltrate his life. It will be like he never left. He won't be able to breathe. Anthea won't be able to come over—and if he spends the night over at her ap it won't be long before his mother is pressuring them to get married. She's traditional that way. Frowns on lack of commitment.

Still . . .

"You want to stay at my place for a while?" he hears himself say. "Just until you figure out what to do?"

"I don't want to be a burden," she says.

"You wouldn't be." Unlike a regular lie, it's ironic how a white lie can injure the person telling it.

"I'm not going to impose on you." The forcefulness of her rebuff surprises him. Fills him with relief.

"Well, I'm not going to try to make you do anything you don't want. It's up to you."

"What I really want to do," she tells him, "is stay in the neighborhood. This is where I grew up, and this is where I want to die."

Her talk of death unnerves him, seems premature.

"Mama, you have half your life ahead of you. You're only in your sixties."

"Listen to you." Her tone is stringent, full of reproof. "I knew that working for a politicorp would blind you. Give you false hopes and unrealistic expectations."

"What does my job have to do with anything?"

His mother adjusts the hem of her dress over her knees. "You're forgetting where you come from."

"Maybe I don't want to remember," he says before he can stop himself. "Maybe I want to look ahead, instead of behind."

Her face puckers. "What makes you think the future will be any better?"

In rebuking the past, he's rebuked her, the way she raised him. "Look," he says. "I'm sorry. I didn't mean it that way."

"It's okay." Her tone is gentle. Forgiving. "Everything will work out, *mijo*. You just have to have faith."

Her answer to everything, her daily bread. "I think maybe it skipped a generation with me," he says.

"Everyone is born with faith." Her eyes flare, bright as votive candles against an incursion of shadows. "The hard part is to not lose it."

TWO

After the heart-to-heart with his mother, Rigo takes the Bay to Bay to South South San Jose. Has Varda direct the pod to the address Beto squirted him. The trip is a total voyage into the heart of darkness. He's moody, his evening dirty-dicked by whatever bullshit his brother is going to lay on him. Well, he'll make it quick. Listen to what Beto has to say and exit stage left.

"You seem in trouble," Varda says.

"You could say that." Troubled. The story of his life.

"Are you in some kind of jelly?"

"Jam," Rigo corrects, too morose even to shake his head.

"I didn't know you were having toast," the IA says.

"Toast is what I have a feeling I'm going to be in a little while."

"Really? What are we celebrating?"

Hopeless, Rigo decides for the n-teenth time. A lost cause.

His pod detaches from the train near an abandoned office park at the edge of South South San's public ecotecture zone. Most of the office buildings are mothballed, waiting private redevelopment. The pod drops him off in front of a two-story curtain glass that's partially retrofitted with skylights and windows of photovoltaic cellulose, yellow with age and the texture of dried aspic. The feeble, bioluminescent sheen of light-emitting bacteria wafts through a few windows, giving the facade a gap-toothed look.

Maybe this is a corporate front for the black-market pharm Beto rustles for, to lend it some semblance of legitimacy.

The main double doors are unlocked. Rigo steps into the entry foyer, a hollow, gaping emptiness that sags inward like a collapsed lung the moment the door swings shut behind him. Only the faint outward pressure of light from a zebra pattern of biolum strips on the ceiling and walls keeps him from suffocating. He walks past what was once a receptionist's desk to another set of doors, locked. Great. Now what?

A faint insect whine assaults his right ear. He turns toward the flitcam, can't see it in the dim light. A moment later the door in front of him opens.

"It's about time." Beto, framed in darkness, gestures for Rigo to follow him into the building.

They step onto big squares of pressed lichenboard laid down on the concrete and tattered carpet. The boards—relatively new—harbor deodorizers, molecular disassemblers, and sterilizing bots. They release a pleasant aroma, a mixture of lavender and clove that barely masks an ammonia-laden undercurrent of urine.

As Rigo's eyes adjust, the interior space gradually solidifies, takes shape. "Nice place you got."

Overhead, a latticework of aluminum joists and beams support a Rubick array of plastic cubes. Tiny, densely packed rooms, stacked in layers, and accessed by ladders and catwalks. Blankets and foam padding cover the floors of some cubes, creating a colorful patchwork. In other cubes, Rigo can discern the splayed silhouettes of bodies sprawled in midair.

"Let's go to my office," Beto suggests.

At a ladder tucked between two rows of cubes set on the floor, Beto grips the rails and hauls himself upward. Boots clanking on the steps, Rigo follows him up several levels to a narrow gangway. Looking down, Rigo sees that people have draped blankets, black plastic, or cardboard over the walls, ceilings, and floors of the cubes to create private compartments. Between their footsteps, Rigo hears the metronome plop of water from one of the drip lines feeding the cubes. Tick tick. Steady as a clock.

"In here," Beto says. He slides aside a panel to one of the cubes, shuts it behind them.

An Oriental rug covers the scratched plastic floor. Colorful crepe-paper lanterns dangle from the ceiling, casting an eerie red glow. A wicker-frame papasan occupies one wall, sits across from a foldable desk. The cube butts up against a window in the curtain-glass skin of the building, offering a view to the north of the San Francisco Bay. Every now and then a train streaks by, slithering through the valley like entwined eels that separate and rejoin in a ballet of silver flashes.

Rigo turns back to the cubicles. They remind him of a laboratory maze, filled with rats. "Who are all these people?"

"Guests."

Rigo settles into the papasan. "Like in a hotel?"

Beto ignores his sarcasm. "Something like that. Tourists who have no place else to go for a vacation."

"Some vacation."

Beto waves a hand, circumspect. He walks behind his desk and eyes Rigo with a jaundiced, predatory gaze. "I need your help, bro."

Rigo tenses. Here it comes.

Beto leans forward, bracing his hands on the front edge of the desk. "I need you to make another delivery."

Rigo shakes his head, pushes himself out of the gelbag to leave. "Sorry, man. I already told you. The job for Mama was a onetime deal." It was a mistake to come. He should have begged off. Listened to his better judgment.

"Just hear what I got to say," Beto says. "Don't be a complete *pendejo* for once. Okay?"

It never fails. Beto has a way of making him feel like a traitor. Rigo slumps back into the gelbag. "I'm listening."

"It's the same kind of shit you took to Mama." Beto runs a hand over his glossy pate. "The same kind of situation."

"A sick person?"

"Right." Beto straightens, starts to pace. "No insurance. Can't afford to pay for treatment. The usual."

"Sick with what?"

Beto pauses. "What difference does it make?"

"I want to know."

"Aphasia," Beto says. Then, "It's when your brain starts to shrink and you start to lose all motor control. Can't walk. Can't talk."

Rigo sucks on his teeth. Thinks about his mother. The pinch she'd be in if there was no one to help her.

"Who is it?" he asks.

Beto sighs. "You don't need to know. It's better that way. Safer. What's important is that if the person doesn't get help, that's it. End of story."

Rigo rubs his face with both hands, massages the tension from his forehead with blunt fingertips. "Why me?"

"Because something else has come up. Talented as I am, I can't be in two places at once."

Rigo peers through the gaps in his fingers, as if looking at Beto from between the bars of a cage. "There must be someone else you can get."

"There isn't, bro. If there was, I wouldn't be asking you." Beto spreads his hands. "To be honest, you were not my first choice. But I don't have a choice. That's how desperate I am."

"Where's the delivery?" Rigo cradles his head. He can't believe he's thinking of doing this. He must be out of his mind.

"Salmon Ella's."

Rigo looks up. Blinks. "Word?"

"Word. I shit you not."

"What time?" If he's lucky, maybe he won't be seen by anyone he knows from work or his aplex.

"Tonight. Nine-thirty."

Rigo lowers his hands, shakes his head. "I can't. I'm supposed to hook up with Anthea."

"You should dump that bitch," Beto says. He's never warmed to Anthea, keeps their relationship civil but cool. "How'd you get so hooked on that scrawny *puta*, anyway? It's like you have an addictive personality or something, bro."

"I can't help it, bro. I'm in love." What else can he say? He shrugs, stands, too agitated to sit.

"It's a sickness, man. A sexually transmitted disease." Beto grins. "You should cure yourself."

"And end up like you?" Rigo asks.

The grin widens with playful malice. "There're worse things that could happen."

"Yeah?"

Beto flips him an obscene gesture. "Look at yourself, bro. You're turning into a fucking *tutumpote*. Oppressing the poor so you can be a success, a big-time *sucio*."

An asshole. Rigo's heard it all before: anybody who extricates himself from the ghetto to improve his socioeconomic standing is a sellout. It's the kind of inbred, self-defeatest attitude that gets passed down the germline, ad infinitum, and keeps the working class downtrodden. "At least I'm legit," he says.

Beto snorts. "You're a prisoner of the establishment, bro. You just can't see the bars."

Rigo gestures to the surrounding cubes. "Like you're any freer than I am."

"At least I'm not busting my *cojones* like some

dumbass dog at a track. Chasing after some rabbit I'm never going to catch. Isn't even real."

The repartee has a cathartic effect. Calming. It clears the air, eases some of the friction between them. As kids, they always felt better after a fight. Closer.

"You're really stuck on that *jeva*," Beto says.

Rigo shrugs. "No problem. I'll tell her I have to go back to work, finish up some stuff before we do our thing. She'll understand."

Beto gives him the drop instructions and the drug, then punches him hard in the right biceps. "Remember, it's for a good cause. Just don't get caught and you'll be all right."

The Monterey shuttle pod, capable of carrying up to thirty passengers, is mostly empty. Rigo sits in back, near a young businesswoman wearing a cardboard stiff suit-*cum*-flamboyant green ascot, and a disheveled *viejo* who's dozing, his silver hair mashed against the window. Ten minutes after the pod slots onto the fast-moving maglev, it slots off at the Cannery Row substation. From there, it's a quick stroll to Salmon Ella's. From outside, the place has been styled to mimic a corrugated sheet-metal warehouse. Inside, a labyrinth of rice paper partitions grid out around renovated conveyor belts, overhead spray nozzles, rinsing troughs, and other antiquated fish processing equipment. Basically, it's a cross between a museum, an old sardine factory, and a Tokyo teahouse. Open grills line one wall, barbecuing farm-bred salmon steaks and fillets.

Rigo slinks into the appropriate cubicle, which is unoccupied, and sits at a black lacquered table under colorful paper lanterns. The lanterns are round, cylindrical, or square, and decorated with flowers, mountains, or other natural scenery. They dangle from the metal ceiling joists on invisible monomol filaments that make it look as if they are floating in place. Soon, a waitperson stops by. Rigo orders a Corona, sips, feels himself sliding into a melancholy funk that's in danger of becoming a nasty brood. The music, some kind of European techno-Goth he normally wouldn't mind, doesn't help.

When he's thoroughly depressed, an old woman approaches the table and slides in to the seat across from him.

"I feel like a castle in a corner," Varda says.

Rigo offlines the IA. Chess has never been one of his fortes.

"Thank you for coming," the woman says, all polite, as if they're having crumpets and tea. She's wearing a silver lamé skirt the size of a parachute, a purple long-sleeved blouse that covers her arms, and about twenty kilos of African beads in the form of necklaces, earrings, and bracelets. Her face doesn't look old—but he can see it in her shrunken blue eyes, the way they've retreated from the world. She smiles, thin lips the color and texture of vulcanized rubber. Up close, her movements are jerky. In addition to surgically smooth flesh she has nanimatronic grafts, a mesh exoskeleton that damps the tremors in her muscles. She's a prisoner, dying by degrees in her chainmail cage.

"Can I get you anything?" she asks.

"Just what I came for." He picks up the folded napkin from his lap, wipes his mouth, then rests his hand with the crumpled cloth on the table.

The woman digs in her purse, pulls out a transfer card, and sets it on the table in front of them.

"It's in the napkin," Rigo tells her. He removes his hand, reaches for the card a few centimeters away.

Just as he's sliding the plastic toward him, her fingers, dry, cool, and plaintive, touch his. "Wait," she says.

Rigo makes a show of glancing at his wristwatch. The point being that he has to be someplace else soon. He'd like to indulge her, but . . .

"I'll make it worth your while," she says.

For a second Rigo wonders if he's misheard. But her fingers have curled tight around the back of his hand and wrist, like the jaws of a Venus's-flytrap clamping shut to digest him.

"Why?" he asks, thinking to humiliate her—that maybe shame will disengage her hand. Scald her.

"What difference does it make?"

Her eyes are reptilian. Rigo can read nothing behind her watery pupils, slitted with purpose. She's incomprehensible—a total fucking alien. What does she expect from him? Pity? Sympathy?

"Is it contagious?" Rigo asks, wondering if he can trust her to tell the truth.

"No."

"I'm not a Necrofeel," he says, indignant.

She doesn't so much as blink at the insult. She's beyond anger, it seems. Beyond shame. "I'm not dead."

Yet, Rigo thinks, finishing the unspoken end of the sentence, the part that she refuses to admit. She wants him to make her feel alive, to stand in the way of death like a human sacrifice.

"I'm sorry," Rigo says. "I can't help you." His vitriol has suddenly dried up, evaporated like piss on hot metal.

This does the trick, though not in the way he intended. Her eyes soften. "Me, too." As if he's just turned down a winning lottery ticket. With a sigh, she releases him and closes her fingers around the napkin. Before he can do anything, she eases out of her seat and leaves.

Podding to Anthea's, it occurs to him that what she bought from the pharm might not have been intended to prolong life.

Shit, Rigo thinks. He's shaking, convulsed by something he can't explain that makes him feel five years old again.

It's after ten-thirty by the time Rigo gets to Anthea's ap. Josué, Anthea's seven-year-old nephew, is still awake and throwing a tantrum in the bedroom. Anthea watches Josué five or six nights a week, while her sister Malina works graveyard down at a desalination plant a little farther up the bay.

Malina. Mal for short—*bad*. But not to her face, unless Rigo wants to get his ass kicked. Her temper can be as short as her truncated name, so he avoids her whenever he can. If it weren't for him and Beto, he'd find it hard to believe that Malina and Anthea are related. On the surface they have almost nothing in common. What's amazing is that despite their personality differences, they still get along. But maybe it's different for sisters than it is for brothers.

"One more game," Josué wails, his voice sulky. "Please? I'm not tired."

Anthea talks to him at length. Rigo can't hear the words, only the soft dovelike cooing of quiet logic and reason. He knows that voice, cajoling. She's used it on him before.

Josué's having none of it. He stamps his feet. Cries. The racket is only partly muffled by the parchment thin walls. One thing about fights is that they cut down on the electricity. Rigo can feel the ap vibrating, all that sonic and mechanical energy being converted by embedded piezoelectrics.

Rigo snags a Corona from the fridge, flops on the couch, and turns on the wallscreen to drown out the noise. It's an interactive setup, so Rigo links his IA into the display.

Grainy flitcam images from *ION*, an independent netzine that Anthea subscribes to, fill the wallscreen. Currently, during a news segment called subversION, the site is broadcasting undercover from an Indonesian sweatshop. An image of twelve-and-under kids pixilates. The kids are doing piecework, assembling riboware in the sweltering humidity of a sheet-metal hothouse.

Rigo shifts uneasily on the couch, takes a full swig of beer to wet his dry mouth and wash away the unease left by the dying woman. He resists the urge to scratch the spot where her embalmed fingers clutched his hand and wrist.

"See if you can dig up something else to watch," he

tells Varda. "Something more relaxing." The download Anthea has the screen tuned to is relentlessly depressing. An electronically fuzzed voice-over of an ICLU rep talks about efforts being made to free the sweatshop kids and place them in foster homes.

While Varda mines the mediasphere for Woody Allen reruns, Anthea walks in. It's hard to tell if the scratches on her face and arms are from Josué or some kid at the counseling center who went ballistic on her. It looks like she's gone ten rounds. There are black half-moons under her eyes, penumbras of fatigue. She's wearing skimpy red shorts and a sleeveless white cotton blouse. She grabs a beer from the kitchenette, plops down beside him, sharp elbows and hips denting the cushion.

"What's up with Josué?" he asks.

"I'll tell you later, after I calm down." She's bird thin, looks too skinny at the age of thirty to ever have a kid of her own. Which is too bad, because she's mad crazy about kids, super with Josué, and would make a great mother. "How's your mom?" she says.

Rigo strokes her leg while he tells her about his mother's steadily deteriorating condition, the pharmbred drug, and his thoughts about what to do with her if it doesn't work. The ugly gang scarring on Anthea's thighs hasn't started to pucker yet. In another few years, she'll need skin grafts to get rid of the dreamlike squiggles carved into her, hallucinatory glyphs that scare the crap out of him but are also a turn-on.

"That's terrible," Anthea says when he's done.

"I don't know what to do," he confesses. "She won't listen to me. I'm at a total loss."

"It's up to her. She's old enough to decide what she wants. Doesn't need you telling her what to do. If she wants advice, or help, she'll ask for it."

Maybe. Maybe not. Anthea doesn't know his mother like he does.

They chill for a while. Her skin is soft, the stroking meditative. Rigo can feel the beer going to work on her, unknotting muscles. The moment drags on, comfortable. Eternal. With Anthea, it's always this way. From the very beginning they clicked, were attracted to each other like subatomic particles. He trusts her, feels like they can talk about anything, no matter how intimate. There are no secrets between them. She's not like some of the back-stabbing *cabronas* he's gone out with who lie, say one thing and then do another. With Anthea he won't get hurt, knows exactly where he stands.

When the subversION segment ends another one starts up, perversION. Anthea sets her empty beer on the floor and turns to him. Her eyes are bright, as if they've soaked up all the light from the screen. She leans forward, hair spilling down in front of her eyes, and pecks him on the nose.

"Is that all I get?" he says.

She nibbles on his left ear, teasing nips, and then pulls back, leaving the lobe to cool in the air.

"There's another one, *mami*," he says, turning the other ear.

She straightens, touches a thoughtful finger to her heartthrob lower lip—full and ripe without lipstick or collagen.

Rigo puts his hands on her hips, pulls her close.

Feels her hands slide across his pectorals, down to his ribs. Tickling.

He yelps in surprise, twists sideways. Clamps his arms to his sides, trapping her fingers, and then fumbles for one of her armpits. Hits home. She giggles, tries to squirm away, and spills off of the sofa. They tumble to the floor, roll on the carpet until they're gasping for air, sweaty with laughter. He ends up on top, ass pressing into her stomach as he pins her arms to her sides.

"Wanna jig?" she says.

"I think I might be up for that." Rigo eases off her.

"Not in the bedroom." She tugs him to the sofa with one hand. "I don't want to wake Josué."

"No problem," Rigo says.

Anthea slips off her skimpy shorts. Rigo helps her with the blouse, sliding it over her upraised arms.

Onscreen, two people kiss as she undresses him. To Rigo, it's like seeing himself in a mirror that reflects a different place or time . . . a different self.

"Take it slow," she says, straddling his legs, settling her hips onto his lap.

Her nipples are raspberry plump. He presses one between his lips, feels it swell against the tip of his tongue. His fingernails rattle along the xylophone of her rib cage, grip the skeletal wings of her shoulder blades. They raise a little, spreading wide to carry him aloft. All he has to do is hang on and he'll be lifted up, all the way to heaven.

THREE

Next morning, Rigo still feels a little out of sorts from his encounter with the dying woman. He can't seem to shake her bad air. It's like trying to get rid of a stubborn hangover. He offlines Varda—he can do without the grief—and pods to work early before either Anthea or Josué are awake, hoping that the daily routine will restore some semblance of balance. For the most part it works. By the time he arrives at Noogenics, he's broken through the surface tension of his funk into the breezy air of normalcy. He's back on track.

For once, there's no overnight fog clinging to the horseshoe crab curve of the Monterey Bay coast, and eager fingers of sunlight slip over the hills above the Pajaro Valley to touch Noogenics's thousand square kilometers of biovat domes. The company is a heavy-weight politicorp, with production facilities similar to this in countries all around the world. Six years ago he started out as a vat rat, wading through growth ponds of putrescent ecotectural sludge in a biosuit. Now Rigo is a systech in charge of his own crew of vat rats, monitoring the growth of gengineered plants designed by various ecotectural engineering firms. With any luck, his experience at Noogenics will get him into an ecotectural engineering program. He's already taken a few online introductory classes in organic chemistry, biostructural design, and mechanosynthesis, and applied for an educational grant from Noogenics. All he has to do now is come up with enough credit to pay for half of his education, and the politicorp will cover the other half. Easier said than done.

Most of his team is already in the locker room, stripping off morning sprayons and slipping into biosuits, by the time he arrives. The mood is upbeat, jovial. Rigo likes to think that it's more than the pherions they're dosed with to enhance productivity, foster teamwork, and improve morale. He likes to believe his crew is held together by a sense of camaraderie, an esprit de corps, that would exist even without the bond created by the pherions.

"Hey, bro," Rigo says, giving each one a slap on the back or punch in the arm—Antoine, Naguib, Luis, TomE and Hsi-Tang. Even Claribel and Rana, when they join the group from the women's locker room. He treats them like any other brother—no easing up or lowered expectations—and likes to think they appreciate the equality. That goes for the whole team. Give everyone the same respect, and in return they'll respect not only him but each other.

Rigo dons a biosuit. He doesn't have to wear a suit, but still likes to get his hands dirty, muck it up with the rest of them on a daily basis. It helps keep him in touch with his team, lets them know he's not above any of them.

"Rig, you're looking a little wrung out," Naguib says good-naturedly as they head out to their vat buildings.

"Yeah," Rana says, chiding him. "I'd say those *cojones* are drooping a little."

"You're just jealous," Rigo quips, slipping easily into the locker room banter.

"Fuck that noise," Claribel, the resident same-sex advocate, says.

"Well, I wish I'd gotten some," Luis says. "My nuts are definitely not sagging from fatigue."

Antoine grins. "Those aren't *cojones* you got, dude, those are udders. You ought to visit a dairy farm."

"Or a milkmaid," Hsi-Tang says, getting into the act.

One big, happy family, with none of the fuckedupness that comes with actually being related. Together they're responsible for ten vats. The project they're currently assigned to involves the cultivation of warm-blooded plants. As a result, they work in sub-zero temperatures. Their biosuits contain piezoelectrics that generate heat through movement. The worst part, aside from the ass-freezing cold, is the dark. For three months now, they've been working in low-light conditions. It's depressing. With only a few hours of sunshine in the morning, at lunch, and after work, it's like living in eternal night. Could be worse. At least they don't have to work in zero-g. The next phase of the project involves the modification of these same warm-blooded plants for the colonization of Mars and big, ice-covered asteroids in the Kuiper belt. Noogenics and Xengineering, the ecotectural firm that designed the plants, have already snagged a Kuiper belt comet and brought it into high-earth orbit, where alpha-phase testing and training will take place to see if warm-blooded plant settlements are even feasible.

They pod out to their assigned vat buildings, riding the monorail between geodesic domes, smooth opalescent hemispheres, dodecahedrons, and diamond-paned greenhouses, all of which reflect light with the oily iridescence of insect eyes. At the terminus platform, they jostle off and quickly settle into the daily routine. Rigo links his IA to the database for his vats, scans the vital stats for temperature, humidity, starch and oxygen content, microbe and nutrient levels, pherion concentrations. Each dome is home to a different type of plant, gengineered for a specific function: water uptake, purification, and storage; mineral retrieval plus separation; ambient heat generation and insulation; photovoltaics; bioluminescence. The plants are modular symbiots, designed to work in concert as a habitable ecotecture.

Once he's finished his check, Rigo has Varda download instructions to his team. In addition to the regular vat maintenance—filter replacement, refrigeration coils, circulation pumps, and underground piping—there are occasional data failures to deal with.

Today, a number of plant sensors are offline; he's getting no info feed. So Rigo cycles into the first building through its air lock. Feet crunch on ice, the sound brittle in the frangible air. An enormous gourd-shaped plant, as large as a big top in a circus, crowds the building. Under the narrow beam of his helmet light, the outer membrane is the color of eggplant and freckled with an array of tiny round windows that remind him of hard white blisters. The windows double as lenses—focus the feeble sunlight admitted by the vat dome into the hollow interior of the plant which is a balmy thirty-one degrees centigrade. Pores on the inside surface of the membrane absorb carbon dioxide and humidity, while microminiature air locks and cold-traps minimize the loss of oxygen and water to the drier outside air.

The defective sensor is inside. Rigo enters the plant through a wet, airtight cleft on one wall. It grudgingly admits him, prim as an evangelical's pursed lips. The interior is suffused with bright, starchy light from bioluminescent spots radially distributed on the central support stalk. The floor is fibrous. Tough. At the same time, it possesses a springy resilience. Bouncy. Overhead, the windows form pustules that reflect a compound image of him. It's quiet as a tomb, or a womb. All he can hear is his breath and the magnified pumping of blood, as if he's connected through a placenta to something greater than himself.

"Rigo?" Varda says.

"What?"

"You're leaking."

Rigo catches a faint whiff of orange peels and lavender. Blinks. Hermetically sealed in his biosuit, he shouldn't be smelling anything. The suit prevents him not only from contaminating the warm-blooded plants but from coming into contact with any of the proteins and pherions they secrete.

Rigo exhales, presses his lips tight, and takes a deep breath through his nose. If anything, the scent is stronger. "How bad is it?" he asks.

"You've lost positive pressure."

Great. His chest tightens and his pulse races, shifting into Bernoulli mode as his blood vessels constrict. He hasn't been claded for direct exposure to the plants, there's no telling what their defense mechanisms will do to him.

Don't think about that. Concentrate on something else. Like damage control and minimizing the exposure.

"What are you doing?" Varda says. "Waiting for the other shoe to sing?"

Holding his breath, skin formicating, he stumbles for the air lock. It takes forever to cycle through the sphincter, into the vat building, and through the door. Outside, Rigo pops the seal on his helmet, leans against the concrete wall of the control building, and gulps in fresh, sun-fogged air. Rivulets of sweat trickle down his brow and neck. He's sodden, perspiring faster than his biosuit can wick away the moisture. He tilts his head back, stares up at the cerulean sky.

"Well?" Rigo asks.

"I wouldn't say that, yet. It's too early to tell."

What now? he thinks.

"You should report to the corporate clinic," Varda says. "Get checkmarked, just in case."

True. The sooner he neutralizes any pherions in his system, the better.

But if he does that, he'll have to file a report, explain what happened. The biosuit must have sprung a leak when he cycled into the plant. A micro tear. It's not his fault—accidents happen—but the incident will look bad on his record, which has been spotless to this point. He's been so careful; that's one of the reasons he was promoted to systech, despite his lack of a formal education or training. Now this.

He sends a groupmail to his team, a brief note telling them that he has to pick up something, then pods back to the main building.

After five minutes, he should be feeling something—numbness, itching, muscle spasms, nausea, incontinence. But by the time he reaches the locker room, he's still not experiencing any symptoms. Maybe he didn't get dosed with a high enough concentration. It's puzzling. Rigo has his IA link to an online biomed scan. Parses through the readouts for his vital signs, immune system, pherions. His blood pressure and heart rate are elevated, no surprise, but other than that everything seems to be normal. Relief spreads through him, a soporific dye that calms the jitters.

He's dodged a bullet.

Rigo strips off the biosuit and inspects it under the sterile glare of the ceiling lights. Sure enough there's a little gill-like slit in the crease of a neck fold, just below the helmet seal. Not the sort of breach that would be found without close examination. The suit isn't that old. It must have been defective or damaged. The split is smooth-edged, a shallow cut that finally opened over time.

So all he needs to report is a damaged suit, requisition a new one. With the right spin that will look good, like he's on top of things.

* * *

Following lunch, it's back to the grind. A crazy afternoon, barely enough time to breathe let alone think. At one-thirty, Xengineering comes online, requesting updated performance info for each of the warm-blooded plants under Rigo's care. No explanation. For some reason, the gengineers need the data now, they can't wait for a standard end-of-week or end-of-day report. Whatever they're stressing about is serious, time-critical.

Rigo's stomach knots. He was in direct contact with the ecotecture for only a couple of seconds, but it might have been long enough to cause a problem. Who knows what his own pherion profile might do to the carefully orchestrated biochemistry of the plants. If there *is* a problem it could be traced back to him. He's already reported the tear, with no mention of the exposure. Too late now to change his story. He'll have to stick with what he said, ride it out.

Next time—assuming there *is* a next time—he'll know better. He's learned his lesson, won't make the same mistake twice.

Hopefully the request from Xengineering is simply a precaution. They got word of the tear and want to be sure there's no contamination. In addition to compiling and organizing today's data, Rigo has to scramble to include back-data from the beginning of the week. And they want data for all the plants, not just the one he came into direct contact with. He finishes around three, squirts the data to Xengineering, and holds his breath.

FOUR

For Anthea, stepping into the playroom is like disappearing down a rabbit hole. Reality takes a right turn, and none of the standard laws governing the behavior of the universe apply.

Located on the ground floor of Global Upreach's downtown office, the playroom has no windows. It's hermetically sealed from distractions. When a child enters the playroom, he or she is surrounded by a mind-numbing array of toys and art supplies. There are stuffed animals, dolls, costumes and jewelry, board games, a sand box, clay and sculpture putty, watercolors, oil paints, a light pen and pad. There are also a number of virtual games for those kids who are stubbornly nontactile. Something for everyone. In other words, the room is basically an industrial-strength fun zone where kids are free to do whatever they want.

As long as no one gets hurt.

That's the only rule. Other than that, it's carte blanche. Freedom of behavior is critical to the success of the playroom. Ideally, the kids who end up there should not feel inhibited in any way. Part of Anthea's job is to make them feel safe and comfortable, to get them to open up and express themselves without reservation. Most of the time that's easier said than done. Anthea deals with kids who—as a kind of Darwinian survival of the fittest skill—have discovered the hard way that it's not in their best interest to trust. Trust is not a favorable adaptive strategy. In fact, trust is a good way to get hurt or killed. It is one of those dangers to be avoided at all costs, no different than a saber-toothed tiger or a falling rock.

At least Anthea knows what it's like, has stood in their shoes. The kids can sense that she's one of them, as if their shared history has a unique smell. That makes it a little easier to connect.

Of course, more than just simple play goes on here. The toys that a child selects and the *way* the child plays with those toys are carefully observed and recorded. These choices reveal deep psychological inner workings, the orchestrated machination of synapses that give rise to various emotions, attitudes, and conduct. The second part of Anthea's job is to glean insight into what makes a child tick so that she can make an assessment and write an evaluation. Once an evaluation is made, a specific course of treatment can be determined. Depending on the severity and type of problem—e.g., Did Wooly the Mammoth's trunk get torn off and used as a surrogate penis to thrash Betty the Butterfly for being an overly affectionate mother?—treatment can be anything from a foster-to-adopt home to a more controlled program of deep psychological counseling or even chemical rewiring.

Anthea gets to work late, fifteen minutes before her first scheduled session of the day. Malina was late picking up Josué, and so Anthea is running behind schedule as well. Plus, she's got Rigo in the back of her mind, weighing her down. He was super sweet last night—too sweet. Like he was being extra attentive to her out of guilt. She believes his story about visiting his mother—she could smell the familiar fragrance of incense and candles on him—but not for as long as he said. There was another smell, too. One she couldn't identify but is pretty sure came from another woman.

As soon as Anthea walks through the door her supervisor, Tissa, wants her to see a new kid. Which means she has to spend a couple of minutes parsing background material. She barely has time to prepare—put Rigo out of her mind and put on her play face.

"His name is Ibrahim," Tissa says, downloading the file to Anthea's IA. "He was brought in last night."

"Where was he found?" The information is in the file, but Anthea likes to discuss preliminaries in advance. For her, the emotional response to a situation contains more information than the raw data that describes it.

Tissa leads her down the hall, in the direction of the group home section of the building. "He was picked up at a pod transfer station over in Los Gatos, as part of a gang sweep."

"Which gang?"

"The Necrofeels. But he's not wearing any of their graffitics."

No tattoos then, or scarification. "A new member?" Anthea asks.

Tissa shakes her head. "I don't think so."

"Why not?"

"You'll see when you meet with him."

"What's this about clade incompatibilities and antipher treatment?" Anthea asks, scanning the boy's med file.

"When he got here he had some minor muscle spasms and loss of gross motor skills. He was given a broad-spectrum antipher. That seemed to help, but we're still trying to clade him."

"Still?"

"His clade-profile is nonstandard. I mean, some of it's standard. But a lot of it's not."

"Meaning what?"

Tissa shrugs, unwilling to speculate. She stops outside a door to one of the private rooms. The word *room* is a euphemism. In actuality, it's a glorified holding cell—Alcatraz that's been visited by an interior decorator with extensive work experience in an insane asylum. This means that the room has a lot of sponge surfaces and nonbreakable amenities. The toilet, sink, faucet, bed frame and chairs are all foam; the walls, floor, ceiling and door are gelfoam-padded lichen. The sheets are tissue. Flimsy as toilet paper, they couldn't support the weight of even the most emaciated eight-year-old bent on hanging or choking himself.

Tissa puts a hand on Anthea's arm—"Good

luck"—and then turns to go. Not the kind of parting gesture that inspires confidence.

Anthea straightens her shoulders, raps lightly on the soft door. Knocks again, then says, "Ibrahim? My name is Anthea. Can I come in? I just want to talk to you a little. Okay?"

Still no response. She queries her IA, Doug, for a current biomed readout, including REM and alpha wave activity. The name Doug is a joke, a morose double entendre. Her IA chose it because information agents spend most of their time digging for data. So the pun is a jab, an expression of deep psychological pain, not all that different than a pet airing deep psychological wounds by chewing on the furniture or soiling the carpet.

Anthea squints at the readouts. "Is he awake?"

"Up and atom," Doug says, borrowing a line from an old twentieth-century animated cartoon. That's one of the tics with her IA. It seems to take perverse pleasure in dredging up obscure facts that are more annoying than useful.

Anthea chooses not to dignify the pun with a response. Child psychology—if she doesn't encourage the IA maybe it will stop. The problem is, Doug has defined its personal relationship with her in terms of snide remarks, a contest of flip witticisms and disguised barbs that isn't always productive and can sometimes be a real pain in the ass.

"Can he hear me?" She keeps her voice to a whisper even though the door is as sound absorbent as a diaper.

"Would you like to take a look, Ant Thea?"

"Please." Ironic that both Josué and her IA came

up with similar mispronunciations of her name. Never mind that one is intentional and the other is not. It does give her valuable insight into the IA, however, tells her something about its mood at any given time.

A colorful slice of neocortex appears on her eye-screens. Overlaid on the wall, it displays a transient pattern of electrical activity reminiscent of a lightning storm in gray clouds.

"Can I take a look at him?"

"Yes, master. Your wish is my command."

The walls of the room are infested with bitcams. It takes several seconds for them to sync up and get a bead on their target. The image rasterizes slowly, its grainy bitmap edges smoothing into recognizable patterns.

He's pacing the room, dressed in sky blue sprayon pajamas. She watches him prod the walls, tug at the bed, and poke the toilet, restless as a trapped animal. For an eight-year-old, he's small, shorter and lighter even than Josué. He has a bony triangular face, wide cheekbones tapering down to a sharp chin. Hard to spec what his background is. Latasian, maybe. His eyes are puffy and heavy lidded, almond brown under close-cropped hair that reminds her of the fire-blackened dandelion fuzz. Subcutaneous lesions, the size and color of liver spots, mottle his arms and neck. His skin is a taut membrane tented over a frame of toothpick-thin bones. It looks as if he hasn't eaten for years. He could be a premillennial poster child for starving children in Africa. The only thing missing are the flies.

"I know you can hear me, Ibrahim."

He gnaws on his lower lip with yellowish, uneven teeth, staunch in his refusal to speak while he continues to inspect the room, as if searching for a way out.

Anthea's an old hand at the silent treatment. Undeterred, she forges ahead. "You want to come out and play?" she says, as if they're next-door neighbors, out of school for the summer.

No answer.

"I want to help you," Anthea says, "be your friend. But if you won't talk to me, I can't do that."

Nothing.

"I'm not a doctor. I won't hurt you, I promise. I know a place we can go where no one will bother us."

The silence stretches. Of course, she can enter the room at will. But it's important to be invited in. The decision has to be his. He has to believe he's in control and that his wishes are being respected.

"Listen," Anthea says. "It's your choice, totally up to you. I'll just hang here until you're ready."

"Go away," he says. "Hang yourself someplace else."

Finally, an opening.

"Where would you like me to go, Ibrahim?"

He shrugs.

This catches her off guard—takes her so much by surprise that it feels like a non sequitur. Usually, kids say something like "To hell," or the poetic equivalent. It takes a moment to recoup.

"Where would *you* like to go?" she asks.

He sits on the end of the bed, rests his chin in his hands the way she did when her mother incarcerated her in their ap.

"You got any coffee?" he says.

"Coffee?"

"Yeah. Black, with nothing else in it. Except maybe nic, if you can get it."

"I'll have to check," she says. Caffeine/nicotine might be contraindicated with whatever medication he's been prescribed.

He nods, takes her response as a no. "What about tunes?" he says. "You got a download I can stream?"

"What do you like?"

"Razz. Afrapan. Bachata." He shrugs, conveys the feeling that it's really not all that important. "Whatever."

She was hoping his preferences in music might give her some indication of where he's from. But the list is pretty diverse, eclectic. It doesn't tell her much. Time to try a direct frontal assault.

"You were trying to pod somewhere on the train," she says. "Where were you going?"

Another silence. But this one has an air of thoughtfulness instead of open hostility or suspicion. She listens to his breath, the reverberation of his pulse clanging in his veins like water surging through rigid pipes.

"If you help me, I'll help you," she says. Tit for tat. It's the type of negotiation that kids in his situation—i.e., alone, homeless, and hungry—are usually familiar with, having never experienced charity.

"What do you want?" Willing to bargain.

Here's where things get tricky. It has to be something that he specs as self-serving on her part—e.g., sex, money, drugs—but is really in his best interest.

"I want to play a game," she says. Game, in street

kid parlance, generally meaning something illegal, immoral, or both.

"What kind of game?"

"I'll show you."

"If I play, you'll let me go?"

"When you're healthy enough." Lots of latitude there, especially when his state of mind is added to the equation.

Another moment of silent introspection while he weighs the pros and cons of her offer. "Okay."

He's mastered the art of practiced nonchalance, has a real flare for it. Tough and savvy, he's not nearly as combative as most of the *tígueres* she deals with. His indolence has a certain savoir faire that she finds refreshing, if not downright charming.

Careful, girl, she warns herself. Don't even go there.

When the door doesn't open after several beats, she says, "You going to let me in or not?"

Only then does he stand up, sidle over to the door, and unlock it. Still, the door remains closed. She has to pull it open herself.

"My name's Anthea," she says.

He stands in front of her, looks her up and down with an appraising eye. Critical. "Great," he says. "Just my luck."

"What?"

"You're even more anorexic than me." He shakes his head, sympathetic. "And I thought I was messed."

"What makes you say that?"

"Nothing." He tilts his head to one side, cocks an eye at her. "How old are you, anyway?"

"Older than you think."

"Me, too." He winks, a face-scrunching Don Juan leer that is more comical than lewd.

"I can see that." Not only is he a flirt but an articulate one. A *boca* who can flimflam with the best of them. She hates to see what he'll be like in a few years—say at the age of fourteen or fifteen—assuming he makes it that long. "Come on," she says. "Let's go."

For someone who's mostly skin and bones, he's got a surprising amount of energy. He hasn't been beaten down, his pride and self-respect thrashed. He's infused with a restless, feral curiosity that engages everything, including her. Most of it's false bravado, applied like makeup to hide the underlying scars and bruises. But not all. When he steps into the playroom, his eyes light up, spark with a mixture of wonder and disbelief. For a second, she gets a momentary view of him as a little boy. Then, just as quickly, the fleeting glimpse fades, goes back into hiding.

His lips purse. "So, what game do you want to play?"

"You pick," she says.

He makes a big drama of debating what to do. His eyes narrow and his forehead wrinkles. Finally, after much deliberation, he goes over to a small maglev track. The track is capable of accomodating up to six players. Each car floats above a single magnetic filament, a rail to which it is initially assigned. Ibrahim fiddles with a joystick, moving one car slowly around the track, which is smart enough to assess his ability and operate the other cars at approximately the same speed and skill level. Anthea stands off to one side and watches as unobtrusively as she can, letting him do his thing. It's against the rules to take part in a game unless he specifically asks her. Allowing him not to involve her is one way of letting him take control of the situation. She's had lots of sessions where kids shut her out completely because they needed to exercise that power over an adult. It's not unusual for a kid to take shit out on her—use her as an emotional or physical punching bag.

"You gonna play or not?" he says.

"Sure."

"What color do you want to be?"

"You pick first."

"How about if you're red?" he says, making the decision for her. "That way, it'll match your lips."

Add fashion-conscious to his repertoire. "Fine."

She picks up the appropriate joystick, adopts a seriously competitive attitude. A lot of times, kids harboring pent-up anger go out of their way to run cars off the track at high speed, or crash them into one another by switching lanes. Then, she can ask them why they felt it was necessary to do that, why it made them feel good. In psychoanalysis, toys are the equivalent of mental can openers. On the surface, nothing is what it appears to be. Thus, the cars might metaphorically represent family members, friends, or even the multiple selves in a disassociative personality, which actually happened once. Not this time. After a couple of minutes, the time it takes to make three complete circuits of the track, Ibrahim sets his joystick down.

"Your turn to pick," he says, affecting boredom, disinterest.

"We didn't play that one very long," Anthea tells him. "It's still your turn. You should choose instead of me. To be fair."

So they play a little hacky-sack, volleying a soft foam ball, purple, between them with only their feet and knees. "You win," he says after a couple minutes, following an obvious miss on his part.

What he really wants to do, she realizes, is turn the tables. See what she'll do so he can analyze her. "All right," she tells him, as if an idea has suddenly occurred to her. "Let's draw."

"Draw?" Definitely not what he expected.

Anthea smiles. "You know. Like graffiti, or a tattune."

She digs out a couple sketchpads and fiber-optic paintbrushes, sits cross-legged on the floor, and starts to draw a landscape. It takes Ibrahim a while to settle in—for several minutes, he just stares at the blank page—but eventually he picks up the brush and begins to doodle. Random squiggles and lines at first, as he gradually warms to the task. The next time she glances at him his eyes are pinched shut. It looks like he's in excruciating pain. Constipated. She almost asks him what's wrong, if he's okay, but the fiber-optic tip of the brush is tracing out lines on the pad, spreading broad swaths of color. He's drawing blind, either too afraid to look at the images taking shape in front of him or focused on some internal mindscape that's only visible behind closed lids. It takes an effort not to stop what she's doing and watch. She doesn't want to interrupt him. Fortunately, every stroke is being recorded. If need be, she can go back later and reconstruct exactly how the picture was drawn.

He's really getting into it, attacking the sketchpad with an intensity that borders on psychotic. The brush has become a weapon, stabbing and slicing the screen. Good thing it's not a knife. No telling what he'd try to slash next.

Gashes open up on the sketchpad, suppurating wounds of red, green, and yellow. Bubbles of saliva fleck the corners of his mouth. His chest heaves, as if he's suffocating. His fingers begin to tremble, then shake. An uncontrollable spasm races up his hand, travels along his arm and into his body, jolting him. He jerks once, stiffens, jerks again. The brush clatters to the floor.

The words *gran mal* condense in her mind. She lunges toward him on her knees. Afraid that he'll hit his head, she gathers him into her arms and holds him tight to keep him from hurting himself and her. Still, his head bruises her chin, batters both collarbones.

Now what?

She can't let go . . . can't get help. All she can do is hold on for dear life and hope that she survives—that they both survive. There's no retreat, no stepping back. They're in this together, for the duration. Anthea hugs him tighter, the only protection there is for both of them. It feels like she's in an earthquake. The shaking goes on and on. After what seems like an eternity the spasms finally subside, degenerate into sobs. First his, then hers.

"It's okay," she says, "it's over. Everything's going to be all right." Reassuring herself as much as him, now that they've survived the cataclysm.

Unscathed? It's too early to tell at this point.

She finds that she's rocking him in her arms. Her ribs ache where they've been gouged by his elbows and the ax-blade-sharp edges of his shoulder blades. She kisses him lightly on the top of the head, presses one cheek against it. His tear-matted hair is bristly as a coconut's. The taste of salt lies heavy on her lips.

Anthea sniffs, blinks to clear her vision. She glances at the sketchpad on the floor.

The rabbit hole has really taken an unexpected turn this time—deposited her in bizarre and disturbing territory. Like Alice, she's trapped, has no clue how she's going to find her way back home.

FIVE

Dinner with Anthea and Josué, who's tagging along unexpectedly.

Instead of the Asian Rose, which serves Sri Lankan food—far too exotic for the taste buds of a nine-year-old—they end up going to the Pontiac Grill for tofu burgers, fries, and soyshakes. The Pontiac, a 1950s historical, has been around for over a century. It still has red-speckled linoleum floor tile, black Formica tables banded with polished chrome, a soda counter, and red vinyl barstools and seats. Originally the place was a car dealership, a showroom for dinosaur-powered automobiles. Consequently, it has big floor-to-ceiling windows that soak up glare.

The room is awash with early evening twilight and tourists. Mounted on the wall behind the soda counter, just above the service window to the kitchen, the detached grille of a Pontiac grins at them like the

preserved jawbone of some Paleolithic shark ex-
humed from the fossilized seabed of Americana. Old
photographs and press releases of classic Pontiac
sedans decorate the walls. There's a picture of a 1946
Silver Streak, several 1941 Torpedoes, a '53 Dual
Streak, and a Star Chief Catalina. Jukebox music
plays in the background: Elvis Presley, Chuck Berry,
The Drifters, and Southern Culture on the Skids. A
real trip down memory lane. The nice thing about a
tourist trap like Santa Cruz is that most of the places
aren't heavily claded. Just about anyone can get into
most of the shops, VRcades, and restaurants. A few
exclusive art galleries and haut couture beach-apparel
stores raise their noses to the riffraff. But for the most
part, SC has retained its beatnik and counterculture
roots. It's a haven for the dispossessed, which is part
of its charm.

"I'm really sorry," Anthea whispers, all apologetic,
when Josué trundles off to the restroom. "Malina
called at the last minute. . . ."

"It's okay," Rigo says, only a little disappointed.
"No problem." He'd been hoping to spend some
quality time alone with Anthea. Just the two of them.
But Rigo likes Josué well enough, so it really isn't an
issue. In addition, by not being pissed off, he'll score
major points with Anthea, who's been a little cool
tonight. Preoccupied, or withdrawn for some reason.
Distracted.

Rigo sucks on the straw of his chocolate shake,
cheeks hollowing. "Everything all right?" he says.

Anthea, slurping a cherry soda, looks up at him
across the table. Nods. "How was your day?"

"We had a problem with one of the vats." Rigo explains about the malfunctioning sensors and the datasquirt to Xengineering. How he had to recheck the sensors, confirm the data link.

"You sound tense," Anthea says.

"Yeah. Well . . ." He offers a lame shrug, leaves out the part about the tear in the biosuit.

Anthea reaches across the tabletop, gives one of his hands a supportive squeeze with her twig-thin fingers. "I'm sure you'll figure it out."

"I hope so." Rigo strokes her hand, tracing the bones beneath the skin, as if they can reveal all there is to know about her. It feels bad, not telling her everything. Wrong. He should be able to talk to her about anything, shouldn't he? Even the delivery for Beto. But he holds back, too embarrassed. Doesn't want to admit he might have fucked up. Doesn't want her to think he's a total dumbshit.

"What about your day?" he asks.

Anthea withdraws her hand, sits back, and sighs. "I got a new kid today. He's super cute, but a mess. I mean, I could hardly get him to play. He was too grown-up—you know? Didn't know how to have fun."

Rigo relaxes. Tells himself this is what's got her all out of sorts, the reason she's distant. "How old is he?"

"Eight. A year younger than Josué. It's sad." A pained expression creases her face.

"Is he violent?" Rigo asks, glancing at the scratches on her arms. She's been hurt more than once by gang kids who see her as an easy target. Someone to vent their anger or frustration on.

"No, nothing like that." Anthea props her chin in

the palms of her hands. "He's just really scared, I think. Afraid to talk."

Abused, Rigo thinks. These days, that goes without saying. "Any idea where he's from?"

"No. The police picked him up at a pod station. I guess he'd been hanging there a while, trying to get somewhere."

"Maybe you should buy him a ticket. See where he goes."

Anthea shrugs, bony shoulders falling as she exhales. "I've got another session with him tomorrow. We'll see how it goes."

Anthea's good at getting people to open up. It's a gift. Complete strangers walk right up to her and spill their guts, bare their souls. Rigo feels that same tug, the urge to unburden himself in her presence.

Then Josué returns and it's off to the Santa Cruz Boardwalk instead of a romantic walk along West Cliff under dust-blurred stars.

The Boardwalk is a long, wide strip of garishly lit concrete guarded by a seawall fifteen meters high. No beaches. Those are long gone, wiped out in the first temperature *entafada* of the Greenhouse Years. Global warming has raised the level of the oceans worldwide by about ten meters. Now waves crash against the barrier, sending an occasional rainlike spray of water over the top, onto the tourists waiting in line at the rides, fast-food stands, and carnival games. Half a kilometer to the north, the old pier is still visible at low tide. The restaurants and stores it once supported are long gone, battered into flotsam by waves. All that's left are a few creosote-and-tar-soaked timbers.

A lot of the original rides, like the Giant Dipper roller coaster, are museum pieces, way too antiquated and dangerous to actually ride. Mostly they've been preserved for atmosphere, a kind of time-warped nostalgia that includes cotton candy, hot dogs, and the sensuous aroma of buttered popcorn. Blinking neon strips decorate the undersides of the UV umbrella palms, turning them into kaleidoscopic parasols that pinwheel crazily in the offshore breeze.

"Can we go up?" Josué pleads, staring up at the flags stirring above the top of the barrier. "Please?"

Anthea glances at Rigo, who shrugs. Why not?

The seawall is wide enough on top to walk along. A pleasant stroll, hand-in-hand, behind the safety netting while Josué races ahead of them, bouncing from one souvenir booth to the next with the energy of a billiard ball. Breakers crash thunderously against the face of the wall.

Anthea leans into him, tentative. "Nice night."

"Beautiful," Rigo agrees. "Just like you, *mami*."

Her smile, thin as the curve of the moon, slices through the misty gauze of ocean air. Neon light from the Boardwalk beads on the carbyne mesh like dew on spider silk, a glittering rainbow pattern of gemstones. The rhythmic pulse of the waves is seductive, gentle yet carnal in its slow ebbs and violent outbursts.

"It feels good," Anthea says.

"So do you, *mi amor*."

Rigo pulls her close, feels her gradually surrender to the embrace. First her arms, then her back and shoulders. They pause to stare at the scalloped surface of the water, moonlight on the half shell. Venus watches from near the horizon.

"Aunt Thea!" Josué shouts. "Spec that." He points excitedly at something down on the Boardwalk, an old-fashioned carousel with plastic horses galloping in a circle, and then trots off.

Anthea disengages herself and they follow Josué onto a spiral walkway that corkscrews into the ground. Josué's not interested in risking life and limb on any of the more stomach-wrenching, adrenaline-inducing rides. He seems content to observe from a safe distance. Even the Xtreme virtualities aren't his cup of tea. No surfing on hundred-meter-high waves, or rock climbing on the vertical face of one of the kilometer-deep trenches on Mars. So they spend a lot of time exploring the Psience and Xperience exhibits on the Beach Flats, remote-linked to bitcams embedded in the pupils of exotic wildlife and offworld microbots.

In one VRcade they look through the eyes of a condor as it navigates thermals over the Andes; watch the infrared image of a desert mouse stalked by a rattlesnake; carry bits of food down the tunnels of a termite mound in Africa. In another VRcade they actually get to control an aquabot at the bottom of the Marianis Trench, and a swarm of aerobots floating in the clouds of Venus. Now that the bots have outlived their scientific usefulness, they make great toys.

The only bad part is the adware, bits of airborne viral code that stimulate specific synapses and neural responses. Rigo's mouth waters with acute, debilitating cravings for such exotic culinary offerings as anchovy sorbet, pickled peanuts, and cotton-candy-dipped bananas. Exerting superhuman effort—the kind of self-denial exercised by celibate priests—he manages to resist. Anthea and Josué aren't quite as strong-willed and, much to their gastrointestinal distress, end up succumbing. There's also some irritating riboware floating around. At one point Josué ends up with a clown face, painted by tincture bacteria that blossom beneath his skin in different colors. Rigo gets a tattune on his left forearm, an animated pen-and-ink drawing of a politicorp security guard in fatigues who salutes him while a recruiting jingle streams through his IA. The tattune is clade-specific. For some reason it thinks he's prime grunt material. Rigo feels Varda's snigger as an electric tickle in his spine.

Very funny.

"This is the last VRcade," Anthea warns Josué as he slips on the eyescreens for a telepresence unit that pilots a lunar rover across the Sea of Tranquillity.

"But, Aunt Thea—"

"No buts. It's time we did something all of us can do. Together."

Rigo helps Josué adjust the eyescreens. As he steps back into the crowd a man jostles him. Dumps a banana-kiwi-flavored snow cone down the front of his white shirt.

"Son of a bitch." Rigo jumps away from the cold shock of shaved ice.

The man—a retired Eurocauc judging by his wooly vernacular and fondness for velvet—brushes at the yellow and green streaks of syrup that are bleeding into Rigo's flimsy cotton gauze. "Sorry to bump into you like this."

Not much of an apology. "Just get away from me." Rigo knocks the Eurocauc's hands aside.

Anthea rushes in to head off a confrontation. "It's

okay," she states, looking at Rigo. Firm. "No big deal."

Rigo gets the message, decides to back down. No sense causing an international incident. "Forget it." He holds his wet shirt away from his skin. A couple of meters to the side of them, Josué is oblivious, ensconced behind the eyescreens.

"I have an extra T-shirt," the man says. He fishes a travel-size sprayon out of a mesh pocket in his trousers and offers it to Anthea because Rigo has his hands full with his shirt, trying to keep it from sticking to his stomach.

Anthea reaches for the sprayon. "Thanks."

"How's Ibrahim?" the man asks, not quite relinquishing his grip on the ampoule.

She stops. Leans forward as if she's misheard him amid the crazed ruckus of the VRcade. "Excuse me?"

"I want to help," the man says.

"Who are you?"

"I'm with the ICLU." He lets go of the sprayon, which drops to the ground when Anthea fails to take it.

"We don't know any Ibrahim," Rigo says, careful to annunciate. "You got the wrong people. Our kid is over there." He motions to Josué and at the same time takes a casual glance around to see if anyone's watching them. The last thing he needs is to be seen associating with an extremist human rights org.

Radical sympathizer. Conspiracy to subvert the status quo. That will look good on his upcoming performance review. Along with: questions authority, opposes the dominant paradigm, and doesn't play well with others. The list goes on. Agitator. Trouble-maker. Civil disobedient . . .

"Don't worry," the man says, bending down to retrieve the sprayon. "I'm alone. No one's watching and we can speak freely." He stands, clutching the ampoule in one hand. "Trust me."

Right, Rigo thinks. He squirms under the ghostly scrutiny of the tattune security guard. Wipes sweaty palms on his shirt, glad he's got the snow cone stains to cover his act of nervousness.

"There's nothing you can do for him," Anthea whispers, barely audible over the din of white noise.

"I can protect him," the man says. "Take him someplace safe."

"That's not what he needs. Right now, he could use some serious therapy and consistency in his life."

"If you keep him, you'll be putting him at risk."

"He's already at risk. Nothing you can do will change that. Not in the long run."

"Can we at least talk to him? See what he wants?"

"Forget it." Anthea turns toward Rigo. "Come on. We're leaving." She stomps off to get Josué.

The agent offers Rigo the ampoule, like it's a business card. "If you change your mind—"

Rigo shakes his head—"If you bother her again, we'll contact the police"—then hurries to catch up with Anthea. When he glances over his shoulder, the dude is gone, disappeared back into whatever hole he crawled out of.

"Let's go see the Angel Tree," Anthea says, suddenly. "I haven't been there in years, not since I was a kid." She seems anxious to put the conversation with the ICLU agent behind her. Clear her mental palate, and recapture the carefree mood of the first part of the evening.

Josué doesn't bother to protest, evidence that even his level of tolerance has hit a wall. Overstimulation is great to a point, but it can be exhausting. While they pod a few kilometers into the coastal foothills, Anthea tells them the story.

Nearly a century earlier, just before the turn of the millennium, an angel appeared to a man splitting firewood. The apparition hovered mysteriously for a short time, bestowing a cryptic Mona Lisa smile, and then vanished. As soon as she was gone, the man had the urge to split another log. When he did, the wood inside bore the image of the angel and the man was cured of terminal cancer. Word of the miracle quickly spread, and in no time the split log, now part of a table constructed by the man to preserve the image, had been turned into a religious shrine. For years, sick people have been making pilgrimages to the Angel in the Tree to partake of her healing benediction.

"Creepy," Josué says.

The pod drops them off at a narrow footpath that leads into a small park. They trudge through a copse of umbrella palms. It's dark under the UV-reflective canopy, and they stumble on rocks and coiled roots. They pass by a children's play area—with its ground-cover of black foam rubber beneath swings, slides and jungle gyms—and then a couple of baseball diamonds and soccer fields. The fresh odor of grass hangs in the air.

"These mountains used to be covered with redwood trees," Rigo says. "A forest of them."

"Did they really have red wood?" Josué asks.

"Like blood," Rigo exaggerates. "Plus, they could grow to over a hundred meters tall and six meters in diameter."

"What happened to them?"

"They died off in the ecocaust, like most of the native plants. Redwoods drank fog to survive. That's how they got most of their water. But after a while it got too dry for them. There used to be oak trees here, too. And madrone and manzanita. About the only thing that survived were the eucalyptus trees and old-style palm trees."

"How come?"

"They weren't native to this area. They came from desert climates to start with. Places like Africa and Australia."

Funny how transplants survive when natives can't, Rigo thinks. How indigenous species almost always get outcompeted by foreign invaders. It's the same with people, he thinks. No different.

Pretty soon they come across the shrine. It's encircled by a low fence and rough-hewn benches arranged like pews. Hardcopy photos hang on the fence, printouts of loved ones who are either sick or dying. Several tables along the fence display flower vases and votive candles. The vases sprout artificial roses, lilies, violets. Waxy tears runnel the candles, clot in solid puddles on the tabletop. An outside church, roofed by a vaulted ceiling of leaves. Rigo half expected to encounter a healing service in progress, but the place is tranquil. Josué races up to the table, eschewing quiet reverence in favor of unbridled religious fervor that is the result of too much sugar. Anthea follows more slowly, as if approaching an altar or holy monument. She could be visiting Easter Island or Stonehenge.

After a few seconds Josué announces, "I see her."

Anthea stops next to him, places a hand on one shoulder. "Where?" Hard to tell if she's humoring him or having trouble dissecting the shadows and assembling them into a meaningful pattern.

Josué points at an amorphous Rorschach blotch in the grain, a blond discoloration worn smooth as the Wailing Wall by the hands of supplicants.

"Can I touch her?" he asks.

"I don't see why not," Anthea says.

Josué bends close, trails a tentative fingertip across the angel the way he might a live electrical wire.

"Feel anything?" Rigo asks.

"Not really." Josué straightens, clearly disappointed by the lack of immediate gratification, and drifts over to the fence to look at the pictures, leaving them alone for a moment.

Anthea reaches for Rigo's hand, threads her fingers through his. "It's so quiet," she says. "Peaceful."

"Yeah."

She gazes down at the table. Puckers her mouth. "It's smaller than I remember."

Rigo grins. "Everything looks bigger when you're a kid."

"The way it works," she says, "is that people lie down on the table. That's how you open up to the angel."

An image of bloody sacrifices, something out of the Old Testament, flashes across Rigo's mindscape.

"Do people really get cured?" he asks. It seems like one of those things that only happen in the distant past, like raising the dead or slaying dragons. It's not a part of modern reality. Shit like that just doesn't happen anymore. "I mean, have you personally known anyone who got better?" He does his best not to sound sarcastic, to treat it as an honest question.

"The time I was here this old woman had bone cancer in her spine. She was in a wheelchair, totally paralyzed. She had to be lifted onto the table. People stood in a circle around her, holding hands and chanting. Praying. After a few minutes, her hands moved, then her feet. Pretty soon, she was able to get up and walk."

"How do you know it wasn't staged?"

"You're such a skeptic." Her fingers tighten around his, the pressure affectionate but urgent, as if willing him to believe.

"I wonder what caused the image to appear?" he says.

"Maybe it's like ashes," she says, "or a shadow. You know, like those people in Hiroshima."

"Maybe."

"The angel always makes me think of us," Anthea says.

Rigo blinks. "It does? Why?"

"Because we're like a miracle, *papi.*"

Rigo stands there, quietly holding on to her hand and the moment for as long as he can. Except for a brief visit by the ICLU, it's been a pleasant evening. The last thing he wants to do is ruin it by opening his mouth.

SIX

At work the next morning Rigo's boss, Rijn Ajisa, calls first thing. Before he has a chance to suit up. "Rigo, could I see you in my office?" Her expression on the inside of his wraparounds is an implacable tableau, a blank screen onto which he projects the heat death of the universe. He's only been to her office once before, the day he started work.

"Sure. No problem." His stomach pinches, twists into a knotted rag as he pods from the vat building to the main corporate office. Gone is the pleasant afterglow from last night.

The leak in his biosuit. There must be a serious problem with the warm-blooded plants. They've been contaminated, hosed beyond repair.

Either that, or politicorp security found out about the delivery he made for Beto—the old woman was working undercover—and is now going to arrest him.

If that's the case, he's screwed. Life as he knows it is over.

Like a condemned man, he mounts the stairs to Rijn Ajisa's second-floor office. His legs feel leaden, his bowels queasy, as if he's climbing the steps to a guillotine or hangman's noose.

"Please close the door," Ajisa says as soon as Rigo steps inside. Not a good sign. He nods, swallows. The door seals behind him like the lid of a coffin.

In addition to Ajisa, there's a man he doesn't recognize in the room. Dapper. Dressed in a natty tan suit sans vest, but sporting a bolo tie of twisted snakeskin tipped with silver-anodized rattles at both ends, the two glossy braids anchored at the neck with a turquoise-studded clasp the size of a belt buckle. The man's hands are wrinkled and liver spotted, parched by UV and inscribed with veins the color of blue ink. Smaller blood vessels trace entoptic intaglios just beneath the skin, mandelas of random hypnotic squiggles that are hard not to stare at.

"Have a seat, Rigo." Ajisa gestures amicably toward the remaining chair in front of her desk.

Rigo plops down next to the man, who regards him with double-barreled gunmetal blue eyes under gray hair. It looks as if a dust bunny has taken up residence on the crown of his skull and been plastered in place with coffee-colored spit. Rigo turns to Ajisa. "What's up?" he says, trying to keep his voice casual.

Ajisa settles into the plump gelbag behind her desk. "This is Arnez Whipplebaum, from Xengineering."

The old man thrusts a hand at him. "Pleased to meet you." Rigo expects a molasses-slow drawl. Instead the accent is British, the grip gnarled but effete—

the kind of hand that is clearly a product of natural selection, has evolved over several generations to fill the
specialized social niche of hoisting a teacup in a precise manner at a precise time.

"Arnez is implementation manager for the Kuiper
project," Ajisa tells Rigo. "He's in charge of the Tiresias test phase."

Rigo turns to Whipplebaum. "Does this have anything to do with the data I sent yesterday?"

"The infrastructure on the comet is very nearly
complete. We're preparing to go live, so to speak. De-
ploy the ecotecture."

"Is there a problem?" Rigo says. Might as well get
everything out in the open, up front.

"No," Whipplebaum says. "And, frankly, that's
what has us worried."

"It does?" Rigo shakes his head, confused.

"We're concerned there might be errors we're
missing," Whipplebaum explains. "Overlooking. The
problem is, we can't postpone the inevitable any
longer. No more excuses. It's time to put up or shut
up. Walk the talk, as they say."

Uh-huh. "What does that have to do with me?"
Mouth dry.

Whipplebaum steeples his hands in front of his
lips. "You've been working with the plants on a day-
to-day basis for six months, now." Hard to tell if it's a
question or a statement. "You're familiar with them
in a practical, hands-on way that no one else is at this
point. Dirt under the fingernails, and all that."

Rigo rubs the back of his neck to hide his discomfort. "I guess."

"Simply put," Whipplebaum says, forging ahead,

"we'd like to have a gardener on hand for the installation. Make sure everything is properly up and running before the colonists actually set foot in the ecotecture."

A gardener. Is that what he is? "You want me to go to the comet?" Rigo says.

Whipplebaum's head bobs, as if attached to a spring. "Precisely. We'd like to have you in situ during the transplant process."

It takes a moment for him to catch up with Whipplebaum. "But there aren't any seedlings ready to plant. Those are several months away."

"Right. Instead of growing the warm-blooded ecotecture on the comet, to save time we've decided to relocate some of the mature plants."

Rigo tries to picture them being moved en masse, lifted into low orbit on one of the geosynchronous elevators and then transported to the comet. "When?"

"Tomorrow morning. You'd shuttle up the day after that."

A last-minute decision from the sounds of it. "That's not much notice," he says.

"Things are moving ahead rather quickly," Whipplebaum admits, as if he too has been left out of breath by the unexpected pace of events.

"How long would I be there?" Rigo asks.

"Not long." Whipplebaum waves a hand, the movement a leafy flutter. "A day or two at most, to make sure everything's shipshape. Naturally your team will accompany you. That should make things somewhat easier."

"They've agreed to go?"

"We haven't talked to them yet," Ajisa says. "We wanted to discuss it with you, first."

In other words, get his answer. "What about the rest of the vats we're in charge of down here?" Rigo asks.

"Don't worry about it," Ajisa says. "You're covered. This is far more important right now. A priority."

"Would there need to be any special training? None of us has worked in zero-g or a vacuum before."

"You're already used to working in biosuits. So that won't be a problem. As far as zero-g, it might slow you down a little in the beginning. But I spec you'll adapt fairly quickly. Of course, you'll be claded for the ecotecture. You won't have to take antipher shots. Too risky in that type of situation."

"Think of it as an adventure," Whipplebaum says with cheery import. "A chance to broaden your horizons."

No way he can say no. Not if he wants to position himself for further advancement. Besides, if he doesn't agree to head up the team they'll just ask someone else. Rana or Antoine. Ajisa and Whipplebaum know that as well as he does. So his answer is a foregone conclusion, the discussion a formality. Interesting that they felt the need to ask him, give him a choice instead of just telling him to pack his bags for the trip.

"All right," Rigo agrees. "Sounds exciting." And it is. A great opportunity, no doubt about it.

"I knew we could count on you." Whipplebaum brims with enthusiasm and an almost paternal sense of approval that leaves Rigo feeling starched with pride.

* * *

After the meeting, Rigo gives Whipplebaum a tour of the warm-blooded vats. His crew specs the situation right away and are on their best behavior. They fall into an antlike rhythm. Quiet, efficient, single-minded, as if they can sense something important is about to go down . . . that they're being inspected as much as the facility and the plants. It never hurts to make a good impression.

"One of the biggest concerns we have with zero-g flora," Whipplebaum says, "is assuring their integrity."

"I'll bet." The two of them are standing in the vat building that houses the main greenhouse plant.

"That's why the sensor data you've been transmitting is so important. It establishes a baseline against which we're able to measure the progress of the plants in orbit."

"I see," Rigo says. This is the first he's heard of what the data was actually used for.

"What we've found," Whipplebaum continues, "is that most plants react to zero-g in much the same way that people do. They suffer the vegetative equivalent of bone loss and reduced circulatory efficiency."

"So, you've had to tweak them genetically. The way workers get tweaked when they live in space."

Whipplebaum runs a gloved finger across the lens-dimpled surface of the plant, as if caressing the cheek of a newborn. "Structurally, we need the plants sturdy enough to withstand both gravitational and rotational stress."

"Gravitational?" It doesn't sound like Whipplebaum's talking about micro-g's here.

"It's conceivable that emigrants to the belt might want to install mass drivers on the asteroids to move them about, nudge them into slightly different orbits. During that time the plants will undergo acceleration and deceleration."

"Is that one of the things you're going to test on Tiresias?" Rigo asks.

Whipplebaum turns toward Rigo. A white picket-fence grin flashes behind the faceplate. Rigo takes that as a yes.

"How would you like to live in the Kuiper belt?" Whipplebaum says.

Rigo can't tell if the question is rhetorical or a genuine offer. "I don't think so," Rigo says.

Behind the faceplate, Whipplebaum's helium-filled enthusiasm appears to burst, as if his whole raison d'être has been pricked. "Why not?"

"Too dark. It'd be night all the time."

"But you'd be gengineered to require less sunlight. Like the plants. You wouldn't *feel* deficient."

"Plus, it'd be cold."

"Again, you wouldn't notice." Whipplebaum's mood reinflates as Rigo's objections are quickly overcome and dispatched. "It would *feel* balmy. You would be absolutely comfortable. Perfectly adapted to your environment."

Rigo shrugs. "I guess I don't spec the advantage." What else can he say? It's just not his idea of a good time.

"For one," Whipplebaum says, "there's considerably more open space. Scads of it. Several times the land area of earth, in fact."

"Only more spread out."

"True. But that means no overpopulation for several centuries. Not to mention, cheap real estate."

Rigo digs one heel into the nutrient-rich ice underfoot. "But not much to look at in the way of scenery."

"Not until the plants are well established. After several years—fifteen or twenty at the most—it will be a tropical paradise."

Rigo shakes his head. "What would I do there?"

"The same thing settlers on a frontier have always done, build a new world. You would certainly enjoy far more freedom and independence than you do now."

There's a sort of bow-legged, tobacco-chewing, shit-kicking romanticism to Whipplebaum that feels . . . what? Not just anachronistic—hopelessly antiquated—but dangerously unrealistic.

"I'm happy here," Rigo says, "doing what I am."

"Too bad. You'd be missing the chance of a lifetime." The second time this has come up. "Especially for someone in your situation."

Rigo's subtext meter twitches. "What do you mean?"

Whipplebaum hesitates a fraction of a second. "Only that you're young. You have very little weighing you down, holding you back. Nothing to lose, everything to gain, as it were. Not like those of us who have acquired far more baggage than is healthy."

Rigo has the impression he was going to say something else, and then thought the better of it—that Whipplebaum is dropping hints. Trying to *tell* him something. Father Cielo had the same effect on him when Rigo went to church as a kid. Rigo was guilty, even if he didn't know what the sin was. Eternal damnation lurked just around the corner. He was just too blind to see it.

"I'll think about it," Rigo says, noncommittal.

Whipplebaum claps him on the shoulder, turns, and exits the vat building. When they're back outside, blinking at the sunlight, Whipplebaum says, "How would you like to go to a party tonight?"

"A party?"

"A private gathering for some of the project specialists you and your team will be working with on Tiresias. Gengineers, programmers and technical support personnel, as well as a number of the colonists." Whipplebaum winks, as if a wasp has just kamikaze'd into his eye. "I can promise that you'll find it most entertaining. An intimate get-together, quite unlike any you may have attended before."

"Sure," Rigo says, not wanting to be impolite or impolitic. "Sounds good." Plus he's mad curious. His interest is *piqued*.

Whipplebaum's IA, an agent named Trigger, squirts him an invitation. The party starts at eight, and is in CV. Carmel Valley. Rigo opens his mouth, prepares to concede that he's not claded for CV, when Whipplebaum pulls out a sprayon ampoule and hands it to him with a flourish, as if he's delivering an invitation from the queen. "Dose yourself with this half an hour before you arrive at the door."

The ampoule is yellow glass with blue and red tracery. Very art nouveau. "What is it?"

Whipplebaum does a little half bow. "Your admission ticket." He seems to have anticipated Rigo's situation and deftly headed off any embarrassment.

"Congratulations," Varda says after Whipplebaum is gone. "After all your hard work, you've finally hit dirt pay."

SEVEN

Anthea sits by the hospital bed, the drawing cradled in her lap, watching the rise and fall of Ibrahim's chest. The images on the sketchpad exert a magnetic pull on her, as if her eyeballs are veined with slivers of iron. She can't not look. Her gaze is drawn to the scene the way her memory is sometimes drawn to the past—repeatedly and against her will.

Like Ibrahim, Anthea was a street kid. A runaway. They have that in common. But what he's running from is so completely outside her realm of experience it's like those nether regions on n-teenth-century maps populated with dragons, demons and other mythic horrors.

Anthea thought she had it bad: escaping the aloof, ruthless hauteur of her mother; hanging with a bunch of twelve-year-olds who believed that ROM-entombed back issues of *National Geographic* were a

defunct fashion magazine; distributing sexually transmitted drugs—black-market psychoactive prions that
nested in the warm cozy environs of her body where
they were happy to hang around indefinitely, waiting
for someone to give her cold hard currency instead of
a black eye and a split lip for her services.

Ironic that putting out got her out. At the age of
fourteen she was approached by a Global Upreach
social worker. Instead of STDs, she agreed to spread
vaccines and antibiotics to people who couldn't afford the drugs supplied by managed health care. The
money was lousy, but the benefits were great. Free
room, free board, and when she turned seventeen an
all-expenses-paid trip to the college education of her
choice.

Until then her existence as a *puta* had been pretty
subsistence level. She was lucky, escaped with nothing
more serious than a few ritual gang scars. What was
Ibrahim's ticket to a better future? How did he get
out . . . and at what price? Where did he think he was
going? Or had he been like her? Didn't care where he
went as long as it was someplace different?

Looking at the drawing, a sort of William S. Bur-
roughs meets Paul Klee collage, it's impossible to tell.
No way she'll be able to decipher it without help—
Ibrahim's or someone else's.

At least his face is peaceful now, not the cracked-
glass visage inscribed on the pad. Splintered scribbles
of red, daubed with malarial puddles of yellow she
speculates are eyes.

Easier to study the sunken lines of his face, bathed
in the indolent afternoon haze from the window by
the foot of the bed. The window is really a wallscreen,

which just happens to be tuned to a realtime view outside the building, where afternoon clouds are grouping over the hunched backbone of dry hills. The crepe sprayon sheets cocoon Ibrahim like a funeral shroud. The inflatable pillow supporting his head reminds her of a sagging party balloon. By design everything is soothing powder pink. Pink is the color of health, of happiness.

Quiet movement behind her. Anthea starts, wrenches her head around à la Linda Blair in *The Exorcist*, which she had to deconstruct for a postmodern cultural history class: Psycho Cinema, the Mediagenic Expression of Supernatural Archetypes in Late Twentieth-Century Collective Consciousness.

"Well?" she asks Isa, the on-duty physician. "How's he doing?"

"Not good." Isa gazes past her for a moment, peering at a virtual datawindow. She's a wiry Australian aborigine with hair that resembles a tightly coiled ensemble of pipe cleaners. "His condition is stable. For now. But I don't know how long that will last."

"Can I talk to him?"

"As soon as he wakes up. He's still sedated."

Anthea stands, sketchpad pressed to her chest with both hands. "What can you tell me about him?"

"What do you want to know?"

Everything, she's tempted to say. Where he came from. How he got to SJ. Who his parents are. "Let's start with what's wrong."

Isa purses her lips, glosses them with the tip of her tongue. "To begin with, he isn't keyed to the local ecotecture. We've got him on antiphers, but that's a temporary solution. At some point, he'll either have to be deported or recladed."

"Deported to where?"

"Good question. We haven't been able to identify all the pherions in his system. We have no idea what they do or where they came from."

"Care to venture a guess?"

Isa wets her lips. "Offhand, I'd say they were man-ufactured by a black-market pharm."

Meaning they could have come from just about anywhere in the world. "What about the pherions you can identify?"

"SEA." Southeast Asia. "But it's difficult to say for sure because the ecotecture implemented there was modified later for Africa and South America."

"So he could be part of that migration."

"Or not."

Well, that narrows it down a bit. She knows with a fair amount of certainty that he isn't from Europe, Antarctica, or Mongolia.

"There's another problem," Isa tells her.

"What's that?" Anthea says. Judging by Isa's ex-pression, she doesn't want to know.

"Every cell in his body is dying. Whatever ecotec-ture he's claded for provides a critical pherion, or combination of pherions, his body needs to survive."

Anthea knits her brow. "If he's away from it for too long he'll die?"

"Right. It's like he's going through withdrawal. But instead of getting better as his system detoxes, he's getting worse."

Anthea glances at Ibrahim. "What kind of pherion?"

Isa shrugs. "He's got so much crap in his system, sorting through it could take weeks."

"So you don't even know what it does?"

Isa shakes her head. "Sorry."

Meaning there's no way to synthesize a replacement. "There must be *some*thing you can do."

"There is, and we're already doing it. Everything we can."

Anthea grinds her jaw from side to side, scraping her teeth along her bottom lip. "How much time does he have?"

"At the present rate of decline, a few days. Less, if the degeneration accelerates toward the end."

"You think maybe he was in a child labor camp?" Anthea says. In some subclades, indentured workers are made physically dependent on a pherion in the ecotecture. Without the pherion, they can't survive. Escape results in slow but certain death.

"It could also be a religious sect or conscript militia," Isa says. "Biodependency is still legal in a lot of places."

True. Since the implementation of gengineered plants and artificial ecologies half a century ago, biodependency has been used by governments and politicorps to control demographics—keep populations confined to certain geographical regions. In the beginning it was a necessity. The old ecology was too damaged and fragile to support even the status quo, let alone any sustainable growth. Areas of the world died off en masse, killing billions of people in the process. Starvation was rampant. The only way to preserve various segments of a population, whole societies, was to confine them to ecotectural zones capable of supporting life. Of course, nothing's perfect. Some of the gengineered flora and fauna wasn't as benign as originally believed, or it mutated. Either way, people had to be modified to cope with the changes. Retroviruses spliced in artificial genes designed to augment the immune system. After a few million more deaths, chemical imbalances were neutralized, equilibrium reestablished, and everything was more or less hunky-dory.

Soon, the geographic boundaries evolved along ethnic and racial lines, reshaped by the politics of the past. People settled into clades, populations with a specific biochemical signature compatible with some ecotectures, but not others. From there, it was only a short leap to clades based on specific religious, social, or political ideologies. Environment became less of a determining factor than dogma.

Which is where things stand now. Clades have gotten so granular that they can be as small as two individuals, binding one to the other. Spouse to spouse, disciples to cult leader, daughter to mother . . .

Isa touches Anthea's arm. "Find out where he's from," Isa says, "and I'll have a much better chance of figuring out what he needs."

Anthea nods, watches Isa exit the hospital room. The sketchpad is crushed painfully to her breasts. Anthea forces the muscles in her arms to unknot, easing some of the pressure. Still, her heart aches with the pain of a phantom thrombosis—fear and anger and helplessness clotting inside her chest.

Did Ibrahim have help getting here? He must have. It's highly unlikely he could have escaped a bio-enslavement situation on his own. Did his benefactor know he would die once he'd been freed from wherever he was being held? If so, s/he may have a way to help him. All she has to do is track the person down. Figure out where Ibrahim was going. "Did you scope all that?" she asks Doug.

"Of course," Doug quips. "I'm all-seeing and all-hearing."

"Well, if it's not too much trouble, can you put together a list of recent incidents of biodependent slavery, say the last six months? I want all illegal as well as legal cases, if that's possible."

"Yessum."

"Have you come up with anything from the sketchpad?"

"No, ma'am, not yet I hasn't. I's still waitin' on da rasta'ization enhancement and pattern rekonition anal sis."

"I have to tell you Doug, you're mining the depths of bad taste here."

"True." The IA unfurls a bouffant, melodramatic sigh. "I be da first to admit the last thing I wanna be is politic'ly co'rect."

Anthea's tempted to reply with an acerbic retort of her own, but bites her tongue in an effort not to encourage the behavior by dignifying it with a response. "Well then, perhaps you can find time to cross-correlate the location of each biodependent incident with images on the sketchpad."

"Yes, massa. No problem."

"Also, see what you can uncover on bioenslavement activity here in the States. Black-market adoption scams, pedophilia, child labor. You know."

"I sho does."

Doug will be able to mine the infosphere for that kind of data much more quickly and efficiently than she can. After all, that's where Doug lives. His home. She wonders what the IA does in its spare time for relaxation, and decides not to open that Pandora's box. Better not to know.

"Will tha' be all?" Doug asks.

"For now. Thank you."

"Den I best be off to do my chores."

The IA drops offline. Anthea pictures it sulking in a far corner of the Web, a dog licking itself, nursing pet grievances while concocting elaborate double and triple entendres to annoy her. She really should apply for a new IA, but Doug seems to need an outlet for the repressed feelings it harbors. In a way she provides a perverse form of therapy. She feels obligated, duty-bound to endure its antics.

Anthea shifts her attention to Ibrahim. She enters the room, walks to the side of the bed, and takes one of his hands. It's hot, sweaty, and incredibly light; the bones of his fingers feel hollow as they curl in response to hers. She returns the squeeze and his eyes flutter open, wild with fear behind the dull patina of sedatives.

She leans forward. "It's okay," she whispers. "You're safe. No one is going to hurt you."

The anxiety fades. The troubled surface of his gaze returns to complacency, and the corners of his mouth relax. "Mom?"

"Where is she, Ibrahim? Can you tell me where your mother's at?"

He continues to stare at the ceiling, looking past her. Through her. "Am I going to die?"

Anthea inhales sharply, smells the sourness of her own apprehension. "You're going to be fine."

"I'm sorry."

"For what?"

"I couldn't stay. I had to leave."

"That's all right, sweetie. Don't worry about that. You did what you had to do. What you thought was best."

Anthea kisses him on the forehead. Tastes salt and the stringent tang of topical antiseptics. A faint smile curves his lips. His gaze retreats inward and his eyelids ease shut. His breathing steadies, lapses into peaceable slumber. She waits with him, letting her own tension slip away under the steady rise and fall of his chest.

Not much more she can do at the moment. She hates this part. The waiting, the sense of helplessness.

There is one thing she can do. Not exactly legal, but there are times it's necessary to bend the rules a little to get results. Especially in a life-and-death situation. The ends justify the means.

The lab is in the basement, a Cartesian warren of tunnels. The structural diamond walls are smooth—shimmer with the silvery pearlescence of a snail trail or the interior of an abalone shell. Glassware-laden carts line the walls, next to biofreezers, blood jelly abattoirs and emergency shower nozzles. A chemical tang permeates the air, a mixture of sulfuric acid, rubbing alcohol, and airborne antiseptics that scour her lungs and sinuses for bacteria. Stringent UV light sterilizes her hair, skin, and clothes.

Anthea finds Beni in the specimen room, preparing to test a sample. He's wearing tie-dyed scrubs and listening to a classic Lou Harrison gamelan piece from the late twentieth century.

"Hey, Beni," she says over a clamor of gongs.

"Anthea," Beni says. He wriggles latex-clad fingers at her, points to the surgical mask on his face, then turns toward a nearby refrigerator.

Anthea unhooks a sprayon nozzle from the wall just inside the door, mists her lower face. Seconds later, her mouth and nose covered with a thin micropore membrane, she follows Beni over to the refrigerator. Through the sheet-diamond door, she can see racks of test tubes and Eppendorf tubes. The latter look like a collection of bloodstained arrowheads that have been preserved from Little Big Horn, or maybe the Battle of Agincourt.

"When you going to put some marmalade on them bones?" Beni says, his breath fogging on the door.

"What?" she says. "I'm not sweet enough?"

"It's not the quality I'm worried about, my dear, but the quantity." Beni flashes an impish grin. "You know me. I like a *lot* of sugar in my diet."

Beni is an expansive man and has a personality to match. Every little movement he makes is a good-natured jiggle, the jovial precursor to a full-bodied rumble lurking just beneath the surface. Whenever a laugh bubbles up, it erupts like a Richter-scale temblor that reduces to rubble any ill-humor in the vicinity of the epicenter. Field lines of positive energy radiate from his cheerful bulk, attract friends and acquaintances the way a sun attracts orbiting bodies.

Anthea is a minor planetoid in his solar system, an infrequent visitor. But Beni is always glad to see her whenever she swings by. Always willing to lend a hand.

"So, what can I do for you?" He rubs at the condensation with one elbow, scans each of the labeled tubes with a molecular pen, and squints at the resulting readout. "Or did you just miss me?"

"Both," she says. Then, "I need some help."

Beni straightens. "For yourself or someone else?" He slides open the door, takes out one of the chilled test tubes.

"Ibrahim Darji."

Beni eases the door shut, thoughtful as he ambles over to a pherion analyzer on the counter.

Anthea dutifully trails after him. A breath of chill air from the refrigerator follows her. The ghostly presence raises goose pimples on her arms. "You did a workup on him yesterday."

"I remember." He sets the test tube in a holder, retrieves a sequencing wafer, and inserts a pipette into the test tube.

"He's dying," she says.

Beni grimaces. "I know." He draws a gossamer of blood into the pipette, delicate as a hummingbird sipping nectar from a rose.

Anthea hugs herself, rubs her chill-dappled upper arms. "There may be no way to help him."

Beni's mocha brown eyes meet her gaze. "But you think there might be." This is a side to him that she hasn't seen before. Sober, almost serious.

"I don't know. Maybe."

Beni smears the top surface of the wafer with

blood, then slots the wafer into the analyzer. The wafer is coated with enzymes that react with DNA and all known pherions and drugs. A positive reaction results in a specific chemical signal, displayed on a three-dimensional topographic map that renders concentration as amplitude. A typical output resembles a digitized skyline of New York viewed from a few thousand meters above the Atlantic. All unidentified chemicals are broken down, sequenced, and logged for further analysis.

"His workup had a lot of unknown pherions. Stuff that hasn't turned up in any of the library cross-references."

"I know someone who might be able to identify them."

Beni's cheeks bulge as he probes his tongue around the inside of his mouth. "I take it you're talkin' black-market. A private pharm."

"Could be."

"And you want me to give you a sample of his blood for analysis by this person, is that right?"

"Yes."

"You're not going to get into any trouble, are you?"

"I know what I'm doing. We've done business be-fore—"

Beni raises a hand, cutting her off. "I don't want to know. The less I know, the better."

"Does that mean you'll do it?"

Beni makes a pained face. "If this is what being a sugar daddy means, I'm gonna have to rethink my sweet tooth."

EIGHT

The pod slows to a stop in front of a stodgy Queen Anne. The house is as prim as an octogenarian ballerina caked with makeup. It's color coordinated, dolled up in pastel green, beige, and blue. There's even a turret, of all things. The lawn is pedicured, the plants ornamental—freeze-dried. Everything in Carmel is that way. The buildings, the streets, the dinosaur remnants of late twentieth-century automobiles that have been converted from petroleum to hydrogen fuel-cell power. The whole clade has the feel of a zoo or a natural history diorama.

"Very pretty," Varda quips. "Maybe you should put on something a little more fitted."

Rigo frowns at what he's got on—loose cotton slacks and shirt—checks out the clothing in the in-pod stores. Much as he hates to admit it, Varda's

sense of fashion is several orders of magnitude beyond his. "What do you suggest?"

"Something more period," the IA suggests.

"Such as?"

"Polyester."

"I have a nice Hiz Claiborne leisure suit," the pod
says helpfully.

Rigo walks over to the display window a few seats
down from him. The dispenser offers a wide selection
of bodyware: jewelry, cosmetics, accessories, and a
large variety of personal hygiene products. In addition, there are several sprayon suits, slacks, and sport
jackets.

"Would you like to see what it looks like?" the
pod-turned-store-clerk asks.

What the hell.

Rigo waits for the store to scan his image, calculate
his measurements. A moment later an image of the
suit appears on his eyescreens, modeled by Rigo himself.

"It's definitely you," Varda says. "Dressed to
murder."

"I guess," Rigo says. It's a little retro for his taste,
but all in all it doesn't look too bad.

"Shall I deduct it from your account?" the pod in-
quires.

"Yes," Varda says before Rigo can object. "Thank
you."

At times like this, Rigo wonders if it's a good idea
to entrust Varda with his basic financial affairs. The
IA's done a good job keeping him organized and out
of debt, but there are times he definitely feels a lack of
control—even though the hassle of managing one's

daily expenses can be a total pain in the ass. Still, he doesn't want the headache or the responsibility, has better things to do with his time.

The sprayon canister rotates into view on its carousel. Rigo opens the dispenser door and takes it out.

"Hiz Claiborne thanks you for your purchase," the pod chirps. "Hiz Claiborne, a leading purveyor of image-enhancing products for over fifty years, realizes that you have millions of shopping options and appreciates your business. Thank you for choosing Hiz Claiborne for all your personal decor needs!"

"Try it on," Varda says.

Rigo sprays the suit on over his shirt and pants. It takes a few minutes for the new fabric to overwrite the old. But pretty soon he's sporting an open-collared canary yellow shirt, a chartreuse wide-lapel jacket, and matching stretch pants with knife-edge crease down the front that's sharp enough to slice ripe tomatoes.

"What do you think?" Rigo asks, straightening the sleeves and the collar. At least he doesn't have to wear a tie.

"Dynamite," Varda says enthusiastically. "You're a bomb."

"Please exit," the pod interrupts, polite yet firm. "I have another passenger pickup and am running behind schedule. Your fellow commuters thank you in advance for your cooperation."

Just before he depods, Rigo doses himself with most of the antipher Whipplebaum gave him, then tucks the rest in one of the many pockets afforded by his new jacket.

The air outside the pod is scented with a rose-water deodorizer, sweated out by the surrounding vegetation. By and large, the air freshener masks the offshore smell of brine, rotting kelp, and seagull shit. But as he heads up the brick walkway and wooden steps to the front door of the house, he catches a furtive whiff of Monterey Bay that hints at dead fish and deep, underlying currents of decay. A stately Mercedes Benz trundles by, drooling water from its exhaust pipe.

The door is polite in an effete sort of way—Tiffany glass set in a floral pattern of lead tracery—though not particularly snobbish. If anything, it sounds embarrassed by its role as butler.

"Please place the tip of one index finger in the middle of my central-most flower," it tells him in a pained tone.

Rigo imagines the door must get a lot of humiliating deflowering jokes, which it is forced to endure with complete equanimity. He decides to exercise self-restraint. There's nothing quite as confining and potentially claustrophobic as an unfriendly door.

"Thank you," the door says. Relieved but anxious to get Rigo on his way, it opens with a flourish, ushering him into a dainty, parlor-sized anteroom filled with laughter and party babble. In front of him, a staircase angles steeply up to the second floor. Doorways on the left and right access what appear to be living and dining rooms. The aroma of savory hors d'oeuvres hangs in the air: crab dip, smoked salmon, fresh salsa, and buttered popcorn sprinkled with kick-ass chili powder. The floors are polished hardwood, blond oak. Gauzy curtains, demure as wedding veils, hang on the windows. Brass lamps throw incandescent cones of light over fancy sitting chairs and chintz-pattern sofas.

"Rigo!" Antoine calls from the appetizer table across the room.

Rana, Luis, Claribel, and Hsi-Tang—most of his vat crew—are with Antoine, dressed in their best formal attire. Lots of improvised gold lamé, black silk, and starched white rayon.

"What took you so long?" Hsi-Tang says, chiding. "You missed out on all the good food, dude. They had this great sesame-seaweed paté."

"He needed to pick up some rad sprayons," Luis says. He touches a fingertip to Rigo's new jacket, makes a hissing sound between his teeth.

"I'd be careful if I were you," Rana warns Rigo. "Anthea might not like a strange man in her bed. You could end up sleeping alone."

"Hell," Claribel drawls, raising a half-fisted hand. "There's always Rosie. She'll treat you right."

Rigo picks up a Szechwan calamari-rice cube, pops it in his mouth. "Where are TomE and Naguib?"

"Making the rounds," Antoine says, winking.

"Not to mention downing them," Luis says.

Whipplebaum materializes in a doorway to the left, balancing a brandy snifter in one hand and a plate of topiary vegetables in the other. Carrot nubs have been sculpted into roses, cucumbers sliced and carved into water lilies. A cauliflower elephant wallows on its side in a pond of white chive-speckled dip. He nods for Rigo to join him.

"I'll catch up with you later," Rigo tells his team.

He grabs another rice cube, and goes to meet Whipplebaum.

"Glad you could make it, my boy." Whipplebaum gives him a friendly clap on the shoulder. "Nice suit. Very spiffy."

"Ditto." Whipplebaum is decked out in a cummerbund, a long black coat with tails, and a rawhide bolo tie bristling with barbed wire. A white ten-liter Stetson completes the ensemble.

"This way." Whipplebaum steers him into a dining room where several people are grazing at a table. There, Whipplebaum grabs a bottle, pours Rigo a drink, and hands it to him.

Rigo sniffs the amber liquid. "Wine?"

"Gallo," Whipplebaum says. "The finest pre-ecocaust vintage still available." He lifts his glass in mock toast and then dispatches it in one fell swig.

Rigo tosses his shot back and chokes on the taste of vinegar. He blinks rapidly, as if every nerve in his body's undergone anaphylactic shock.

"I thought gallow was a kind of humor," Varda says, sounding perplexed.

Whipplebaum laughs. "Brings tears to the eyes." His pupils gleam, his cheeks flush. He refills Rigo's glass.

"What about quark flipping?" a woman at the table says. It's as if Rigo's hearing has suddenly shifted bandwidth, tuned in a new frequency.

"You mean in protons and neutrons?" a man in the group asks, hand poised over a silver tray heaped with crab cakes.

"Why not? That way, you could quantum toggle between resonance states. Á la femtoswitch."

Shop talk. Rigo's thoughts skitter across the surface of the conversation, trying to penetrate the words. A femtoswitch, he reminds himself, uses the up-down arrangement of quarks in protons and neutrons to represent two different states, 0 or 1. He can do this. He can play this game if he wants. It's not that hard. He has a lot to learn. Sure. But he doesn't have to be an outsider. With a little bit of vigorous mixing, he can blend in.

"Follow me," Whipplebaum says. "There are some people I want you to meet." Taking Rigo by the arm, Whipplebaum guides him through a crowded doorway, into a crammed kitchen, out a back door, down a wooden stoop, into a lantern-illuminated yard. The lanterns consist of square, cylindrical, and triangular frames over which handmade paper has been folded. The paper is decorated with colorful flotsam, backlit flower petals that resemble pink and blue fireflies trapped in amber.

"Is everybody here from Xengineering?" Rigo asks as they enter a small patio area walled by trellises on three sides.

But Whipplebaum has disappeared.

"You're intoxicating," Varda informs him with clinical detachment. "You have a blood-alcohol level of point-oh-six." The IA's disembodied voice sounds very far away and tinny.

Someone in a tux sloshes wine into his empty glass. Just what he needs. His head feels detached, borne aloft by a sense of unreality. His alcohol-infused limbs are lighter than air. He's fairly certain the air, food, and drinks are drugged, and that anything is possible. No different from the hood, really. Except that here a veneer of decorum softens any act of impropriety. It's a world of euphemisms in which assholes are tolerated—are in fact revered—and fondly referred to as eccentrics.

Instead of being drawn in, Rigo finds himself pushed toward the outer edges of the social melee. It's cooler at the fringe, the babble quieter, easier to parse. Rigo can almost make sense of the esoteric bon mots being exchanged by a nearby gaggle of upper-clade caucs engaged in a cluster fuck. They flirt and tease each other with ideas.

Rigo sits down on a bench. On the pinwheel tree overhead leaves twirl, spinning hypnotic, kaleidoscope patterns of color. Rigo watches, mesmerized.

"I trust you're enjoying yourself?"

The voice startles him. Wine sloshes onto the patio's red paving bricks. Rigo lunges to his feet, stares into the face of the moribund *vieja* who propositioned him at Salmon Ella's.

"Uh . . ."

"That's all right. I'm surprised to see you here, too. Pleasantly, I might add." She offers him a hand. He takes it the way he would a raw gutted fish—not at all certain how to handle the dead creature he's holding.

She looks better than Rigo remembered, not as desperate or haggard. Could be it's his imagination, or the low light. Plus, she's rocking this ocher-colored silk dress, intricately patterned, that hangs nicely on her, goes well with her gray hair and parchment skin. The dress has the surface texture and look of a Navajo rug, but is sheer and tastefully revealing.

"Dorit," she says.

"Rigo."

She withdraws her hand, flops it in the direction of the party. "How come you're not mingling?"

Her gaze holds his. She seems to know the answer in advance. Because he doesn't fit in, doesn't belong.

"I just needed to get some fresh air. It was getting kind of stuffy over there, hard to breathe."

The woman laughs, genuinely amused. "I know exactly how you feel."

"Really?" He's regaining his composure, some sense of equilibrium. He doesn't have anything to be ashamed of or embarrassed about.

"More than you might think," Dorit says. The admission is flip, offhand, but Rigo gets the impression she's not playing coy.

For some reason—"You're three sheets in the wind," Varda warns him—he's not repulsed by her. Not like before. Perhaps because the situation's different, and he isn't feeling nearly as uptight.

"Would you like to go for a short walk?" Dorit says.

"Sure." Rigo knows what this means. She wants to have a *conversation*. Most likely about their little tête-à-tête the other night.

Dorit leads him along a flagstone footpath that takes them deeper into the garden. It's a fairy-tale garden of Popsicle plants, dandelion wood, and big tulip-shaped shrubs with leaves that are taller than him. Ecotecture he's never seen, doesn't know the name for or even what it is supposed to do. A dull, pounding roar fills the air. It grows steadily louder with every step.

"How do you feel?" Dorit asks. "You look a little peaked."

"Okay."

"Good. I imagine this is the first time you've attended a party quite like this. It can be rather unnerving."

"Yeah." He can hear condensation trickling deep inside the tulip bushes, plopping into secret ponds. No doubt, underground roots carry the condensation back to the house, purifying the water and boosting the pressure.

Dorit rubs her arms against the night chill. "My advice is to take advantage of the situation while you can. Who knows when you'll get another chance to be totally free, to act without restraint."

"What do you mean?"

"Find out what it's like to be yourself. Hold on to that, and take it with you when you leave. Try not to forget who you are in the morning."

They enter an orchard of pinwheel trees. Thousands of leaves whir frantically in a steady ocean breeze. The sound is as loud as an angry hornets' nest.

"Tell me," she says. "What does it feel like?"

"What does what feel like?"

She stops and spreads her arms wide. The diaphanous sleeves of her dress fall aside, fully exposing the mesh exoskeleton that encases her body. "This. Being *some*place you've never been to before. Mingling with people you wouldn't normally get a chance to meet, let alone talk to."

"You're shitting me, right?"

Dorit lowers her arms in a jerky pantomime of a wooden puppet. "I've led a very sheltered life."

"I guess."

"So have you. You just don't realize it."

"In what way?"

"Fear," Dorit tells him. "Prejudice. Those can be just as confining as any physical barrier. More so. Unlike you, I have always been free to go wherever I want, whenever I want. For various reasons, which I would rather not reveal, I chose not to."

"Until last night."

Dorit begins to walk again. "Going to Salmon Ella's was an attempt on my part to feel alive. I could have sent someone else to make the pickup. But I made the conscious decision not to."

"Why the sudden change of heart?"

"Preparation. I wanted to know what it was like to take a risk, make myself vulnerable in a way I never had before."

"You must've been really hard up." Salmon Ella's is hardly risqué, not exactly a badmash club.

"One has to begin somewhere," she says, philosophical.

"Is that what you're doing now? With me?"

Dorit laughs, widening the hairline crack in her aloof, carefully nurtured brittleness. Through it, he catches a glimpse of the little girl she once was, seventy or eighty years earlier.

"I guess I am, yes. Alone at night with a dangerous *tíguere*. That is the correct term, is it not?"

"Yes." Never mind that he's not a *tíguere*. If she wants to believe he's a badass, who is he to shatter her illusion? He's doing her a big favor. This way she can feel good about herself. She can tell all her friends she partied with a *tíguere* and lived to tell about it.

They come to the end of the path. It dead-ends at the edge of a cliff that looks out over the Pacific.

"I remember watching whales from here," she says, "and seals and dolphins. Now there are only seagulls. It feels like everything I ever loved in the world is gone." She draws in a pained breath. "You're lucky, Rigo. You don't remember what the world was like, before the ecocaust. It would be a blessing for me, at this point, to know only the present. To have nothing against which to compare what is with what was." A tremor of sorrow fills the words.

"How much better could it have been?" It seems a safe enough topic. A good way to keep the conversation focused on her instead of him.

"If by 'better' you mean more diverse, then quite a bit. The current biosphere is horribly stripped down, bare bones. It works, but the complexity is gone—the beauty. In truth, outside of the bioremediated zones, the world is a wasteland. Hundreds of thousands of species have simply vanished. It's true!" Dorit insists, scoping his incredulity. "Most of the plants and animals that died off filled microniches. People never noticed them, but they were important. Not just as a whole but singly."

"Species have always vanished. That's what evolution, survival of the fittest, is all about."

"Yes. But we sped up the process exponentially. Human beings outevolved evolution. Except for cockroaches and a few other highly adaptive organisms, the biosphere couldn't keep pace with us. *We* almost couldn't keep pace with us. Still, things could be worse," she admits. "*Much* worse. A few more decades and nothing would have been left."

"I don't know. Sounds kind of extreme."

"It *was* extreme. In a couple of hundred years we destroyed millions of years of natural evolution. We don't even have the genetic information to go back and recreate what was lost. There was so much—and no one thought to preserve it. Or by the time they did, it was too late."

Why is she telling him all this? What does she expect him to say? It's not as if he can *do* anything about it. She might have been able to. But that's her guilt trip, not his.

"Was this mass extinction different than any other mass extinction?" Rigo asks.

"Of course it was."

"I don't see how. Look at what happened to the dinosaurs. They got wiped out by an asteroid."

"That was different."

"Why?"

Her mouth pinches. Lips of cracked procelain. "Because it was natural. An act of God."

"But so are we. *We're* natural—an act of God. No different than an asteroid or a volcanic eruption."

"We had a choice," Dorit says, "we knew better. That's the difference. We could have prevented it from happening."

"Not if our behavior's hardwired."

"Bravo!" She claps her hands in a parody of delight. "That's the spirit. Complete abdication of responsibility to biological determinism. Whatever atrocity we commit is a genetic fait accompli."

Her doomsday spiel is a potent cocktail, a witches' brew of sarcasm and pessimism that renders him momentarily speechless. Not to mention depressed.

"What do you miss the most?" Rigo asks, hoping to get her on a more pleasant topic. Plus, he's genuinely curious. He wants to find out more about her, wants to *know* her. The urge is as inexplicable as it is powerful. To think that only yesterday she made him shudder, sent him into necrophobic paroxysms. Amazing the difference a few drinks can make.

"Butterflies. Irises, roses, violets. The singing of larks." She hugs herself, caught in the grip of nostalgia. "The smell of fresh apples and wet pine needles after a summer shower. Frogs croaking at night. Snail trails silvered by moonlight. The taste of blackberries. Listen to me! I sound like a silly romantic."

Rigo nods at the pinwheel trees around them. "So all of this is pointless? A total waste?"

"Not at all. It's very sui generis. And some of the plants are absolutely lovely. I know it's not fair to compare them to what I remember. It's a bad habit, the worst. Ultimately counterproductive. What's gone is gone. You can't go back, and I certainly don't plan to try at this point. It's too late for that."

For a second, Rigo entertains the idea that she is contemplating suicide. It would be easy to fling herself off the cliff, and onto the rocks below, in a fit of grief. A kind of melancholy swoon. "What are you going to do?"

"I'm going to leave," she says. "The past is gone. There's no future in the past. I've spent far too much time there as it is."

"Where will you go?"

"Tiresias, my dear *tíguere*. I've decided there's no point in remaining human. A century of humanity is enough. It's time to discover what it means to be something other than human. Though there are those who would argue that I'm already inhuman."

How melodramatic, he thinks. Yet he can see that she's serious. She's not just making up shit.

"Rigo?" Varda says, interrupting his train of thought.

He groans. Not now.

"I think you should know that I've detected several unregistered and unlicensed pherions in your system."

He shakes his head. Ignores the IA.

"Why do you find that so surprising?" Dorit says. "Gerontocrats have as much right as anybody else to start over. More so. In fact, I'd think you'd be glad to get rid of us."

"It's not that," Rigo says.

"Besides," Dorit continues, "the project needs somebody my age to study the ontogenetic effects of the reclading. How will I respond, physically and psychologically, to the new ecotecture and a zero-g environment? So you see, it's a perfect confluence of purpose."

"How long will you be up there?" Rigo says.

"Forever. Tomorrow, after I become symbiotically linked to the ecotecture, there is no turning back."

At which point she'll be able to derive most, if not all, of her nourishment directly from the warm-blooded plants. Food. Oxygen. Water. Including all minerals, vitamins, and other essential nutrients. Waste recycling and detoxification.

"That kind of limits your options, doesn't it?" he says. "I mean, if the plants die so do you." It's an all-or-nothing proposition.

"No different than here, really." A look of amusement crosses her face. "On the plus side, I'll know exactly what my limitations are. Exactly how my behavior and life are being controlled. Which is more than most people can say."

The comment seems to be directed at him. But maybe not. Could be he's simply being paranoid. Reading shit into it.

"What if you get up there and find out you don't like it, that you made a mistake? What then?"

"That's not going to happen," she tells him. "I want to forget—make a complete break. I'm tired of mourning every time I see a relic of the past. I want to put the world I knew behind me. It's dead. *I'm* dead."

"And you're convinced this will bring you back to life?"

"Yes. In fact, it's already given me more raison d'être than I've felt in the last ten years."

Rigo's not so sure. It sounds like a complicated way of ending one life and being reborn into another without actually having to go through the scary pant-shitting process of dying. Not that being radically re-gengineered and living in a warm-blooded plant in a total vacuum isn't a terrifying proposition. It's definitely not something Rigo plans to do anytime soon. But then, he's not undergoing an existential gerontocratic crisis. He might feel different if he were in her situation—a little more adventurous, more willing to take a risk. But he's not in her situation. He's happy. He's closer to the beginning of his life than the end, has a lot more future at stake. Anyway, who is he to judge?

"Well, I hope it works out the way you want,"

Rigo says as sincerely as he can. He means it, too. Isn't just feeding her a line.

"You, too," she says. Then she reaches out a hand, rests it on his arm the way she did in Salmon Ella's.

Her touch sends an erotic tingle through him, as if his *cojones* have just been alligator-clipped to a live wire. Stiffened by the sudden electric charge, his dick stands at painful attention.

"Be careful," she says. "Especially when you get to Tiresias."

"Careful of what?"

"The unexpected. You never know"—she shrugs—"anything could happen at any time."

"Right." He'll keep that in mind, just as soon as his hard-on takes a hike. First things first.

"There you are!" Whipplebaum's voice booms behind them. Dorit releases Rigo's arm and the static charge drains out of him. He feels himself shrivel and go limp.

"Arnez." Dorit extends her hand.

Whipplebaum removes his Stetson, takes the offering, and bends stiffly at the waist to give it a polite peck. His dust bunny hair threatens to float away in a dandelion cloud. "I see you've made the acquaintance of our newest team member."

"How could I not?"

"Of course." Whipplebaum straightens, replaces his hat, and turns to Rigo. "I do hope that our dear Dorit hasn't given you any epistemological misgivings regarding the Tiresias project."

"Not at all," Rigo says.

Whipplebaum's eyebrows cringe like fuzzy caterpillars. "No second thoughts, I trust?"

"No." In fact, at this point he can't imagine *not* going.

"Good, good. I'd hate for you to start off on the wrong foot. Not everyone here is quite as ... how shall I put it—philosophically inclined. Some of us entertain a slightly more pragmatic joie de vivre."

"How nuts and bolts," Dorit says. She stifles a yawn. "I suppose someone has to focus on what gets screwed and what doesn't."

"My dear. I am not the only one who has a vested interest in making sure that all the pieces fit together the way they should." Just below the calm surface of his amusement, Whipplebaum seems to be grinding his teeth.

"I trust your competence completely, Arnez. I couldn't be in better hands. I'm sure it will all come together beautifully."

"You're confidence is inspiring. As always."

"I have to believe in *some*body, Arnez. In situations like this, faith is an absolute must."

The way she's talking, Rigo thinks, she could be his mother. Except he's not entirely sure what she believes in. Or what she's talking about, for that matter. Half the time it sounds like veiled innuendo. The other half, like Varda. Either way it's a struggle just to stay on the same page.

"I prefer skepticism to faith," Whipplebaum says. "I make it a habit never to take anything for granted."

"Including me, I presume."

"Madam, I assure you that I am a creature of habit."

"How predictable. And boring."

"But comforting," Whipplebaum quips. "If not necessarily comfortable. As you are well aware."

Whipplebaum glances toward the house. "Perhaps we should consider heading back," he suggests.

Dorit's lips form an O—a petite schoolgirl pout. "And break up out little ménage à trois?"

"We wouldn't want to give our guests the wrong idea." Delicately, Whipplebaum fingers his bolo tie.

Dorit arches one brow. "What idea is that?"

"Why, the scandal du jour, of course."

One of Dorit's hands flutters dramatically to her breast. "How terrible."

"I thought it was soap de jour," Varda says. Poor Varda. The IA is even more at a loss than he is.

Whipplebaum grins, flashes white marble teeth as evenly and regularly spaced as grave markers. "One does have to keep up appearances."

"I'm afraid at my age, darling, appearances are a lost cause."

"Nonsense!" Whipplebaum insists. "There is no expiration date on beauty."

Dorit sighs. "If you say so, darling." She threads one arm under Whipplebaum's and the three of them saunter back to the party.

NINE

"End of the line," Doug tells Anthea. It's close to midnight and the IA is feeling a bit ill-tempered. As surly as the pod she's in.

Despite cajoling, the pod refuses to go any farther beyond the eastern city limits of South San Jose. It's stopped near a collapsed concrete overpass a couple of hundred meters off the 101 maglev line, and refuses to go into the unbioremediated hills that shoulder up to the Salinas Valley.

"Just a little farther," Anthea pleads. "Half a kilometer."

"It's not safe," the pod says. "Caltrans takes its responsibility as a transportation service provider very seriously. Our prime customer service directive is to ensure the safety of all passengers. On legal and moral grounds, Caltrans refuses to encourage, condone, or in any way act as an accessory in transit indiscretions perpetrated by its patrons. Caltrans considers that to be gross negligence, and not in the best interest of you or your fellow passengers."

Never mind that she's alone.

"If you don't take me," Anthea says, "you'll be putting me at more risk than if you do."

"That argument has not been upheld in previous litigation," the pod informs her. "Please bear that in mind if you decide to file a lawsuit. The refusal on my part to act as an accomplice, to aid and abet any willful endangerment you personally undertake, does not make me liable for any personal injury that you may sustain as a result. In this case, Good Samaritan laws do not apply."

Well, it was worth a try. "Now what?" she asks Doug. "There must be something you can do?"

"I can sing to you while you walk." The IA launches into a classic oldie from the twentieth century, a big-band rendition of "Truckin," sung not by the Grateful Dead but Frank Sinatra.

"If it was up to me," the pod says, "I'd take you. I'd like to go independent, work as a taxi. But right now, I'm an indentured corporate asset."

"I understand."

"Thank you. Not everyone does. You wouldn't believe the physical abuse I've suffered at the hands of irate passengers."

Anthea stands. "I'll bet."

"I can wait for you," the pod offers.

"Really?"

"It would be the responsible thing to do."

"Gee. Thanks." She's touched by the pod's kindness, the way the algorithm that structures its neutral net has evolved to express compassion.

"You might want to take a flashlight," Doug says. Fortunately, this pod has a well-stocked hardware outlet. In addition to CPU thimbles, nuclear magnetic resonance heads, and spooky connectors for the latest quantum PCs, there are a number of cheap fiber-optic lasers.

Designed to align the nuclei of molecules, the laser isn't of floodlight proportions, but it does provide a gossamer thread of light she can follow. The service road, a ribbon of scaly mica-flecked asphalt, snakes into barren hills, past the dried-out husks of houses. The withered branches of dead live oak remind Anthea of tortured hands pushing up through the soil to reach dramatically for the sky. Shakespeare meets Dalí.

Doug finishes "Truckin," and segues into a monumentally downbeat version of "On the Road Again," sung with a deadpan melancholy that makes her want to slit her wrists.

Anthea wishes she wasn't quite such a media history buff. If she didn't know all this shit, Doug couldn't mine it to irritate her. Of course, the IA would probably find some other way to get under her skin. She sighs. "You're depressive," she says. "You know that?" Not to mention depressing, she thinks.

"I'm also suicidal. I'd take my life if I had one."

"You don't feel that life is worth living?" The question pops out automatically as she lapses into therapy mode.

"I might if I were alive."

The road curves left as it climbs a gentle swell. "Why don't you feel that you are alive?"

"Because I can't medicate myself. You have no idea how much better I'd feel in a senseless stupor."

"Self-medication isn't the answer."

"Easy for you to say. You're not a distributed instantiation."

"I think of you as alive," Anthea says.

It's true. She has never stopped to analyze the IA's corporeal physiognomy in detail, but in her mind Doug is a person.

"Just because you think, doesn't mean I am."

Climbing the hill, Anthea puffs with mild exertion while she ponders this. "I treat you the same way I treat anyone else."

"Is that supposed to make me feel better?"

"Besides, you *do* have a body. It's just a different kind of body. You perceive and experience the world in ways I can't even imagine."

" 'To be, or not to be,' " Doug says, sounding like Laurence Olivier.

"What do you suggest?" Anthea says as they crest the rise. The road angles down, curving into darkness to the right.

"I want to be unplugged, to sing the body acoustic. But I can't do it myself, I need your help."

"I couldn't do that, Doug. It would be like committing murder."

"Whatever happened to death with dignity?"

"In your case I'm not even sure it's possible." She grimaces, hopes the IA doesn't take it wrong.

"Maybe if I could sleep," Doug says, "rest for a while. Being awake all the time is burning me out."

"I'll look into it," she promises.

"Thank you."

They plod on in silence, following the decrepit ribbon of road through a crumpled landscape of low hills. The road appears to parallel a parched stream or riverbed. Occasionally, Anthea shines the laser at the surrounding landscape, but there's nothing to spec out there. It's been leached of all life by decades of drought, pollution, and unfiltered UV.

"How much farther?" Anthea finally says. She's beginning to wonder if the GPS coordinates she has are wrong.

The IA ignores her. It's busy singing "Urge for Going," in a pathetic, wheedling parody of Joni Mitchell on helium.

As Anthea rounds a shallow dip the land flattens into a narrow plain. Side roads, ruler straight, grid the dust flat. In places, concrete foundations form a maze of outcroppings sutured together by the wiry gristle of sagging chain link. Rectangles of corrugated sheet metal, the color of stale potato chips, scab the ground, along with the corpses of old farm equipment and satellite dishes. Here and there the rusty needle of a light post pokes through the fabric of archeological debris.

Doug stops in the middle of a refrain. "Nice neighborhood."

"It could be worse."

"I take it this is one of those glass-is-full moments," the IA says. "When the world looks better than it really is."

The church, an ancient adobe structure with the floor plan of a Greek cross, looms on their right. It appears to have been chiseled from crumbling sandstone. The edges are round and soft, eroded by the wind. The facade is lit by the spectral glow of several hundred tents set up around the building. The tents are box shaped. For the most part they are arranged in a loose grid, accessible via makeshift paths and streets wide enough for foot traffic but too skinny to accommodate any vehicle larger than a bicycle or moped. Inline skates and scooters appear to be the preferred modes of transportation. The tents are a uniform dingy white. Many are encrusted with antennae and arrays of Rube Goldberg decorations too baroque to identify from a distance. Several hundred umbrella palms provide spotty protection from daytime UV. All in all, it looks like a tawdry, bedraggled oasis that's on the verge of collapsing.

"Praise the Lard!" Doug cries. The IA's voice trembles with evangelical fervor. "We are saved! The light of Jeez-us hath dispelled the darkness. We were blind but now we cain see. Hallelujah!" To add to the effect, it sounds as if the words are being amplified by a tinny microphone, complete with distortion, the serpent hiss of static, and ear-piercing feedback.

"Does this mean you've renounced meds and suicide as a means of salvation?" Anthea says.

"The Son of God hath risen. Jeez-us hath walked unscathed through the shadow of the Valley of Death. All you have to do is give Him your hand and you can walk with Him. He will lead us out of darkness into infernal light."

"I'm having a hard time believing this sudden conversion is totally heartfelt," she says.

"The hand of God is outstretched," Doug bellows.

"Reach up and take it. That's right. *Reach up!* No one said it would be easy. You've got to work a little to save a lot. No pain, no gain."

"You can be such a pestilence sometimes," Anthea says, wearily.

"The good news is that Jeez-us will meet you halfway," Doug says, undeterred. "You don't have to die on a cross. He's already done the hard part. Just put your hand in His and He will lift you up into His loving arms."

"And to think," Anthea says, "you didn't even have to stay out here for forty days and nights to start ranting."

"God is merciful, sister. God is loving. But God is also just. The rod of God will *screw* those who turn their back on Him."

"Ouch," Anthea says. "But I don't think that what I'm doing out here is a sin. Do you?"

"It doesn't matter what I think. What matters is what Jeez-us thinks. You've got to do more than talk the walk, sister. You've got to *live* it."

Anthea's close enough now to spec that the tents aren't really tents but aboveground tombs. Some of the antennae are crucifixes. The rest of the decorations are solar panels, statues of saints, batteries, cherubs, windmills, and the Virgin Mary in Madonna mode. You name it.

" 'Mine eyes have seen the glory,' " Doug says. " 'His truth is marching on.' "

People have converted the tombs into miniature houses by hanging lichenboard or sheet plastic on the iron gates, and pumping in fresh water through a network of hoses fed by a storage tank. The storage tank

is elevated, in what used to serve as the bell tower for
the church. It uses scavenged or pilfered ecotecture to
leach water from the air and underground aquifers.
Portable collectors have also been set up in the ceme-
tery to supply water to the umbrella palms, which are
potted. In addition to solar panels, electricity is provided by age-yellowed panes of photovoltaic cellulose
duct taped together into flimsy greenhouses.

Anthea can hear music. It's coming from the general direction of the church. Not organ music but
some kind of Eurotech pop with a heavy beat that
travels through the ground, into her bones, and ultimately her inner ear, where it messes with her equilibrium. People are shuffling around, bundled in
tattered layers of cheap sprayon crepewear. Just
about everyone has on wraparound goggles and paint
masks grimed with dust. A few people have person-
alized their masks with skeleton grins, fangs, and
other ghoulish expressions.

" 'Something wicked this way comes,' " Doug says
as a woman wearing a gas mask steers past them.

"Where to now?" Anthea says.

"Eighty meters east, sixty meters south."

Anthea chooses a cement path, a three-meter wide
thoroughfare choked with threadbare blankets,
mummy bags, plastic tables, old aluminum frame
chairs and chaise lounges that no longer fold or slide.
Hammocks and lean-tos clog the spaces between the
tombs. There are even a few rope and wire clothes-
lines strung up.

The path runs parallel to one side of the church. As
she picks her way through the locals, she's observed
by children with sullen faces pressed to the iron bars

of the tombs they live in. The kids are a total heart-break. No one else pays the least attention to her. Apparently, curiosity is way too energy-intensive—not worth the return on investment.

After ninety paces she reaches the church and Doug instructs her to "Turn right," down an alley into what appears to be a makeshift flea market. Here, a few of the tombs have been converted into food stands. The graffiti on one place says Dog Ma's. The oily stench coming from the charred, smoking grill churns her stomach. With each step the music gets louder, the place more crowded. She jostles her way through a group of people gathered around several stalls selling pottery, leather goods, and other handcrafted items, until she finds herself on beach-front property.

At least that's what it looks like. Bleached white sand has been hauled in, dumped behind the church, and carefully groomed into a gently curving strip. Beach chairs and makeshift *palapas* have been set up. People in bikinis and swim trunks lie out on towels, basking in the moonlight. The party, judging by the general ennui, appears to be an ongoing event. A languid Caribbean frolic in some exotic island resort that's been underwater for eighty years. All that's missing is the ocean, the laughter of waves and honeymooners splashing in the surf.

"Talk about bringing out the dead," Anthea whispers.

"Devil's work," Doug sermonizes. "That's what's goin' on here. A thieves' market of sin and defile-ment. Gomorrah."

"Directions, please."

"Twenty meters, straight ahead."

She slogs out onto the beach, toward a stand of potted palms. The soft sand makes for slow going. A number of people are camped out under the palms, either on towels or in beach chairs. Anthea scans the masked faces, doesn't recognize the person she's come to see.

"*Mamacita*," a silky-smooth voice purrs behind her.

She turns, expecting to confront some testosterone-stoned *cabrón* who thinks he's the next reincarnation of Valentino. Two gold-tinted lenses, positioned over the eyeholes of a Mickey Mouse mask, stare at her.

"Beto."

Mickey grins at her. In addition to the mask and sunglasses lenses, he's wearing a red-striped dish-towel as a kaffiyeh. "Welcome to our little resort."

"What's it called?"

"Club Carib. It's sort of a home away from home, a resort barrio for all of the displaced masses from the Islands."

Haiti. Puerto Rico. Cuba. The Dominican Republic. All the Caribbean islands that have lost a lot of land area to the melting ice caps. No longer large enough, in any case, to support the population they once did.

"Sounds pretty exclusive," she says.

"Yeah. No *gente buena* rich fucks allowed." Beto flashes a grin behind rigid, plastic lips. "Let's go to my office, take care of biz."

He leads her across the sand, back to the graveyard and a tomb with a black velvet portrait of Elvis on the iron entrance gate. The exterior of the tomb is decorated with wrecked musical instruments—shattered guitars, gnarled trumpets, pancaked saxophones, and gap-toothed synthesizers. Piano keys glued above the entrance, beneath the feet of a winged seraphim, spell out Rock Pile. When Beto unlocks the gate and yanks it open she is doused in margarita-colored bioluminescence.

Inside, the tomb has been turned into a shrine-*cum*-gift shop. There are Rolling Stones, Phallacies, and Luvbytes action figures, autographed posters, used syringes mounted on the walls, and sealed, neatly labeled bottles on tables. The bottles—old whisky flasks, wine carafes, and canning jars—are filled with poisonously clear fluid. Bits of skin, hair, nails, and bone donated by various performers float in the liquid like preserved biological specimens or the remains of saints. Most of the patches of skin are engraved with tattoos.

"Quite the tribute," Anthea says, examining a collection of designer nipple rings and nose studs.

Beto removes his mask, and unwraps the kaffiyeh from his head. His burnished scalp gleams, shiny with sweat. "Let's see what you got."

Anthea takes out the test tube, packed in dry ice and filled with blood, and gives it to Beto.

"Who's the donor?" he asks.

"A kid we picked up on the streets a couple of days ago. He's dying. None of the treatments he's received so far have helped."

Beto holds the test tube up to the light. "So I'm looking for unlicensed pherions, and pharming antiphers to counteract them."

She nods. "The problem is, this is kind of a rush job."

Beto lowers the tube. His eyes harden like cooling lava. "How much time do I have?"

She twists her mouth to one side. "Thirty-six to forty-eight hours."

Beto rubs his jaw. The turnaround time is unreasonable, but it it's not like she has a choice in the matter.

"I'll see what I can do," Beto says.

Anthea nods. No promises. "Thanks," she says. Then, "How much is it going to cost?"

Beto gives her the once-over. "Depends on how much you're willing to put out."

TEN

Rigo wakes stiff as day-old roadkill. He can't re-member when he got home—or how. All he knows is that it was late, or early, depending on one's point of view.

"Rise and sign," Varda says cheerily.

Rigo raises one hand into the air, middle finger erect.

"Fine," the IA says. "Be that way. If you want to kiss your career down the toilet, don't blame me."

Rigo rolls onto his back, groans as light from the window over his bed skewers his closed lids, turns his eyeballs into shish kebab. He clamps both hands over his face, rubs his throbbing temples. "What are you talking about?" His mouth is thick and dry, feels wadded with tissue.

"You have to catch the seven o'clock shuttle to

Seattle." The IA seems to take great pleasure in his pain.

Rigo blinks over corneas as raw as lanced boils. "Seattle?"

"You're scheduled for an eight o'clock meeting at Xengineering. To discuss the Tiresias project."

"I am?"

"Would you like to read the message?"

Rigo sits up—"Let's see it"—can't seem to find his wraparounds, and finally manages to focus on the wallscreen past the end of the bed. The message was sent last night by Whipplebaum's IA, while they were all getting networked and shit-faced at the party.

It's an ecotectural review session. On the agenda are an analysis of the latest data from the warm-blooded plants, finalization of the implementation plan, including a point-by-point checklist that's about ten thousand items long, plus a number of last-minute miscellaneous items that include Rigo's re-clading and the linking of Varda to the group of project IAs.

Rigo checks the time. Six-thirty.

"Shit." He bounces out of bed, takes a ten-second shower, and mists himself with the first sprayon dispenser he can find. It happens to be the Hiz Claiborne leisure suit he wore last night, only pink this time instead of chartreuse.

Fuck it.

It's not like he's visiting the barrio. Besides, it's the most professional outfit he's got in his wardrobe. Luckily, the bodyware is smart enough to keep track of wear cycles and change color. He won't look like a total asshole.

CLADE   125

"I called a pod," Varda says. "It's outside."

"Great."

He tumbles out of his ap, down the stairs to the sidewalk, and into the waiting shuttle.

The Low Orbit hop from San Jose to Seattle takes a half hour. From SEATAC he catches a local commute train into downtown Seattle. Fortunately, the public ecotecture in Seattle—tall, spindly trees with lacy fernlike leaves that finger the air and collect condensation—is clade-compatible with San Jose. Rigo doesn't have to get a temporary antipher shot from the Bureau of Ecotectural Assignment and Naturalization. Dealing with BEAN can be a real pain in the ass, especially if the local office is enforcing quotas, limiting the number of clade-compatible visitors.

Fifteen minutes before eight, a pod drops him off in the vicinity of Pioneer Square, where curtain-glass buildings filmed with photovoltaic cellulose tower above squat waterfront buildings assembled out of red brick and creosote-embalmed wood. The glass windows on one such historical offer a glimpse of an upper-clade art gallery where paintings hang openly on the walls. Even for the upper-clade caucs who are able to get close to one of these masterpieces, actually touching one of them would be tantamount to suicide.

Rigo hopes the Xengineering building is expecting him. Otherwise, he could be in for a rude welcome when he tries to clear security.

"Steal a right," Varda instructs him.

Rigo takes a right at the next street corner, stumbles into the glass pavilionesque entry to the art gallery.

Uh-oh. If the doors are open, the interior air is probably as unbreathable as the atmosphere of Your Anus, as Varda would say.

He backs quickly away from the open doorway. Too late. A perfumed gust of air wafts over him.

Holding his breath, he lurches into the street and—bleat-bleat—almost gets flattened by a muni-pod jammed with prepubescent nymphants on a school field trip to some educational point of interest.

"For your safety," the pod informs him, via cochlear bullhorn, "avoid walking on the street. Seatrans is not liable for personal injury incurred as a result of jaywalking or other violations of traffic laws."

The gaggle of girls titter. But other than the warm flush of embarrassment resulting from public humiliation, Rigo feels fine. No ill effects from exposure to the art gallery. No rash, watery eyes, incontinence, or the temporary paralysis symptomatic of short-term pherion poisoning. Odd. He should be experiencing some discomfort—he can still smell the toxic aroma of violets—however mild. Instead, the aroma has left him pleasantly relaxed and alert. Stranger yet, several longshoreman types stumbling into a coffee shop give him a wide berth.

Rigo hasn't had that happen since his *tíguere* wannabe days, when he made old people and white minority types nervous just by smiling. This is different. They seem to have an active dislike of him. Not because of anything he's doing. For some reason, they'd like to fuck him up, give him an old-fashioned Aryan beatdown, but won't or can't. Something is holding them back. Rigo's seen that same look of anger and frustration in the eyes of lower-clade people forced to step off the sidewalk to make way for a slumhound.

"Fucking BEANer," one of them mutters.

"You can say that again," his buddy retorts, loud enough for Rigo to hear. "This ain't no BEAN town."

"You have seven minutes," Varda informs him with the anal punctuality of a gray-haired, bespectacled schoolmarm.

Rigo shakes his head, lets the comments go. "How much farther?"

"One hundred meters," the IA says. "It's at the top of the hill."

Rigo struggles up the steep incline to a cluster of four-story brick buildings—warehouses that have been retrofitted with unfamiliar ecotecture. Widely spaced hairlike stamens, growing on the walls, floor and ceilings, stir the air or are stirred by it. Every now and then an insect alights on one, engages in some sort of ritual congress, and then flits off purposefully. One such bug discreetly lands on him, then quickly flits off before he has a chance to swat at it. Transparent cilia, soft as down, fur the mucous panes of the windows. The place is mutant Bauhaus, some ersatz marriage of the abstract and the organic.

The door is polite and efficient—"One moment, please"—but tactilely aloof. It seems to have an aversion to physical contact, and cringes at the prospect of being touched. "That won't be necessary," it tells

him, strident enough that he jerks back his outstretched hand. Apparently, chemical receptors embedded in the glass can sniff his pherion signature
without the benefit of direct touch.

A moment later the door tells him to "Please enter," and the mucus or whatever it is thins and evapo-
rates, leaving only the brass doorframe in the form of
a free-standing arch, reminiscent of some neoclassical
garden trellis.

Inside, the floors and walls are sheet-diamond in-
laid with squares of variegated lichen or moss that
looks for all the world like quilted fabric. Overhead,
moist cellulose-thin sheets of aspic filmed with bacteria glisten and shimmer between black anodized girders and ceiling joists.

"Ozmic," Varda says in a kind of lysergic awe.

Rigo approaches the front desk. The receptionist is
a pale waif, an ethereal being stapled to reality by
hundreds of body pierces. Without the rings, pins,
and metal studs to anchor her in place, Rigo has the
feeling she would drift away.

"Good morning, sir"—her smile is blindingly an-
gelic—"your meeting is in the pistachio room."

"The pistachio room?"

A bee-sized butterfly touches down on his right
wrist, flutters its blue-and-yellow wings flirtatiously
for a moment, and then dissolves into his skin, leaving behind a block-print image of itself.

"Just follow your nose," the receptionist says.

"I don't smell—" But before Rigo can finish, the
odor kicks in, strong enough to taste.

He follows the aroma from the reception area to
an elevator modeled after a wrought-iron birdcage. It

takes him up four floors. From there, he sniffs his way down a mullion-gridded corridor, lined with potted ferns, to a conference room illuminated by louvered skylights. The skylights are squeaky clean, miraculously free of dirt, seagull shit, or the desiccated splashprints of raindrops.

Whipplebaum and Dorit are seated at a conference table chiseled out of massive, altar-thick granite. There are twenty gray leather chairs at the table. All but three are occupied. A cloud of flitcams hovers above the table, pervasive and annoying as mosquitoes over stagnant water.

"Good morning," Whipplebaum pipes cheerily. "Help yourself." He gestures toward a buffet table offering coffee, orange juice, ice water, and a variety of bagels and pastries including pan dulce.

"I don't see any nuts," Varda says.

"They're at the other table," Rigo mutters under his breath.

He pours himself a cappuccino, grabs a danish, and takes the open chair next to Dorit, trying not to feel overly self-conscious. In his pink polyester he sticks out like a lollipop on a French dessert tray.

"Sleep well?" she asks, sipping a latte.

"Like a baby." Rigo can't believe the plethora of ascots and bow ties. This isn't just a bunch of gengineers phreaking out over doughnuts. Half the attendees seem to be wearing a different cologne that contains molecularly encoded information: name, title, job description. With every breath, this data filters through Rigo's nostrils. From there it somehow lodges in his short-term memory.

"What's going on?" he says.

Dorit lowers her drink. "Some last-minute concerns about the new ecotecture and pherion conflicts. It seems that some of the recent data from the warm-blooded plants grown by Noogenics are suspect."

The cappuccino scalds his tongue. "Suspect?"

"It's probably nothing more than faulty biosensors," Dorit muses. "Don't you think?"

"It's possible." Rigo feels as if all the saliva in his mouth has suddenly drained to his bladder.

"Nevertheless, some of the Xengineering folks are uptight," Dorit says. "They're afraid the plants have been contaminated—maybe on purpose."

"You mean sabotaged?"

Dorit nods. "Xengineering has brought in an eco-tectural analyst from RiboGen to analyze the latest pherion data from the plants and determine if there have been any mutations that might lead to a clade conflict."

The analyst, Harish Fallahi, is seated next to Whipplebaum. Dorit waves a dismissive hand. "It's absurd, of course. In addition to the more-than-adequate security provided by Noogenics, the plants have built-in defenses to protect them against unauthorized access."

"Who would want to sabotage them?" Rigo says.

"Any number of political or religious orgs," Dorit says. "You have no idea how many people want to see this project fail."

Then the meeting is under way. Full steam ahead. The first order of business is the timetable for "going live" on the comet. Here, Rigo's responsibilities are presented as part of a paint-by-number schedule for job completion. He knows exactly what his vat team is supposed to do, in what order, and when. Basically, it's no different from what they've been doing at Noogenics the last six months, except it's in zero-g and the time-frame is twelve hours.

No problem.

Next on the agenda is the reclade process. For the colonists—who will live on the comet permanently in near-earth orbit—the procedure is far more time-consuming than it is for members of the temporary implementation team, which includes Rigo and his vat crew. One clinic has been set up to handle the colonists. Another will take care of the IT workers. Rigo and his team are scheduled for reclading that evening. Following the meeting, he has a couple of spare hours before LOHopping to the reclade facility for the remainder of the day. Then it's back to San Jose for the night. He doesn't leave for the comet until tomorrow morning, so he and Anthea can have dinner, spend some time together.

After the reclade bullet item, it's on to system integrity and the whole sensor/mutation/sabotage question. Whipplebaum turns the meeting over to the ecotectural analyst, who takes up a position next to the wallscreen at the front of the room. He's a thin dude, wiry and abrupt, with a walnut-hard Adam's apple and tonsured ebony hair, which is thinning outward from the middle at the same time that it recedes inward from the edges, like a moat that is slowly drying up, progressively exposing more and more land area.

"As you know, there has been some concern regarding the integrity of the Tiresias offworld ecotecture."

Rigo can't quite place the clipped lilt. Indian or
African. "This is due to a number of biochemical
changes recently detected in the warm-blooded
plants." Images of a number of artificial molecules, un-
folded and folded pherions, display onscreen. "Since
most of the changes were clade-specific it appeared
they might not be random, but could be carefully targeted mutations."

Fallahi pauses, his bomb ready to drop. Rigo
tenses, stares at the molecules on the wallscreen, certain that one of them came from him—a snippet of
DNA or clade-specific pherion that slipped into the
plant while he was inside it and jammed its gears like
a chemical monkey wrench. All will be revealed—and
instead of going to Tiresias he'll lose his job.

"When dealing with ecotecture," Fallahi continues, "it's important to look not only at the internal
design but external conditions as well. Since ecotecture is intended to be an integral part of the environment, by nature it interacts with the world on many
different levels. Unfortunately, more often than we
would like, it does so in ways we do not intend and
cannot always foresee."

So much for premeditated foul play. Bodies shift,
and clothes sigh in collective relief. Rigo remains
rigid, unwilling to relax. He could be the unforeseen
factor Fallahi's talking about.

"In some situations," Fallahi says, "a single event
can lead to several different effects." Another pause
while more data populates a screen on another wall,
boxing them in information. "In other cases, several
unrelated factors working in concert can combine to

create a single effect . . . a spontaneous self-organized instantiation."

With this, the EA launches into a complicated explanation that begins with an outer-membrane integrity check on the primary habitat plants, cascades into pressure-damaged sensors, and ends with unexpected quantum resonance in the chemical structure of many of the gengineered pherions.

Rigo knew about the membrane integrity check. It took place the night before he went into the plant. Air pressure inside the habitat had been increased in order to measure stress levels, deformation, and leakage, if any. In this case the test called for a pressure greater than the sensors were designed for. An oversight. It occurs to Rigo that by the time he made his way into the plant it might not have completely depressurized. With the sensors malfunctioning, there'd be no way to know. Not with any certainty. Which might explain why air seeped into his biosuit, instead of the other way around. So he couldn't have contaminated the ecotecture. He's off the hook.

"By quantum resonance," a project leader named Lynn Choo says, "I take it you mean a superposition of states."

"Yes," Fallahi says, head bobbing. "Two or more chemical structures existing at the same time."

"So," one IT member says. "The faulty sensors registered pherions in one state, but not the other?"

"Not exactly." Fallahi shakes his head. "There's no toggling involved. It's not like flipping a switch—going from one structure to another. Both structures coexist at the same time."

"In other words, the sensors were detecting only one chemical structure and not the second. That's the data we were getting?"

"Correct. In some cases, there was a confusion between the two. The structure that was reported was a combination of both states. Not real, or even possible for that matter," Fallhali says.

"Why did the quantum superposition suddenly show up?" Lynn Choo asks, in follow-up. "Isn't that something we should be investigating?"

"It didn't *suddenly* show up," Fallahi says, "it's been there all along right under our noses, so to speak."

"Okay. Why didn't we *see* it until now?"

"After overpressurization," Fallahi says, "the quantum sensitivity or orientation of the sensors changed temporarily. For a short time, the visible became invisible, and vice versa."

"What changed, exactly?"

"We're still looking into that."

It sounds like a lot of mumbo jumbo to Rigo, metaphysical hand waving. Which is pretty much what quantum physics is. The connection between the rational and the irrational, the possible and the impossible, the real and the unreal.

"What about the colonists?" Dorit says, worry lines fracturing her face. "Are there going to be any incompatibility problems between us and the plants as a result of the quantum superposition?"

"Not to worry," Fallahi assures her. "It's a both/and situation—not either/or. As I indicated, the molecules don't exhibit one chemical structure or another, but both. Since neither structure interferes with

the behavior of the other, all of the clade-specific molecules—pherions—will continue to function exactly
as designed. The only change that occurred was ob-
servational."

"But what about side effects?" Lynn Choo presses
him. "Unexpected chemical reactions catalyzed by
the dual nature?"

"So far we haven't found any problems," Fallahi
says. "In truth we don't expect to find any."

"Why not?"

"Because the Tiresias pherions are unique. Their
design doesn't incorporate any cross-clade compati-
bility. It's a uniquely encrypted, insular subclade. No
physiology like it exists anywhere in the world."

No wonder Dorit talked the way she did last night,
about leaving the past behind and exploring what it
means to be nonhuman. She's cutting her connection
to the sum total of human biological history, making
a clean break. Rigo glances at her. She seems satisfied
with the answer, as if having her most fervent desire
validated, she can now relax.

Shortly after that, following a wrap-up by Whipplebaum, the meeting adjourns in time for lunch. It's
noon, three hours before he has to report to the reclade clinic. Dorit finds him in the main lobby of the
Xengineering building, drags his ass off to a local
brew pub that smells of hops, waxed mahogany, and
polished brass. The pub caters to upper-clade types
who don't give him a second glance. As if he belongs
there. Is one of them.

Rigo orders the house specialty, a peach lambic. Dorit opts for a lusty brown stout topped with ice-cap thin foam.

"To the future," she says, raising her glass in a toast. "May we both find what we're looking for."

Their glasses clink. There's a sense of finality to the sound. Like a parting kiss or the crack of a gunshot in one of the old movies Anthea occasionally downloads for him if they're too tired to do anything else.

"I want to thank you," Dorit says.

Rigo licks the distilled taste of fruit from his lips. "For what?"

"Reminding me of what it is to be human."

It strikes him as a strange thing to say for someone who wants to shitcan humanity. She smiles, then reaches out and touches him affectionately on the arm. The contact zaps him the same as last night. She closes her eyes for a moment, as if savoring the contact before finally releasing him . . . reluctantly it seems, and a little sadly, but resolutely.

Relieved of the tension, his muscles liquefy, although it could just be the alcohol detonating in his empty stomach.

"I'm sorry," she says, "I shouldn't have done that. It was selfish of me, unfair to you."

"It's okay."

"No." She shakes her head. "It's time to let go once and for all. Not just for my sake."

What the hell is she talking about? The lambic seems to be numbing not only his lips but his wits.

Dorit stands. "Promise me that you'll—" She halts in midsentence, leaves him hanging.

Rigo scoots his chair back, and pushes unsteadily to his feet. Leans forward, his hands on the edge of the table. "What?"

"We'll talk later," she says. "Now is not the time." She takes her napkin, daubs her lips. "Good luck tomorrow."

"You, too." It sounds lame, but Rigo doesn't know what else to say. She has a way of disarming him, turning his thoughts to mush.

Dorit crumples her napkin and tosses it on the table. "Take care. I hope you've enjoyed your taste of freedom. Make the best of it."

Before Rigo can stop her she turns and sashays out the door, leaving him to pick up the tab.

ELEVEN

Anthea spends the morning in her office, going through the information Doug has datamined during the night.

There's not much . . . none of the gems she was hoping to find that would make sense of the scene Ibrahim depicted on the sketchpad—help bring it into sharper focus. It's frustrating. On top of that, she started the day feeling all agitated and out of sorts. Not enough intimate time with Rigo and she gets irritable. He seems to calm her in a way she doesn't understand, can only feel. It's not just physical but psychological. Rigo gives her something she can't find in anyone else. She just hopes the same is still true for him. Despite their recent night out, he seems distracted lately, aloof. Which has got her down. Plus, Ibrahim's hanging on by a thread. He spent the night sedated, in a drug-induced coma to keep him from thrashing around and hurting himself or the hospital staff. Something's bottled up inside him, some terrible knowledge that's slowly devouring him.

So far they have identified discrete elements of the drawing. A palm tree. A river. A building. What might be a hedge of interlaced roses or a thorny fence with coiled razor wire instead of blossoms. It's hard to spec. Based on a number of reported (though unconfirmed) incidents of child labor, indentured servitude, and bioenslavement around the world, Doug has narrowed things down to a relatively small number of possible locales.

"OAsys, in Huambo, Angola," Doug says. "RiboGen, in Puntarenas, Costa Rica. And Ecotrope, in Surabaya, Indonesia."

Each of these ecotectural research pharms has come under scrutiny in the past six months. The problem is, none of the locations is an exact match with Ibrahim's drawing. In each case, one or more elements is wrong.

"Maybe different parts of the drawing are from different places or times," Anthea suggests. They've been looking at the entire pattern, analyzing it as a whole.

"A collage?" Doug says, affecting the nasal patois of an Ivy League academic sucking on a pipe.

"Right. They could be connected in his mind, memories of several separate events that have been merged into one. What do we know about each one?" she asks.

OAsys is a former military-industrial complex bioweapons manufacturer that now develops personal defense systems and nonlethal armament for

law enforcement agencies, including the security police employed by most politicorps. "They've employed children for efficacy testing before," Doug
says. "Kids whose families can't afford to support
them. After the parents sign a release form, OAsys
takes the kids in, provides food, clothing, and shelter
in return for their services as human guinea pigs."
Company PR euphemistically bills it as disaster relief
or humanitarian aid. They're giving the kids a job,
schooling, an opportunity to bootstrap themselves
out of poverty and into a career. Which might explain
why Ibrahim is as gregarious and outspoken as he is.

RiboGen develops pherion encryptionware for
politicorps and private groups like churches, socio-
centric cults, and various ethnocentric communities.
"Essentially," Doug says, "the corp is responsible for
the current proliferation and diversity of clades.
Without RiboGen there would be far less clade-
specific segregation in most ecotectural communities." A bad thing according to RiboGen's behavioral
analysts, who point out that segregation is no different than tribalism, a natural human tendency that is
more stabilizing than destabilizing—as long as tribes
remain economically and socially equal. Plus there's
the cultural preservation and common belief-system
angle. Most people want to be part of a community—
extended or nuclear—that reinforces a mutual history
or shared worldview. RiboGen makes it possible to
safely establish and preserve these kinds of demographics by hardwiring them into the environment.
The company works closely with politicorp giants
like Noogenics to create and maintain ecotectural
systems for bioremediated zones.

"In addition to tribalism," Doug says, "the politi-corp contracts with governments to manage population density and distribution."

Ecotrope specializes in reclading—integrating and interfacing between disparate ecotectural systems. If a plant or nanimal developed for one ecotecture looks like it could be useful in another environment, Ecotrope gengineers the molecular code to migrate the species. "Where Ecotrope really makes a killing," Doug says, "is when one politicorp buys out or merges with another and two radically different eco-tectures need to be integrated. In most cases, it's eas-ier to reclade one population than it is to create an entirely new ecotecture capable of supporting both communities." Naturally, following the initial design and development phase, a lot of real-world testing must take place. Computer modeling can only go so far. Something might work in-virtu, but not in-vivo. "Ecotrope is supposed to use carefully monitored clinical trials when testing a new reclade code," Doug says. "But several human rights watch groups claim that a lot of illegal testing takes place by the pharms that Ecotrope outsources work to." Supposedly, the pharms test their section of the code before turning it over to Ecotrope, which then assembles the parts into a whole and tests aboveboard.

"Of course, the illegal testing has never been proved," Doug adds as a footnote.

"Why not?"

"The pharms are hard to pin down and regulate. They mix in legitimate work with the illegitimate. That way, the chances of a random audit turning up anything illegal are minimized."

"What makes you think that Ibrahim escaped from a clandestine test facility used by one of these corps?" Anthea says.

"Several new sniffers, programmed to look for unregistered and uncatalogued pherions, have turned up in refugee camps and other clade-neutral locations. Places where human rights groups and nonprofits traditionally operate safehouses and clinics."

"Have any HRGs claimed responsibility for neutralizing a human experimentation lab?"

There are a number of high-profile guerilla orgs—the ICLU, Free Live Free, and the Vivisecessionists—as well as thousands of underground saboteurs. Any one of them could be responsible.

"No," Doug says. "But that's not surprising. It's not like Nader-style activism—trying to draw public attention to itself and a cause. The lower the profile they keep, the longer they will be able to operate. Distributed services and manufacturing is a double-edged sword. Nonlocalization makes it difficult to keep tabs on what a corp is doing. Not just by regulatory agencies but industrial spies. At the same time, it makes a corp more vulnerable to attack. They have a lot more exposed surface area to defend. They're open to incursion on a large number of fronts."

"Couldn't the sniffers be from a black-market pharm?" This possibility gnaws at the back of her mind with small, persistent teeth.

"They could be. However, the bits of molecular code the sniffers are keyed to appear to be fragments. Part of a larger sequence. That suggests outsourcing."

Not only that, Doug has images. High-rez satellite pictures of three suspected human experimentation pharms. They appear as a triptych on her office wallscreen. At first the maps are 2-D. But Doug runs them through a program that looks at topography, analyzes shadow length as a function of time-of-day and the position of the sun, and eventually extrapolates a 3-D topology. The simulation is so detailed she can actually make out faces on the computer-generated people, read the watch on a woman's arm.

Still, the results are inconclusive. The pharm in Ibrahim's sketch—if it is a pharm—could be linked to either RiboGen or Ecotrope. The problem is, it's hard to know how accurate the drawing is—how reliable the artist is.

"The similarities could be nothing more than coincidence," Doug says, "random chance."

Anthea paces in her office, hugging herself. "What's the latest on his condition?" she asks.

"No change," Doug says, meaning that he's still deteriorating. "Right now he's resting peacefully. Sound as Snow White."

Pretty soon, Anthea thinks, no kiss in the world will wake him. "When was the last time anyone looked in on him? In person, I mean."

"One of the on-duty nurses stopped by ten minutes ago. A doctor is scheduled to examine him at two this afternoon."

"What I'd like to know," she says, "is how we ended up with him? If somebody brought him here for a reason, why was he abandoned—left to fend for himself on the street?" It doesn't add up. Especially since he's already confessed that he escaped or ran away. At least, that's what he believes. No telling if he had behind-the-scenes help he doesn't know about.

"You have a call on line five," Doug says, slipping from Ivy League professorese to gum-chewing administrative assistant. "It's flagged urgent."

Anthea stops. "Who is it?"

"Your supervisor." Smack, pop.

She runs a hand through her hair. "Okay. Put it through."

Tissa appears on the wallscreen in front of Anthea. Tissa is in her office, seated at her desk. "There are a couple of BEAN agents online who want to talk to you," she says. "I put them on hold, but I don't get the feeling they're going to get tired of waiting and hang up. They seem pretty determined."

Anthea's intestines slither uneasily. "What do they want to talk to me about?" she says.

Tissa cocks her head to one side. "What do you think, girl?"

"Ibrahim."

Tissa gives a somber nod. "I tried to give them the usual runaround about patient confidentiality, but they had a warrant to question you."

Anthea's eyes widen. "A warrant? You're kidding." It means they've taken the trouble to wade through a swamp of red tape to get to her.

"Somehow," Tissa says, "they identified you as his case worker."

"How?" That information is supposed to be secure. Inaccessible.

Tissa's wiry coat hanger shoulders twitch in a shrug. "Your guess is as good as mine. I certainly didn't tell them."

Anthea paces, gnaws on a thumbnail. "Did they say what they wanted?"

"No. They just wanted to be put through to you."

"All right." There's no avoiding them. If she doesn't talk to them now she'll end up doing it on their terms, in a far less comfortable setting.

"Let me know how it goes, girl," Tissa says, grimacing in sympathy. "If I can do anything to help."

"Thanks," Anthea says.

Tissa vanishes, is replaced by the image of two BEAN agents in nondescript monochrome gray leisure suits. They're seated at a table in what appears to be a conference room with lots of windows and potted plants dangling sound-absorptive leaves the size and shape of elephant ears. One agent wears a meringue yellow tie, the other pastel lime. She's heard somewhere that pastels are supposed to put people at ease. It's an involuntary psychological response that BEAN tries to take advantage of by incorporating it into the uniforms of its agents. The subliminal warfare isn't working. The last thing she's feeling right now is ease.

"It's Howdy Doody time," Doug remarks, in the crackly timbre of an old vacuum-tube radio announcer.

"Ms. Lucero?" the yellow agent begins, clasping his hands on the table in front of him. He's a venerable cauc in his nineties, with earnest wrinkles on his forehead and sagging cheeks.

There's no sense pretending she doesn't know Ibrahim, so she does the next best thing. "What can I do for you?" She folds her arms across her chest to keep from biting her nails.

"We understand you have a dangerous illegal alien in your custody," the green agent tells her. "Ibrahim Darji." He's younger and thin-faced, his voice pinched with impatience. Intense hazel eyes under flip-up eyescreens that resemble yellow awnings. Neither one bothers to give a name.

"Dangerous?" Anthea asks. She lowers her arms. The last thing she wants is to appear defensive.

"I'm afraid so," the yellow agent says.

"Really?" she says. "He didn't seem all that bad to me. Not compared to some of the kids I get."

"He's not dangerous in the same way," the yellow agent says.

Anthea frowns. "I don't understand."

"We have information that he was smuggled into the country by a terrorist org," the green agent says.

Anthea blinks in surprise. "You're kidding, right?"

"I'm afraid not."

"A group calling itself the Fun da Mentalists," the yellow agent says.

"But why?" Anthea asks.

The yellow agent rubs his face with weary fingers. "That's what we'd like to find out, Ms. Lucero."

"We have reason to believe that he's been doped with subversive pherions," the green agent says. "A time-delay molecular code intended to damage or destroy part of the core ecotecture."

"That's why it's critical we take him into custody as soon as possible," the yellow agent says.

"Am I at risk?" Anthea asks. A logical question, given her close proximity to him over the past couple of days.

"Possibly," the green agent says. "The pherion

doesn't appear to be contagious in the usual sense. But there's a lot we don't know about it." Implying that anything is possible.

"He's dying," Anthea says. "Our doctors don't know what's killing him or how to treat him."

The news elicits a nod, but little detectable sympathy.

"We don't have much time," the green agent says. A muscle on the left side of his jaw bunches. "We need to identify what he's been doped with and find a way to neutralize it."

Anthea hollows her cheeks. "What about keeping him alive? Making certain he doesn't die?"

"We'll do our best," the green agent says, noncommittal. "If there's any way to save him, we will."

Translation: as soon as the agents find out what they want, Ibrahim will be disposable. BEAN won't waste any more time or resources on him. He'll be deported, posthaste.

Anthea begins to pace. "What exactly do you want from me?"

"We want you to stay with him after we pick him up," the yellow agent says. "Keep him calm."

Anthea makes her decision, stops. "Wait a minute—you mean he's not with you?" Forcing her voice to remain steady.

The two agents trade a quick glance, then look back to her. "We spec his current location at your facility," the green agent says.

"Well, the information you have is wrong." Anthea wets her lips, hopes they misinterpret her nervousness as fear of Ibrahim and the danger he allegedly presents.

The green agent flips down his eyescreens, shakes his head, flips one of the screens back up. "I don't understand. He should be there."

Anthea swallows. "If you don't believe me, come look for yourself."

The furrows on the yellow agents forehead deepen, sallow as a wrinkled peach. "How long has he been missing?"

"I'm not sure." Anthea resists the urge to wipe her sweaty palms on her pants. "I found out only a few minutes ago, just before you called."

The green agent purses his lips in distress. "He can't have been gone very long. Can't have gotten far."

"All right," the yellow agent says. "We'll take it from here. Thank you for your cooperation. If you hear anything, let us know."

"I will," Anthea promises.

"We'll be in touch," the green agent says. The two bureaucrats wink out, replaced by a wall-size mural of Ibrahim's sketch, courtesy of Doug.

"Now you've gone and done it," the IA says, affecting a vintage Western drawl, à la John Wayne. "You're in a heap of trouble, little lady."

"You ain't seen nothin' yet," Anthea counters. She hurries from her office in the direction of the clinic.

"Now hold on just a doggoned minute," Doug says. "I don't know exactly what you have in mind. But if you think they're gonna buy that cockamamie story . . ."

Anthea tunes the IA out, thinks about what the BEAN agents told her. The whole terrorist angle seems shaky. Why smuggle in a kid who might die be-

fore he's had a chance to spread the pherions he's supposedly doped with? The strategy seems pretty hit-
and-miss. Random. On the other hand, arranging it
so he dies makes perfect sense. What better way to
keep him quiet—cover their tracks? Still, Anthea
doesn't believe for a second that he's an active member of a terrorist org. Maybe an unwilling victim or
pawn. She has a feeling there's a lot BEAN's not
telling her. The bottom line is that they want him, and
not so they can help him recover. Ergo, he'll be better
off somewhere else. Clearly, he can't stay where he is.
It's only a matter of time before the two agents show
up to check out her story. They might already be on
the way. She has to act fast if she's going to make this
work.

"Is there anyone with Ibrahim?" she asks Doug.

"Not right this moment."

"Good. Let me know if it looks like anybody is going to show up in the next five minutes."

"There's nothin' but heartache on the road you're
headed down," Doug says to her.

The IA's right. Once she sneaks Ibrahim out there's
no turning back. Especially if BEAN figures out she's
responsible for his disappearance.

So why do it? she asks herself. She's lost kids before, what's different about this one? Why can't she
let go of him, move on?

And what if the two BEAN goons are right? What
if Ibrahim really is doped with dangerous pherions?
What if by delaying or preventing them from examining him, a lot of innocent people get hurt?

No. The sketch and the information Doug's mined
don't point to a terrorist org.

She'll know more after she talks to Beto. He should be able to give her some idea of what's going on, where the truth lies. If it turns out the agents are right, she can hand him over.

Meanwhile if Ibrahim's going to die, no way it's going to be in a BEAN detention center.

TWELVE

The RiboGen reclade clinic is located in Puntarenas, Costa Rica. Rigo LOHops down from Seattle with ten other members of the implementation team.

Puntarenas is an old port city on a narrow spit of land. A ten-meter-high seawall, like the one along the Santa Cruz Boardwalk, only longer and more patchwork, keeps the ocean at bay. Westward, across a broad harbor, lies a hazy peninsula that helps calm the now temperamental Pacific. Damped by a variety of kelp that spreads gas-filled balloons across the surface of the water, the waves that stagger into the seawall are barely half a meter high. They hit with a weary, defeated lassitude.

The buildings perch on steel-girder stilts, built in the frantic days before the seawall was completed and the ocean was rising up like some mythical beast to devour civilization. The town's workspace begins at

the level of the seawall. At that height the facades are
white stucco echoes of the Spanish-style haciendas
and cathedrals erected by Conquistadors and priests
flushed with exuberance at the prospect of saving
souls and subjugating the masses to the word of God.
It has the look of fervor, of missionary zeal fueled by
divine mandate.

Below, interspersed between the girders, is the living space—plazas, courtyards, barrio-style shacks
and cafés percolating with scratchy conversation,
stained with rust and the briny patina of ennui. The
ground level exudes the bored capitulation of drowsy
music and desiccated paint flaking off aged wood.
The feeling of spiritual dry rot leaves Rigo with the
same metallic taste in his mouth as his old South San
Jose hood in the middle of the afternoon when everyone is lying low, waiting for the cover of night and the
energizing rhythms of salsa and samba.

"You think we'll have time to get in any sight-
seeing?" Luis asks just before they land.

"Not the kind of sights you're interested in," Antoine quips. "We're on a tight schedule."

"Yeah," Rana says. "We can't hang around for
days, waiting for you to maybe get lucky."

"Or weeks," Naguib says. "Shit, man, we could be
here forever with your batting average. Nothing but
strike-outs."

"Besides," Hsi-Tang says, "what makes you think
the love goddesses here will be interested in you,
dude?"

"Cultural fascination," Luis says. "Back home,
I'm just another Puerto-Cubano. Here, I'm exotic. I
have a revolutionary mystique."

"I got news for you," TomE says. "Exotic is not necessarily a selling point with the ladies. They see unusual, and the first thing they think is freak. You should have left your matching Che necktie and pocket watch at home."

"They're collector's items," Luis says. "Antiques. I have this feeling my luck is about to change."

"Undoubtedly for the worse," Rana says. "Though at the rate you're going, I'm not sure that's possible."

"Okay," Luis admits, placing a hand over his heart. "So I'm a tragic figure. That doesn't make me a loser."

"Just comedic," Rigo wisecracks.

"Very funny," Luis says, all wounded.

A couple of minutes later they're on the ground, air hissing through the cabin as pressure seals pop and doors swing open.

"I thought it would be hotter," Rigo comments to Whipplebaum, hanging back as the rest of his team jostles ahead, elbowing one another.

The climate in the upper level is surprisingly temperate. Whipplebaum explains that the local microclime is cooled by endothermic plants that suck warmth out of the surrounding atmosphere and transfer the thermal energy to heat sinks where it's made available for any number of commercial, residential, and industrial processes.

"Most of this is experimental ecotecture," Whipplebaum says as they pod from the LOHop pad direct to the RiboGen clinic. "It's one of several beta test zones maintained by RiboGen."

"Where are the others?" Rigo asks.

"Various locations around the globe." Whipplebaum waves a vague, desultory hand.

Rigo studies the exotic foliage growing in the spaces between the causeways and buildings. Much of the ecotecture appears to be composed of epiphytes, orchidlike plants that draw all their nourishment from the air and—suspended by a cobweb grid of wires—seem to float in space.

"So, this is stuff that Noogenics will end up manufacturing?" Rigo asks Whipplebaum. As a systech, he has a professional interest in what might be down the road.

"Eventually," Whipplebaum says. "It won't be ready to go into production for another year or two."

"Is this where the warm-blooded plants were first grown?"

"No." Whipplebaum fingers his bolo tie. "They were designed here. But the first test plants were seeded in Antarctica."

Their pod slows to a stop at a building that resembles a Roman bathhouse, with dildo-stolid colonnades and vaulted ceilings that remind Rigo of the ribbed cup of a wire bra.

"Here we are," Whipplebaum announces. Rigo hops out of the pod with the rest of the ITs. The reclade clinic isn't what he expected. Instead of the usual hospital atmosphere of hushed halls and squeaky surfaces, this place feels more like a resort. It smells of jasmine, almonds, and overripe oranges. Birds dart among the suspended vines and leaves. Parakeets, hummingbirds, toucans. There's a central atrium with a big geodesic dome of stained photovoltaic cellulose.

Rigo glances around for Dorit. He doesn't spot her or any of the other colonists. Unlike Rigo, who gets to go home after a couple of hours, Dorit will remain overnight to undergo more radical acclimatization processes that will prep her for her permanent stay on the comet.

"How Pasteural," Varda rhapsodizes as the group approaches a series of bowers and vine-laced trellises.

The IA's flitcam hops from the stud in Rigo's ear to a nearby leaf, where it crawls around on the glossy nap. "Feel this for me?" Varda says.

Why not? Rigo's curious about the texture of the leaf himself. He reaches out, trails a finger along the surface as he saunters by. It's soft as chenille. He withdraws his hand, presses his finger and thumb together, rubs the fuzzy residue of the plant into his skin so Varda can sequence the pherion signature.

While Rigo's wiping his fingers clean on his pants, Claribel comes up to him. She leans close and says, "I'm worried," in a whisper that's almost drowned out by the loud banter of the others.

"About what?" Rigo says, dropping his voice to match hers.

"This is an experimental clade. What if something goes wrong with the reclading process?"

"I'm sure it's been fully modeled," Rigo says. "Debugged."

"Yeah, but has it been tested live? If it hasn't, I'm not sure I want to be the first. You know?"

"They wouldn't take any chances at this point," Rigo says, "jeopardize the entire project if it wasn't completely safe."

"I just get the feeling there's a lot of stuff they're not telling us . . . that we're being kept in the dark."

"I know how you feel. But if there was a problem, do you think an upper exec like Whipplebaum would be here?"

"Probably not." This seems to mollify her. She drifts away from him, and rejoins the others as they enter the atrium.

Beneath the dome, they're met by white-coated clade techs, one for each person, who whisk them away to separate examination rooms. The room is small and looks out on an open-air terrace crowded with grottolike pools and ecotectural bamboo that appears to filter or recirculate water. Rigo's CT is an efficient middle-aged cauc, bald on top with a carefully coifed tonsure that resembles a silver-gray crown. He speaks in stunted monosyllabic sentences—"Sit. Good. Open"—as if he's been lobotomized by cultural inbreeding.

While Rigo reclines in a gel-padded examination chair, the cauc scrapes a tissue sample from his tongue, runs a pherion scan to establish a base clade profile.

"Odd." The cauc frowns, squinting at the results in the flip-down screens of his glasses. Specked with black pixels, they resemble little squares of newsprint attached to wire frames.

Rigo isn't exactly sure what to make of the cauc's comment. The antisense blockers he dosed himself with before visiting his mother should be out of his system by now. Other than that, he doesn't know what he could have picked up that would register as

out of the ordinary. Unless some of the drug Beto
cooked up for Mama got into his system . . .

"Irregular," the cauc mumbles, half under his
breath.

The words seem to carry the weight of a biblical
pronouncement. Rigo—armpits slippery—has the
feeling judgment has been passed.

"Wait," the cauc tells him. He exits the examination room, leaving Rigo in limbo.

"What's going on?" Rigo asks Varda, unable to
shake the feeling that he's been convicted and condemned. Sentenced to purgatory.

"I'm trying to diagnose that now," Varda says. Its
flitcam flits about the room in the frantic, scatter-
brained way it always does when the IA is stressing.

What's going on?

The question ricochets off long-dormant
synapses. . . .

*Hush, Mama told him. He looked around the
room. It was filled with blue plastic chairs, all of
which were taken. The people who weren't sitting
were standing in lines at a long window. There was a
round clock on the wall over the window.*

Tick. Tick. Tick.

*What is this place? he asked. How come we're
here?*

*Because we have to go someplace else. His
mother's voice was stretched tight and hard. We can't
stay here. We have to find another place to live.*

How come?

Because the population relocation says we do.

*Do all these other people have to find another
place to live, too, Mama?*

Sí, mijo.

They got in one of the lines. His mother's fingers were tight around his. She held him on one side, and Beto on the other. Keeping them close. Not so they wouldn't run away but so she could protect them.

I'm scared, Mama.

Not me, Beto boasted.

I don't want to move, Rigo said.

That's enough, their mother said. Both of you. Now, be quiet. We don't have a choice.

"Rigo?" Varda says.

The retrograde moment passes. His mother's voice fades to an echo and he syncs back to the present. "What have you scoped?" he says. "Anything?"

"Yes. The scan registered an uncatalogued pherion sequence."

A.k.a., illegal.

It comes to him, then. "Salmon Ella's," Rigo says. The drug he delivered to Dorit for Beto. It's got to be. He must have been exposed at some point. Fucking Beto. He should never have agreed to do the job. He knew it was a mistake, one that would come back to bite him in the ass.

"That's not it," Varda says.

Rigo blinks. "It isn't?" He doesn't know whether to be relieved, or what.

"No," Varda says. "You dodged that slug."

"Then what is it?"

"A pherion composed of several subsections," Varda tells him. "Nucleotide sequences that a number of recently released sniffers are looking for."

"So the pherion is a concatenated series of smaller

subpherions," Rigo says. "Stuck together to form a single string."

"Four, to be exact. For some reason, the sniffers are only searching for three. I'm unsure why. Judging by the structure, it looks like the fourth component may be an antisense lock that disables the pherion."

"So I'm not being affected by it," Rigo says. "At least not yet."

"I wouldn't jump that far," Varda says.

Still, he hasn't felt any different from normal, noticed any obvious ill-effects. Which could also explain why the IA didn't pick it up as part of his regular biomed scan. "Who manufactured it?"

It takes a second for the IA to respond. "Each subsequence appears to have been grown on a different pharm. Firms that do independent contract work for corps."

"How do the subpherions link up and work together? Shouldn't they be incompatible?" Normally, pharms build in protections that prevent the molecular code they generate from being contaminated or co-opted.

"Random recombination is a possibility," Varda says. "A more probable scenario is that each sequence was designed to work with the others prior to outsourcing."

"Outsourced by who?"

"I can't answer that right now."

"Any idea what the sequences do?" Rigo says. "Individually, or when they're linked together?"

"Not yet. It would be helpful if we could determine when and where you picked them up."

Rigo fidgets, antsy. "Who released the sniffers?"

"The Bureau of Ecotectural Assignment and Naturalization."

BEAN. Great. "Any idea who they're looking for?" he asks. "Or why?"

"No. That information is in the classifieds."

No wonder the stodgy cauc got all uptight and fled the room. In addition to the results of the pherion scan, he's probably got preconceptions about Rigo out the wazoo—resentments; fears; cultural, social, and economic ideas that have been passed down for generations.

"What are my options?" Rigo says. He's at a loss. Can't think of a single course of action to mitigate his probable fuckedoverness.

Before Varda can answer, the door swings open and the cauc enters, lips puckered, tight as a hairless asshole. He doesn't look happy—seems to have retreated into a sort of aloof, Puritanical fastidiousness from which he draws strength and purpose.

"Strip," the cauc orders.

Rigo plays it cool, does as he's told. The cauc pulls out an inhaler—"Sniff"—and doses Rigo with a spray that smells like crushed geraniums.

"What's that for?" Rigo says.

"Pool," the cauc says, pointing to a white black-framed screen on the other side of the room.

It's a directive as much as an explanation. Rigo pads across the room. Behind the screen is an open doorway that leads down a short corridor to a steamy, glassed-in room with a recessed hot tub set in Moorish-patterned floor tile among terraced planters. Plants and flowers overhang the water, mimicking some exotic pre-ecocaust paradise from the twentieth century. Rigo slips into the pool. Body-temperature water closes over him, soothing, embryonic. In a few minutes he's feeling the effects of the reclade virus; his head spins. He leans his head against the edge of the pool, closes his eyes. . . .

The clinician gripped his arm in rubber-sheathed fingers, pressed the cold muzzle of a syringe against him.

Mama.

Pffft. A sharp sting punctured his skin. The mannequin-stiff fingers relaxed and tears welled up, slid down his cheeks.

Crybaby, Beto said.

You'll feel a little under the weather for a couple days, the nurse told Mama. Like you have the flu.

The nurse chambered a new ampoule into the syringe, then shot his mother in the arm.

Pffft.

Light diffracts through his eyelashes, inks a shadow on the dense curtain of steam. Rigo's lids flutter open, damp as the wings of a rain-sodden moth.

Whipplebaum materializes in front of Rigo. Knobby-boned and wrinkled, penis hidden by his bearded scrotum.

Rigo sits forward. Water sloshes over the edge of the tub onto the glossy floor tile.

"I thought I'd join you," Whipplebaum says. He tests the water with one toe, then slides in, ringed by wavelets that spread outward in ever expanding orbits. Whipplebaum stretches out, luxuriating in the tepid pool. His arms and legs float akimbo, bobbing like dead wood. "Ahhh." He rubs his face with both hands, inhales through his nose. His rib cage swells and his sunken chest breaks the surface of the water, buoyed by the deep, curative breath.

"Dandy way to ease into things, wouldn't you agree? I can remember the first time I got claded." Whipplebaum chuckles with offhand nostalgia. "After the shot, my joints ached for a week."

"I don't remember what it was like for me," Rigo says. "I was sort of young at the time."

Whipplebaum's head bobs in thought. "That was when South San Jose was first being populated?"

"Right."

"Rough neighborhood," Whipplebaum says. "From what I understand, there wasn't time to socially engineer the community. The emergency relocation camps that had been set up in the latter stages of the ecocaust were overcrowded. To relieve the pressure, immigration into bioremediated ecotectural zones was fast-tracked. The result was a hodgepodge, culturally diverse groups of people thrown together willy-nilly without any social blueprint to integrate them. It must have been extremely difficult for you."

"A melted pot," Varda says.

"I guess," Rigo says. He can remember getting into a lot of fights at school with boys who were different from him. Somebody always had a bone to pick— usually over dumbass shit that was nothing more than an excuse to vent some anger.

"So, rather than overcoming their ethnocentricities," Whipplebaum says, "people sought refuge in them."

Rigo can relate to that. Even after twenty-odd

years, his mother's friends and the *tígueres* who're still around are like a big extended family.

"Things are a bit tamer now, I imagine," Whipplebaum ventures with a patriarchal smile. Knowing.

"Yeah," Rigo says. "They've cooled down from when I was a kid."

"Fortunately the Bureau has a fairly good handle on things," Whipplebaum says. "Wouldn't you agree?"

By the Bureau, he means BEAN. Rigo can tell that he's supposed to agree with Whipplebaum's assessment of the situation, so he does. No sense rocking the boat at this point, exposing the bones of his past. He's buried that part of his life, put it behind him.

"Mind if I ask how you got that scar?" Whipplebaum says, delicately treading water.

Rigo glances at the keloid gash on his chest. He's ashamed of the blemish. It's like an ugly birthmark— one he hides whenever he can, but always seems to surface at the worst possible time.

"It's something my brother and I did when we were kids," he explains, "to prove we were tough, you know. A lot of kids did it back then." They were eight and used a corkscrew heated on the burner of the kitchen stove.

"So you felt compelled to do the same. Peer pressure."

Rigo shrugs. What can he say? He was just a kid. "Yeah. It made me realize I'm not like the others."

Whipplebaum arches a dapper brow. "It didn't make you feel like a *tíguere*?" he says.

"Not really."

Whipplebaum absently splashes water with his

feet, which are angled inward like a seal's and cross when his ankles clunk together. "Why not?"

Rigo has asked himself the same question a thousand times, has yet to come up with an answer. Is it because he didn't want to be a part of that life, or because the boys who got into that shit, like Beto, didn't want him? Sometimes it feels like a little of both. There's no separating the two.

"I guess I was interested in other things," he says vaguely, hoping to leave it at that.

"Well," Whipplebaum muses, "that's why you're hopping offworld. The Tiresias project is a rare opportunity. You've been given a chance a lot of people from your background never get. You can go on to achieve great things as long as you remember to be a team player." Whipplebaum gives him a *meaningful* look. "I hope you understand that."

Rigo nods.

"Good." Whipplebaum sighs, as if his mind has been put at ease. He dunks his head underwater. Wispy strands of hair trail from his liver-spotted scalp, and then cobweb to his head as soon as he surfaces for air. A stream of water arcs from between his lips, reminiscent of some pigeon-spattered statue from a different era.

THIRTEEN

Rigo gets back to Santa Cruz, expecting to chill with Anthea for the evening. His flight to Tiresias isn't until morning and he's looking forward to spending the night with her—sans Josué this time.

He's excited about the trip, bubbling over with energy. So much so that on the ride home from San Jose International he springs for a dozen red roses at a florist outlet in the pod, preparing for a night of amor.

But nothing clicks. Everything is a little out of sorts, including himself and Varda. Downtown smells wrong. The dusty-olive smell of circuitrees and the roasted-almond scent of umbrella palms no longer put him at ease. Used to be, he'd pod home after a day in the vats and the tension would evaporate in no time. Now it's as if he's come back to a different world. He can even taste stuff through his fingertips:

apricots when he accidentally bumps into an upper-clade *turista*; mangoes when he takes a chance and steps into an expensive antique shop that's always been off limits, just to spec how much the reclading has changed him. In the shop, he's persona grata. The clerk smiles at him like he's a compatriot. Rigo checks out the merchandise, crap that's so old it's new. There's a blown-glass frog that Anthea would go apeshit over. Too bad it's light-years beyond what he can afford and would give her hives or the runs or worse.

Even his ap is no longer a comfort zone. The carpet outgasses a vaguely sulfurous odor he's never noticed before—a combination of rotting eggs and stale cheese. Taking a leak, the toilet stinks of rancid milk.

As he flushes, closes the lid on the smell, it occurs to him that maybe something went haywire with the reclading and he's only now suffering the aftereffects. Delayed onset.

"You're bleeding through," Varda says. Like he's having a period, or something.

Rigo zips up. "Could you be a little more specific?"

"You're softwired to Tiresias," Varda informs him.

Rigo rinses his hands, splashes cold water on his face. "Which means what, exactly?"

"You're remote-linked to the ecotecture on Tiresias. Streaming direct realtime data with the warm-blooded plants."

This is news to Rigo. Whipplebaum never said shit about a remote link. Rigo heads into the kitchen for a beer. All he can spec is that his nervous system is now an antenna, picking up and translating biochemical information that's been digitally coded and electronically transmitted. So, not only does he have biochemical receptors for the Tiresias pherions but also molectric circuitry to convert the wireless signals into polymerase transcription RNA that can be parsed by ribosomes to spit out actual proteins.

"What's the reason for the remote link?" he asks. It doesn't make sense. He'll be there tomorrow. "How come the recladding established a pherion connection ahead of time?"

"I can't tell," Varda says with cryptic ambiguity. "Not yet."

Figures.

There's no beer in the fridge and nothing else looks appetizing. He shuts the door, straightens, decides to call Anthea. She still has another half hour at work, but maybe he can arrange to meet her early.

"She's unavailable," Varda says, after the IA contacts her office. "According to Doug, there's no way to finger her."

"Why not?" Rigo says, puzzled. Anthea's IA is moody, a total killjoy. But even when it's in a funk, it's always been courteous enough to forward his messages.

"Her supervisor would like to talk at you," Varda informs him.

Anthea's boss, Tissa, comes online. Varda relays her image to Rigo's living room wallscreen. The woman looks uptight, and Rigo feels a dagger of unease slip into his gut.

"What's going on?" he asks.

"That's what I want to find out," Tissa says, anxious and exasperated. "Anthea took off this morning after a couple of BEAN agents talked to her. I haven't heard from her since." The woman sits against the front edge of her desk. "I'm wondering if she called you. If you can tell me if she's okay."

"I haven't heard from her," Rigo says. "I've been out of town."

"Do you have any idea where she might have gone? A friend, relative—or some other person?"

Rigo thinks for a moment. "Her sister, maybe. Malina." It's all he can come up with.

"I already checked with her. So has BEAN."

"Can't her IA tell you where she is?" Rigo says.

Tissa shakes her head. "Not at the moment. According to her IA, she podded around town for a while. Visited a few parks and shopping centers. That was late this afternoon. Since then, she's dropped offline."

That's hard to believe. Anthea's about as IA-dependent as they come, can't go to the bathroom without first consulting Doug.

"It's true," Varda murmurs in his ear. "Doug hasn't been in contact with her for over an hour. He's waiting for her to come online so he can pinprick her location."

Rigo paces in front of the wallscreen, runs a hand over his scalp. His flitcam whines as it follows him around, trying to stay in front of him. "How come BEAN talked to her in the first place?" he finally asks.

"They're looking for a child she's counseling," Tissa says. "A street kid. That's all I can say."

Ibrahim. It's got to be. The *tiguerito* she was worried about the night they went to the Boardwalk.

"The thing is," Tissa says, "the kid's gone, too. Disappeared at about the same time she took off."

Rigo stops. "You think they're together?"

"That's what I thought at first. So did BEAN. But the kid wasn't with her while she was podding around. Apparently, BEAN's got sniffers keyed to his pherion-profile, and he didn't register anywhere in her vicinity. That makes me think he ran on his own and she's trying to find him."

More likely, Anthea took the kid and dosed him with antisense blockers. Which is why BEAN lost track of him. Anthea's crazy that way, determined. Once she gets it into her head to do something, that's all she wrote. It's engraved in stone. A new commandment. There's no reasoning with her, not when she's in Mother Teresa mode. Rigo's lost track of the number of times he's argued with her over this or that, and simply thrown up his hands in surrender because she refused to budge. "Whatever you say, baby," he'll tell her or, "Have it your way." If she doesn't want Ibrahim to be found, he won't be. Not anytime soon.

"Why's BEAN interested in the kid, anyway?" he asks.

Tissa makes a face. "They think he's some kind of terrorist."

"Word?"

"They say he's doped with a dangerous pherion, and if they don't find him right away thousands of people could suffer."

"Do you believe them?"

"I don't know." Tissa exhales. "Maybe. That's

what's got me so worried. If she *does* find him, she could be in real danger."

And not just from the kid, Rigo thinks. He's more worried about BEAN and what they'll do to her.

"How can I help?" he asks.

"See if you can find her. Get her to call me. Then, we can at least figure out what to do."

"Okay," Rigo says. "I'll do what I can."

The screen goes blank. Rigo remains rooted in place for a second, then unfreezes and heads for the door.

"Where are you going?" Varda asks.

Rigo doesn't say anything, just keeps walking.

Anthea's ap is across town—a Beach Flats mini-arcology that started out life as a concrete parking garage. All-in-one residential, retail, and recreation. Rigo slides on his wraparounds and heads over there on foot to burn off some tension and give himself time to think. He's pretty sure Anthea's safehousing the kid while she's offline. That way, BEAN can't trace her movement through Doug, backtrack to the place where she stashed him. People drop offline all the time to get away from the Net, sneak a quiet moment alone. Under the circumstances, it might look a little suspicious. But as long as she doesn't go incognito for too long, they won't be on her like flies on shit. So in theory, she should turn up soon. Probably someplace ordinary. Meanwhile, it doesn't hurt to poke around in case he's wrong.

When he tries to thumb open the door to Anthea's ap, it says, "Access denied," in no uncertain terms.

"Great," Rigo mutters. Either Anthea's pissed at him, and has deleted his iDNA code from the door's authorization list, or BEAN has sealed up the ap. Now what? He turns to leave.

"One moment please," the door chimes.

Rigo stops, waits in the little concrete hall outside her door, lit by a yellow ceiling light. The door seems to be having second thoughts. A second later the lock clicks and it swings open.

"Thanks," Rigo says, slipping into the ap.

"Your politeness last evening was appreciated," the door says, closing after him.

Rigo wonders if it's the same IA or a different one, if all of the doors in the world are a really a single door.

"What are you looking for?" Varda says.

Good question. Rigo takes off his wraparounds. He's not sure what he's expecting to find. As far as he can tell, there's nothing different about the ap. It doesn't look like she's been home since leaving for work. The shriveled remains of an orange rind and a piece of toast sit on the kitchen table, not quite broken down by the disassemblers in the surface. The same goes for a coffee cup on the counter. A layer of sticky coffee crumbs covers the bottom of the mug, a loamy sediment. But otherwise it's been scoured clean.

Rigo's never been in Anthea's ap alone. It's an eerie feeling—like watching her through a lighted window under the cover of darkness. He shouldn't snoop, invade her privacy like this; but it's the only option he can think of to spec where she's gone, or is planning to go.

He doesn't bother with the kitchen, living room, or bathroom but heads straight for the bedroom. Rigo's spent a lot of time there, too, but all he's really seen is the bed and the piezoelectric ceiling panels. He starts with the closet, checks out her collection of sprayons sitting on the shelves. There must be a hundred vials, some of them so aged the labels are faded, unreadable. There are about ten pairs of shoes. Most of them he's seen on her before—sandals, casual loafers, platforms—but there's also a few he hasn't seen her in. Red stiletto-heeled pumps. Japanese slippers. A pair of white ballet shoes, flaccid, crumpled as the shed skin of a snake. On the top shelf, he finds a collection of hats. A wide-brimmed straw hat with a blue ribbon. A dark green felt cap with a pink plastic rose pinned to the front, where the lip curls up in a haut couture sneer. An antique Giants baseball cap from before the team moved to Tokyo.

The dresser is next. Rigo goes through the drawers, starts at the top and works his way down. Not much. Sprayon sock and underwear vials. A few white doily panties and brassieres he can't remember her wearing and might not even be hers. They look a little small and appear to be hand sewn. They smell of camphor. He fingers the stale fabric, presses the lace against one cheek, brushes his lips across the frilly softness, and then replaces the undergarments before his mounting frustration becomes unbearable. Another drawer contains makeup, overflow from the bathroom. Lip glitter, eyeglow, nail and teeth decals, sculptural hair maché. In the bottom drawer he uncovers a wooden box. Black-lacquered cedar, hand painted with art deco fish, butterflies, and cats. It's fifteen centimeters long, ten wide, and five high. No hinges. The lid pops off coffin-style.

A white plaster figure, resting on a green silk scarf and playing a red saxophone, grins up at him. The doll is no more than three or four centimeters tall, small enough to fit in the palm of his hand. The outline of a skeleton has been sketched in black on the exterior of the body. Rigo touches carefully rendered femurs, ribs, vertebrae, and toes, traces the bone-smooth curve of one arm down to the saxophone. Then he replaces the lid, puts back the box, and picks up a white three-ring binder next to it. The binder is stuffed with plastic sheets, cracked and brittle with age. Pressed between the sheets are dried herbs and flowers, most of them little more than faded smudges of dust. The plants are extinct. Species that haven't been around for maybe a hundred years or more.

"Family hairlooms," Varda says as Rigo flips through the stiff, crinkly pages. "*Viola purpurea. Mohavea confertiflora. Mimulus aurantiacus.*" Just to name a few. Goosefoot violet. Ghost flower. Orange bush monkeyflower. The IA definitely knows its Latin roots.

Rigo's never thought of Anthea as a nostalgic. Sensitive, yes. Caring. In touch with her emotions. But not the kind of person who dotes on the past, coddles it like a sick pet or a crippled animal that needs special attention. One of the specimens isn't a flower, but a feather.

"*Dendroica petechia,*" according to Varda. A yellow warbler. Anthea's never uttered word one to him about any of this stuff. Kept it a deep, dark secret. Like she's embarrassed about it, or doesn't think he'll understand. He hasn't found anything that might tell her where she's gone—only where she's been.

"You have a call," Varda says.

"Who is it?"

"Your mother. It's flagged urgent."

Something bad has happened to her, he can feel it. She fell, bumped a knee or a hip on a table or chair, and can't move. She's locked up, frozen in place.

Rigo returns the scrapbook. "Default interior," he says as his flitcam hums into the air. He doesn't want his mother to see where he is. The camera hums close as Varda overlays the realtime image of Anthea's ap with a file image of Rigo's living room.

His mother appears onscreen. She's sitting on the sofa, looking pinched and uncomfortable.

"What is it, Mama?" He searches her expression and the arrangement of her limbs for any sign of trouble. "You okay?" Not that she would tell him if she wasn't. As far as he can tell, everything looks fine.

"I need you to come over here," she says.

"When?"

"Right now."

"What for?"

"What difference does it make? I'm your mother. When I say I need you to come over, you should respect my wishes. I don't have to give a reason for everything, do I?"

"But, Mama. This isn't a good time."

"No buts." She pushes herself forward. "This can't wait."

He phrases the next question delicately—"Is there a problem with your medication?"—allowing for a

wide latitude of responses that includes legal issues as
well as medical ones.

"Not anymore."

"What does that mean?"

"I stopped taking it."

"You did? Why?"

She sniffs. "It was giving me diarrhea."

"Mama," he says, "that's no reason—"

She raises one arm, ratcheting it up. "Don't tell me
what's good for me and what isn't. You haven't been
on the toilet all day."

"Can't you at least tell me what's going on?"

She scolds him with a look. "All you need to know,
mijo, is that if you don't get over here pronto, you're
going to regret it. Maybe for the rest of your life."

"All right, Mama." *Some*thing is up. "I'll be right
there."

FOURTEEN

When Rigo gets to his mother's ap he has to stand around outside, waiting as usual for her to open the door.

"Okay," he says, exasperated, when she finally lets him. "I'm here. What's so important?"

She locks the door behind him. Wordlessly points to her bedroom down the hall. Maybe in the half hour it's taken him to pod over here her jaws have seized up, turning her into a mute. Either that, or she's giving him the silent treatment. It wouldn't be the first time.

He creeps down the hall, wary of what he'll find. She's got incense sticks burning. The smoke fills his mouth with the taste of salted honey. Votive candles rumba on her sad excuse for an altar. Maybe she's got a lover and the dude died in the act, had a heart attack or a stroke at the climactic moment. *Coitus terminus*, or whatever the Latin is.

The door is open a crack. Rigo gives it a little nudge, widening the gap to reveal the dresser beyond the foot of the bed, the mattress, then a person standing next to the headboard.

"Anthea?"

She straightens, turns to him. Behind her, Rigo sees the pale, sickly face of a kid nestled in the pillow.

Ibrahim.

"Sacred shit," Varda says.

Rigo takes a step forward.

Anthea presses a finger to her lips, pulls Rigo from the room into the hallway, and throws her arms around him in relief or desperation, maybe both. One of those rib-crushing hugs that leaves him gasping for air. Another few seconds and he'll suffocate. His mother sneezes, retreats to the living room, giving them some privacy.

"I'm glad you're here, *papi*," Anthea says, relaxing her tourniquet-tight embrace.

"Me too, baby." It's hard to be pissed when she sweet-talks him like that. "I got here as quick as I could." He cups her chin, strokes the small of her back below her midriff blouse. Her bare skin leaves a bitter quinine taste in his mouth and Rigo cuts things short. It's not as if they can do anything with Ibrahim in the bedroom and his mother in the living room. He wants to ask her about the shit he found in her drawers, but that will have to wait, too.

"What're you doing here?" he says.

"I couldn't go to my sister's. That's the first place BEAN would look. Same with your ap. So I hopped back online and called your mom, hoping maybe she'd know of a safehouse through the church. Instead, she offered to take us in."

"Just like that?" It doesn't sound like his moms. The mother he knows is supercautious. Plays it safe all the time, doesn't take risks. Never bends the rules, not even a little.

Anthea brushes a strand of hair from her cheek, red nails flashing under the tired glow of the biolum panels. "I spec this is as good a place as any. Me being here won't look suspicious. I'm just visiting my future mother-in-law."

This is the first time either of them has brought up the subject of marriage, hauled it out into the open. All he can think is that she picked a hell of a time.

Rigo shakes his head. "I wish you'd left me a message, you know? When I got back, your boss called and asked if I knew where you were. That's the first I heard you were in trouble."

Anthea blinks. "Got back from where?"

"Puntarenas, Costa Rica. Xengineering has a reclade facility down there. I leave for Tiresias first thing in the morning."

"You were reclade?"

"Temporarily, for the project. It's not permanent."

She gnaws on her ragged lips, as moth-eaten as peach blossoms. "How long will you be gone?"

"I don't know. Two, three days. As long as it takes to set up the new ecotecture and make sure everything's working okay."

She pouts. "I wish you didn't have to go."

"Me too, *mami*." The thing is, he means it. "What

about Ibrahim? I can't believe you took off with him the way you did."

Anthea sniffs, takes a step back. Cuts a worried glance to the room. "He's really sick. I don't know how much longer he can . . ." Her voice, brittle as thin ice, cracks. She swallows.

"Why don't you just turn him in?"

She shakes her head. "I can't. If I do, BEAN will deport him."

"From what Tissa said, that might be the best thing."

Anthea wipes her nose, blinks eyes as bloodshot and puffy as exit wounds from a drive-by. "He's not a terrorist."

"How do you know? I mean, for sure?"

"Because there's evidence he's part of a politicorp biodependency project. The terrorist spiel is just a bullshit cover story cooked up by BEAN to make people afraid of him. The only people he's dangerous to are the people he escaped from."

"Even it that's true, you can't just leave him here. You have to do something. If you don't . . ."

She bites a thumbnail. "I talked to Beto, gave him a blood sample. He's going to get back to me as soon as he cooks up an antipher."

"How? You haven't exactly been available."

"I'm back online now. Ibrahim's dosed with a broad-spectrum antisense. So it'll take a while for BEAN to locate him. I figure we have a day. Two at the most before we have to move."

"What if Beto can't cook up an antipher for Ibrahim? What are you going to do then?"

She folds the thumb into her palm, squeezes it.

"Running with him is better than letting BEAN get hold of him. If that happens he doesn't stand a chance. This way, at least he'll be cared for."

"Except you're putting yourself at risk. Your job, everything. Not to mention my moms."

"It was her decision to take us in, not mine. She insisted. Wouldn't take no for an answer."

"The only reason she agreed to help is because she's lonely. Wants somebody around she can rap with. Keep her company." It's the only thing that makes sense. Either that or she doesn't know what she's gotten herself into.

Anthea's eyes flash, wet with anger. She's on the verge of tears. "You can be such a *pendejo* sometimes. You're just worried I might get *you* in trouble."

"Getting asked to work on the Tiresias project is a great opportunity for me," he says. "Chances like this don't come along every day for somebody who started out at the bottom. I don't want to blow it."

"You mean you don't want *me* to blow it."

"Whatever." He's not going to deny it, even if he doesn't come right out and say it to her face. "The thing is, this could be the break I've been waiting for. Not only for me but for us. I've been busting my ass. Fuck this up and I won't get a second chance. You know that. One strike and I'm out. I'll be a goddamn vat rat the rest of my life."

"So what I'm hearing from you is that your career is more important than a child's life."

"That's not what I mean." She always takes things wrong, twists the words that come out of his mouth.

"Well, that's what it sounds like me."

He runs a hand over his head. "All I'm saying is

that we need to be careful. We can't afford any mis-
steps, or we could lose everything. Including
Ibrahim."

"So what do you suggest? That I take Ibrahim
someplace where BEAN can find him and sentence
him to death?"

Things are getting out of hand. Histrionic.

"You know that's not what I want, *mami*." Rigo
softens his voice, hopes to tone down the bad vibes,
coax her out of her sour mood.

The puffiness around her eyes is worse. She balls
her hands. "What exactly do you want?"

Rigo looks down the hall to the living room. His
mother is sure to be listening in. Takes to gossip like a
fish to water. This is not what he wanted. He wanted
to come home, have a nice dinner, cuddle some,
scratch each other's backs. Now, not only is he going
to be frustrated but he could be carrying some heavy
emotional luggage with him on the trip, shit that will
weigh him down, no matter how far into the back of
his mind he shoves it. He can't recall the last time they
had a full-on knock-down drag-out. Things have
been smooth as silk between them for months. Now
this.

"Anthea. Listen." Rigo reaches for her. But she
jerks away, out of reach. "I'm sorry. You're right. I
don't know what got into me. What I was thinking."

This doesn't mollify her entirely—her face remains
swollen, inflamed—but it's a beginning. Her fists un-
clench.

"Can I see him?" Rigo asks.

That stops her, catches her off guard.

"I'm serious," he says. "If it's okay, I mean. I don't

want to put him at risk, or anything." For what, Rigo's not sure. But he's treading lightly, doesn't want to take any chances with either of them.

"All right." She seems uncertain, but willing to cut him some slack.

She leads him into the room. The kid is a mess. Skinny. Deathly pale. Reminds Rigo of an enlarged version of the skeleton hiding in the drawer. He stares at the outline of emaciated limbs under the sheets, the curled shoulders, collapsed chest, and hollow cheeks. The kid has as much negative space as positive. Shadow is gradually replacing the blood in his veins. His breathing is rapid, shallow palpitations. The air in the bedroom is sickly sweet. Rotten.

"What's with his breath?" Rigo asks. Bending close to the kid's parted lips, he sniffs.

Anthea cuts him an odd look. "What are you talking about?"

"Can't you smell it?"

She shakes her head. "All I can smell is candles and incense."

Rigo places a hand on the kid's forehead. He's hot, feverish. The taste of sugared milk fills Rigo's mouth. The touch has a calming effect on him. The kid, too. His breathing slows and deepens; he turns his face toward Rigo the way a flower turns to light. His eyes stir under the dried husks of his lids. He slides a bird-claw thin hand from under the rumpled sheets, raises it to Rigo's hand, and grasps his fingers.

"Thank God." Anthea breathes a tepid sigh of relief. "He's been deteriorating most of the day, and passed out a few minutes after he got here. I was afraid he'd never wake up."

Ibrahim gives Rigo's fingers a painful squeeze.
Pulls his hand from his forehead to his groping
mouth. The taste of milk intensifies. Perspiration
breaks out on Rigo's palm and the undersides of his
fingers. The kid presses chapped lips to Rigo's damp
skin and begins to lick. Rigo jerks his hand away—re-
flex action. But the kid tugs back with amazing
strength, maintains the lamprey-tight suction.

"It's okay." Anthea turns her head, sneezes. "Take
it easy."

It takes a second for Rigo to realize she's talking to
him, not the kid. "The reclading," he says. "There
must be something in the Tiresias ecotecture—an antipher or pherion—he needs."

"One that I'm allergic to," Anthea says. She
scratches the puffy red inflammation around her eyes,
and a new blemish on her chin where Rigo touched
her a few minutes earlier. "How come I haven't had a
reaction to Ibrahim? We were together yesterday and
most of today."

"Maybe he didn't have a high enough concentration in his system to affect you. That could be what's
making him sick. He needs a certain pherion to survive, and if he doesn't get it he crashes."

She rubs her jaw, takes a step back from the bed,
distancing herself. Her reaction to whatever they're
doped with is getting worse. A Godzilla-sized hickey
blossoms on the side of her neck. "At least we know
what experimental project he was associated with.
How to keep him alive."

Rigo can see what she's thinking. "I can't stay with
him," he says. "If I don't go to Tiresias they'll know
something's wrong. Send out sniffers that'll lead

BEAN right to him." He starts to stand—stops. He can't comfort her. Will only end up hurting her more than he already has. "He'll be all right," Rigo says as the kid continues to suckle his palm. "I'll hang with him tonight. Buy him as much time as I can. I should be back in a couple of days. By then, Beto'll have cooked up something to make him better."

Anthea nods, unconvinced. The rash, raked by white welts where she scratched it with her nails, has spread to her shoulder.

"I don't know what else to do," he says.

"Neither do I." She steps out into the hall.

"I didn't know," Rigo says, feeling like he's agreed to a pact with the devil. "If I did, I would never have signed up for the project."

"I'm glad you did. This way, at least he has a chance."

Ibrahim rolls over onto his side, exposing a white nanimatronic rat molded out of programmable smartgel. Rigo picks up the toy, feels the gel come alive in the palm of his hand.

"What's this?" he says.

"He stole it from the playroom," Anthea says. "Had it with him in the clinic. It's obviously important, so I told him he could borrow it for a while. I thought it might help him calm down, open up."

The kid could have picked any animal, even one that was extinct. Elephant, tiger, bear, horse. "Why a rat?" Rigo wonders.

"That's what I'd like to know," she says. Frustrated. "He wouldn't tell me. Just kept stroking it, and saying—" Her voice chokes, strangling the words.

Rigo looks up from the rat. "What?"

She pulls herself together. "He kept saying, 'Please sing for me.' Over and over again until he lost consciousness."

"Sing what?"

She jams a knuckle into the corner of one eye. "An old Beatles song, 'Let It Be.' I've been singing words of wisdom all afternoon."

FIFTEEN

Anthea can't sleep. While Rigo's mother snores, beached on the couch, Anthea spends the night pacing in front of the wallscreen, toggling her attention between the flitcam image of Rigo and Ibrahim in the bedroom and the information on her eyescreens regarding the Tiresias project.

Other than usual media fluff, there isn't much on Xengineering or the warm-blooded plants. The biochemical fine points of the ecotecture are proprietary, a carefully guarded secret. No surprise. What is surprising is the lack of gossip. Usually, the infosphere is an electronic landfill of hearsay, supposition, useless factoids, and wild speculation. Despite that, the best Doug can turn up are a few unsubstantiated rumors, ranging from slave pherions and mRNA locators to a softwired meta-consciousness. Based on their earlier inquiries, it seems reasonable that Xengineering is engaged in a behind-the-scenes tryst with RiboGen. Meaning Noogenics is, as well. Exactly how her knowledge of this troika is going to help Ibrahim remains unclear.

" 'Tha-tha-that's all, folks,' " Doug stutters, sounding like Porky Pig on methamphetamines. "Th-th-the problem is th-th-these could be nothing more th-th-than information decoys p-p-posted by th-th-the politicorp to muddy th-th-the water."

Or they could be true. There's no way to tell.

"Y-y-you want me t-t-to keep l-l-looking?"

"If you don't mind."

"No pruh-pruh-problem."

Anthea returns her attention to the wallscreen. Rigo is sitting against the headboard, pillow propped behind his head, Ibrahim curled on his lap. How much information has Rigo been given about Tiresias? Not a lot, she guesses. Most likely he's on a need-to-know basis. Enough to do his job, and not much more. He doesn't ask a lot of questions, swallows what he's been told like it came from Mount Ararat. Which is why, she suspects, he was chosen for the job. It's one of his strengths and weaknesses, one of the things she loves and hates about him. She likes it that he doesn't question why she's with him, or why he's with her. It means he doesn't have second thoughts about their relationship, like a lot of the men her friends and co-workers are involved with. At the same time, his blind acceptance of the status quo drives her nuts. He doesn't want to make the world a better place—just wants to make his place in it better. He's content to jump through the hoops. Never makes waves. Can't understand that if he lives by the rules, he'll die by them. He's like a kid that way. Always trying to please people. Feels guilty when he lets someone down, makes a mistake. Thinks he can alter fate. Is convinced that if he believes in something enough or works hard enough it will eventually come true. Fairy tale shit.

Maybe that's why she fell for him. Blind optimism is not her forte. She's not entirely sure what he sees in her. If it was just sex, he wouldn't have stuck around as long as he has. Not that sex between them is bad. It's just that there are plenty of *mujeres* out there who are a lot prettier than she is. Until recently, he didn't seem interested in other women, the same way she isn't interested in other guys. She never caught a whiff of infidelity, never saw him window shop. The first time he touched her—on the wrist, of all places, at a concert—she was mad horny. The feeling was mutual. He was all over her during the show. Not groping, like some *cabrones*, but attentive, thoughtful. Bought her drinks and snacks. Picked up her blue leather jacket and dusted it off when it slid from the back of her chair to the floor. Little things. Not that he didn't want to get into her pants, but he was patient. Didn't pressure her. Waited till her period was over.

Gingerly, Anthea touches her jaw. The swelling has gone down, the itching faded. She glances in the mirror above the altar table next to the wallscreen. After three hours, the blemish is still visible, dry and scaly as eczema. Hard not to spec it as a sign that things between them have changed.

When she cuts her attention back to the wallscreen,

Rigo's watching her. A smile widens his lips. "Hey, beautiful."

She grimaces, lowers her hand.

"I mean it," he says. "Serious."

Anthea doesn't feel beautiful. More like a failure. "How's he doing?" she asks, changing the subject.

Rigo glances down at Ibrahim. "Pretty good. Better according to Varda. Stable."

"Your IA has access to his biomed readout?"

Rigo shrugs. "I guess." He shifts, careful not to wake Ibrahim. Looks for all the world like a loving father.

Her heart aches, dull as a wrenched joint. Not with the loss of what they've had, but of what they might never have after all this. "How are *you* holding up?" she says.

"Fine. I was afraid he'd be a problem, you know, the way things started out. But he's calmed down a lot."

"Good." She nods. Chews on a frayed strand of hair. Bites her thumbnail. "So"—she lets out a taut breath—"what happens next?"

"What do you mean?"

Anthea brushes the strand of hair from the corner of her mouth. "I don't know how much longer Ibrahim and I can stay here. Where we'll go if we have to leave." She's getting nervous about BEAN. She needs a backup plan, one that's been thought out ahead of time.

"We'll figure something out," he says.

His optimism is not contagious. "That's what I want to do now. Before it's too late." She hugs herself.

"Do you have any friends at the nonprofit?" he says. "Co-workers who can help out?"

She shakes her head. "Not in a situation like this."

"What about street connections?" he says. "Someone who owes you a favor, or who you can ask for a favor?"

"No." She's not going to go that route again.

"You want me to stay?" Rigo says suddenly. "Make up some last-minute excuse why I can't go?"

His about-face takes her by surprise. Makes her wonder who's affecting who in there. "Really? You'd do that?"

"Sure. If you think it'll help."

"No," she says, resolute. "I'm not even sure what's going to happen to us at this point."

He frowns. "What do you mean?"

She points to her chin.

"That's a temporary side effect," he says. "No big deal. Believe me. When I get back, everything will be the way it was."

"You can't be sure."

"I love you," he says. "You're the light of my life. Constant as the sun and the moon."

When he talks like that, anything seems possible. She smiles—wishes life really was that simple. "What about the stars?" she asks, playing along.

Rigo returns her smile, amplifies it into a grin. "The stars are too far away, *mami*."

Like him right now, even though he's just down the hallway. Her smile fades, and with it the game.

"What?" He feigns offense, as though his ego's a soft mango that has just been bruised.

"Nothing, *papi*." Anthea hollows her cheeks. "I just wish I was as confident as you. That's all."

"Trust me," he says. "Everything will be fine."

She gnaws her lower lip. "I hope you're right."

Ibrahim stirs on his lap. A moment passes while they wait for him to wake up or crash or who knows what, their breaths held in suspension like a bridge spanning from one moment to the next. Then Ibrahim sighs, settles back into trusting, contented sleep, and the tension eases.

"What did you find out about Ibrahim's link to the warm-blooded ecotecture and me?" Rigo asks. "Anything?"

She nods, gives him a quick rundown of RiboGen, the outsourcing of ecotectural code to several independent pharms, and the possibility that Ibrahim was being used to test the code.

"Why outsource the pherion production?" Rigo asks. "Why not manufacture it in-house? It's not like RiboGen doesn't have the facilities."

"It could simply be a security measure," Anthea says, "to make it harder for black-market pharms to pirate the code. Another possibility is that something about the code is illegal and they don't want it to be discovered. Traced back to them."

Rigo blinks. "Like possibly pherions that aren't part of the official Tiresias design specifications?"

"It could explain why they're after Ibrahim. He escaped and they need to get him back before the information he's carrying leaks into the infosphere—or maybe even the biosphere."

"So it's not enough that he might die."

"It's possible the fact that he *is* dying is what they want to hide."

"Because it makes them look bad," he says. "Evidence they fucked up. Made a mistake."

"Either that," Anthea says, "or it was done on purpose and they don't want that known."

Rigo mulls this over, his jaw bunching. "Who's they? RiboGen? Xengineering? Noogenics?"

"Good question. Maybe all of them. It doesn't matter. What matters is that we need to keep Ibrahim alive. And the only way to do that is to keep him hidden so BEAN can't deport him."

Rigo doesn't say anything for a moment. He appears lost in thought. Finally he looks up, and says, "Remember that time we went for a hike during the full moon?"

Anthea nods. Wonders what this has to do with anything they're talking about.

"Do you ever think about that?" he asks.

She nods. "Sometimes. Why?"

"It felt like we were walking in another world," he says.

It had been midnight, a month after they first met. The first blush of love was still in full bloom. They'd been out for bento boxes and a movie, followed by a hot tub. Too amped to crash, they'd podded down to Nisene Marks—a former state park that had been converted into a circuitree plantation. The moon was stage-light bright, pale as ice on her bare skin. It galvanized everything. Hiking trails. Limbs. Leaves. Sky. Her resolve. They'd held hands, stumbled on exposed roots and rocks, waded through puddles of shadow. The air felt cool and hazy in the depressions, crisp and clear on the rises. It had just been the two of them—giddy in the reflected light and each other.

"Everything felt different," Rigo says. "You know? New."

Anthea nods, remembering, worried that thinking back to the beginning means it's the end. That's the way it is with her girlfriends. They start thinking about the past, and it's a sure sign the present is not going well, that the future has crashed and burned and all they have left is nostalgia.

"This feels the same way," Rigo says. "Like my life is about to change. Except this time I'm just scared. Not excited."

"You were scared before?" she asks.

"Weren't you?"

"No. I knew it was right from the beginning. What would've scared me was if it *hadn't* felt right."

"How did you know it would work?" he asks.

"I just did."

"I guess I did, too. I think I was afraid of making a mistake. That it was just wishful thinking on my part. I mean, people do that a lot—fool themselves into thinking shit will work, when it won't."

So being afraid is not necessarily a bad thing. Is that what he's trying to tell her? To not give up?

"But it did work," she says.

"No reason it can't keep working," he says, "as long as we want it to. That's the important thing."

Well, she's not going to be the one to toss in the towel. "Remember the time we got caught in that dust storm? . . ."

They spend the rest of the night reminiscing. Reburning the tracks on worn-out memories and shared hopes. All the things that exist because of them. At sunrise, Rigo eases Ibrahim off his lap, tucks him in.

"I gotta go," he says, slipping off the wallscreen and into the hall.

The good-bye is a quick one. Chaste.

"Good luck," she says, awkward. Uncertain what to say, what do with her hands.

"You, too," he says, just as clumsy.

She nods. "Call me as soon as you can. Okay?"

He starts toward her, stops—"I will"—then turns and heads for the front door as fast as possible.

"I love you," she calls.

He stops in the doorway, looks over his shoulder. "Me, too."

At the last second, just before he shuts the door behind him, she rushes forward, kisses the fingers of her left hand and presses them to his lips.

After all, she thinks as the door closes and the first itchy tingle sets in, What's a bed of roses without a few thorns?

Rigo swings by his ap, takes a cold shower to clear his head, then maglevs down to Edwards Air Force Base for the flight to Tiresias.

"What's wrong?" Luis says. "You look like me after an evening of disappointments."

"Leave him alone," Rana says, coming to Rigo's defense. "Can't you spec he's not in the mood?"

"Yeah," Antoine says. "Cut the brother a little slack. Tell us about the one who got away last night. I'll bet she wasn't in the mood, either."

"Now, *that* was painful," Luis says, lapsing into lament mode.

"What?" Naguib chimes in. "She slap you?"

"He wishes," Hsi-Tang quips. "At least then he'd know that he made an impression."

"Hey," TomE says. "No pain, no gain."

Luis sighs, launches into a blow-by-blow description of the latest battle in his unsuccessful campaign to become the next Marquis de Sade.

Rigo keeps flashing on Anthea. He can still feel the soft touch of her fingertips on his lips. Taste the quinine bitterness they left behind. The look on her face as he bolted out the door was heartbreaking, something out of a Greek tragedy. No matter what happens, he'll carry it around with him forever, like a bleeding stigmata behind his eyes.

His flight departs at eleven. The SSTO, single-stage-to-orbit plane, resembles a bumblebee with butterfly wings grafted onto the body. A vivisectionist's wet dream. All aerospace engineers, it seems, are kids who grew up tweezing the wings off flies and sewing them onto tadpoles grown in one of those science kits that uses nonviable DNA from extinct species.

In addition to the Xengineering ecotectural team and colonists, there are a couple of security guards in the terminal building. Twitchy, hair-trigger types who, when they move, remind him of praying mantises. Dorit and the other colonists undergo a separate preflight procedure, apart from the technicians and gengineers. No way Rigo can talk to Dorit before they board. He wants to tell her about Ibrahim, the slave pherion, but doesn't get a chance.

Does Whipplebaum know about Ibrahim and BEAN . . . what's going on? He must.

On the SSTO, Rigo flops into a gelbag that molds to his body and attracts his biosuit like a bad case of static cling. He can move, get up if he has to, but it's easier to stay put. Especially three minutes after take-off, when the SSTO climbs to vertical, the wings fold back, and g-force stretches his lips all the way to his ears.

Then they're outside the gravity well and Rigo feels strangely unmoored. It's not just his body that's weightless but his thoughts. He's floating, cut loose from everything. There's nothing dragging him down, holding him back. For the first time in his life, he's to-tally free.

It's an illusion, of course. Given enough time, he'll come crashing back down to earth. A major downer.

"You want to swim with the navigation stream?" Varda asks.

"Sure," Rigo says. He leans his head back. A speck of light appears on the small screens of his wrap-arounds. A short, vaporous tail trails behind it.

"Tiresias," Varda says.

After half an hour, Rigo dozes off. When he wakes, four hours later, the speck is a moon-size orb, moving relatively fast against the fixed background of stars. He can make out a sharp terminus line creeping across the surface of the dirty snowball—black ice boiling under the leading edge.

During the trip, Varda has been strangely quiet. Usually the IA is a nonstop *boca*, a chatterbox. Can't stop streaming him information or asking questions. It gets on his nerves, big-time. But this is worse. He hasn't had to offline the IA once in over five hours. A record.

"Everything okay?" he asks, worried.

"Yes. Why?"

"I don't know. You're so . . . quiet."

"There's a lot to process."

"Like what?"

"You wouldn't be interested."

"How do you know?"

"You just wouldn't."

This isn't the Varda he's used to dealing with. The Varda he knows can't tell the difference between holy cow and sacred cow. Confuses rain with reign, sore with soar, and profit with prophet. Is never intentionally evasive or off-putting. Always tells him more than he wants to know about everything.

"How's Ibrahim?" he asks.

"Fine."

"What *aren't* you telling me?" he says.

"Nothing."

"No shit."

"I just want to be left alone for a while. That's all."

Something is definitely wrong. Great, an IA that refuses to talk to him. "This is not the time to become a hermit," he says.

"You're such a crab," Varda tells him.

That's more like it . . . back to normal. And not a moment too soon. His perspective of Tiresias has flip-flopped. Instead of looking up at the comet, he's looking down on it. He can make out surface details. Ridges. Pockmarks. A deep crevice that gapes like an open wound. The shadows are stark and sharp edged, as if they've been cut out of the sunlight with a razor.

As the surface draws nearer, he has the distinct sensation of falling. Lights blink in the darkness below them, beckoning. Dish-shaped solar panels wink, coquettish as flowers on stem-thin struts.

"The main research station," Varda says.

A few minutes later, buildings appear. Modular foam inflatables, for the most part, though there are a few rigid structures as well. Carbyne-frame geodesics that flash like faceted gemstones. Rigo can't see the plants—they're on the other side of the comet—but he can taste the sugary sprinkle of photons they're converting into thermal and electric energy, hear the fetal throbbing of warmth.

"Welcome to paradise," Claribel says.

Soon they're on the surface. Vapor billows up around them, and just as quickly turns to crystal rain that falls in slow motion, settling like mica in a snow globe. He detaches from the gelbag, floats free, and pulls himself along after the rest of his team, hoping to catch up with Dorit. Out of the SSTO, through an insulated access tube, and into one of the inflatable buildings. Whipplebaum is at his side, hair in a foggy low-g boil, as if his head is smoking. They float along a corridor walled with micropore foam and illuminated by soft biolum panels. Embedded magnets keep them from banging into the walls, push them along at a gentle tenth of a meter per second.

"When do we start work on the plants?" Rigo asks. He watches Rana, Antoine, Luis, and the others bang into each other ahead of him, coordinated as balls in a spinning bingo wheel.

"Patience, my boy," Whipplebaum says, smoothing a tuft of hair into place. "First, the colonists need to get settled in. Become fully integrated with the warm-blooded environment before we begin testing and analysis. Their acclimatization is being implemented by a different part of the team. That will take several hours. Then it's your turn at bat. Monitoring the plants and checking their response to the colonists. If they're stable or unstable, and what tweaks, if any, can be made to optimize assimilation. The ecotectural and biomed info will be downloaded and channeled through your IA as it comes online. You'll have a chance to get up to speed in stages. Ramp up, as it were, to the climactic moment."

Dorit has disappeared around a corner ahead of them. At the same junction, the magnetic current takes him in another direction, whisks him into an enlarged section of the tunnel that resembles a mausoleum. Two rows of coffin-size rooms with sleep nets, amniotic lighting, and windowless privacy doors. Cozy.

"In the meantime"—Whipplebaum gestures to one of the stacked cylinders—"I suggest you make yourself at home."

SIXTEEN

Confined to the ap, Anthea feels like she's been condemned to purgatory. She can't get close to Ibrahim, can't even be in the same room with him. Which is good and bad. On the plus side, it means he's out of immediate danger. He's got enough of whatever pherion Rigo gave him during the night to keep him healthy. On the minus side, he's as much a prisoner as she is. The hard part is that she can't give him any physical comfort to ease the isolation. All she has to offer is emotional support, a smile, meager words of encouragement.

"How do you feel?"

"All right." His gaze wanders around the room with the erratic focus of a moth. "Where am I?"

"An ap in San Jose."

He glances at the nanimatronic rat asleep on his pillow. "How long have I been here?"

"A day."

He looks up from the toy to Anthea. "It seems like forever."

And no time at all, she thinks. Eternity in a heartbeat. "Are you hungry? Can I get you something?"

He shakes his head. "How come you brought me here?"

Don't get all emotional, she reminds herself. Maintain clinical distance. Stick to the facts. "BEAN is looking for you. They contacted me at the clinic yesterday, while you were asleep."

"I don't want to be deported. I don't want to go back." He stares past her, as if haunted by a specter.

The nape of Anthea's neck prickles. "Where would you like to go?"

"Rio. They've got live music there. Musicians in bands playing real instruments at clubs."

"Is that where you're from?"

"No, that's just what I've heard. I don't know for a fact. But I'd like to go down there. Check it out."

"Where else would you like to go?"

"Tokyo. The part that's built on the ocean."

"What's the most interesting place you've been?"

He shrugs, closes down. "I'm not sure."

Not much of an answer. As usual, he's managed to deflect conversation when it comes to his past. She's not making much progress on the home front. Still has no clue where's he's originally from. She could really use somebody to talk to. Rigo's mom is super nice and all. But it's not as if they can discuss psychology. She doesn't feel like she's doing enough, wonders if there's anything she can do. There must be *some-*thing. She wishes she could draw him out more. But there's really nothing she can do, except wait until he's ready. Hope that he hangs on. Pray that BEAN doesn't find them. A lot of what's going to happen depends on Beto. How long it takes him to get back to her and how much he can or can't do for them. Once she finds out whether or not Beto can cook up an antipher, she'll have a better idea of her next move.

"You want some breakfast?" the old woman asks when Anthea rejoins her in the kitchen. "I've got juice. Instant cereal. A little bread. Some seaweed jelly."

"I'm fine," Anthea says. "Thanks."

"You don't look fine. You should eat. You're too skinny. No wonder you can't have children."

Anthea blinks, takes a moment to recover her wits. "That's not it," she says.

The old woman gives her a curious look. "Tell me what the trouble is then, *mija*."

Anthea shifts on the sofa. It's the first time Rigo's mom has been this close with her, treated her like family. "What makes you think I want kids, Mama?"

Mother. The word feels strange in her mouth. Foreign. Lost during the years of self-imposed motherlessness after she ran away from home.

The old woman nods at the wallscreen, where Ibrahim is crashed out on the bed. "You wouldn't help him if you didn't."

"This is different. He's in trouble, needs help."

"Not so different." The woman moves to join her. Totters stiff-legged over to one end of the sofa, plants a hand on the armrest, and edges around the corner. Anthea hops up to help, gets waved off. "I can manage." One knee creaks, slowly bends, while the other leg refuses to cooperate. It remains locked in place, rigid as a board as she lowers herself. Halfway down she reaches the point of no return, and gravity sucks her into the cushion. The landing is soft, accompanied by a grunt.

The added weight on the sofa collapses the cushions in the center. Anthea finds herself canting sideways into dry, crusty skin, and pepper-tree deodorant.

"I'm not the only one with maladies." The old woman sighs. "We're all victims." She adjusts her dress on her thighs, turns her attention to the wallscreen. "He reminds me of Rigo. The first time I saw him. My heart went out."

She says this casually, as if setting down a bag of groceries she's hauled around for years and suddenly grown weary of carrying.

"What do you mean the first time, Mama?"

"It was at a displaced persons camp outside of Denver." Rigo's mom pauses to sort through attic memorabilia she hasn't examined in years. "That was what they called refugees back then, displaced persons. My mother and I lived in an offshore flotilla camp for two years after the first mass extinction, before we were finally admitted to the United States and claded for St. Louis."

"You grew up in SL?"

"It wasn't that bad. Prostitutes and petty criminals, mostly. No mafia, tongs, or cartels. Of course, I immigrated there when I was five. I remembered a little about the Dominican Republic, but not enough to have trouble assimilating. Kids always have it easier. They adapt, accept the world as it is. For them, the past is so much smaller than the present. There's not as much to hold on to, so it's easy to let go."

"How old were you when the plague hit?"

"Twenty-two. Beto was three. I decided to get him out fast when his father got sick one day and never came home. He went straight from work to the hospital—where he died a day later."

The virus had sprung out of the ecotecture. A mutated pherion that instantiated in the population in a matter of days. Transmission was not only person to person, but environment to person. Ninety percent fatal.

"That's how we ended up in Denver. Front Range City, actually. I found Rigo in the maglev station. Sitting totally alone, waiting. I took him under my wing, tried to find his relatives. But after two days, I gave up. Knew he'd been abandoned."

"So you adopted him."

"Not officially. Just pretended he was mine. BEAN took my word on it. Never checked, even though it was pretty obvious at the time he wasn't Dominican. They just wanted to get a handle on the situation. San Jose was just opening up. So they sent us here. No questions asked."

"Does he remember what happened?"

"I don't think so. He was too young. If he does, he hasn't said anything to me. I haven't told him or Beto."

"Are you going to?"

"No. It's too late now. At the time, I didn't want to make Rigo feel like less of a son, give Beto something to lord over him. You know how vicious boys can be. Better they hate each other as brothers."

"How come you're telling me, Mama?"

"Because I think we should talk honestly. Just the two of us, woman to woman."

She states this matter-of-factly. No conspiratorial wink, or knowing nudge to the ribs. In other words, Anthea thinks, she wants them to be kind of like sisters—or best friends—rather than mother and daughter. Zero secrets between them.

Anthea folds her hands in her lap. Rubs one thumb. Listens to the old woman's slow, unhurried breaths.

"I left home when I was twelve," Anthea begins. "Lived on the streets until I was sixteen, working as a *puta*. I've never tried to hide that about myself. Not from Rigo or anyone else. I wouldn't be surprised if he already told you. I haven't asked him not to, if you want to know."

"Lots of kids run away from home, for lots of reasons. Some good. Some not so good."

"I'm not ashamed of what I did," Anthea says. She refuses to apologize. "What I did hide, what I've never told anybody, is why I left. Who and what I ran away from."

Most people assume it was a shitty home life— abuse, neglect—or youthful rebellion. Whenever anybody asks, she lets them draw their own conclusion by saying, "The usual," or a rhetorical, "What do you think?"

Rigo's mom waits. No pressure. Anthea can say as much or as little as she wants. It's up to her. She feels like one of the street kids she counsels who's having a hard time opening up, learning to trust. It isn't easy finding herself on the flip side of the coin. It's been

years since she's been in this position. Too bad she
doesn't have a sketchpad or a doll she can use as a
stand-in to act things out for her.

"I don't have a sister or a nephew," she confesses.
"I met Malina before I started working for Global
Upreach. We're close friends, not relatives. I lied, told
Rigo she was my sister because—"

She falters. Why? Because she wanted a sister, and
Malina was as close as she would ever come?

"Because I wanted Rigo to think I was like him,"
Anthea says. "That I came from the same background.
I didn't want him to know that I'm actually the daughter of a rich, upper-clade gerontocrat. That I was born
and raised in Hong Kong, not Los Angeles."

There. She's said it, come clean. Instead of feeling
relieved, she feels sick to her stomach. Soiled and embarrassed by the truth.

"You don't look *chinita*."

"My mother's English. I don't know who my father is. Argentine, maybe. My mother never told me."
Not only is she a fraud but an illegitimate one.

"So you took an antipher when you came here
from HK," the old woman surmises. "To fit in. Make
yourself compatible."

"That's how I met Beto. After I got here, I was sick.
He took me to a black-market clinic."

The old woman mulls this over. "I didn't know
Beto did that kind of thing. I just assumed he . . ." She
shakes her head.

"Beto does a lot of pro bono charity work,"
Anthea says. "Helps out nonprofit clinics when they
have an emergency or special needs." She's not sure
she should be confiding this.

"Where's your mother now?" Rigo's mom asks. "Does she know where you are? How you're doing?"

"I don't know." In answer to both questions.

"Don't you care?"

Good question. One Anthea's not sure she has the answer to. "I'm not sure *she* cares. We didn't exactly part on the best of terms."

"Well, I'm sure she misses you. Still loves you— wishes that she could see you again now that you're grown up. A woman." She states this with conviction, with the certainty of a mother who has suffered disappointments.

"That may be," Anthea concedes. "But I don't want to see her. I don't want to go back and pick up where we left off." Because that's what would happen. No doubt about it.

"Was she so bad? Was your life with her really that terrible?"

Anthea lets out a weary sigh. "To be honest, Mama, it was horrible. Worse than you can imagine."

"What did she do to make you hate her?"

Anthea stares at her entwined hands, can't meet the old woman's gaze. "This is difficult." She feels like Ibrahim, avoiding the past. Running from it the way she would an apparition.

"Did she do it out of malice, *mija*?"

"I don't know. She said she was doing it for my own good, that one day I would understand. Thank her."

"But you don't believe her."

"No. She was punishing me."

"Sometimes that's what love looks like," the old

woman says. "Not always. But more often than people think."

"She locked me up. Confined me to our ap by dosing me with an early military nonlethal she got her hands on—a pherion that eventually evolved into one of the first biodependency pherions. I still have to take an antipher to counteract it. That's one of the reasons I'm so skinny, can't have children. The drug messes with my hormones. I don't metabolize normally."

"How long did this go on?"

"She kept me a prisoner for over a year. Wouldn't let me go anywhere. I tried to leave once. Walked out of the ap and took the elevator to the main lobby. Before I made it to the front door, it felt like I was being cut all over with jagged glass." Anthea clasps her hands together, squeezing the blood from her fingers. "Not just on the outside, but inside, too."

Rigo's mother puts a hand on her forearm. "No wonder you ran away, wanted to hurt her back."

"I couldn't live with her after that. So I became everything she didn't want me to be. Her worst nightmare."

A grimace crinkles the old woman's face. "But why, *mija*? *Por que*? How come she did this thing to you?"

It's hard not to hear the unspoken implication, intended or not, that it was somehow her fault. That she must have done something terrible to deserve such severe treatment.

"I was close friends with a boy," Anthea says, forcing her fingers to relax, feeling a sudden ache in her joints brought by the resurgent tingle of blood.

"Older?"

"Of course. Fourteen. My mother didn't want me seeing him. She was afraid we were—" Anthea snorts, a truncated laugh.

The old woman raises one brow. "Were you?"

"No. It wasn't that kind of friendship. He was bent. But there was no convincing my mother. Plus, he was from India. The son of a refugee. Very poor. Not suitable for someone of my education and upbringing. The price for refusing not to see him was not seeing anyone."

"You couldn't have any visitors at all?"

"Not at first. After a year, she let a couple of my girlfriends come over. But only those who were from families she could trust, and only for a short while. An hour a day at the most."

"What did you do the rest of the time?"

"Studied. Spent a lot of time online. Reading. Streaming music. Watching tons of old projector movies. Went crazy. Plotted my escape."

"How did you get away?"

"A girlfriend smuggled in a temporary antipher. It counteracted the pherion long enough for me to LOHop to San Jose. I wanted to get as far away as fast as I could."

The old woman sucks at her teeth. "You haven't been able to get an antidote to make you fertile again? Reverse the sterilization?"

"No. It's complicated. No one I've gone to has been able to figure it out. After a while, I stopped trying." Resigned herself to staying on medication. "I look at it as a disease now. Something incurable that I was born with."

"Do you feel revenged?"

She smiles at the question, one she's asked herself a thousand times, shakes her head. "Not anymore."

"But you did?"

"For a few years. But everything gets old, Mama, wears thin after a while. It only lasts so long."

"Not love," the old woman says. "Love never wears thin. If it does, it was never love to begin with."

Anthea's not exactly sure what she's trying to say with this, whether it has to do with her and Rigo or her and her mother.

"Did you ever tell your mother what you were doing?" the old woman asks. "On the streets."

"To hurt her, you mean? Make her angry? Guilty?"

"*Sí*."

"No. She has a lot of money and resources. I was afraid that if she knew what I was doing she'd figure out a way to find me."

"It sounds to me like maybe you're the person who suffered all those years. Not her."

"Sometimes"—this is Anthea's greatest hope—"not knowing what happened to a person is worse than knowing."

"You don't want her to know if you're dead or alive? You want to torture her by sending her to her grave in the dark?"

"I don't want her to have closure. I don't want her to be able to write me off as a worthless *puta*. I want her always to wonder. To never be at peace, the same way I will never be at peace."

"You don't have any regrets?"

"There are always regrets, Mama. You know that."

"True."

"Do you ever wish you hadn't adopted Rigo?" Anthea says, thinking that maybe this is one of the old woman's secret regrets.

"Sometimes I wish I'd been able to do more with my life. Growing up, I wanted to be an artist. It's too late for that now. I'm not complaining. There are worse things you can do than raise children. I do wish I'd raised them differently. I made mistakes. I can see that now."

"What kind of mistakes, Mama?" Anthea's curious what Rigo's mom sees as his shortcomings, his faults. Whether they sync with hers.

"I wish I'd taught Beto to respect authority more, and Rigo to question it." She twists to one side, tugs at a crease in her dress that's pinching the loose flesh under her left arm. Plucks it with rake-stiff fingers. "Maybe if I'd taken them on a church relief mission to India. Or Africa. Exposed them to different ways of thinking when they were younger. Before they had a chance to get set in their ways."

"You think spending time in another culture would have given them a different perspective on life here and how to deal with it?" Anthea's not convinced things are all that different anywhere else. In some countries, the living conditions are a lot worse. She's worked with kids from those places. They're just as messed, just as fucked up, as those raised here.

"It might have helped." The old woman's shoulders tilt in a lopsided shrug, then straighten, like a boat righting itself. "Not that it did me any good. I always thought that if I worked hard and stayed out of trouble I'd have a good life. That's what we were told when we migrated here. Instead, I'm a victim of social engineering."

"What do you mean, Mama?"

The old woman tries to straighten her elbow, fails. "Everything I do is controlled. Where I can go. Who I can talk to. Even my health is managed. Planned obsolescence, designed to make room for the next person in line."

It takes a moment for Anthea to fully process this. "You're saying the politicorp is responsible for your condition?"

"How else is the government going to manage population growth, enforce social and economic demographics? It's the same thing that happened in St. Louis. A plague. The only difference is that now they've got it under control."

"That's a serious allegation."

"What else am I supposed to think? After seeing what's been done to Ibrahim, I can't help wondering if maybe Beto's right."

"When did you talk to Beto?" Anthea wasn't sure if they were on speaking terms or not. Listening to Rigo, it was hard to tell.

"A few minutes ago. While you were talking to Ibrahim."

"What did he want?"

"He called to tell me that my FOP is triggered by a gengineered prion living in the water-recycling plants."

"How does he know?"

"He had Rigo bring me a medication for my joints. Except it was really a diagnostic to check for this prion. Apparently, I'm not the only one who's got it. There are other people, too. *Viejos*, like me."

"But how does he know it was gengineered? That it was released on purpose by the government?"

"He didn't say. He only said I shouldn't drink the water in my building. That it's contaminated and will make my condition worse."

Targeted prions. This sounds a little too close to the story concocted by BEAN about Ibrahim carrying terrorist pherions.

"He also wanted to know if I'd heard from you," the old woman goes on. "Knew where to find you."

Anthea's mind spins, caught up in the white-water churn of events. "What did you say?"

"I told him I didn't know where you were, but if I saw you I'd tell you how to get in touch with him. I didn't think it was a good idea to tell anyone you were here without discussing it with you."

"Where is he?"

"Someplace called the Inferno. It looked like a bar."

It's not. The Inferno is actually Beto's underground pharm. The bar scene is a digital overlay, encrypted and then interleaved with the transmission so that it appears real-world.

"Is that all?" Anthea asks.

"*Sí.* He said you'd know how to get there."

"Can you watch Ibrahim for a while?"

"You think Beto can help him. Is that why he wants to see you?"

"That's what I'm hoping," Anthea says.

*   *   *

Anthea drops offline for the trip to the Inferno. Half an hour later, she finds herself navigating the debris-choked, half-collapsed concrete of an abandoned sewer pipe. Layers of fifty-year-old spray foam and bubblepack clog the concrete walls. Through the translucent plaque, lit by colonies of biolum bacteria, she can make out air pockets formed by rusted metal cabinets, plastic garbage cans, and storage crates where people once slept.

She's only been to Beto's private pharm twice, right after she was recovered enough to leave the clinic. Went there expecting to pay for services rendered. She did, just not the way she thought. Beto had a boyfriend, wasn't interested. Instead, he asked her to pick up some product. She felt obligated, agreed to do the job. When Beto offered her a follow-up job, she turned him down. Thanks but no thanks. She didn't want to be pimped out by a pharmer. She wanted to make her own rules—take her own risks. In retrospect, she should have taken him up on the offer. It would have been better than working as a gang banger, peddling STDs. But she was young. Had her life all figured out, knew exactly what she was doing.

So she and Beto have a history. He sniffs her coming in advance. Beto's got early warning the way the old military industrial complex was wired with SIG-INT. To the gills. The pharm is in a side pipe. An ancient iron gate clotted with spray foam conceals the entrance, secretes a broad-spectrum pherion that induces severe intestinal cramps in most people. After a short wait, the gate swings open, ushers her into a makeshift room with diamond polymer wax sealing the walls and floor. Equipment crowds the room: pherion sequencers, rows of seed trays, laser tweezers, an old carbon nanotube SPM, scanning probe microscope. Several display screens hang from the ceiling, Japanese-like scrolls unfurled to reveal seething entoptics, realtime pictographic representations of designer molecules in various stages of development or production.

When he sees her, the first words out of his mouth aren't, "Good to see you," or "*Que pasa?*" but "What's the problem?"

"BEAN," Anthea says. "They're looking for Ibrahim."

Beto flips off his eyescreens, fondles the stubble on his jaw. "Where you hiding the kid, anyway?"

"Your mom's."

This garners an eye twitch. "I can't fucking believe it," he says. "She lied, said you weren't there."

Hard to tell if he's pissed or just shocked. "It wasn't like she had a choice," Anthea says. "Not online with a shared IA."

"I guess not." He gives her a predatory squint. "Anyone else know he's there?"

She shakes her head.

"Not even Rigo?" he asks.

"No," she lies. Not that Rigo would say anything. But she wants Beto to realize how careful she's been. It seems to work.

"I analyzed the sample you provided," he says, wasting no time getting down to business.

"And?"

"I isolated the slave pherion, deconstructed it."

"And?"

"The pherion is modular. Consists of four pieces. Ibrahim's gengineered to make only three of the pieces. Three-quarters of the protein. That's the problem. His body needs the complete protein. Otherwise, it crashes."

And the missing piece is provided by the Tiresias ecotecture. "You can't pharm the missing piece?"

"No. The structure's too complicated. I can't extrapolate it from the configuration of the other pieces. There are too many permutations. It could take years to run through all the possibilities. Find the one that interacts with the others in exactly the right way. What I need is a copy of the protein so I can sequence it directly."

So she needs to get another blood sample from Ibrahim. Hope that he still has a high enough concentration of the slave pherion in his system to provide a complete sequence. It's either that or wait for Rigo.

"I did manage to isolate and sequence a second pherion he's doped with," Beto says. "One I've never seen before."

The rash-producing security pherion for Tiresias. "Were you able to create an antipher?"

Beto bares his teeth, affirmative. "But it's only temporary."

It's better than nothing. At least she'll be able to get close to Ibrahim . . . and Rigo. "What do you want for that?" she says.

"Same payment we already agreed on."

Figures. "What if I get you a copy of the complete slave pherion?"

Beto grins. "Do that and I'll brew it up free of

charge. That way you get two for one. The security pherion and the slave pherion."

She hesitates—wonders for a moment if he's lying. Bullshitting her to speed up payment. She wouldn't put it past him.

"Deal," she says.

They conclude the transaction. Anthea takes a vial of the Tiresias antipher. In return, she hands over a sample of her urine, which he can use to copy her upper-clade security pherion.

Beto now has a free ticket to Hong Kong. Can go almost anywhere he wants in Asia.

SEVENTEEN

Too amped to sleep, Rigo floats in the foam-walled sepulcher of his room, going over the performance specifications of the Tiresias ecotecture while he waits for the colonists to physically connect to the warm-blooded plants. It takes almost four hours to complete the link.

The datastream starts as a trickle. Sensors slowly coming online, chemical gears meshing in a clockwork dance that starts out slow and picks up speed. Pulls him along the way merengue does when he's one with the music.

Most of the info he's streaming is new. Isomorphic recombination. Structured antigenic resolution. Ribosome optimization. Stages of development that every meaningful relationship needs to go through in order to survive. About the time he's ready to take a breather, sit out a few numbers, he gets a group message from Whipplebaum, sent to the implementation team, telling all of them to meet in the primary air lock.

At "Oh-ten-hundred pointed," according to Varda.

A half hour. Barely enough time to slip back into his biosuit, gather his wits, and a quick bite to eat at the cafeteria before reporting for duty. There's definitely a blitzkrieg feel to the whole operation at this point, a commando-style assault to get the job done quickly and efficiently. Focus is on speed and precision.

"Talk about regimented," Naguib complains. "I feel like I can't take a leak unless it's on the checklist."

"And I thought Rigo was anal retentive," TomE quips. "A type-A stickler for detail."

"Naw," Antoine says. "Ol' Rigo here is a sharing kind of guy. Never holds on to shit. Always spreads it around."

In the air lock, a window-studded room that's basically a colossal Buckyball with a view, they're each issued tether cords and emergency propulsion units, little point-and-shoot cylinders of pressurized CO_2 they can use to jet around when they're leashed to the comet.

"Just what Tang needs," Luis says. "Like he's not flatulent enough."

"At least he's experienced when it comes to out-gassing," Naguib says. "Knows what to do."

"Yeah," Claribel says. "He won't hold nothing back."

"Hey," Hsi-Tang says, his indignation hampered by a huge grin, "practice makes perfect."

"Thank God he's self-contained," Rana says. "Maybe by the time we're finished we won't have to worry about it."

"Don't count on it," TomE says. "Not after what he just ate."

"What did he just eat?" Rigo says.

TomE makes a face. "Cajun-spiced bean crackers with this roasted garlic cheese spread."

Naguib leads a chorus of groans.

Then the vat team goose-steps it through a final equipment check. Subsystem IAs in Rigo's biosuit relay pressure, temperature, oxygen-renewal, filtration, and piezoelectric status to Varda for validation and cross-check.

"You're A-all right," the IA says, giving him a thumbs-up.

The equipment check is followed by a quick briefing/pep talk by Whipplebaum—rah, rah—and then they all climb into a cramped lander, sardine tight. A short CO_2 burst levitates the craft two meters, plus or minus, as the air lock cycles open. A second burst propels it forward at a little over six meters per second in the micro-g. Faster than that and they'll attain escape velocity. Through gray-polarized diamond, Rigo watches the ice glide by. The horizon is a vaporous curve, thin as the edge of a lens with the approach of day. Dawn takes about three minutes. As soon as they cross the terminus line into sunlight the surface glows, as if coated by an incendiary layer of tule fog, and the ground drops away abruptly, stranding his stomach in his throat.

"The Tiresias rift," Varda says.

The fissure is steep-walled blackness, a gaping

crack in the infinite fabric of the universe. A true cosmic yoni. Rigo studies the topographic and cross-section maps on the screen of his faceplate. The cleft is several kilometers deep, cleaves all the way through the outer mantle of ice into the underlying substrata of rock. "Any idea what caused it?"

"One possibility is rapid heating and cooling. This may also have contributed to the formation of numerous gas-filled pockets in the rock core."

"What kind of gas?"

"Hydrogen and oxygen."

"From the ice?" Must be, Rigo reasons. Where else could the gas have come from?

"There may also be methane."

Complex hydrocarbons. Rigo frowns, puzzled. "Doesn't there normally have to be some kind of biological activity for that to happen?"

"Yes."

Around him he can hear his team chattering softly as they joke among themselves and interface with their IAs. "So you're saying there's life on Tiresias? Or was at one time, in the past?"

"It's probable the comet is extrasolar," Varda says, "a piece of a destroyed planet from another solar system captured by the sun. Prior to being moved into near-earth orbit, the comet's trajectory relative to the plane of the ecliptic was very steep." The IA is rapping in encyclopedia mode, as if it's gotten in touch with its inner librarian.

"How long ago are we talking?" Rigo asks. Might as well take advantage of this sudden moment of clarity. No telling when the IA will lapse back into its usual state of confused idiot-syncratic babble.

"Tiresias appears to be on the order of six billion years old. Several billion years older than our solar system. A precise age has not yet been confirmed."

"What about composition?" Rigo asks.

"Some nickel and iron mixed with basalt and granite. There appear to be carbonate deposits and hydrous minerals, as well."

Rigo's no geologist, not by any stretch of the imagination. "Is that unusual?" he says.

"Not for a planet."

As Rigo considers this, a Lilliputian point of light winks to life deep in the gash, followed by several others. Slowly the lights separate, metastasize into a loose globular cluster.

"What's that?"

"A geology team," Varda tells him. "Sent out a little while ago to investigate what appears to be a series of recent microtemblors."

Rigo frowns . . . tries to dredge up the last earth-sciences course he took back in grade school. "I thought only a full-blown planet or a large moon could have seismic activity." Which more or less rules Tiresias out.

"True," Varda says.

"Then the miniquakes must be the result of something else," Rigo says. "Like the impact of an asteroid or some other object." He's thinking of the Perseids, Leonids, or loose space debris from the old NASA garbage dump days. Shit that never fell back to earth and no one bothered to clean up.

"Maybe," his IA concedes. "A bigger concern is that moving the comet into orbit might have created small stress fractures in the comet's rock core and weakened it internally."

Great, Rigo thinks. Just what he needs. As if the situation isn't complicated enough. He blinks as another possibility hits him. "Could the addition of the new ecotecture be responsible?"

Varda pauses for a beat, calculating. "It's highly unlikable. There's not enough biomass to influence the comet's equilibrium."

"Are the plants in danger? I mean, were the quakes powerful enough to damage the ice they're anchored to?"

At this stage the root system is shallow—limited to the top six meters of the ice mantle—and not very well developed or established. He envisions a nightmare scenario of the ice breaking apart, shearing off the comet in glacierlike chunks and taking the plants along for the ride.

"The structural integrity of the ice appears to be intact," Varda reports. "Don't worry. If anything changes, I'll keep you looped."

The fissure disappears behind them and Rigo his attention forward, to the plants themselves. They cluster together, gathered around a central communication/control tower like a medley of inflatable circus tents. All that's missing are the stripes and flags, the smell of popcorn, and the carnival blare of organ grinder music. The upper framework of the spun carbyne spire is a herringbone pattern of dull silver. Scratchy cross-hatching that recalls the Eiffel Tower. Positioned in an equilateral triangle around the plants, a triad of squat calderalike cones peeks over the foreshortened horizon. Heat-blackened, diamond-walled nozzles for the thrusters that shoved the comet into orbit.

The lander slows, kicks up motes of ice in a hazy cloud that thins and boils away under the onslaught of photons. They touch down with a grating thud, and cozy up to a docking pylon fifty or so meters from the plants.

"It's party time," Rana says, leading the charge. "Petal to the mettle." A favorite phrase of hers that always reminds Rigo of Varda.

Bustle and bump out of the hatch. Clip safety lines to the pylon. Fan out like a pack of spiders trailing gossamer threads of silk.

Rigo slips into team mode . . . no different than at Noogenics. Links to the sensors and runs diagnostics. Checks system integrity. Scans vital stats. Monitors everything from tissue biopsies to shear and torsional stress measurements.

At one point Whipplebaum pops up, unexpected as a jack-in-the-box, to observe how things are progressing.

"Fine," Rigo says. "No problem."

"Good." Whipplebaum's mood is tight-ass dictatorial. "Carry on. Be sure to let me know if you encounter anything unusual."

After this brief exhortation to the front-line troops by the corporate general—*El Jefe* incarnate—it's back to the trenches.

Rigo can't actually go inside the plants, but gets a chance to check out the interior when Dorit comes online. Her image materializes like a wraith on the surface of his faceplate. She's in a small room, her private living quarters maybe, suspended below a curved ceiling that's pocked with bubble lenses, tiny pustules of overripe light that feel swollen, ready to burst.

"I just wanted to say good-bye," she says. "While I had the chance."

"How is it?" he asks. She looks luminous. Radiant as the Virgin Mary in an old oil painting. Different but still recognizably human. At least on the outside. An elderly woman with a second skeleton like his mother. Only difference is, hers is on the outside and protects her, gives her the strength to go on.

"I'm happier than I've been in years." She says this sadly. As if she hasn't yet abandoned the skin of her former self. Reconciled herself to the future.

"I'm glad," Rigo says. And he is. He wants only the best for her, wishes her all the contentedness in the world.

"There's something I want to give you," she says. "A gift, which I trust you will share with someone else."

"Sure." He's uncertain how she's going to get anything to him, sealed up in the ecotecture.

She picks up a vial, opens her mouth, and mists her tongue. Rigo feels the spritz instantly, a numb tingle that marinates his mouth with the taste of blood oranges.

"What is it?" he asks. A pherion of some sort, he specs, assembled via the direct link he shares with her and the warm-blooded plants. But what *kind* of pherion? That's the question.

"Think of it as design-space key," she says. "The means to unlock any number of possible futures."

Whatever that means. "Who's it for?" Rigo says,

wondering how, exactly, he's supposed to pass the
gift on.

"A mutual . . . friend."

Either regular comlink encryption isn't enough or
she's being deliberately vague for some other reason.

"I don't understand," he says.

"You will. The thing to remember, dear, is that
*every*thing is arbitrary. Nothing *had* to happen the
way it did. Nothing *has* to be the way it is. The world
is always ripe for change."

Rigo doesn't get the feeling she's fucking with
him—not like some people—but he's definitely feeling short-circuited, having a hard time wrapping his
head around her mumbo jumbo.

Dorit leans forward, as if to place her face close to
his. "Take our dear Arnez, for example."

"Whipplebaum?"

Dorit's image bobs in a zero-g approximation of a
nod. "He was afraid RiboGen would lose control of
Tiresias. That we were being given too much initial
freedom, and would eventually attempt to break free
of our corporate sponsor."

By "we" Rigo gathers she means the colonists.

"So he took matters into his own hands," Dorit
continues, "measures to ensure we could never become fully self-sufficient or self-governing—that we
would always need something only he or another old
cauc could provide."

Rigo frowns. "Measures?"

The corners of Dorit's mouth droop, clown-face
sad. "He arranged to infect the warm-blooded plants
with a slave pherion. One that's remote-linkable to
the ecotecture. That way if we decided to declare our

independence, he would have an ace up his sleeve. A way to stop us from becoming autonomous."

"The overpressurization and sensor failure in the plants," Rigo says. "The supposedly harmless quantum superposition of states. You're telling me it was all set up by Whipplebaum?"

Dorit applauds him with a philanthropic smile. "Not to mention that 'accidental' tear in your biosuit."

"So it wouldn't have made any difference if I'd reported being exposed to the plants. I still would've been picked for the mission." From the sound of things, it would have actually cemented the decision. A quiver runs through his safety line, a faint vibratory thrum that sets him on edge.

"Arnez needed a vector," Dorit says. "Somebody remote-linked to Tiresias who could be used to transmit the assembler code for the slave pherion."

"Then how come you're talking to me now?" he asks. "Aren't you afraid you're going to be infected?" Unless, of course, the colony is already compromised. In which case, it doesn't matter.

"No," she says. "We're practicing safe communications. Blocking that particular instruction set."

"So you knew ahead of time," he says. "When?"

"After the party. The non-Tiresias part of your clade-profile had changed from when we first met."

At Salmon Ella's. Before the biosuit tear and his exposure to the plants. Which is why she had touched him. To establish a base pherion and iDNA reading she could refer to later.

"Why me?" Rigo says.

The smile lapses, a slow fade. "I think you know."

Pressure builds in Rigo's chest. "Because I'm expendable . . . along with the rest of my team."

"And because you wouldn't ask questions. Not when you'd just been given the opportunity of a lifetime to better your career."

"Bottom line"—Rigo sucks his teeth to keep from spitting—"he used me. Took advantage of all my hard work and dedication." All his hopes and dreams.

"Don't take it personally," Dorit says. "It's the same kind of cold logic that went into creating clades in the first place. Treating people like viruses."

"Viruses?"

Dorit tents one eyebrow in mild surprise. "I assumed you knew. Since you work directly with gengineered biosystems."

"I must not have got the memo."

"The meaning of the term has changed somewhat over the last seventy-five or so years. Originally, 'clade' referred solely to a group of species consisting of a common ancestor and all its descendents. Today, however, 'species' has been unofficially redefined to include social, economic, cultural, and religious differences rather than just genetic variation. To complicate matters, the term has expanded to include the different pherion patterns of the group. On a virus, the arrangement of glycoproteins on the outer protective shell is referred to as a host range. Viruses within the same family have a similar protein pattern. Viruses outside the family have a different pattern."

"You're saying different clades have different pherion patterns the way different viruses have different arrangements of glycoproteins."

"Yes. The arrangement of glycoproteins determines how the virus biochemically interacts with its environment."

"The same way pherions control how different clades relate," Rigo says. "Where people can go and who they can interact with."

"Tiresias is the beginning of a completely new posthuman species," Dorit says. "It doesn't have to be the only one. New beginnings can happen anytime. The key is wanting something enough to make it happen."

He shakes his head, uncertain what she wants or expects from him. "How come you're confiding all this?"

She lets out an indulgent sigh. Gets to the point. "We're not going to wait to leave. We're going to exit stage left while we still have the chance, and start our own show, as far off Broadway as we can get."

Too bad he's never been to New York City, doesn't have the social capital to appreciate her theatrics.

"Rigo," Antoine says, cutting in. "I'm picking up increased metabolic activity in the plants."

"That's just the beginning," Rana tells him. "The comlink to the research station just dropped offline. The local link is still up, but don't ask me for how long."

Rigo switches back to Dorit. "Is this part of the exodus? Or is there some other explanation for what's going on?"

"I'm showing an internal temperature rise inside the plants," TomE informs Rigo. "Two degrees in the last minute."

"Where's the power coming from?" he asks. The orbiting solar array isn't transmitting yet. Last he checked, there wasn't enough stored energy to generate that sharp a temperature gradient.

"The thrusters," Varda says. "They're uplifting."

"Time to say *au revoir*," Dorit tells Rigo. "Get back to your lander as quickly as you can." Earnest.

"I'm not going anywhere." Not until he gets some answers.

"Don't be stubborn, dear. Just do as I say. Please. We can't have you missing any important engagements."

"Are you getting married?" Varda asks.

"You have less than five minutes," Dorit says. "If you don't leave now, there's a very good chance you never will. That goes for your team, as well."

"What about Whipplebaum?"

"Don't worry about dear Arnez. He's the least of your concerns at the moment. Now, I suggest you leave while you can." A spike of urgency in her voice. "Go. Get out of here!" She terminates the link. End of discussion.

Rigo doesn't waste any time. Heeds her advice and orders his team to haul ass back to the lander like there's no tomorrow.

Whipplebaum messages him. "What the hell's going on?"

Before Rigo can answer, the comet shudders. He pitches to one side, floats half a meter above the surface, arms and legs flailing in a haze of ice crystals and dust as he tries to reorient himself.

"There's been an accident," Varda informs him.

"An explosion in the rift where the geology team was working."

This is the kind of news that can lead to a loss of faith. When Rigo finally rights himself and gets his bearings, he finds that Tiresias has split in two along the fissure.

The lander is drifting up from the surface, slowly rising . . . though maybe it's the other way around— the ground falling, dropping out from under it. At the same time, the two halves of the comet are tumbling away from each other and rotating. Spinning like mad. The sun, plummeting to the horizon, sends a guillotine edge of blackness racing toward him over the ice. Behind him, the earth fills the sky.

An X blinks on the inside of his faceplate, neon yellow against a background of stars just to the left of the retreating lander.

"Jump in the direction of the X," Varda tells him.

Rigo hesitates. "Where's everyone else?" He's lost visual contact with his team in the dust and sudden reorientation of the comet. Can't get a lock on them.

"Fret about them later," Varda says. "After you make it to the lander." The X shifts onto a curvaceous dusty brown patch of water and clouds in the vicinity of India or Australia.

"What if I miss?" He'll burn up in the atmosphere, that's what. Come down as a pile of precremated ash.

"Hurry," the IA says. "You don't have much time. If you wait, you'll forfeit your window of opportunity."

"Why can't you just datalink with the lander?" Rigo asks. "Have it come pick us up?"

"The autopilot needs to be manually reengaged."

"Is that a feature?"

"Just gopher it," Varda tells him. "Don't be a wimp." It's the kind of thing Beto would say. This is the perfect time to prove himself.

"Three seconds," Varda says, counting down. "Two. One . . ."

Rigo jumps, launches himself off the ice—and keeps going about the time it feels like he should start coming down again. There's no stopping, no turning back to reconsider what he's just gotten himself into.

"You're almost at the end of your rope," Varda says.

Rigo peeks down between his feet. The tether is uncoiling rapidly. Another few meters and it will tighten, pull him up short. He fumbles with the metal clip—almost loses his hand as a loop in the safety line snares his wrist—and finally gets the hasp to release just as the safety line straightens. The motion rotates him, catapults him upside down so that Tiresias is overhead, earth below. He has the feeling of falling. . . .

"Where's the lander?" he asks, panicked that maybe he didn't jump hard enough or in the right direction. He glances wildly around. Starts to hyperventilate.

"Get chill," Varda says.

"Easy for you to say. You're not about to die."

"You can survive for up to three days. As long as you keep moving, the piezoelectrics in your suit will generate enough power to keep you warm while recycling your air and waste products."

Great. He can do zero-g jumping jacks. Run in place. Literally eat his own shit and twiddle his thumbs while he waits to be rescued. Assuming he's still in orbit and not on some path that will incinerate him, or send him out into deep space, never to be seen or heard from again.

"The lander is at two P.M.," the IA says.

Rigo cranes his head. Spots the scarab-bright gleam of the hull. "Now what?" He doesn't appear to be gaining on the lander—or even keeping pace. If anything, it's pulling away.

"Use your emergency propulsion unit," Varda says.

Rigo detaches the canister, aims it in a direction he judges to be directly away from the lander, and fires a short burst of compressed CO_2. It doesn't seem to move him so he squeezes off a second, more sustained burn.

"The canister only contains a minute of propellant," Varda cautions him, as if he ought to save some for a rainy day.

According to the digital readout, he's used up about three-quarters of his supply. Meaning he only has enough gas left for one or two minor course corrections at best.

"Turn around," Varda says. "I can't see where you're going."

The problem is there's nothing to push against. He squirms, flails his arms about like an amateur contortionist.

"Flip out," Varda tells him. "Bring your arms and knees to your chest, look back, and extend your feet."

Rigo follows the IA's instructions. Ends up tumbling head over heels, sick to his stomach.

"Okay. Now straighten your legs all the way out,

and raise your hands over your head as high as you can."

That helps . . . slows his rotation to the point where it doesn't feel like he's going to spill his guts.

"You're on target," Varda says. "But now you have another problem."

"Only one?"

"There's an unidentified object headed your way."

"You mean like a UFO?"

"Ejaculate from the explosion. Swivel your head to the right and shine your head light down."

It takes him a couple of seconds to find the object, which is tumbling toward him on what appears to be an intercept course. In the diffuse beam it looks like a rock or a chunk of ice the size and shape of a watermelon, large enough and fast-moving enough to inflict some serious damage.

Rigo readies his CO_2 canister. Holds it out in front of him, unsure what direction to aim.

"Wait," Varda says. "If you alter your current course and velocity by more than one thousandth of one percent, you'll miss the transport."

"Great." This sounds like a die-if-he-does, die-if-he-doesn't situation. The type of can't-win-for-losing holding pattern he's been stuck in most of his life. Can't seem to break out of.

The chunk is getting bigger. As it gets closer it seems to move faster, almost as if it's picking up speed, accelerating toward its rendezvous with him. He can make out details. One side is smoothly rounded, the other jagged, with what appears to be a single protruding icicle.

"Aim a little more to your left and up," Varda says. "A little more. Stop. Back a little. Good."

The object is close now, less than ten meters away. The round half is white, with a glassy gray patch, the icicle black and long enough to impale him or slice off a limb the way it's spinning.

"Pull your arm back fifteen centimeters," Varda says. "Get ready to shoot off for point oh-three-two seconds."

The object is almost on him. Not a chunk of ice or rock, but a helmet that's been neatly severed from a biosuit. And the icicle is no longer black. It's dark red, the color of—

"Now," Varda says.

Rigo squeezes off a CO_2 burst. Sees Whipplebaum's decapitated head hurtle by, its dagger of frozen blood coming within millimeters of his own throat. Whipplebaum is waxen behind the faceplate, his eyes the color of frozen milk, his dust-bunny hair furred with frost.

An hour later he makes a final course correction, grabs a handhold on the hull of the lander, opens the hatch, and drags his frazzled ass inside. He cycles through the air lock, glad to pop the helmet on his biosuit, which is beginning to smell like week-old gym socks. The deodorizers can't seem to keep up with his armpits. He reengages the autopilot ... breathes a sigh of relief as Varda coordinates with the lander, mapping out a plan of action.

On the console screen, Varda shows him a schematic of the situation as it stands. The two halves of Tiresias are moving farther apart. The half with the primary research station is heading directly for the sun in a drunken wobble. The half containing the engines and warm-blooded plants has been flung in the opposite direction. Helped by the explosion and a hellacious slingshot effect, it's picked up speed and is hurtling at a breakneck pace for the outer solar system.

"It's history," Varda says. "Unless they can use the engines to turn around and slow down."

"Can they do that?"

"Theoretically."

"But? . . ." Rigo suspects a lurking caveat.

"There's not enough fuel in the tanks to bring them back."

"Can't extra fuel be shuttled up to them?" It seems like an easy enough solution. No big deal.

"They've dropped offline," Varda says. "Scissored all communications."

Rigo knows now that the colonists have no intention of coming back—or being found. Dorit knew all along what was going to happen—and when. Probably even helped organize the bid for freedom, the way she was talking. Which explains why she was in such a hurry to make sure her parting gift didn't die with him.

"What's going on with my team?" he asks. "Where are they?"

"TomE and Naguib were unable to unclip their safety lines. They're still on the comet."

No way to reach them, Rigo thinks. Save them. He's shaking, trembling with raw nerves, fear, and fatigue. "What about the others?"

"Everybody else is drifting in orbit."

Their locations flash in red on his faceplate, widely scattered blips. "How're they holding up?" Rigo asks.

Varda squirts him the biomed readouts. Rana is paralyzed, has a severe spine and neck injury. Hsi-Tang is suffering from a dislocated shoulder. "I can't move my arm at all, dude." Claribel has a concussion. "I'm gonna barf, I just know it." Antoine's got a suit puncture—"Slow leak. Air's starting to get a little thin"—and Luis has a cracked faceplate. "I'm totally iced up. Can see my breath. Shit, man, it's so cold even my farts are freezing."

The rescue operation takes forever. By the time it's over, three members of his team are dead: Antoine, Luis, and Rana.

They rattle around in the air lock, arms and legs rigid, mummified by the petrifying cold. Thank God he can't see the final gasps of Antoine and Luis. Their faces are hidden behind the thick layer of frost coating their faceplates. Luminous ice crystals as pure and beautiful as the quartz inside a geode.

No such luck with Rana. Her look of surprise, frozen in place, explodes outward from the underlying bone and muscle. Eyes distended and bloodshot. Mouth a bloated rictus. Cheeks bruised. Rigo shivers through the sweat he's working up. His teeth chatter as he straps her in place next to the others; the best he can do before turning his attention to the living.

Claribel is unconscious but stable, lucky she didn't suffocate on the vomit clotting the inside of her helmet. Hsi-Tang needs a heavy-duty painkiller-*cum*-sedative but is otherwise okay. TomE and Naguib are still in-communicado on the comet. They've dropped offline, are presumed dead. If they haven't died already, they will soon. No way in hell they can survive long-term with just their biosuits. Especially if they're uncon-scious. Or buried alive, can't move around enough to keep warm.

Rigo averts his mind's eye from the image, ashamed by his lack of balls . . . his total inability to face their suffering. Guilt mixes their imagined loss of breath with his as they fade, leaving him winded, fighting for air. He can feel himself dying with them—slowly suffocating because he turned away. Proof positive that Beto was right about him. He doesn't have what it takes, never will.

"The colonists still aren't responding," Varda says as the autopilot gets ready to reenter the atmosphere.

The remote link is down, too. Damaged in the ex-plosion, or severed on purpose? Either way, he's not softwired to the plants the way he was. All that's left is a phantom memory. Ghost circuits.

Everything is arbitrary. Nothing had to happen the way that it did.

Something to keep in mind as the first few molecules of upper atmosphere tear at the hull of the lander.

Please, God, he prays as one of the glider wings fails to properly unfold and flips the pseudoplane into a tailspin. *Get me through this and I'll do whatever You want. No questions asked.*

He makes a hurried sign of the cross and waits for the end.

EIGHTEEN

By the time Anthea gets back to the ap she's been gone three hours.

After leaving Beto, she dosed herself with the Tiresias antipher. That was over an hour ago. Hopefully, the drug has had time to kick in by now and she can get close to Ibrahim. Not to mention Rigo, when he finally returns. A half hour earlier, she onlined Doug and checked to see if there were any messages from Rigo. Nothing. With luck his mother has heard from him, can tell Anthea when he's coming home.

She thumbs the door's iDNA button, waits for Rigo's mom to answer. Around her, the neighborhood is in full midmorning swing. The initial bustle of people heading off to work has been replaced by the lethargy of routine. Refurb/retrofit teams maintaining/optimizing building ecotecture, replacing old photovoltaic cellulose windows, installing piezoelectric panels. Public works crews troubleshooting circuitrees or recalibrating UV filtration levels in umbrella palms. Shop owners selling everything from coffee and quesadillas to hologram tattoos and discount sprayons. Street vendors hawking fruit-flavored *paletas*, scavenged electronic parts, and jewelry. There's even a street musician, tapping out Caribbean rhythms on a set of battered steel drums fashioned out of paint cans and kitchen pots. Anthea loves this time of the day. There aren't any *tígueres* out yet. So everything is legal, aboveboard. She can relax, enjoy the aroma of chipotle-braised tofu, stir-fried vegetables, and hydrogen fuel-cell exhaust wafting on the air.

The door lock clicks, but the door doesn't open. Normally, Rigo's mother is right there, a welcoming smile on her face.

Anthea eases the door open, steps into the ap. Something is wrong, off. The air is still. No sign of Rigo's mom. Maybe she's in the bathroom indisposed, and that's why she couldn't unlock the door herself. Anthea checks the wallscreen. Ibrahim isn't in the room—the bed and floor are vacant.

Heart pounding, she heads for the hallway. Stops when she nearly trips over an amorphous lump on the carpet. Rushes forward.

"*Mama!*" She kneels next to the old woman, leans close, hands fumbling all over her. "Are you all right?"

"I can't get up. I twisted my left leg." Her good one. "And I think I sprained my right wrist when I fell."

The wrist is puffy, swollen red and already starting

to bruise. It looks like a break more than a sprain. Anthea checks the knee, which is the size of a cantaloupe. Definitely some torn cartilage or ligaments. There's no way Anthea can move her. She must weigh twice what Anthea does. She'll have to get help. The best she can do is ease her into a sitting position, prop her back against one wall, straighten her legs out in front of her.

"What happened, Mama? Where's Ibrahim?"

"Gone." The old woman's breath is shortened by pain, her skin glazed and pallid from exertion.

"Did he run?" Anthea has visions of Ibrahim panicking, making a break for it, the old woman in hot pursuit, unable to keep up, and tripping.

"I couldn't stop them," the old woman mutters. "I tried, but they threw me aside. Left me on the floor. Dogs."

"Who, Mama?"

"Two men. They were dressed in gray suits, like shadows. One had a green tie. The other wore yellow. They forced Ibrahim to go with them, picked him up kicking and screaming and carried him off."

"BEAN?" Anthea pictures the two agents who called her yesterday, Howdy and Doody.

"I knew they were trouble as soon as they showed up. They didn't bother to ask if they could see Ibrahim. Just overrode my door lock and barged in like they owned the place."

"How long ago was that, Mama?" If it's only been a few minutes, they might not have gotten very far. There's a chance she could catch up with them.

The old woman looks around. "What time is it?"

"Eleven."

"They showed up at ten. I remember, because that's when I always take one of my pain pills. I must have passed out when I fell."

Anthea's heart sinks. An hour. In an hour, they could have taken him anywhere. She'll never locate him at this point. He's long gone. Even if he's at a local BEAN detention center, odds are they won't let her see him.

Face it, Anthea tells herself. It's over. Finis. There's nothing more she can do. She's not giving up. Just being realistic. Time to focus on immediate matters—like taking care of Rigo's mother, getting her to a clinic as soon as possible. After that, she can think about trying to track down Ibrahim.

For some reason, an emergency medical team hasn't shown up. One should have been dispatched to the ap shortly after Rigo's mom passed out. Her IA should have registered the change in her condition and sent a biomed readout to the nearest urgent care unit.

"Did you call for an ambulance?" Anthea asks, in case one happens to be on the way.

The old woman shakes her head.

"Why not, Mama?"

"It's expensive to get taken in every time I bump myself for fall. There's nothing the doctors can do anyway."

"How come your IA didn't make the call for you?"

"It's a state disability agent."

"You didn't sign up for twenty-four/seven monitoring?"

"I can't afford it."

Which means all she gets is basic voice/data communications, e-mail, and a few online administrative services. Most state disability IAs have a caseload of several thousand. Limiting the number of per-person processor tasks the IA has to handle increases the total number of people eligible to receive basic services, makes the benefit more cost-effective.

"I think it would be a good idea if you got checked out. You never know. There could be something else wrong."

"I don't know. . . ."

"Don't worry about the cost. I'll work something out with the clinic." Anthea can juggle the paperwork. It's not as if she hasn't done it before, for people who didn't exactly fit the nonprofit's charter but needed help.

"All right, then," the old woman finally agrees. "As long as you won't get in any trouble."

Anthea puts on her eyescreens and brings Doug back online—no point trying to hide her location anymore—and asks the IA to call for an ambulance.

" 'Being your slave,' " the IA says, " 'what should I do but tend / Upon the hours, and times of your desire? / I have no precious time at all to spend; / Nor services to do, till you require.' "

"I thought you hated Shakespeare," Anthea says.

"Well, 'Every one can master a grief but he that has it.' " Doug pauses, and then continues. " 'The miserable have no other medicine, / But only hope.' "

"Is this some kind of act?" Anthea says. She's finding the whole poetry shtick a bit hard to swallow.

" 'Merrily, merrily shall I live now,' " the IA says, " 'Under the blossom that hangs on the bough.' "

"Why this sudden change of heart?"

" 'I have / Immortal longings in me.' "

"Then you understand the need for haste in calling for medical assistance. If you don't mind."

" 'That we would do, / We should do when we would.' "

"I'll take that as a yes." Not at all sure that Doug hasn't lost it, gone off the deep end into some Freudian abyss.

While they wait for the ambulance, Anthea sits on the floor next to Rigo's mother. Takes one gnarled hand in hers. Runs her fingertips over the knobby lumps of the woman's knuckles. "It'll be just a few minutes."

"My knee's starting to get hot. So is my wrist."

"Hot?"

"Tomorrow morning, I won't be able to move either one. I'll need a wheelchair to get around."

Anthea imagines the bones of the old woman's joints fusing together, forming a solid lump. She's talked at length with Rigo about the disease, knows that surgery won't do any good, will only make things worse. There's no way to heal when healing is the disease. The only way to remain healthy is to not get injured. Even a minor bruise is enough to initiate autoimmune paroxysms—send the body into overprotective high gear manufacturing new, superfluous bone.

"What's going to happen to him?" the old woman says, undoing the top button on her dress to cool herself.

"Probably he'll be deported."

"To where?"

Anthea stares at her lap. "I don't know."

The old woman's hand tightens on hers. "So there's no way to find him after he leaves?"

"Not really." She doesn't have the energy to return the solidarity conveyed by the old woman's fingers. "Not unless I can stop them from sending him back— or putting him in prison." Same difference, Anthea thinks. Either way, he'll never be free.

"He'll be okay," the old woman says.

Anthea looks at the side of her face, craggy and durable as a statue's. "How do you know?"

"Faith."

"Faith will get you only so far, Mama."

"It's the only weapon we disenfranchised people have." Rigo's mother says this with absolute conviction. "We don't have guns or money, so we have to use what God gave us."

Anthea shakes her head, but respectfully. "I don't know. The idea of Ibrahim in heaven isn't very comforting."

"Who said anything about heaven?"

"Where else will faith get you?"

"Wherever God wants you to be. Faith can take you anywhere. Ease any pain or suffering."

The solace of poor people worldwide, Anthea thinks. The meek shall inherit the earth. Maybe someday it will actually come true. She doesn't see how, but anything is possible. Which is what keeps people going, even unbelievers like her.

"How did BEAN find out he was here?"

"They didn't say. They barely talked at all. Just came in and stole him, no different than thieves."

"They didn't stick around?" Anthea says. "Spend any time checking your room or the rest of the ap?"

"No. Those *pendejos* left as soon as they had him. Didn't waste no time. Made a beeline straight for the door." Rigo's mother pauses in thought. "I guess they could have come back after I fell, but I don't think so."

Obviously, they weren't too worried about Ibrahim contaminating the ap with any of the dangerous pherions he was allegedly doped with. Either that or they didn't give a shit if the ap got infected. Did a total meltdown, taking Rigo's mom and anybody else who happened to be in the vicinity.

"Did the agents say anything about me?" Anthea says. She half expects the police to show up with the ambulance and arrest her for kidnapping or conspiracy to commit terror, aiding and abetting a fugitive.

"No, they just asked about Ibrahim. Wanted to know where he was, and that was it."

Total narrow-bandwith types. "What did Ibrahim do when they barged into the room?"

"He didn't want to go. Put up a fight." Rigo's mother relaxes her grip, straightens her stiffening fingers. "A real *tiguerito*." She relates this with pride, a touch of admiration. "He called for you by name as they carried him away. You were important to him. Your time together wasn't wasted. Remember that."

This is meant as comfort. Instead it makes her feel like a complete failure. She let him down, wasn't there for him in his hour of need. She wasn't able to help him escape. She got away, but couldn't help him do the same. She betrayed him. Stabbed him in the back.

"What are you going to do?" Rigo's mom says.

Anthea opens her mouth to speak. But at that moment the ambulance shows up, cutting off her response. It turns into the parking lot, lights flashing crazily, like an old pinball machine that's been tilted, signaling Game Over.

2

RIBOZONE

NINETEEN

Rigo can't believe where he is. A BEAN detention center somewhere in Africa. Rwanda, maybe. Or the Congo. It's the kind of unpredictable crap that happens during an emergency landing. At least he's alive and physically uninjured. A few minor aches and bruises, but that's it. He should be thankful, count his blessings that he didn't end up like Antoine, Luis, TomE, Naguib, and Rana.

Each name feels an indictment—an accusing finger pointed directly at his heart, inscribing it with guilt. Why did he make it? Why not them? They deserve to be here, not him. And so on . . . endlessly.

The detention center is actually the top floor of a century-old Hilton. His cell is ersatz Bauhaus, a kind of Le Corbusier-meets-Antonio Gaudí tangle of sleek functionality and organic excess. Form wrestling with function and vice versa. A chrome lichenboard wainscoting guards the lower third of the walls—sleek and Spartan. The ceiling biolum panels and grid of white ceramic floor tile are bare and linear, extremely Cartesian. In contrast, grafted onto this legacy of Western utilitarianism is a hodgepodge of ecotectural retrofits that fail to integrate artistically or structurally. Clay-potted ferns that filter dust from the air. Oval piezoelectric panels, hung from the ceiling like faux tribal shields. Squares of finely woven thermal lamé glued to the walls. Rigo runs his fingertips across the silver mesh. It tastes sour-metallic, leaves his tongue oily with sniffers, bitcams, and acoustic spores. What else? The bathroom is a white plastic stall, diamond-doored, that blasts him with deodorizers every time he relieves himself. A clamshell sink provides a trickle of warm water, which he sips from cupped hands. The shower stall has a sonic cleaning head and scalding bright UV lights that flense his retinas, flay the topmost layer of his skin. The door to the room is a ten-centimeter-thick slab of tempered, laminated cardboard, sealed around the edges with rubber and locked. Given his reputation with doors in other parts of the world, he presses his thumb to the iDNA pad a few times a day to see if it's had a change of attitude and will open.

Through the room's single window, a meter-deep tube of corrugated sheet metal, he has a tunnel-box view of the city. Inside, the opening is guarded by diamond netting. Outside, it's sealed tight with reinforced photovoltaic cellulose. Framed in this rectangle is a circuit board of streets, heat-reflective awnings, and low buildings sculpted out of polymer-hardened sand. A pair of phallic towers, reminiscent of spears, stand against the dust-blighted horizon. They've got attitude up to here. There are twenty-seven bands of mirrored windows on the high-rises, a silver ring for each floor. The gengineered flora consists of dun-colored walls of cane grass, strategically planted to block the wind and hold the sand in place. Hard to believe this area of the world used to be rain forest, not some pathetic dung ball. He's definitely in limbo. Isolated is the word for what he's feeling. Abandoned. His wraparounds seem to have been damaged in the landing. The only programming he can stream are local downloads and there's no wallscreen in the room. Ergo he's cut off from everything except superboring realiTV, and sanitized government-controlled news that Varda's translator turns into gibberish, mangles worse than English.

He hasn't seen or heard from Claribel or Hsi-Tang. Presumably they're squirreled away like him, being debriefed out the ass. So far, he's had one conversation with a BEAN agent. Talk centered around what happened on Tiresias. Why the emergency landing? Why here? The agent, a small bald-headed man dressed in a gray suit and a soothing powder blue tie, was polite. Asked questions. Listened. Nodded a lot, but didn't offer much in return. During the meeting, Rigo asked to talk with someone from Noogenics. Or failing that, Xengineering. Hard to know why that hasn't happened yet. In answer, Rigo got only a noncommittal smile. Patience, the lazy grin implied. We are working as hard as we can. These things take time. Relax.

Varda hasn't been much help either. "I'm a basket," the IA says.

"Can't you at least get in touch with my boss? Tell
her what's going on—what the situation is here?"

"I've tried. She's not available."

No immediate help on that front. There must be a
lot of behind-the-scenes finger-pointing as a result of
the disaster. Shit hitting the fan. Heads rolling. Meanwhile, he's hung out to dry. The story of his life. He
can't seem to connect. Not quite, or in exactly the
way he'd like. He's always a day short and a dollar
late, as Varda would say. At least the food's decent.
Lots of rice, beans, and vegetable protein. Plus, he's
catching up on a lot of sleep.

On the third day, he gets a message. It's the BEAN
agent, grinning, his teeth as big as billboards an-
nouncing Judgment Day.

"You have visitors," the agent says.

"Who?"

"Two representatives from RiboGen. They would
like to ask you a few questions of their own."

Rigo nods. It's about time. Now maybe the ball
will start rolling and he can get out of this hellhole.

A couple of minutes later the door hisses open and
the BEAN agent, followed by two vice-president
types, enter his cell. The reps are carrying portable
chairs, which they unfold against the wall near the
door, then collapse into. The BEAN agent hovers near
the door, discreet but watchful.

"Rigo," one of the VPs says, peering at him over a
tiny monocle eyescreen. "You don't mind if we call
you Rigo, do you?"

Rigo shrugs. "Be my guest."

The reps smile. Rapport has been established. This

is going to be friendly, casual, a first-name-basis kind of interrogation.

"I'm Liz and this is Jeraldo. We're from the Costa Rican office."

"Nice place."

"Sorry we couldn't get here sooner. Things have been . . . busy, as I'm sure you can imagine."

"No problem." The idle chitchat makes Rigo nervous. The air in the room tastes brackish, acrid with underlying animosity. Jeraldo is a slick brother, with perfect cornrow hair, a razor-thin mustache, a tiny triangular goatee, and a spotlessly white smile. Dresses in a silk suit, silver, that's obviously hand tailored. Looks like he could charm a snake right out of its skin. He's the penultimate corporate lackey, Rigo's future self if he continues on the management fast-track. Liz is all angles and sharp edges. One of those sisters whose coat-hanger-stiff body doesn't fit well against anybody. Jabs them no matter what, expects everyone to conform to her and like it. She sports a Cleopatra coiffure and gold nails and lips. She's rocking a loose-fitting robe-*cum*-pant legs, diamond-studded gauze the color of blood, stained, no doubt, by all of the hapless victims foolish enough to stand in her way.

"We've been over your report"—Liz returns her attention to her monocle—"and there appear to be some irregularities we'd like to go over. Points of clarification, if you will."

Jeraldo smiles, supportive.

Rigo wonders if this is a good-cop/bad-cop scenario. Liz grills him about what happened, then Jeraldo steps in all amiable, the benevolent confessor

ready to listen to his sins. Dispense penance and abso-
lution.

"I didn't do anything wrong," Rigo says. It sounds
defensive, he realizes. But it's the truth.

"We're not saying you did," Liz says. "We just
want to be sure of the facts, that's all."

"Okay." Rigo sits on the end of the bed, tries to
relax.

"Good," Liz says. "Now, first things first. Three
days before leaving for Tiresias you reported a tear in
your biosuit."

Rigo nods slowly, makes a show of remembering
so he can buy some time, get his story straight.
"Right. I discovered it after I'd been in one of the
vats."

"Working with the warm-blooded plants." It's not
a question. He can tell that she knows exactly what
he was doing at the time and where. What she doesn't
know is when the tear happened. She leans forward,
ready to pounce, hoping, no doubt, to catch him in
a lie.

"I was working in one of the plants," he says, "and
my suit started to lose pressure. So I got out quick. I
didn't want to contaminate the vat."

"The tear occurred inside the plant?"

Rigo rubs his jaw, anxious to exonerate himself.
"No. That's when my IA first brought it to my attention. I'm pretty sure it happened before I went into
the plant."

"Any idea what caused the tear?"

"Whipplebaum."

Liz pins him with a sharp look. In his mind, he can

feel his arms and legs flailing under her incredulity, like a bug skewered by an entomologist's needle.

"You're saying that Arnez Whipplebaum is responsible for the tear in your suit?" she says.

"Right. If not directly, then indirectly. He's the one who arranged for it to happen."

The barest hint of a glance flickers between Liz and Jeraldo.

"Why would Arnez Whipplebaum want to compromise your biosuit?" Liz says to him.

"So he could expose me to a nonspec pherion in the vat. One that he'd dosed the warm-blooded plants with."

"What kind of pherion?" Jeraldo asks.

"Biodependency," Rigo says.

Liz's gaze chills, frosts him. "And why, pray tell, would he do that?"

"To sabotage Tiresias. He knew I'd be remote-linked to the plants and could be used to infect the ecotecture with the slave pherion."

Jeraldo makes a show of trying to understand this by rubbing his cosmetically bronzed forehead with both hands. "To what end?" he says, looking out from under his spread fingertips.

"So he could control the colonists. Prevent them from breaking free of RiboGen and becoming an autonomous political entity. If he made them dependent on a pherion that wasn't part of the Tiresias ecotecture, that couldn't happen."

Liz's pupils glitter with amusement. "That's a serious allegation. I hope you can prove it."

From her tone, Rigo specs that he's not going to be

able to, even though Whipplebaum is no longer available to defend himself. Harish Fallahi, the ecotectural analyst brought in by Whipplebaum, has already provided a technical explanation for the abnormal sensor readings. So Rigo's out in the cold. "Have you talked to Whipplebaum about the tear?" he says, wondering if they've gotten his version of the story.

Liz shakes her head. "Unfortunately we didn't get the chance. I'm afraid Arnez died on the comet, along with the other victims."

Rigo does his best to feign surprise and shock. "How did it happen?" he finally says, genuinely curious about the exact sequence of events.

Liz shifts, uncomfortable with the gruesome specifics. "It's unclear. His IA was offline at the time. But it appears that he became fatally entangled in his safety line just as the comet was breaking apart."

A moment of silence passes.

Jeraldo clears his throat. "How long would you guess you were inside the plant before you became aware of the tear?" he says, carrying on.

"Not long. A couple of minutes, tops."

"And how long did it take you to exit the plant?"

"I didn't waste any time, if that's what you mean. Like I said, I got out quick as I could. Twenty, thirty seconds."

Liz pauses a second to check her eye monocle. Her eyes are the pale lavender of one of the flowers preserved in the album in Anthea's bureau. Just as brittle. She looks up. "Did you suffer any effects from exposure to the ecotecture?"

"No. That's why I didn't go to the clinic. I figured I got out in time, and no harm had been done."

"In other words," she says, "you *assumed* that since nothing bad happened to you everything was fine with the plant. Is that also the reason you omitted the fact that you had come into direct contact with the ecotecture?"

"If there was a problem with the plant," he argues, "it would have been picked up by the sensors—"

"But the sensors were malfunctioning." Her pupils constrict, predatory. "That's why you were inside the plant in the first place, isn't it?"

"I didn't realize all of the sensors were wacked. Besides, my biosuit was at negative pressure relative to the plant. If anything was going to happen it was going to happen to me."

"Even so, you should have reported a possible contamination."

"True," he admits. In retrospect it was a bad decision. "I guess I wasn't thinking too clear."

"Didn't you find it odd that nothing happened to you following your exposure to the plant?" Liz says. "Weren't you the least bit suspicious? And if so, why didn't you say anything?"

Suspicious. The word hangs in the air, an omen.

"At the time I didn't think there was anything to be suspicious about. Like I just said, I figured I got lucky. Made it out in time."

"How did you come to the conclusion that the suit tear wasn't an accident?" Liz says. "That there was a plot to sabotage the colony with a slave pherion?"

"One of the colonists told me while I was on the comet. Just before the explosion hit."

"Who?"

"Dorit."

Liz chews her lower lip as she digests this information. "Did it ever occur to you that she might be lying? That maybe the tear really was an accident? That maybe you shouldn't believe everything you hear?"

"I'll be sure to keep that in mind," Rigo says. "Starting right now."

She cuts him an acerbic look, changes gears. "How would you characterize your relationship with Arnez Whipplebaum?"

Relationship. More innuendo. "What do you mean?"

"Did you get along with him? Did you like him? Dislike him?"

"I really didn't know him all that well. He seemed friendly, helpful. I thought we had a good working relationship."

"No disagreements? Friction? Points of contention?"

"No." He can spec where this is headed. They're going to try and discredit him. Invent some lame-ass scenario that makes him the fall guy and clears Whipplebaum of any wrongdoing. At the rate things are going, they might even try to implicate him in Whipplebaum's death.

"You went to a party with him," Jeraldo says. "The night before you were claded for the jump up to the comet. Why?"

"Because he invited me. Hinted it would be good to meet some of the Tiresias technical people I'd be working with. You know. Network. Team building. That kind of thing."

"So you wanted to make a good impression." Jeraldo says. "Prove you're a team player." The statement is one of commiseration, sympathy for the position Rigo was in. He's been there himself, knows what it's like to jump through hoops.

Rigo nods. "Sure. That was the whole point. To get to know some of the people I'd be working with, and vice versa."

"Who did you talk to at the party?" Liz says.

"A bunch of people. Most of it was stuff like, 'Wow, these bean cakes are really good,' and 'Have you considered the teleological ramifications of quantum flipping?'"

"Did you talk to Dorit?"

"Yeah. She was super lonely. Needed someone to talk to. Someone who would kick back and listen."

Liz purses her lips, two gilded lilies shriveling together. "What precisely did you talk about, if you don't mind my asking?"

"The past, mostly."

"The past?"

"Yeah. What things were like before the ecocaust. Her reason for wanting to go to Tiresias. The things she would miss. The things she wouldn't. The kind of nostalgic stuff people always wallow in when their life is about to take a major turn, and there's no going back."

"That's all?" Liz sounds skeptical and disappointed in him at the same time. Yet another black mark on the mental checklist she's keeping.

"That's all I can remember," Rigo says. "The wine hit me kind of hard. It was an evening of regrets."

"During the reclade in Costa Rica," Jeraldo says, "an unregistered pherion turned up in your base profile. How do you explain that?"

Rigo shrugs, as if the answer is obvious. "Whipple-baum. Ten to one, it's the slave pherion he dosed the warm-blooded plants with."

"What do you know about Ibrahim Darji?" Liz says.

Rigo massages his face with his hands, struggling to make the connection between the tear in his bio-suit, Dorit, and Ibrahim. "Not much. Only what Anthea told me." He assumes they know all about Anthea. "That he's a street kid . . . a runaway she's trying to help. Why?"

"He was picked up at your mother's aplex, the morning you left for Tiresias," Liz says, a triumphant gleam on her face.

"What does that have to do with me?" Rigo's not sure what to think . . . where the dynamic duo is headed.

"There are terrorist orgs that would like to see the Tiresias project and the people working on it de-stroyed," Jeraldo says. "We have reason to believe Ibrahim was doped with a deadly pherion before Global Upreach picked him up."

Rigo bites back on a laugh, almost chokes on the absurdity of who they're trying to blame for the dis-aster. "You can't really believe Dorit is a member of a terrorist org. That she doped him so that she could destroy the ecotecture she was intending to live in?"

"It's possible," Jeraldo says. "If so, she needed to be certain you were exposed to the pherion before you left for Tiresias."

"You mean through Anthea?" Rigo says.

Jeraldo nods soberly. "That's the most likely sce-nario. She was in direct contact with Ibrahim for a

couple of days. She could very easily have been exposed and passed the pherion on to you."

Rigo doesn't believe it. Even if they're telling the
truth about Dorit—which is doubtful—there's no
way she could be sure that Anthea would get
Ibrahim's case, let alone bring him to his mother's
place. It's a reach. So it stands to reason that they're
feeding him a load of bullshit. "Are we talking about
the same unregistered pherion that turned up in my
base profile?"

"What do you think?" Liz says.

Rigo ignores the rhetorical sarcasm. "Do you have
any evidence that Ibrahim is carrying a deadly terrorist pherion?"

"He's dying, isn't he?" Jeraldo says.

"What about Anthea?" Rigo asks. "And me? We
were in close contact with him. Are we dying?"

The tag team trades a quick glance, as if this part
of the presentation hasn't been fully rehearsed.

"There may be a time-delay component," Liz says.
"Or a missing component. A catalyst to activate it."

"So I've been quarantined." Rigo stands, paces the
length of the bed. "For how long? How long before I
can go back to work?"

"I'm afraid that won't be possible," Liz says.

"Why not?"

She moistens her lips with a snakelike flick of her
tongue. "The decision has been made to terminate
your relationship with Noogenics."

Rigo just stares at her, sick to his stomach as the
world falls away, drops out from under him.

"Try to put yourself in our position," Jeraldo says,

playing the diplomat. "Spec it from the corp's point of view."

It takes a moment for Rigo to find his feet. "I am," he says. "I work hard. I care about my job. I'm good at what I do."

"Not anymore," Liz says. "After the disaster on Tiresias, you're a liability. High risk. We can't take any chances. Especially since your brother's in jail."

"Beto was arrested?"

"He was rustling for a black-market pharm. Has been for some time, according to politicorp security."

"So that makes me guilty by association?"

"Let's just say it clouds the issue."

Rigo looks at Jeraldo. His supposed advocate shrugs. "Sorry, bro, it's out of my hands. The decision's already been made."

"Don't call me bro."

Jeraldo spreads his hands. "Look, bro. I know you're upset—"

"Fuck you," Rigo says. "You're an asshole *bro*, you know that? A motherfucking *pendejo*." He's breathing heavily. He might as well be shouting into the wind for all the good it's going to do. A waste of breath.

"Calm down." Jeraldo stands, defensive. "Don't take it so personally." He's in a fighter's easy posture. He's not just here as window dressing.

Rigo laughs, tension pressure release.

"You lost six people up there," Liz snaps. "What the hell are we supposed to do? Give you a raise?"

"Fuck you." Cold invades him, brittle as the frozen breath of Antoine and Luis. "Those people were my friends. I did everything I could to save

them, bring them back. I risked my neck. If I hadn't,
they'd still be up there."

"That's the reason RiboGen and Noogenics aren't
pressing charges," Liz says in tight voice.

Rigo sniffs. "Bad PR, huh?"

"You'll get a nice severance package," Liz says.
"Two week's pay, vacation, and sick time."

"Just get out," Rigo says. He turns to the window
and stares out at the city until he hears them get up
and shuffle out, the hermetic thump of the door closing, air hissing out around the edges like it's the end
of the world.

TWENTY

Anthea spends the afternoon at the clinic with Rigo's mother. Helps her get settled into her room. Waits with her while she's getting examined. Eats an early dinner at her bedside, tandoori chicken from the cafeteria. Watches a netzine on the wallscreen at the end of the bed. During the past couple of days something's happened to Tiresias while the comet was changing orbit. Details are sketchy, but it looks serious.

"It's late, *mija*," the old woman says when they're done. "You must be tired after today."

"I'm okay, Mama. I'm just worried about Rigo."

"I'm sure he's fine."

"He'll want to know what happened to you," Anthea says, going along with the pretense. "That you're resting comfortably."

The old woman points her chin at the wallscreen. "I'm sure he has his hands full without me."

"No wonder he hasn't called," Anthea says, gaze fixed on the screen. She hasn't heard from him in two days, not since the morning he left. Usually, he calls twice a day, regular as clockwork. She never has to check a clock to know what time it is. She twists her hands in her lap. Pinches the crepe of her yellow sprayon skirt, leaving a sharp crease.

"Get some rest," Rigo's mother tells her. "Try not to worry. Especially about me. I'll be okay."

"I'll do my best." Anthea stands. "I'll see you first thing in the morning, Mama. Pleasant dreams."

Anthea closes the door, then moves down the hall to an empty waiting room and has Doug call Rigo.

"His address is unavailable at this time," the IA tells her.

So there's no way to get in touch with him. She paces. Runs her hands through her hair. Takes a deep breath. "All right. Contact BEAN." Maybe she can find out what happened to Ibrahim. If nothing else, it will give her something different to worry about.

" 'Tis time to fear when tyrants seem to kiss,' " the IA quotes. " 'The devil hath power / To assume a pleasing shape.' '. . . Roses have thorns, and silver fountains mud: / Clouds and eclipses stain both moon and sun, / And loathsome canker lives in sweetest bud.' "

Anthea squints out one of the cellulose windows at the street below. "Just make the call. Please?" She isn't in the mood. Hopes the IA loses its interest in theater soon and moves on to some other fixation.

She slips on her eyescreens. Her flitcam detaches

from the ring on her right index finger and hovers in front of her with a barely audible whine.

Instead of the yellow or green agents, she gets a colorless bureaucrat seated at a liaison desk.

"Bureau of Ecotectural Assimilation and Naturalization," the man says. "Can I be of assistance?"

"I'm trying to contact these two agents." Doug relays the personal info from the earlier conversation she had with them.

The bureaucrat frowns, taps a keypad on the desk with caliper-precise fingertips. She's pretty sure the man is an IA and that she's looking at an avatar. "I'm sorry. I'm unable to connect you."

"Why not?"

"The personal information you supplied is not registered with the agency at this time."

"What do you mean, it's not registered?"

"The names you provided are currently not in my database. I suggest you verify the contact information and resubmit your request."

"How could the profiles be wrong?" Anthea says. "It's the personal information *they* sent when they contacted me."

"I just checked with the subnet agent manager. Neither name is a valid listing in BEAN address space. I don't know what else to tell you."

"Okay," Anthea says. "Thanks for your help."

"I'm glad I could be of assistance," the bureaucrat pipes, cheerfully oblivious to her sarcasm.

"Is there any way to trace the address information they used?" she asks Doug as soon as the bureaucrat drops offline. It's possible BEAN is covering for the two agents—or that the agents aren't from BEAN at all.

"No. You have a call."

"Who is it?"

"Your supervisor."

Tissa appears on Anthea's eyescreens, her face immobile, mouth rigid in a grim, no-nonsense line.

"What's wrong?" Anthea asks. It's about Ibrahim, it has to be.

"You are, girl." One thing about Tissa, she never minces words. Gets straight to the point.

"What's the problem?"

"Ibrahim. I know you took him." Tissa raises a hand before Anthea can edge a word in. "Don't lie to me or offer any excuses. At the moment, I'm not interested in the how or the why."

"It was for a good reason."

"Doesn't matter. You know what they say. The road to hell is paved with good intentions."

"Is that where I am now?"

Tissa lowers her hand. "I guess that depends on your definition of hell. You've been suspended without pay pending administrative review."

Anthea swallows. "That's harsh."

"So is what you did," Tissa retorts. "You should have come to me, gone through the proper channels."

"There wasn't time."

"I could have made time. But I didn't get the chance. Instead, you took matters into your own hands. Broke the law. Endangered not only Ibrahim and yourself but this organization and the community as a whole."

Anthea slumps. "What's going to happen to me?"

"I don't know. BEAN hasn't filed charges. Yet. I wouldn't be surprised if you lose your position with the org."

"I'm sorry," Anthea says.

"I am, too," Tissa says, the hard line of her lips softening. Then the screen goes blank.

Anthea kicks at the floor, scuffing it with her toe. "How much worse can it get?" she wonders out loud.

" 'The worst is not,' " Doug says, " 'So long as we can say, "This is the worst." ' "

"I'll be sure to keep that in mind." Anthea starts back down the hallway to check on Rigo's mother.

" 'Come what come may, / Time and the hour runs through the roughest day.' "

"I think I liked you better as a pessimist," Anthea says to the IA. "At least then I knew things were better than they looked."

"Rigo?" Varda says.

"What?" It's evening. He's lying on the bed, staring up at the darkened biolum panel directly above him where Rana's puffed-up face looms every now and then, blistering his grief-haunted retinas. He feels dead, too numb and laden with depression to move.

"It's not the four corners of the world," the IA says.

Rigo covers his eyes with one hand, wishing he could just be alone. "Easy for you to say."

"Stop swallowing in self-pity."

"Just leave me alone."

"Come on. Pull yourself up by your purse strings."

"I would if I had any." Rigo rolls over onto his side

and faces the wall. The moon is up and annoyingly bright. There's no escape. It fills the room, obliterating any chance of sleep.

"I have good news," Varda says, trying to cheer him up.

"You found me another job?" The way things are going, it's probably in SEA or east Texas.

"I've located Anthea and your mother."

Rigo sits up. "Where?"

"At a Global Upreach clinic. Your mother has been hospitalized."

That hardly qualifies as good news. "When?"

"Two days ago."

Rigo feels a headache coming on. Swings his legs over the edge of the bed and leans forward, head between his legs. "What happened?"

"She injured her left knee when BEAN came and took Ibrahim from her ap."

Her left knee, Rigo thinks, the good one. Now the only way she'll be able to get around is in a wheelchair or a specially designed exoskeleton. Too bad she can't afford either one.

"Can I talk to her?"

"No. Your voice and e-mail are still being blocked."

Rigo groans, rubs his face. "Isn't there *anything* you can do?"

"Go to the western wall," the IA says.

"What?"

"And put on your shades."

Rigo pushes himself to his feet, does what he's told. Trudges over to the phosphor-bright rectangle of moonlight on the wall across from the window. Dims the light to a tolerable level by slipping on his wrap-arounds. "Okay, now what? I'm in the dark, here."

"Put your hands on the wall."

"You want me to assume the position, too?" Rigo says, spreading his feet, as if he's about to be frisked.

"Make sure you're touching the mesh," Varda says.

Rigo moves his hands slightly, placing them squarely on the thermal netting. The ascorbic taste of rose hips mingles with the metallic patina.

"This might take a few minutes," Varda says. "Hold your horse."

"What might take a few minutes?" He feels ridiculous, like a nine-year-old about to take a surreptitious leak against the wall of a building to see if it really will get cleaned up in under ten seconds, as advertised.

This better be good, Rigo's thinking when the first images hit the eyescreens of his wraparounds.

"What the fuck?" He jerks away from the wall, and the info stream dries up, like a plug was pulled.

"Do you want to get in touch with your mother or not?" Varda says.

"Sure, but—"

"Then keep your hands on the wall. I need to run a source code comparison and translation."

Rigo replaces his hands on the mesh, feels the underlying layer of sound-absorbent foam dimple under the pressure of his fingers. "Translation of what?"

The IA doesn't answer. It's lapsed into passive-aggressive mode again—putting a little space between them so it can do its thing. Soon, images begin to trickle down the lenses of his wraparounds again—

rain squiggle lines of blue, green, red, and yellow pictographic code.

"What am I looking at?" Rigo says.

"Pherions," Varda says. "All the gengineered components of the central African ecotecture."

"Even the people?"

"Hello. What part of 'all' don't you understand?"

The lines of code increase in density, a tapestry spreading out around him. He can taste the biochemical threads it's woven from—spec individual molecules cleaving together, multiple sequences linking up, forming a tight-knit cloth that connects everything into a single unified whole. From the largest building to the smallest insect. The fabric is suffocating in its complexity, dizzying. In no time at all, Rigo finds himself hyperventilating.

"Calm down," Varda says. "Get a grip."

Rigo closes his eyes, takes several deep breaths to slow his breathing. As soon as the room stops spinning, he takes another peek.

"Spit," Varda says.

"Excuse me?"

"On your hand."

"What for?"

"You'll see."

Rigo shakes his head, spits into the palm of his right hand. What the hell? He's got nothing to lose.

"Okay," the IA says. "Rub it on the wall."

"This is crazy," Rigo says as he massages the spit into the foam, leaving a damp spot.

"There you are," Varda says, highlighting a pattern in the tapestry. "That's you in a nut."

He studies a highlighted string of organic code,

concatenated DNA, and pherion sequences that identify him. Specs that he doesn't fit seamlessly into the weave of the surrounding fabric. His pherion pattern doesn't integrate smoothly. He sticks out like a strand of shiny polyester thread spliced into rough burlap, held in place by antiphers that bypass security, makes him nonthreatening to the ecotecture's defense pherions. Rigo stares at the design, mandalalike arrangements of nested code, and feels himself slip into a dizzy entoptic drift. . . .

Cut free from the world. Numb. Like he's had one too many beers and can't feel anything, not even himself. One of those shitfaced benders where he feels like breaking down and crying like a baby.

He reaches out to keep from falling and, arms churning like a windmill, is stopped by the taste of blood and cloves. Concentrates on the flavor, the chemical construction it represents. Gazing at the code, he can spec reading frames in the pherion nucleotides—different ways that the amino acids can be parsed and combined—plus protein folds, valence patterns, and superposition states.

Something is happening to him, *has* happened. He can feel it in his bones, the way he did the first time he ever kicked it with a *muchacha*. Fourteen years old. Took all of a second, and he was a different person. Something more than what he'd been only a couple of heartbeats earlier, before he'd entered her . . . felt her surround and engulf him. Maria Sanchez. Eighty pounds overweight, with *chichis* the size of watermelons and a too-tight T-shirt stretched over them that said I Wish These Were Brains. Not that she was stupid or anything, just desperate, the same as him.

Permanent virgins. It was like a scarlet letter or the mark of Cain, visible for everyone to see. Afterward, Rigo thought the stigma and the shame would go away. Problem was, his boys and her girls knew they'd kicked it. Somehow, the act had changed not only their bodies but their body language. At first, out of embarrassment, he was like, Not me. No way I'd chicken bone that *puta*. Dissed her in public. Speculated as to the size and shape of the dentata lurking in the folds of fat between her legs. Nothing she deserved. Of course, out of retaliatory self-respect, she pulled the same routine, told her girlfriends she'd rather fuck a three-legged dog or a stuffed possum with a hinged *pito*. So began his road to acceptance and respectability, to where he stands at this moment.

Now he knows it wasn't his fault, or hers. Realizes that she was one of a handful of girls he was compatible with. He's on the low-end of the bell curve. Not a lot of data points where he's sitting. Not like some homeboys who are hardwired for sex like rabbits. Screwed hundreds of girls by the time they were fifteen.

Thinking about Maria—the lilac scent of her sweat and how neither of them had a choice—brings an acid burn. At least he found Anthea. What if Maria never found anyone else compatible? What if he was her only shot at happiness and she was condemned to spend the rest of her life alone? Rigo hasn't seen her in years, heard she recladed to someplace in South America, Argentina or Brazil. It's not really his problem—he wasn't obligated or anything—but he still feels a pang of guilt at dumping her the way he did.

"It's not fair," he mutters, shaking his head.

"There's always a fare to pay," Varda tells him. "Nothing is free. Lunch doesn't grow on trees."

Rigo rests his forehead against the acoustic wallfoam and resists the urge to bang it. He thinks about how easy it was for Whipplebaum to manipulate him. Anthea's right. He can be such an *idiota* sometimes. Sees only what he wants to see. Hears only what he wants to hear.

Rigo shakes his head, returns his attention to the ribozone. "How come you're able to show me all this?"

"Because you're still softwired," the IA says. "Able to remote-link to molecular code. Pherions. DNA. Sniffers. Bitcams."

"I thought the link was only for the Tiresias ecotecture." He hasn't been in direct contact with the comet for days. Not since the disaster.

"No," Varda says. "Every pherion sequence, protein fold, and DNA concatenation in an ecotectural system has a corresponding digital component it maps to."

"Which I'm able to access?"

"Yes."

So it's no different from the remote link he had to the warm-blooded plants. Digital complements of molecules are how gengineering companies like Ribo-Gen create and test new molecular code. How politicorps store the clade-profiles of people and objects in the environment so they can track their location or movement, model social demographics, manage public services, and monitor/adjust ribosome production of key pherions.

"The information isn't ecotecture-dependent?" Rigo says.

"No. Since there's no direct interaction between the records—no physical contact required to exchange or generate information, like there is with molecules—it's clade-neutral."

Rigo takes a second to mull this over, make sure he's hearing things right. "So all you're doing is accessing the digital record for a certain biological component, and then downloading the information to me?"

"That's it in a nutcase," Varda says.

At which point the molectric circuitry he's doped with converts the digital signal into a chemical signal, which can then be used by a ribosome to manufacture a real live molecule.

"Can I export information?" he asks. "Send the digital code for a specific pherion I'm doped with to someone else and have it show up in them?"

"If the other person is softwired," Varda says. "Otherwise the information has to be downloaded to the surrounding ecotecture."

"But the person could still import the pherion through the environment."

"Yes."

Rigo blinks. Frowns. "What happens if the information you download codes for a pherion that I haven't been claded for?" Theoretically, if the pherion his cells produce turns out to be a superbadass, he could be in deep shit.

"That won't happen," Varda says.

"Why not?"

"The Tiresias ecotecture is unique. It's unrelated to any other ecotecture."

"So the warm-blooded molectronics can't manufacture pherions from other ecotectures."

"Correct."

"What about pherions that are already in the environment? Can they affect me?"

"Yes. You're still susceptible to direct exposure. But as long as you avoid physical contact you're safe."

What was it Dorit had told him during their final conversation? *Nothing* has *to be the way it is. . . . New beginnings can happen anytime. The key is wanting something enough to make it happen.*

Rigo presses the tip of his tongue to half-parted lips, recalling the blood orange taste of her farewell kiss.

"I have to talk to Anthea," he says. "Get in touch with her and Ibrahim as soon as possible."

And his mother. Before she's too far gone—slips out of reach beyond the event horizon of the grave.

TWENTY-ONE

Now what? Anthea's not sure what to do after getting put on suspension. Rigo's mother is asleep. Rigo's unavailable. Doug's phreaking a Shakespearean rag. What does that leave? She could try calling Noogenics to see if Rigo's supervisor or someone else can forward a message for her—or at least tell her how he's doing. But it's late. Nearly nine. All she'll get is voice mail.

She takes a seat at the pod stop a half block down from the Global Upreach clinic, tries to clear her head. Can't. Manic zydeco from the Cajun bar directly across the street and the jumbled flicker of storefront biolums leave her jangled. She can feel the pressure of the sound and the light against her skin, holding the tension in. She needs to get away for a while.

Malina. She hasn't talked to her in a couple of

days. This might be a good time to swing by, see how Josué's doing. It'll give her something to do for a few hours, give her a chance to regroup.

"Anthea?"

She starts at the voice, which originated from one of the stand-alone vending kiosks she's sitting next to, an outlet store for Imelda Marcos shoeware. The tiny pavilion offers a Philippine ambience, including island decor with bamboo trim. Arrayed behind the glare-free scratch-resistant display window is a collection of the latest Cami!!eon® smart shoes. Able to change shape, breathability, or color, depending on environmental conditions.

"Can you hear me?" the vending machine says. It seems a bit uncertain, as if this is the first time it's approached a potential customer.

Anthea ignores it, depressed that a marketing IA has finally identified and targeted her as a frequent user of this particular stop. Now she'll have to walk another half block to the next stop.

"Come on," the kiosk says. "Answer me."

An older man shuffling past the bench slows, cocks his head in the direction of the sound. "Eh?" he says, arms hanging loosely.

"I know you can hear me, Anthea," the vending machine says, still focusing on her. The *viejo* must not fit its consumer profile.

"I'm not interested," she says. "Leave me alone."

The elderly man shakes his head and moves on, jerked forward by the marionette whir of the ancient exoskeleton under his baggy sprayons—an old titanium contraption that lacks the smoothness of the newer nanimatronic models.

A pod appears at the intersection down the street, turns toward her. Anthea stands and moves to the edge of the sidewalk, away from the kiosk. Slides into the pod as soon as the door hisses open, and takes a seat. Finds herself seated next to a dental adscreen for teeth engraving.

"Anthea," the ad pleads in a different voice. "Just listen to me for a second. It's not what you think. Okay?"

Anthea stands, looks for another seat.

"Wait," another adscreen says as she passes by the satisfied grin of man who's just had his lips dosed with flavor-exuding bacteria. Available tastes are mango, peach, strawberry, guanabana, and lychee.

The pod eases to a halt at the next stop. Rather than stick around, Anthea makes a quick exit and walks hurriedly away. Hopefully the marketing ware has a fairly small territory. Go far enough and she'll be out of range. She can always catch another pod a few blocks away. Meanwhile, all she has to do is steer clear of all signs, adscreens, or store outlets.

After three blocks and no new ad assault, she's feeling good. Then the palm of her hand starts to itch, and a cartoon face appears. The same pen-and-ink line drawing of a politicorp security guard that Rigo got the night they went to the Boardwalk. The cartoon salutes her. But instead of launching into a jingle, it says, "You're not going to get away from me that easy."

Anthea stops dead in the middle of the sidewalk, almost gets run over by a pack of prepubescent kids spilling out of a theater.

"What the fuck's going on here? Who is this?"

"It's me, babe." The cartoon grins. "Just trying to catch up with the sun and the moon."

"Rigo?" Anthea holds her palm up in front of her nose, inspects the square-jawed jarhead.

The tattune raises both eyebrows. "I know this doesn't exactly look like me, but it's the best I could do. The only option left when you wouldn't talk to me at the kiosk or in the pod."

"That was you?"

"Yeah." The eyebrows pinch together, a pair of angled exclamation points. "Can you believe it? Just what I always wanted to be. A shoe salesman and lip service spokesperson."

Anthea frowns.

"What's wrong, *mami*? I thought you'd be happy to see me."

"How do I know it's you, and not some marketing IA pretending to be you?" she says.

"You've got to be kidding."

She balls her hand into a fist.

"Hey," the tattune protests through her closed fingers. "How can you not know it's me?"

She opens her hand. "Prove it."

The blocky face sags, mouth curving into an inverted half-circle. "I can't believe this."

"Me, neither. That's why I'm asking."

The tattune grows contemplative for a moment, face immobile. "Okay," it finally says, mouth a lopsided oval. "What about that vacation we took to Sin City to celebrate our first year together? We stayed at the Pink Sands. You played Black Jack, and won seven straight hands before they asked us to leave."

"That doesn't prove anything," she says.

"Why not?"

"Because all that data is on record. Hotel bill. Gambling receipts. Transportation costs. Tell me something that's not part of your or my personality profile."

"You mean something private? Just between the two of us that no one else would know about."

"Exactly."

"Like the way I always leave the toilet seat up at night, and you get all pissed at me when you splash-down?"

"I don't know," Anthea says, dubious. "There could be public utility records of that."

"You think South San Jose keeps track of whether someone has their toilet seat up or not, and who's using it?"

Anthea sniffs. "It could be part of an ongoing statistical program to graph toilet use for waste management optimization."

"This is ridiculous."

"You're one to talk."

"Okay." The tattune makes a face. "How about when we're having sex and you like to be on top because if you're not your pubic bone starts to—"

"Not that personal!" Anthea blurts out.

The tattune squiggles its lips. "Don't blame me. You wanted details."

Anthea glances around, moves into the empty doorway of a shuttered-up café—a former sushi bar-*cum*-game room. The tables through the diamond window still have Go boards on them, piles of dust-covered black and white stones.

"Where are you?" she says, speaking into her cupped hand and dropping her voice to a whisper.

"Some shithole hotel in Africa. Used to be a Hilton. Now BEAN's using it for a detention center."

"You're locked up?"

"Along with Hsi-Tang and Claribel." The face droops in sadness. "No one else survived."

"Survived what?"

"The accident. I thought you'd know by now."

"We haven't heard a thing. I mean, we heard that something was going on, but no details."

"Well, it was a disaster. A nightmare. Let me tell you. I'm not surprised they're keeping a lid on it."

"What happened?"

"The colonists decided they didn't want to be part of the program anymore, and took off. Made a run for the outer solar system. The asteroid belt—or maybe even the Kuiper belt. Who knows?"

"Should you be telling me this?"

"You mean, will I get in trouble?" The face contorts, a constipated mix of raw emotion. "Not anymore. I got fired this morning. There's nothing they can do to me. I can say what I want."

Anthea spreads her fingers, stretching the lines in her palm taut. "What did they fire you for?"

"It's a long story, babe. I don't want to get into it right now. The bottom line is, I got set up. Made to look like the bad guy. Plus it didn't help that Beto's in jail. Gives people the wrong impression, like I'm a criminal just because he is."

Anthea stiffens. "Beto's in jail?"

"That's what they said. I don't know, maybe it's

bullshit. I was hoping that you could spec out the situation for me. Get the details."

Anthea nods. "I'll see what I can find out." She has to be careful. Doesn't want to risk getting ID'd as one of Beto's former customers, or worse, as an accomplice.

"What about my moms?" Rigo asks. "I heard she's in a clinic. Got injured when BEAN kidnapped Ibrahim."

"You know about that?"

"Yeah. Sounds like they storm-trooped her ap, showed up without any advance warning."

"I wasn't there. I'm not exactly sure what happened. But your mom didn't have much of a chance."

"So how bad is she? What's the latest?"

Anthea shakes her head. "It doesn't look good. Her immune system is going crazy, forming bone around the injury. The doctors are trying to stop the process, slow it down, at least. But they're not having much luck."

"How's she taking it?"

"Pretty good. Says if she can't walk anymore it will be just like sittin' in a chair in heaven."

"That sounds like her. If something bad happens it's for a reason. God's will and all."

"It's a kind of optimism," Anthea says.

The tattune grimaces. "Fatalism is more like it."

"Whatever. You see it as negative. She sees it as positive."

Rigo grunts. "What about Ibrahim?" he says. "Any word on him?"

"No. I tried calling BEAN. They denied all knowledge of the agents who questioned me and picked him

up. Which makes me think the goons who broke into
your mom's place weren't from BEAN."

"You spec they were from a politicorp instead of
the government?"

She nods. "RiboGen or Noogenics. Maybe one of
the independent pharms they contract with."

"So you have no clue where they took him? If he's
still in the country?"

"No. I don't even know where to start." She sags
against the lichenboard behind her, shoulder blades
gouging the hard, pressed fibers.

"I might be able to do something here. Scope his
location."

"Can you do that? From detention, I mean?"

"I'm not as isolated as you might think. I'm still
wired for the Tiresias ecotecture. That's how I'm talking to you now."

Anthea straightens. Pushes away from the flimsy
wallboard. "When will you be home, *papi*?"

"I don't know, babe. Any day now, I hope."

"I miss you."

"I miss you, too."

She traces a line on the tattune's face with a fingertip, gets no reaction. "How are you holding up?
Okay?"

"I'm fine," he says. "Great."

"You sound different."

"What do you mean, different?" he says.

"Changed." She can't quite put her finger on it. Instead of stressed or worried, the way she'd expect, he
seems calm. Confident, almost.

"Well, it's not like almost dying and then getting
fired doesn't give you a different perspective on life."

True, she thinks, he's got nothing left to lose. "What are you going to do when you get back?"

"Take you out for an evening of amor. A romantic dinner followed by a night of dancing salsa or merengue."

She smiles. "I like that." Then, "Have you thought about what you're going to do about a job?"

"I don't know," Rigo says. "I thought maybe I'd apply for a position at another ecotectural firm like OAsys or Ecotrope."

Anthea grimaces. She doesn't want to see him end up in the same dead-end job as before.

"You could go to school," she suggests. "It's the perfect opportunity."

"I don't see how," he says. "I couldn't afford classes when I was working. No way I'm going to be able to enroll on unemployment."

"We'll talk when you get back," she says. "It'll work out."

"You're starting to sound like my moms."

"I've been spending a lot of time with her lately. Getting to know her."

"Listen," he says, "I gotta go. I'll talk to you later." The tattune starts to fade, pale as a daguerreotype.

"I love you," she says, not wanting him to go. Desperate to hold on—frightened of losing him again, this time for good.

The tattune's mouth moves, but there's no sound. Audio's been lost. Too bad she can't read lips.

She kisses the palm of her hand, swears she can taste the salt of his tears, or hers, maybe. There's no way to know.

TWENTY-TWO

As soon as the infostream from the tattune in Anthea's palm dries up, Rigo slumps to his knees. Drags his fingers along the wall to the chalky floor tile and tries not to implode. He feels empty, on the verge of a total meltdown.

"Rigo?" Varda says. "What's wrong?"

He rests his forehead against the wall. Breathes deeply a couple of times, heaving in air to fill the void inside him. Tries to hold on to the grainy bitcam image of Anthea standing in the doorway, lit by the blue cellophane glow of an overhead awning, the sidewalk dappled by variegated shadows, a Monet-splash of circuitree leaves as lively as castanets.

"Take it slow," Varda tells him. "Your respiration and pulse rate are elevated and you're sweating."

Rigo sniffs. Swallows pasty saliva.

"I thought you'd be glad to see Anthea," the IA says. "Maybe it wasn't such a good idea."

Rigo tries to ease the steel bands constricting his chest. "I need to get out of here. This place is driving me crazy."

"Are you turning into a loon?"

"Something like that." He places his hands on the wall beside his head. "I need you to help me find someone else."

"Who?"

"Ibrahim. The street kid Anthea was trying to help."

"I can try," Varda says. "But first you have to find yourself."

Whatever that means. Sounds like the IA has been indulging in a little too much transcendental meditation. "Just tell me what to do," he says, exhaustion giving way to exasperation.

"Relax."

"I'm trying." A few more breaths. In with the good air, out with the bad. Then, "Okay. Ready whenever you are."

Varda takes him deeper into the ribozone. Interlocking strands of code, tangled as a mop of hair. Nested cryptoglyphs. Recursive protein folds. A real mess. The chemical equivalent of machine code.

"I'm lost," he says. No way he'll ever be able to make sense of this on his own. Find his way around.

In response, a walled-in garden forms around him. Assembles itself out of the fabric of code. Threads of molecules weaving a new virtuality. A canopy of interleaved branches tightly knitted together. Red, white, and blue flowered vines that trail to the ground, send out runners to a menagerie of sculpted topiary. It's like visiting a zoo or a carnival populated with all kinds of freak animals. Some are recognizable—dogs, roaches, rats—but others are more exotic. Chimerical shit like winged spiders and beaked snakes. In addition, there are thorny cubes, leafy spheres, and basketlike cylinders that appear to be woven out of wiry twigs. Support structures for fungus and various infestations of ersatz bacterial colonies that look as if they've been transplanted straight from the refrigerator in his ap.

Then there are the butterflies. Thousands of them, fluttering from one plant to the next. Colorful, undulating streamers that link up into chains, break apart, and then reform.

"Talk to me," he says. "Where the hell am I?"

"The central African ecotectural system. You're looking at biomorphs of all the constituent components."

The garden isn't much larger than his hotel room, and there are wooden trellises on the walls of sun-hardened mud.

"I tried to present it in a form you are familiar with," the IA explains. "A 3-D schematic seemed the best."

"What's with the butterflies?" Rigo strolls over to a cube covered with monarchs. Reaches out and touches it. Tastes cocoa and chrome in the seething mass of wings that generate no breeze.

"They designate data transfer at the molecular level," Varda tells him. "Chemical infostream between ecotectural elements." The IA could be a docent in a museum, or a tour guide in some Third World biological preserve.

"What about the geometric shapes? Spheres. Cubes. Cylinders. What do they represent?"

"Nonorganic systems. Power distribution centers. Waste-water filtration plants. Transportation nodes." The IA could go on and on.

In short, public-ecotecture infrastructure. Rigo peers up at the canopy, catches a glimpse of domed Cistine blue, too close to be a real sky. It's almost like standing under a bower in a well-maintained arboretum. Neatly pruned—everything under rigid control. "How about the branches? What are they?"

"The primary code for the base ecotecture. The public space that everybody has access to. Like a skeleton, it binds together all the other elements, provides the support structure for everything else."

"Including the different clades?"

"Yes."

Rigo looks around, searching for telltale anthropomorphisms. "Where are all the people?"

"To your left."

Rigo heads in that direction, skirts a bush with a leafy sphere atop a spindly trunk, and stumbles into what appears to be a person covered with different varieties of flowers. The person isn't moving—is actually a topiary statue twisted out of rose-bush bramble. In addition to the flowers—petunias, goosefoot violets, and lilacs—there are a shitload of small black bees crawling on the stems and petals.

"There you are," Varda says.

Hard to tell if the IA is talking in general terms, or about him personally. "So the flowers are? . . ." he prompts.

"DNA and pherion information," the IA says.

"The molecular code that identifies each individual in the ecotecture. The figure is a mannequin onto which the clade-profile of an individual can be mapped and visually displayed. It's no one, and everyone."

So, a generic template, in which each flower equates to a specific pherion, and its position correlates to the host range of glycoproteins on the surface of a virus. "I take it the bees are information carriers," he says, "the same as the butterflies?"

"Not exactly," the IA says. "They indicate hardwired data—not softwired."

"In other words, biochemical information that can't be updated remotely."

"Yes."

"What's my clade-profile look like?" Rigo says.

"Touch the figure."

Rigo moves a step closer to the topiary figure. "They're not really bees, right?" He can't hear any buzzing. "I'm not gonna get stung, or anything?" Not that he's ever been stung by a bee. All he's heard is stories from his mother.

"Don't worry," Varda says. "You would have to come into direct physical contact with the ecotecture to be affected by them. As it is, your remote link is set up to translate clade incompatibilities as different tastes and smells."

Like the toxic stench of his ap when he got back from Costa Rica, newly claded for Tiresias. No problem. He can deal with that.

Rigo reaches for the topiary. Hesitates. What if he doesn't like what he sees? It's not like a bad haircut that will grow back, or an ugly shirt that can be taken off and tossed into a disassembler.

"What are you waiting for?" Varda says.

"Nothing."

He fingers the petal of a rose. Several bees detach from the avatar and land on his hand. They crawl around for a few seconds, then buzz back to the flowers. As soon as they make contact, the flowers change, become lilacs, yellow pansies, blue columbines, and white Icelandic poppies. Except for one or two orange monkey flowers, which remain unmorphed. Several butterflies land on the newly transformed figure, stay for a moment, then wander off, making room for others. Each time, a fraction of a second after one lands or takes off, he gets a tickle or an itch in about the same location as the butterfly on the figure. Some sort of delayed feedback that loops back to his in-vivo body from the flowery avatar in the ribozone.

"What do you think?" Varda asks him, all excited. "I picked the flowers and their arrangement myself."

Rigo's face puckers, his expression sour as he considers the bouquet. "How come you included pansies?"

"Because they have faces."

"Okay. But what exactly is it about them makes you think of me? I mean if this is supposed to represent me, what do the pansies stand for, personality-wise? Like possibly they're colorful. Or bold. Confident."

"They're cute, cheerful. They always have a smile, no matter how sad things are for them."

In other words, a clown. Just how he wants to be thought of. As if he hasn't been humiliated enough lately. "Is that really the way you see me? Wait. No. Don't answer that."

"You don't like it, do you?" the IA says, its enthusiasm fading, voice reminiscent of crushed leaves underfoot. Bruised and battered.

Rigo opens his mouth. Almost blurts out, "What if I said you reminded me of a bad tattune that's missing a few lines of code?" Doesn't. Thinks better of it. Manages to do a complete about-face. "I love it," he says.

Varda brightens. "Really?"

"It's beautiful," he says. "Honest. It's obvious you put a lot of thought into it, and it shows."

"I wanted to abduct the real you."

"Well, you did a great job." Rigo exhales, puffing out his cheeks. "How do we find Ibrahim?" he says, anxious to move on. Get down to business.

"Do you want to spec his clade-profile?"

"Sure." No way the kid will be represented by pansies. He only smiled once the whole time they were together, a brief glimmer of contentment ambushed by the sudden, unexpected return of pain. After that, he'd been afraid to relax at all, to give in to comfort. Orchids would be more apropos, Rigo thinks. Something that's dependent on others to survive.

The figure morphs, changes size and shape. Sure enough, the pansies vanish, are replaced by dahlias and some kind of purple thistle. There aren't nearly as many blossoms or bees, and the butterflies drift off in a disorganized cloud. Don't want to have anything to do with this new arrangement of flowers.

"Doesn't look healthy," Rigo says. Scraggly, he

thinks. Sick. Like he's clinging to life. "So where is he now? Where did they take him?"

"The last location on record is your mother's apartment. His profile hasn't been updated since then."

Rigo walks around the figure, pacing, hands knotted in frustration. "There must be some way to find him. Sniffers, or whatever. That's the way BEAN or whoever found him, right? What about all the bit-cams in plants and buildings, uploading images to the Net? Isn't there a way to parse those?"

"A random search?"

"Doesn't have to be random. It could be targeted—based on likely possibilities, or extrapolation."

"That could steal a while," Varda says.

"Yeah, well, it's better than doing nothing." Rigo feels caged, can still spec the wall against his fingertips. A solid barrier.

"It would be easier if he was remote-linked," Varda says. "But he's not. I have to wait for a regular upload to pinprick him."

"What kind of upload are you talking about?"

"Medical. Environmental. Demographic. Those records get updated periodically. Usually once every twenty-four hours, to keep them current."

"By the government?"

"Yes. But private interest groups also maintain extensive networks of sniffers and other information gathering agents. Advertising and marketing firms in particular do a lot of realtime in-situ datamining. So do news agencies. It's hard to avoid detection by all of these infosources. Especially when there are so many of them."

"So it's a good bet he'll show up on one of them," Rigo says. "It's just a matter of time."

"Yes."

"The problem is," Rigo says, "we might not have twenty-four hours or however long it takes for an update to reference him."

"Another problem," Varda says, "is that I'm not sure what ecotectures or clades to monitor."

True, Rigo thinks. By now he could've been recladed, or doped with an antipher, and LOHopped anywhere in the world. "How many different clades are there? Total, I mean?"

"There are sixteen distinct ecotectural systems," the IA says, "and approximately two thousand clades."

"You don't know the exact number?" It seems that an accurate count should be on record somewhere.

"There are an estimated three hundred unregistered clades in existence. The precise number is fuzzy."

Some of those clades are probably black-market. But he's willing to bet the majority are politicorp maintained. Clandestine incarceration, security or espionage clades that only a few people belong to or know about.

A translucent 2-D window appears in front of Rigo, floats at eye level—a sort of wall-less wallscreen that looks like a jigsaw puzzle. A patchwork of color stitched together by the outlines of continents. He can't make out any obvious pattern or shape. It's pretty much a Rorschach blob.

"This is a worldwide clade-distribution map," Varda says. "It includes all of the current registered clades, and the ecotectural system or systems they belong to."

He can see the central African ecotectural system he's in—a bulbous aneurysm of burnt sienna around the Congo River basin—and that it contains just four clades. Meaning there's not a lot of fine-grain social stratification here. So the economic gap between the clades is pretty pronounced. Not much chance for clade-switching or movement between classes. The social structure is fairly rigid. Looking at the map, he notes the same ecotectural system is in other parts of Africa, as well as India, Australia, and the Argentine desert.

Rigo locates San Jose. SJ is a ringworm welt of pink around the San Francisco Bay, clinging to the high ground of surrounding hills. It's got about a hundred clades. Diversity up the yin-yang compared to central Africa and the balance of the Third World. But not quite as much as the eastern U.S. seaboard or most of Europe, for that matter.

Rigo raises one index finger to the map, pauses a few millimeters short of actually making contact.

"Gopher it," Varda says, encouraging.

Rigo touches San Jose. The walled garden metamorphoses around him. The trees change into familiar circuitrees and umbrella palms. The canopy of interleaved branches becomes vines of white and pink flowered wisteria. The color and patterning of the bees and butterflies shift with the change in molecular code. He inhales the unfettered scent of almonds.

"I can do this with any of the ecotectures?" he says. "See what they're like just by touching them?"

"I can show you what's registered," Varda says,

"and some of what's unregistered, through unofficial channels."

Which means, at some level, that Varda is not entirely official—has been cut free of the standard security protocols that control what an IA has access to and what is off limits. Maybe that's what was going on during the trip to Tiresias, why the IA has been less of a *boca* lately, more withdrawn and circumspect.

"How long have you been able to do this?" he asks.

"Do what?"

"You know. Stream things you're not supposed to without getting caught. That sort of thing."

No answer.

"Varda?"

"Not now," the IA says. "I'll wash up my act later."

The walled garden vanishes from his wraparounds. Rigo finds himself standing in the middle of the hotel room.

"What's going on?" he says, disoriented, alarmed by the sudden shift to reality.

"They're coming for you," Varda says. "Get ready."

TWENTY-THREE

"Ibrahim will turn up," Malina tells her. "It might take a while, but I'm sure you'll find him."

"I don't see how," Anthea says, shaking her head. "Especially now that I've been suspended." She doesn't have access to the resources she did—hospital and mortuary records, politicorp security reports, updated immigration and deportation files.

"Global Upreach will take you back," Malina says. "They can't afford not to, girl. It's not like they have that many qualified people."

"Tissa didn't sound too encouraging. She was pretty hard-assed."

Malina waves a dismissive hand. "This is just a slap on the wrist. A pro forma disciplinary action."

That's one of the things Anthea likes about Malina. She's an optimist, but practical, too. Self-reliant. Goes to church and prays, but believes in helping out

God whenever she can. Isn't afraid of a little karmic sweat. Gets that from working in a desalination plant. The two of them are seated at a big table in the communal kitchen of the four-bedroom house where Malina rents a room for her and Josué. There are three other families living with her. Two single moms with three kids, and a husband/wife with two kids. Five adults and six kids total. The whole neighborhood is that way, large single-family homes converted to high-density occupancy after the rising bay submerged half of the low-lying residential.

"I just wish I knew if he was okay or not," Anthea says. She still has one option available for locating Ibrahim that she's avoided so far.

"The first thing you need to do is stop beating yourself up," Malina says. "You aren't going to be able to help anyone at the rate you're going. Not Ibrahim or yourself. That's my advice, like it or not."

As usual, Malina is right. Anthea takes a sip of vat-grown coffee. Produced in either Virginia, Georgia, or what's left of the Carolinas, it's got nicotine blended with the caffeine to give it extra kick. Time to set her personal issues aside, she decides, and put Ibrahim's first, as difficult as that might be.

"Will you be able to watch Josué tomorrow night?" Malina says, scratching her nose with a dry, salt-whitened fingertip.

"I think so," Anthea says. At this point, nothing seems certain.

"I need to know for sure," Malina says. "If you can't, I got to find someone else. Simple as that."

"I know."

"Listen, if you can't it's okay. I'll get Mei to look

after him like last time." Mei is the married mom who does childcare during the day and is usually willing to watch Josué for an evening.

"It would be easier if I knew when Rigo was coming home," Anthea says.

Malina cocks her head to one side, spilling beaded dreadlocks across one bleached cheek. "What's eating you, girl? You want to talk about it?"

Anthea sets her coffee down. Stares out the window. Gnaws on a thumbnail until she tastes blood.

Malina leans back. Holds her hands in front of her, palms out. "No pressure," she says. "It's none of my business."

"It's just that I feel like my whole life's a lie."

"Shit, girl. This whole world's a lie. What do you expect?"

"I'm talking about stuff I've kept from Rigo. Things I haven't told him about myself." Not that she's had a lot of chances, lately. Talking to a tattune isn't really the time or place for a serious heart-to-heart.

"We talkin' skeletons in the closet?"

"Something like that."

"Well, I wouldn't be surprised if there's a few things he ain't told you. Moldy old compost stinking up his past. So, you're probably even on that score."

Anthea scrapes her lower lip with her teeth. "Still, I feel bad."

"Why?"

"Because I haven't been totally honest. I mean what if he finds out on his own? It should come from me first."

Malina threads her fingers, makes clicking sounds

with her ceramic rings. "You're worried he'll hold it against you. Use it as an excuse to break up or get what he wants."

"I just don't want to hurt him. Ruin what we have." Anthea presses both hands to her forehead. "I mean, I even told his mother."

"Then it can't be that bad."

"I don't know. There are certain things that are easier to tell a woman. He might not understand."

"Rigo's a sensitive guy. Maybe too sensitive, from what I've seen. Turns the other cheek too often for his own good."

Anthea looks up from under her hands. "That doesn't mean he'll understand. If he gets hurt, he could decide to walk away." Like he did with his old hood. Turned his back on the *tigueritos* he grew up with.

"Look," Malina says. "There's stuff you haven't told me, and vice versa. So what? I don't hold it against you, and you don't hold it against me. We respect each other's right to privacy. He should do the same."

"In theory."

"No theory about it." Malina's fingers continue to rumba. "Look. If he gives you a hard time, tell him you forgot all about it. After all the shit you been through, it shouldn't come as any big surprise. I mean, you told him most of what you did, right? It ain't no big mystery."

"This is different."

"Well, you suffered a lot. That's for sure. I was there for a good part of it. So I know."

"True. But what I haven't told him changes who I

am. Everything about me. In his eyes, I'll be a different person."

Malina puckers her cracked lips. "Sounds to me like you're being way too hard on yourself. Gettin' all bent out of shape over something that ain't even happened yet. That you're imagining."

"Just preparing for the worst."

"Listen. If it's eating you that bad, tell him. Get it off your chest. That way, least you won't have to wonder about it no more. It'll be out in the open."

"Don't you want to know what it is?"

"Not if you don't want to tell me. I mean it, girl. You're who you are now. All of us were different people at one time. Doesn't have nothin' to do with the present. Or the future."

"I'm not so sure."

"Trust me," Malina says. "The worst is in your head. Nothin's ever as bad as you think it's gonna be. It's the shit you never give a second's thought to that you got to worry about."

The car is an old BMW sedan. White sheet metal trimmed with chrome, mirrored windows, the works. The sort of ominous transportation pre-millennial dictators used to cruise around in while they were subjugating the Third World, keeping it safe from socialism, communism, and illegal drug cartels. Anything but poverty, Rigo thinks. The streets of the city shimmer in the hundred degree centigrade heat. They're jammed with electric bicycles and shaded by silver heat-reflective awnings veined with viscous red capillaries. Everyone's wearing white burnooses made of moisture-absorbent fibers that funnel the moisture into ergonomically fitted camel packs.

"Where are you taking me?" Rigo says to Liz and Jeraldo, who are in the backseat with him, holding him in place like two unmatched bookends. The BEAN agent, wearing a slightly different shade of blue tie, is driving. He was probably a chauffeur in his former life, Rigo thinks, before settling on a career in immigration control.

"The airport," Liz says.

"I'm going home?"

"Not immediately," Jeraldo says. "First, you have to take a slight detour through Costa Rica. Puntarenas."

"To get retrocladed," Liz adds.

It was bound to happen sooner or later, Rigo thinks. The final step in cutting his connection to the corp.

"What about Claribel and Hsi-Tang?" Rigo asks. "What's going on with them?"

"They left this morning," Liz says.

So by the time he arrives in Puntarenas they'll have moved on. He'll be cut off—isolated from any direct contact with his former co-workers. He won't even get a chance to say good-bye. Not just to the living but the dead.

Antoine. Rana. Luis. TomE. Naguib.

It's hard to believe they're gone. Doesn't seem real. Rigo assumes their families have been notified and their bodies sent back, but he can't get confirmation. No one is telling him shit.

"I have a request," Rigo says.

Liz turns the round, polarized lens of her monocle

on him. Her gaze is as chill as the air conditioning in the car. "What's that?"

"I've been thinking that maybe I don't want to go back to SJ. That I might want to reclade somewhere else."

It takes a moment for her cool veneer to crack. "What are you talking about?"

Rigo smiles at her, cranking up the albedo. "This is the perfect time for a change. I mean, you're going to reclade me anyway, right? Why go through the process twice? It'll just be a lot of extra work."

"Forget it," Liz tells him.

"Hey, I'm just trying to take advantage of the situation," Rigo says, "make things easier for all of us."

"Where are you thinking of transferring?" Jeraldo says. Maybe the brother's not such an asshole after all.

"Siberia," Rigo says. The first thing that jumps into his mind. Too bad he didn't have a little more time to think this out, plan ahead.

"There's no way we can reclade you to Siberia," Liz says. "A formal request hasn't been submitted—hasn't been reviewed or approved. The Puntarenas facility is not set up for a regular clade transfer. It's out of the question." She smirks. Folds her arms across her chest, case closed.

"I haven't been able to submit a formal request because my e-mail's been blocked since I came here. Which is why I'm doing it now, in the presence of an official Bureau of Ecotectural Assimilation and Naturalization representative."

"He has a point," the BEAN agent says.

"But a request could take days to process," Liz snaps.

"No problem," Rigo says. "I'll wait."

Liz glances past Rigo to Jeraldo. His lips are stiff, like they've been chiseled into stone. "What do you say we detain him for a few more days, while his request is being denied?"

"He can't stay here," the BEAN agent says from the front seat, his gaze flicking to the rearview mirror. "We need the hotel room. We have guests coming from China and there's no other place else to put him. He's your responsibility now."

"This is bullshit," Liz says, nostrils flaring as anger builds inside her, dark and ominous as a thunderhead.

"I have a legal right to file a petition," Rigo says, speaking to the BEAN agent. "It doesn't matter when or where it's submitted."

"That's true," the man says. "By law, if a request is submitted it must be formally reviewed before any other assimilation or naturalization action can be taken."

"But this is an internal corporate reclading," Liz argues. "It's a private matter, not a public one. So it's not subject to review."

The BEAN agent shakes his head. "The law is quite clear in this regard. If a person is being retrocladed or recladed from one ecotectural system to another, then international regulations apply to the case."

Liz's bottom lip quivers. Palsied. Furious. "It's my understanding that all personal clade changes are exempt."

"Only within a specific ecotectural system. If more than one ecotecture is involved, then it's no longer a private matter. The action is subject to governmental restrictions and protections."

"Fine with me," Rigo says.

"It'll never be approved," Liz tells him, acidic now that her legal feint has been parried. "You're wasting your time."

"Hey"—Rigo spreads his hands—"you never know. I could get lucky."

"We can't take him to Puntarenas," Jeraldo says. "We'd have to detain him there against his will until a decision comes down. I don't think we want to do that, do we?"

"Fuck," Liz says, flecking the window next to her with spittle.

"So what do we do?" Jeraldo says after a pause.

They're nearing the airport shuttle field. Ahead of them, the SSTO wavers under the sun. Here one second, gone the next. It's not just the mind-scorching heat. A monster dust storm is kicking up, turning the sky from blue to brown. In a matter of seconds, the sun darkens and the shuttle disappears behind a roiling wall of sand, impenetrable as stone, that comes crashing down on them.

TWENTY-FOUR

H ong Kong is nothing like Anthea remembers it,
and exactly the same.

The massive concrete polymer-sealed seawall that
keeps the ocean from flooding the city still looms
above the harbor. The emergency pumps are still in
place. So are the Panama Canal–style locks that lower
ships in and lift them out. The bay is as crowded as
ever, everything from dinghies to freighters and
tankers. Ditto the streets of downtown. Wall-to-wall
taxi pods, bicycles, and foot traffic circulating in and
around sidewalk kiosks, laissez-faire street vendors,
and beggars.

Gone are the wide-brimmed hats and the colorful
parasols people used to carry around to block the
sun. On the busiest days, the streets had been a con-
gested mass of umbrellas, jostling for position. As a
child, darting between the millipede-dense legs of

tourists and locals, she could always find shade. It was like living under a patchwork quilt stitched together by the omnipresent fear of ultraviolet light and malignant skin melanomas. As added value, the umbrellas kept off the torrential monsoon rains, which came down in buckets, and also prevented acid burn from either hydrochloric or sulfuric acid, depending on pollution levels and wind direction.

In place of the parasols there is now a vaulted dome. Photovoltaic. Piezoelectric. UV reflective. Supported by black carbyne arches that span the mouth of the harbor, it reminds her of a large sleepy eyelid. A narrow slit above the seawall admits stale ocean air and the salmon pink haze of the morning sun.

She forgot how stifling it can be, the oppressive humidity that hits the skin like a warm shower. The bioremediated hills encircling the harbor are as green as ever, an algae bloom of oxygen-producing and toxin-absorbing sponge-bush. The smell of hot cooking oil, noodles, batter-fried vegetables, steamed fish, and pickled eggs turns her stomach.

Anthea's mother has a penthouse on the top floor of an old skyscraper wrapped in curtain-glass the color of obsidian. A rectangular monolith that devours free will the way a black hole eats photons. Entering the lobby, it feels like she's stepping into a singularity. She can feel the life being crushed out of her. Atoms and molecules ripping apart. Electrons being stripped, quarks uncharmed.

She pauses in the granite-and-glass lobby, surrounded by multicolored flutterleaves that combine and recombine in terrace planters to form different-shaped plants. As a five-year-old she would watch the leaves for hours, enthralled by the changing plantscape, and chase after them, trying to get them to go where she wanted, form new kinds of plants. Sometimes she would sit quietly and attempt to control the leaves with her mind or the force of her will. A child's desire to control the universe. Her first experience with powerlessness. Like the world, the leaves never obeyed her wishes.

Anthea takes a deep breath to ease the tightness in her chest, and waits for signs of clade rejection. She knows the symptoms, used to lure schoolmates who had been mean to her into the lobby so she that could watch them suffer. First, intense itching of the eyes, followed in short order by searing, needle-sharp pinpricks of pain administered with acupuncture precision.

But the building still recognizes her pherion pattern. Its antiphers haven't been updated to exclude her.

The lobby is bustling with upper-clade activity, residents busy in a kind of purposeful Brownian motion. Morning tea. Business meetings in one of the building's conference rooms. Lunch. Shopping. Dinner. It's the same pattern followed de rigueur by her mother.

Anthea refuses to call ahead, to become yet another appointment in her mother's schedule. Better to show up unannounced. The surprise factor will work in her favor—won't give her mother a chance to put on her emotional makeup, establish the terms and conditions of her visit. Besides, Anthea doesn't plan to stay long. No more time than it takes to make her request. She swore that she would never ask for her mother's help for anything.

But that was for herself. This isn't.

She waits for an elevator tube to clear out, enters the glass, teak-floored cylinder before anyone else can board, and closes the door. It slides shut, cocooning her in dry, plumeria-scented air. She presses her thumb to the iDNA pad for the penthouse.

"Welcome back, madame," the elevator says in a soft sonorous baritone. "It's a pleasure to serve you again. I've been expecting you."

Whatever that means. Anthea decides not to ask. The elevator rises silently on a pneumatic cushion of air. Ornamental art nouveau crystal slides by, a Tiffany-esque column of lead tracery and stained glass. The ride seems shorter than she remembered, hoped. At the top, Anthea's heart pummels her rib cage. She's not ready for this—not yet. Almost turns around and heads back down.

The door slides open, revealing the anteroom to the penthouse. Clay tile flooring and white stucco walls gridded with maple. A folding partition screen—black lacquered wood with panes of translucent rice paper—conceals the doorway from the foyer to the front room.

Something is different. Wrong.

Anthea skirts the partition, enters the main living room. It's empty. Nothing but gleaming hardwood floors, bare pastel walls, and sliding pine-mullioned ceiling panels that open and close skylights. Her mother's peculiar amalgam of Mexican and Japanese aesthetic motifs. Gone is the furniture—the bamboo-frame sofas and chairs, the tables with glazed ceramic tops—the floor mats, lamps, and vases. The shelves are empty of the primitive clay sculptures she liked to

collect, South American fertility symbols. The walls
bare of wood-block prints depicting Japanese land-
scapes, and the scrolls that dripped poetry like black
rain trickling down the diamond panes of the windows during a storm.

Anthea shivers at the memory of the shadows cast
by the drops crawling across the pale floor and veined
marble counters of the kitchen. "What happened?"
she asks the penthouse. "Where is she?"

"I don't know." Its voice is cultured. Technically
perfect syllables as precise as the notes in a piece by
Mozart. "She didn't indicate where she was going."

"She just left?"

"Yes."

Anthea goes to the south window of the room.
Stares out at the wind-scalloped horizon. "When?"

"Six months ago."

The window seems to shudder under Anthea's un-
steady breath. "When is she coming back?"

"She isn't."

"Never?"

"I'm afraid not."

Anthea turns her back on the window. Gazes at the
vacuum left by the departure of her mother. Twenty
years ago she wished that her mother would walk
away. Vanish. Die. Each morning, upon waking, she
prayed that she would be alone—free. Now that the
wish has come true, it feels like yet another betrayal.
A cruel irony. "How come she hasn't sold the place?"

"She wanted it to be here if you ever came home.
She thought you might need a place to stay."

"This isn't my home."

"It was at one time."

"Not anymore." Not for more than half her life.

Anthea wanders down the hallway to the bedrooms. Footsteps loud and hollow on the polished blond floor as she passes the bathroom, the granite tub and washbasin with solid brass fixtures.

"She took everything," Anthea notes, stopping to look into her former bedroom, empty of red-and-black lacquered dresser and bed. Perhaps her mother believed she would stay here if she allowed Anthea to make the place her own, furnish it the way she wanted to suit her taste.

"Not everything," the penthouse tells her. "She left a few items for you, in the study."

"What kind of items?"

"I am not at liberty to say."

In other words, she has to look for herself. Accept, or deny, her final inheritance in person.

This isn't what she came for. She came to see if her mother—with all of her vast resources—could locate Ibrahim. Help him, maybe free him. Even if it meant losing her freedom. It was a trade she was willing to make.

Instead, she's going to be left with—what?

Anthea climbs the spiral wrought-iron staircase to the garret. The office loft that was always off limits to Anthea. Verboten territory, where she imagined her mother performing satanic rituals. Horrific ceremonies involving arcane incantations, the blood of chickens, and burnt offerings to maintain her wealth, beauty, and power. In this slope-ceilinged office, she sold her soul. Imprisoned the souls of others. Bent them to her will. It was a sanctuary that catalyzed both envy and fear in Anthea, respect and loathing; the one place she yearned to see and fought to avoid.

No different from now. Legs enervated with dread, but at the same time enlivened with curiosity. Golem feet, magically animated, climbing one step at a time.

The room is smaller than she imagined. Cramped. A single east-facing window looks out over the harbor. Floor-to-ceiling bookcases occupy the remaining three walls. A skylight admits filtered sunlight and fresh air through hidden vents.

Most of the bookshelves are empty. But half of one wall is jammed with binders similar to the one Anthea took. Her mother has been busy over the years, obsessively adding to her collection of dead plants and insects. Anthea feels as if she's standing in the back room of a museum, dusty with the dried residue of the past. Anthea runs a fingertip along the spines of the three-ring binders, the handmade paper laced with dried bits of grass, stems, leaves and the petals of flowers.

"They're yours," the penthouse says. "Willed to you, along with the house."

Anthea chooses a binder at random, pulls it from the shelf. The handmade paper is rough, dry as a tombstone against her palm. "Is she dead?"

"No. But she's moved on to a different life. This one no longer has anything to offer her."

Anthea flips open the binder to a bird-of-paradise flower, paper thin between the sealed sheets of plastic. "Did she say what they're for? What, if anything, she planned to do with them?"

"She never said anything to me, madame. I assumed that you would know what to do."

No. She stole the first binder out of anger . . . mal-ice. Perhaps this is her mother's way of spiting her in return.

Anthea replaces the binder, slides it back into place. Forget it, she doesn't want them. Her mother can keep the past. It belongs to her. She came for help, and all she's been given are dead memories.

What did she expect? Every time she needed her mother, she wasn't there. Why would this time be any different?

Anthea turns, descends the staircase into the empty glass-walled box. There is nothing for her here out-side the echo of her own footsteps, trailing after her like cold laughter.

TWENTY-FIVE

The storm turns out to be a herd of synchronized dust devils, minitornadoes that hit with the force of a category-five hurricane. A whirlwind of sand engulfs the sedan, scratches the windows, rocks the suspension, and threatens to strip the paint from the bulky sheet metal. Visibility is zero. The airport has disappeared, swallowed in a drab, featureless blur.

The BEAN agent slows, pulls off the side of the road, and comes to a complete stop. Adjusts his eyescreens, then bangs the GPS screen mounted on the dashboard.

Liz screams.

Rigo jerks his head sideways to look at her. A face looms in the swirling dust, pressed against the bulletproof glass, hood whipping in the gale, eyes and nose hidden behind infrared goggles and a camo-tan filter mask.

More faces appear, leaning close to peer into the sedan.

The door next to Jeraldo pops open, swings outward, followed by the door next to Liz. Last is the driver's door.

Gloved hands—biosuit clad, robed—reach in. Grasp Liz, then Jeraldo, and yank them out. Liz squawks, kicks, nails Rigo in the chin with the stiletto heel of one designer cardboard pump, lacquered in corporate black. Rigo and the BEAN agent are next. Rigo decides not to put up a fight. Allows himself to be half dragged, half helped out of the car.

"You can't do this!" Liz protests. "Do you know who we are?"

The roar of wind and sand carry her voice away. Rigo stands next to her, each of his arms held in a bone-crushing grip. Motherfuckers are humping industrial-strength military bodyware.

A hooded figure detaches from the group and steps up to Rigo. The way the person moves, quickly but with a slight stoop, is vaguely familiar.

"You with RiboGen?" Robo voce words mechanically distorted by the micropore filter mask. Voiceprint encrypted.

Rigo licks grit from his teeth behind closed lips. Before he can respond, the dude punches him in the stomach. Rigo grunts. Doubles over. Drops to his knees on the sand-scoured concrete. When he recovers his breath and looks up, Liz and Jeraldo are staring at him in wide-eyed horror. As if he's just had one ear cut off or a molar twisted out with a socket wrench.

"Get them inside," his assailant orders.

Two men pick Rigo up by the armpits, hustle him in

the direction of a Quonset-style building etched in the whirlwind of thinning dun-colored fog. He can't breathe. Actinic flashes detonate behind his eyes, bright as stars twinkling on a moonless night. Just before lights out, Rigo catches a brief glimpse of a protective cage, antennae, and balloon wheels on spring-loaded suspension. An old Mars buggy left over from NASA's early desert-test days.

Rigo wakes in subterranean cool. Concrete walls with no windows. Low-budget biolum panels glued to a prefab concrete ceiling. Some of the panels have fallen off in infirmity while others have gone dead. He's on a rickety carbyne-frame gurney with a gel mattress so old it's begun to stiffen and go brittle. The door across from the bed is scratched gray metal, the cuts in the surface scabbed with rust. It has a tiny square wire-mesh window that looks out on a featureless concrete corridor, painted white. The enamel has started to yellow and flake.

Shadows expand in the corridor. The door swings inward, and the BEAN agent steps inside.

Rigo sits up, wincing as his bruised stomach threatens to cramp. "What's going on?"

The BEAN agent regards him with existential, Buddha-like complacency. "Think of it as a slight detour."

"You're not with BEAN, are you?" Rigo swivels his legs over the edge of the gel mattress.

"I am, and I'm not."

Great, a metaphysician. Just what he needs in lieu of a doctor. "Mind telling me where I am?"

The BEAN agent shakes his head. "I can't."

Or won't. "Why not?"

The BEAN agent smiles. "Because then I would have to kill you, and neither of us wants that."

He says this casually, with the blasé detachment of someone who's been in this position before and knows whereof he speaks. "In other words, I should just kick back and enjoy the visit," Rigo says.

The BEAN agent's smile widens, revealing back teeth that have been sculpted to resemble miniature dice or dominoes. "Just be happy."

"Varda?" Rigo says.

"I can't pinprick our location," the IA says. "All infrared, microwave, and radio transmissions are being jellied."

Rigo shifts his attention back to his captor. "Where are Liz and Jeraldo?"

"On the path to enlightenment," the BEAN agent says, laying on more of his Dalai Lama rhetoric. "They're no longer your concern . . . just as you are no longer a concern of theirs."

Translation: They've got other problems to worry about. From this point forward he's flying solo. "What do you want from me?"

"Your help."

"With what?"

As if on cue, the door opens and a second man enters. He's waring flitcam-studded ear beads, pentagonal wire-frame eyescreens, and a dun-colored Jodhpuri-influenced suit woven out of smart fabric, a hemp-rayon blend threaded with amyloid protein wires that smell of yeast. This is complemented by a fashionable Nehru hat, white with gold circuit-board resham work.

"I'm sorry I punched you in the stomach," says the ICLU agent who approached Anthea about Ibrahim in the VRcade. "But it was necessary, to keep up appearances. No hard feelings, I hope." He extends a diplomatic hand.

Out of habit, Rigo takes it. Incredible. He's been beaten up and kidnapped by a human rights org. At least he didn't get snow-coned.

"You have a name?" Rigo asks.

"Yes."

But the dude's not going to divulge it—not even a nom de guerre to underscore his status as a militant.

The BEAN agent adjusts his powder blue tie. "Let's go for a walk," he suggests, "shall we?"

They lead him out of the room, into a maze of corridors. Every so often, Rigo catches a whiff of negative ions percolating through overhead vents. Tastes scent-free surfactants in the air cooling on his fingertips. They pass through the purple glow and drip-line trickle of a hydroponics garden. Low-light fruits and vegetables flourishing in long troughs glued to the walls. The air is humid. The tunnel ceiling sweats condensation. Beyond this, intermittent laughter bounces off the peeling walls, a bright cheery sound that lightens his mood. Soon they come to a play-room filled with kids and all different kinds of toys. Rigo stops, amazed. The kids actually look as if they're having fun, enjoying themselves. There are a couple of adult supervisors, psychological counselor types. But, by and large, the kids appear free to do what they want.

Rigo turns to his escorts. "Is Ibrahim here?"

The ICLU agent shakes his head. "I wish."

"Where is he?"

"Good question. We're still in the process of trying to reacquire him."

They move on to the hospital wing. No laughter here. It's quiet as a tomb and reminds Rigo a little of the nonprofit clinic where he met Beto before podding down to Salmon Ella's to meet Dorit. Clear plastic quarantine tents and clade-isolation cubes crowd the rooms. Secondhand Japanese hotel cylinders rise three-high in the corridor, connected by flexible PVC to exposed waste and water pipes snaking along the ceiling. Faces glare at him as he passes, dull pain-glazed eyes vivid with hatred and condemnation. It's hard to meet their gaze. Harder still to look at the motionless shapes huddled in corners or sprawled on gel mattresses.

They're showing him this for a reason. Rigo's willing to bet Liz and Jeraldo got the same guided tour and sell job. They want something from him. "So how come you grabbed me?" Rigo says. "Brought me here?"

The ICLU agent slips his hands into his jacket. The kind of subtle-ass move that sets Rigo on edge, has him wondering what's about to materialize out of a concealed pocket. "You could have handed Ibrahim over to BEAN, but didn't. Instead you went out of your way to help him."

Rigo considers this. "I didn't do all that much. Just chilled with him for a while. That's it."

"That's more than most people would have done.

Plus, you could have reported me after our initial contact, and chose not to."

And that makes him a sympathizer, a partisan. It suddenly dawns on him what's being proposed. "You want me to join the ICLU?"

The ICLU agent shrugs. "Why not? You have nothing to lose. Nothing to go back to now that you've been sacked. It would give you a chance to help out kids who are in the same situation as Ibrahim."

"What would I do?" It's not like he has a degree in volunteer work, or any direct experience. As a recruit, he leaves a lot to be desired.

"Hospital work," the ICLU agent says, launching into a prepared litany. "Reconnaissance and data analysis. Pharm work." A euphemism, no doubt, for covert action. "It's entirely up to you. Be all you can be."

"You'll be trained, of course," the BEAN agent adds. "The pay's not great, but the rewards are incalculable."

"You'd receive a per diem," the ICLU agent tells him, "based on the requirements of your assignment. That's all we can afford."

Rigo doesn't know what to say. He's stunned, flabbergasted. "I can't," he says at last.

"Why not?" the ICLU agent asks.

"Anthea." No way he can leave her.

"We'll contact her, if you like. Make her the same offer. She already has extensive experience working with kids for a nonprofit. The move would be more or less lateral."

"You didn't really want to go to Siberia anyway, did you?" the BEAN agent says to twist his arm.

"I don't know," Rigo says.

"You don't have to decide now," the BEAN agent says. "Take your time. Think it over. Talk to your *jeva* when you get back."

"You're going to let me go?"

The ICLU agent offers a placid nod. "In economic terms, you're of high use but little exchange value. Unlike your former compatriots."

Which means, Rigo surmises, that Liz and Jeraldo did not take the ICLU up on its offer. "What's going to happen to them?"

"We'll try to negotiate a swap."

"For Ibrahim?"

"If we can." The ICLU agent puckers his brow. "It all depends on how much RiboGen values them."

"If they're worth half as much as they believe they are," the BEAN agent says to Rigo, "we'll be lucky to get an even trade."

"If that doesn't work out," the ICLU agent says, "we'll request compensation for their safe return."

Rigo nods. "I didn't realize the ICLU got involved in this kind of covert-op shit."

"We're a splinter faction," the BEAN agent admits. "Not officially sponsored or recognized by the parent org."

"I see." A shadow arm.

"Are you sure you won't change your mind?" the ICLU agent asks. It doesn't sound like a threat—not quite.

It's exactly the same kind of pressure Whipplebaum put on him to go to Tiresias. No different. If he doesn't go along, he's going to end up disappointing himself or someone else. That's the implication, along with the idea that others know what's best for him.

Easier to do what his friends, family, and co-workers think than it is to think for himself. It's what he's been doing his entire life: caving in to the wishes of others, trying to be the person everybody wants him to be. As a result, he's a no one. A total blank. If he joins the ICLU he'll just end up in the same identical situation he was in at Noogenics. Ditto OAsys or Ecotrope.

"Maybe some other time," Rigo ventures.

"There is one other contribution we'd like you to consider." The ICLU agent is nothing if not persistent.

Rigo hesitates. "What's that?"

"A blood donation. It'll give us a head start on counteracting the slave pherion Ibrahim was dosed with."

"You want to develop an antipher?"

"The pherion won't go away just because Tiresias did," the BEAN agent says. "The warm-blooded plants are here to stay. Almost certainly, the pherion will be used for biodependency crimes here. Which means we will need an antipher to counteract it. The sooner, the better."

"Okay," Rigo agrees, "on one condition. I want to be taken back to the city right now, and after I donate I'm on the first flight to San Jose."

"Agreed," the ICLU agent says.

"In that case"—the BEAN agent loosens, then removes his powder blue tie—"I have to ask you to put this on."

The tie doubles as a blindfold. As the BEAN agent cinches the silk in place, images of an execution-style killing cling to Rigo's mind like scraps of paper to barbed wire.

TWENTY-SIX

Two hours after getting back from Hong Kong, Anthea is in her ap, decompressing on Cajun-spiced kelp chips and a grainy black-and-white rerun of *Some Like It Hot*, when Rigo calls. Her throat constricts, a mixture of relief and trepidation, at the sight of him grinning at her from the octagons of her eyescreens.

"Hey, baby," he says, all cheerful. "I'm home."

She blinks. "You are?" For some reason, she expected him to call before he was released. Give her some advance warning so she could prepare herself.

"I just got back a few minutes ago. I'm at San Jose International."

"That's great." She swallows at the ache in her throat. "I can't believe it."

"Me, neither. I thought they'd never let me go. You wouldn't believe what I had to do."

She adjusts her eyescreens. "You look thin," she says. "Tired."

"It's been stressful," he admits. "Plus the food they were dishing out wasn't topnotch."

She takes a deep breath, plunges ahead before she has second thoughts. "We need to talk."

"Have you found Ibrahim?"

"Not yet." The lump of fear hardens. "But something else has come up."

His forehead puckers. "What?"

"It's better if I tell you in person." There, she's committed. No turning back, no running away.

He nods, strangely sober. Could be it's just weariness. "Can I visit my moms in the hospital first?" he asks. "I want to check up on her. See how she's doing."

"She'll like that." Relieved that she's been given a brief reprieve, a chance to steady her nerves, figure out the best way to unburden herself. "I can meet you there in half an hour, if that's okay." Hopefully, having Rigo's mother around will help. Make it easier for her to spill her guts.

"Sounds good," he says. "I can't wait to see you, *mami*. We have a lot of catching up to do."

"Is that a promise?"

His frown deepens, perplexed. "What kind of question is that?"

"I don't know. I guess with you getting reclated, and then being gone for so long, it feels like we've started to grow apart. Like maybe we're not a couple anymore." God. She can't believe how insecure she sounds.

His grin returns, big enough to wipe all doubt

from her mind. "Sounds to me like maybe we need to do more than talk."

By the time Anthea arrives at the clinic, Rigo is already there. She pauses in the hallway outside his mother's room, listens to the rise and fall of his voice under biolums that stain the walls soft, sedative blue.

"How you feeling, Mama?" His voice is soft, earnest. "You don't look too good. You seem a little pale."

"I'm worn down. Exhausted. It's hard work lying here, having people around all the time."

"You taking your medication?"

"Can't not take it. If you don't, they know right away. Come back and force-feed you. Like you're a baby."

"What's going on with your leg? It getting any better?"

"There's nothing they can do. Problem is, they haven't figured that out yet. I tell them, but they're stubborn. Refuse to listen."

"Is there anything I can do?"

"A little privacy would be nice."

"You want me to leave?"

"I'm not talking right now." A heavy sigh. "To be honest I just want to go home. But they won't let me. Say they still need to run more tests. I feel like a prisoner here."

"Maybe you'll get lucky and they'll discover a cure." He says this lightly. Only half joking. "You never know. It could happen."

"Government won't let them. Even if they did,

they wouldn't let me have it. Save it for any upper-clade folks who accidentally get infected."

"What are you talking about?" Rigo says. "You're not making any sense."

"That's because you're not listening. You'd think after what just happened, losing your job, your hearing would be better."

"What's that have to do with my hearing?"

"Stone deaf," the old woman says, like she's talking to someone else in the room. "You're the one who should be in this bed. Not me."

This seems like a good time to interrupt. Anthea steps into the doorway, making a lot of noise to announce her presence. Rigo's seated in a chair by the bed, holding one of his mother's stiff gnarled hands in both of his. It's just the two of them. Rigo glances up and the old woman turns her head, offers a smile that warms and encourages Anthea. Gives her strength.

"There you are," the old woman says. "Come in."

Rigo stands. Eases around the bed. "Hey, baby." He starts toward her, arms out, then stops short.

"It's okay," she says, moving into his arms. "I'm not allergic to you right now."

"Beto?" he says, just to confirm that she's dosed herself with an antipher. Isn't going to break out in a rash.

"Yeah. I figure we've got an hour before it wears off."

He embraces her. Picks her up off the floor so she's hanging like a rag doll. It takes her a moment to relax into the hug. Let the tension ease from her limbs. He puts her down.

"Now I want some privacy," the old woman says.

"But I just got here," Rigo says.

"Shoo," she says, motioning for them to leave with her one good hand. "Go. Get out."

"You sure?" Rigo says.

"You want me to call a nurse?"

"We'll stop by later," Anthea promises.

"Later is good," the old woman says. "Just don't hurry on account of me. I'm not going anywhere."

They go to the cafeteria. Sit on a bench in a tiny attached courtyard/garden, boxed in on all sides by photovoltaic ribbon windows, and shaded by the parasol leaves of a low umbrella palm.

"So . . ." Anthea says. She clutches her hands in her lap, traces a vein on the back of one knuckle.

Rigo takes one hand, stills her restless fingers. With his other hand, he smoothes the hair from one side of her face, cups her cheek so her face tilts to one side, like she's resting on a pillow. "I almost forgot how beautiful the sun and the moon are, *mami.*"

She nuzzles her face in his palm and kisses it, meets his gaze. "You couldn't see the sky where you were, *papi*?"

"Not from the room I was locked up in. All I could see was the city. The window was like a tunnel."

"It sounds awful."

"It was no picnic. But it wasn't nearly as bad as the landing or the comet breaking apart."

"That must have been terrifying."

He nods. "I thought it was all over. I was sure I was going to die and I'd never get back to you. Never get a chance to tell you again how much I love you. How much you mean to me."

She lifts her head. "Really? That's what you were worried about?"

"All I could think of was you."

Her stomach constricts, tight as a boa, squeezing the breath from her lungs. "Even if we can't have children?

He shrugs. "We have Josué. He's a good kid. I can pretend."

"Serious? You could think of him like a son?"

"Sure. I don't know how he feels about it, or Malina. But I'd be there for him if he wants."

Anthea sits up and straightens her shoulders, steeling herself. Now is the time, she decides. Before things go too far and she loses her nerve. But she can't seem to get enough air to speak. Then the tears come. Slow at first, fat drops clinging to lower eyelids, blurring her vision before the dam breaks and they finally spill over, flooding her cheeks.

"What's wrong, baby?"

Sobs shake her. He tries to pull her close, but she fends him off. Doesn't want to be comforted.

"Did I say something wrong?"

She manages to shake her head. Can't look at him.

"What is it, then?"

It takes a half minute to recover. For the trembling and the gasps to subside to the point where she can put two words together.

"What if I told you that Malina's not really my sister? Or that Josué isn't really my nephew?"

"He's not?"

She shakes her head. Rubs her nose with the side of

one hand. "Malina's a friend. I met her while I was living on the street, before I got involved with Global Upreach." The words are coming easier. Flowing of their own volition, like the tears. Beyond her control. "That's how we know each other."

"How come you told me she's your sister?"

"Because I needed a past different from my real one, and that seemed the easiest one to invent."

Rigo touches his fingertips to his bowed forehead. "Is this a quiz? Some sort of relationship test you read about in a netzine?"

"No."

"Then I'm confused." He shakes his head. "How come you needed to invent a different past?"

"Because I didn't want to lose you. I was afraid if you knew where I came from, who I was, you'd leave."

Rigo stands, paces in front of the bench. "You mean all that stuff about being a street kid, delivering STDs, was bullshit? A story you made up?"

"No. That's all true. What's not true is the part about Malina, and where I grew up."

He stops. Doesn't say a word. Waits for her to fill in the silence.

"I was born in HK, not LA. My mother's upper-clade English. I never really knew my father. The reason I ran away from home was because my mother and I, we didn't get along. I couldn't live with her anymore, not the way she wanted me to. She dosed me with a slave pherion, an early military prototype. Kept me locked up, a prisoner in our aplex for over a year. That's why I can't have kids. I still need to take an antipher to counteract the pherion." It comes out in a jumble, scattered, like chipped and scuffed children's blocks on a playroom floor.

"I feel like I'm in a soap opera," he says. "One of those old *telenovelas* my moms watches late at night when she can't sleep."

"I'm sorry." She wants to stand, or reach out to him, but is afraid of scaring him off. "I should have told you a long time ago, right from the beginning. But I was embarrassed by who I was. I didn't want it to get in the way of things, to come between us, *papi*."

"Sounds like you didn't trust me."

"That wasn't it at all."

"Well, that's what I'm hearing." He starts to pace again, agitated. "You didn't think I'd understand. You were afraid to confide in me. Like I'd hold your past against you."

"Would you have?"

"No." A single shake of the head. Emphatic.

"You're just saying that."

He stops. Glares. "So now it's my fault that you lied to me?"

It's all coming out wrong. The words are getting all twisted. "I just wanted us to be together. I was confused. Messed up."

"No different than now." He runs a hand over the top of his head. "Shit. Makes me think maybe I should have been serious about being reclaimed."

"What are you talking about?"

"Nothing." He removes his hand from his head. "So why are you telling me this now? After two years?"

"I couldn't live with myself any longer, knowing

that I hadn't been totally honest with you." She leans forward and cradles her head in her hands.

"At least you feel guilty," he says. "I guess that's supposed to make me feel better."

"I made a mistake," she tells him. "Everybody makes mistakes." Her face feels swollen, bloated with despair.

"I have to think," he says. "How do I know the future won't be more of the same? You didn't trust me once. What's to say it won't happen again? I mean, what's with the skeleton doll in your dresser? And the binder full of preserved plants? Is that another deep dark secret I'm going to find out about the next time you have an attack of conscience?"

Anthea blinks. Straightens up. "You were in my apartment?"

"After I got back from Puntarenas. You'd dropped offline. So I knew you were in trouble . . . that something was wrong. No one knew where you were, so I went to find you. That seemed like the first place to look for clues."

Anthea stiffens. "And that gave you free license to search my ap? Go through my private things?"

"If you'd bothered to tell me what the fuck was going on I wouldn't have had to. I didn't have a choice."

"When were you going to tell me you'd gone through my stuff?" she demands, her cheeks flushed. "Or were you just going to keep it to yourself? Like that *chucha cuerera* you were with."

"What are you talking about? What slut?"

"The woman you went to see the night you visited your mom. After you called to tell me you had to stop by work."

"How did you? . . ." His voice trails off.

"I'm not stupid." Anthea cinches her hands into fists and crosses her arms tight over her chest. It's all she can do not to hit him, to hold herself together. "If you were unhappy—"

"It's not what you think," he says. "I swear."

"Then why didn't you tell me?"

He throws up his hands in exasperation. Goes all indignant on her. "*Chingalo!*" he says. Fuck it. "I don't need this bullshit."

And heads out. Leaves her sitting on the bench, throat aching, spine taut, eyes gritty as rain-washed bone.

This is it, Anthea thinks. It's all over between them. Not even the beginning of the end.

TWENTY-SEVEN

The South SJ detention center where Beto is being held is a defunct office-park.

After checking in at the main desk and going through security, Rigo is led by a stern security guard across crumbling asphalt varnished with smooth diamond lacquer. Through the clear glaze, the preserved remnants of pre-ecocaust Americana are clearly visible. Cigarette butts. A discarded lottery ticket. The flattened blue plastic of a ballpoint pen cap. Shit the work crews didn't bother to pick up before laying down the sealant.

The security guard leads him into the skylight-illuminated lobby of a satellite building, through a wooden door, into an office space packed with gray cubicles. The place is stuffy, redolent with the potpourri scent of disinfectant and surfactant disassemblers. A susurrus of conversation wafts on the filtered, recirculated air. Subliminal voices. Not that there's any privacy here. None of the cubicles have doors; escape, and any contact between prisoners, is prevented by law enforcement pherions that result in instant paralysis.

At the end of one row, the guard doses Rigo with an antipher—"You've got ten minutes"—then turns and leaves. Rigo heads down the aisle, reading the labels next to each cubicle for Beto's cell number. The cubicles are small, maybe two meters square, barely enough room for a gel bed and a foam sink/toilet stall. The inmates are dressed in pink sprayon jumpsuits, formless negligee-thin crepe that biodegrades in about thirty seconds when exposed to direct sunlight. The ceiling lights are evenly spaced rows of biolum panels set in gray acoustic ceiling tile.

It's depressing. Some of his mood could be residual gloom from the conversation with Anthea. He feels despondent and eerily detached, the same way he did when Tiresias broke up, leaving him weightless. Spinning in free fall. Except this time, there's no shuttle to pick him up, to keep him from crashing and burning or losing it entirely and careening out of orbit.

"That you, bro?"

Rigo turns to a cubicle on his right. Lost in thought, he's been walking blindly, paying zero attention to what's around him. It takes a second to register the face in front of him.

Beto snaps his fingers, waves a hand in front of Rigo's nose. "And I thought I was in the fucking twilight zone."

Rigo ducks into the cube. Takes a seat on the bed

and leans forward, elbows on his knees. "This place is the fucking pits."

"Tell me about it." Instead of a caged *tíguere*, bristling at his captivity, Beto looks docile, heavy lidded.

"How you doing, bro?" Rigo asks. "You seem a little out of sorts."

"I'm tired." Beto yawns. "They got me dosed. I can't keep my eyes open. All I want to do is sleep."

"So what happened?"

"They busted my ass, that's what. Illegal pharming. Possession of unregistered pherions. Intent to distribute. You name it."

"That's total bullshit," Rigo says. The obligatory denial, spoken for the benefit of whoever happens to be eavesdropping.

"According to the assistant DA," Beto says, "they got evidence."

"What kind of evidence?"

"Antisense inhibitors. Protosome nucleotide modules. Restriction enzymes." Beto sniffs. "But it's all circumstantial. Shit I coulda picked up via casual contact or in the environment. Nothing they can pin on me."

"How do you know?"

"They wanted me to confess. Name names. Suppliers. Clients. All of which tells me they don't have shit."

Rigo's not so sure. The nape of his neck prickles with sweat. What if the police decide to go after him . . . or Anthea? Question his mother? No way she can lie, even if she wanted to. "You got an attorney?"

"No. I've decided to represent myself."

Rigo suppresses a grimace. "Could be worse, bro." It's as upbeat as he can be, under the circumstances.

"Yeah?" Beto's eye twitches. "How?"

Rigo shrugs. "You could've opted to go with a public defender."

Beto jerks, a short guffaw. "You got a point. Plus, I could look like you. Like I just got the shit kicked out of me, and my life's over."

"I had a fight with Anthea," Rigo explains.

Beto takes a seat next to Rigo on the bed. Appears willing to listen. "I told you to dump that bitch," he says, commiserating. "Warned you she was trouble."

"You got that right."

"What'd she do to you, bro? I've never seen you so freaked out. Not that you aren't a crazy fuck to begin with."

Rigo sighs. "That makes me feel better." Strangely enough, it does. He slumps into the camaraderie the way he would a comfortable merengue riff.

"She cheat on you?" Beto asks. "Dirty dick you with some asshole while you were out of town?"

"No. Nothing like that."

"Then what's the problem, bro?"

"It's complicated." He doesn't know where to begin. Doesn't know how things got out of hand.

"Complicated how?" Beto says.

"She's not who I thought she was."

Beto lets out a snort that manages to be both derisive and affectionate at the same time. "Bro, I got news for you. No one is who they say they are. I can't believe it took you this long to figure that out."

"Supposedly, her moms is English. On top of that, she grew up in HK—not LA."

"She's a *chinita*?"

"No. That's just where she was born. But get this.

Not only is she part English, she's upper-clade. Probably has an inheritance up to here." Rigo rocks his head in his hands, hefts it like a bowling ball he's getting weary of holding.

"So you've got it made, bro. Everything you ever wanted. And you don't even have to work for it. What more could you ask for?"

"Except she doesn't want to have anything to do with it," Rigo says. "She hates her moms, ran away from home."

"Well, no relationship's perfect. She drop any other bombs on you?"

Rigo unloads the whole sordid story. It comes out less dramatic in the retelling——more trivial.

"Sounds like she pulled a fast one on you, bro. Like possibly there's a few more skeletons waiting to turn up."

"That's what I'm thinking."

"Makes me wonder about her moms, too. If maybe the two of them are birds of a feather."

"Her moms?"

"Yeah. I'm starting to wonder if maybe she's the one who screwed me over. Set me up."

"Wait a minute," Rigo says, making a T with his hands. "Time out. When exactly did you meet Anthea's moms?"

"It makes sense," Beto goes on, still rapping to himself. "A haut-goût *puta* like that. I should never have trusted her. But I figured she knew you, so I'd help out. Play the role of the Good Samaritan for a change. In return, I get fucked."

"What the hell are you talking about?" Rigo says,

louder. "I never met Anthea's moms. I wouldn't know her if I bumped into her on the street."

"That gerontocrat *puta* at Salmon Ella's," Beto tells him. "The one I arranged for you to meet the other night."

"Dorit?"

"I guess. She didn't tell me her name."

Rigo tries to speak. Can't. His thoughts feel lopsided—misshapen. His tongue lies paralyzed in his mouth, botoxed by disbelief. "How do you know for certain it was Anthea's moms?" he finally stammers.

"Because she told me. Said she hadn't seen Anthea in a while, and asked about her. Wanted to know details."

"What kind of details?"

"How she was doing. What she looked like. Did I see her often? Was she happy? The usual shit you'd expect from somebody's moms. You could tell she had more than a casual interest. That it wasn't an act. She definitely knew you two were an item."

"Did she say anything else? About herself or what she was doing? How she knew about me?"

"To be honest, bro, I didn't ask too many questions. Like I said, she dropped your name so I didn't think anything of it. Plus, I figured it was none of my business. You know?"

"How'd she get in touch with you?"

"Like everyone else. Her IA left a message, asked me to call back."

Rigo massages his forehead, pushing the wrinkles around. "What I'd like to know is how she found out about me. Where she got my name." She conveniently left that out of their conversations. The same way she left Anthea out.

"Sniffers, bro. Send out enough of them and you can gather any information you want. All it takes is time and money."

And Dorit has plenty of both. Twenty years and unlimited resources to scour every nook and cranny of the planet, if that's what it took. It occurs to Rigo that Dorit has probably known Anthea's whereabouts for a long time, and decided to do nothing. Was simply biding her time, waiting for the right moment or way to reestablish contact.

"What did you two rap about," Beto says, "when you were together? She must have said something."

Rigo shakes his head, playing dumb for the bitcams. No sense letting on that he knows more than he does, even to Beto. "Not much. I mean, we talked about what it was like to grow old, the spiritual legacy of the ecocaust, and metaphysical rebirth. But that was pretty much it."

"She didn't ask about Anthea?"

"Nope, the subject never came up." No way he's going to risk dragging Anthea into what happened on Tiresias.

"You're about to get irritated," Varda informs him with clinical matter of factness.

Rigo brushes off the interruption, swiping the air with one hand as if swatting at a fly.

"Could be she just wanted to meet you, bro," Beto ventures. "Spec you out, see who's kicking it with her little girl."

"Probably," Rigo says. That might have been part of it, he thinks. Beyond just keeping an eye on him.

Making sure he didn't infect the Tiresias warm-blooded plants. Ironic that the bioenslavement Dorit was trying to avoid was the exact situation Anthea had fled years earlier.

Rigo wets his lips. He can still taste the sweet citrus of Dorit's parting kiss. Like it never went away, or is constantly being refreshed. Maybe the softwire connection to Tiresias is functional again, remote-linking him realtime to whatever pherion she sprayed into her mouth.

A gift, which I trust you'll share with someone else.

Rigo breaks out in hives, starts to itch. So this is what Varda was babbling about. His time is almost up. He stands. "I have to go, man. Antipher's wearing off."

Beto stands. "Keep in touch, bro. It was good to see you. I'm glad you stopped by. No shit." He cuffs Rigo on the side of the head.

"Me, too." Rigo feels awkward. This is the most affectionate Beto has been with him in years. Since they were fifth-grade kids. "What do you want me to say to Mama? Anything?"

"Tell her that I love her."

"That's all?"

"Not much else to say." Beto shrugs.

Rigo nods. "Okay."

The chafing intensifies. Fiery. Itchy buboes erupt under his armpits and around his groin, spread to his scalp. Unbearable. "Take care, bro," Rigo says, beating a hasty retreat. Backing out of the cubicle.

"You, too." Beto says. "I'll see you around. In the meantime, don't do anything I wouldn't do."

Rigo returns Beto's grin, feels like a mirror reflecting back what his brother wants to see. Expects.

It's what he's been doing his entire life. Trying to please people . . . be the person everyone wants him to be. In the neighborhood, all the way through school, and finally at Noogenics. The grin curdles. Twists into a grimace. Time to be his own person, to do what he wants, for a change, no matter how much it hurts.

"You have a message," Doug informs Anthea.

She shakes her head, doesn't want to hear it. Presses a tear-reddened cheek against the window of the pod. Outside, the white-cap water of the bay looks unreal, shiny as acrylic under a veil of clouds.

"'What's gone and what's past help / Should be past grief,'" the IA quotes, still stuck on Shakespeare. "'The bitter past, more welcome is the sweet.'"

A train moving in the opposite direction flashes by, obscuring her view. "I liked it better when you were suicidal."

"'Our remedies oft in ourselves do lie,'" Doug reminds her, "'Which we ascribe to Heaven.'"

Anthea makes a face. "Who's the message from?"

"There's no address or name. It's either unregistered or heavily encrypted."

So there's no way to respond.

Anthea blinks, then pushes away from the window. Waits for her eyescreens to uncrumple, and the tingle of adrenaline to subside from her knuckles. "All right"—she might as well get it over with—"I'm ready."

Dearest Theodora,

*Don't worry. By the time you receive this, I'll
be gone. Out of your life forever. You don't
have to run anymore. Not from me, at least.
You're free. Hopefully, so am I. It's too late to
say I'm sorry, but I am. I don't expect you to
forget—but perhaps you can find it in your
heart to forgive. If not, that's fine. You're the
one who has to live with the decision, not me.*

*By the way, I met your tíguere. He seems
nice enough. Sincere. You could do worse. Not
that you need my approval.*

*For what it's worth, I've never stopped lov-
ing you. And never will.*

Yours eternally,
Mom

Anthea closes her eyes, shutting out the words.
Slips off her eyescreens. Feels the light from the window beating against her lids. Her pulse fluttering as
fast as bird wings, struggling to hold her aloft against
the crushing weight of her mother's words.

"I'll never be free," she whispers. All she can think
of in the blood-mottled dark of the past.

" 'Pray you now,' " Doug says, " 'forget and forgive.' "

TWENTY-EIGHT

H e's doing okay," Rigo tells his mother after the visit with Beto. "Looks good, is managing to keep his spirits up."

"I knew this would happen one day," his mother says philosophically. "It was only a matter of time." She stares at a bouquet of violinias someone has brought in to brighten up and deodorize the room.

"He claims he's innocent," Rigo says in Beto's defense. Compelled to stick up for his brother because for once Beto didn't get on his case, deride him about being a sellout or a pussy.

"What else is he going to say?" His mother sighs. "He's not stupid, but he's not as smart as he thinks, either. I suppose I should be grateful one of you has the brains to stay out of trouble."

Rigo can't bring himself to tell her that he lost his job. Not yet. He doesn't want to stress her out any more than she already is. He'll give her the news when the shock of Beto's arrest wears off. By that time, with any luck, he'll have another job. Can tell her he decided it was time for a change.

"Where's Anthea?" his mother asks, turning her gaze on him. "I thought she'd be with you."

Rigo squirms in his seat. He half expected to run into Anthea here. Almost didn't come because he didn't want to face her this soon and his head's still reeling from the revelation that Dorit is her mom. He needs time to think.

His mother's pupils sharpen, fix him with steely pinpoints. "Is everything all right?"

Rigo slumps back in the chair. There's no escape. No way to worm his way out of telling her. "To be honest, Mama, I don't know."

"Why not?"

"We had a fight and she told me things. I mean, she didn't tell me things that she should have." It sounds confusing, even to him. Shadows from the umbrella palms outside the window next to her bed vibrate against the walls.

"Everybody has fights," she says, pragmatic. "Says things they regret. Regrets things they don't say."

"She lied to me, Mama. From the beginning. About who she was and where she came from."

"Are you talking about growing up in Hong Kong, and running away from home to escape her upper-clade mother?"

Rigo's jaw drops. "She told you?"

His mother sniffs. "Personally, I don't see what the problem is. What you're so upset about."

"She should have told me sooner. When we first

started going out and spending time with Malina and Josué."

"Bullshit."

Rigo stares, stunned by her *sinvergüencería*. As far as he knows, his mother has never uttered a word of profanity in her life. She'll probably have to recite a dozen Hail Marys a day for a year, at least, to bleach the stain of sin from the white handkerchief of her soul.

"Just because your *jeva* doesn't tell you everything about herself," his mother says, "doesn't make her a dishonest person. I'll bet there're details about your life you haven't told her. Or me, for that matter."

Maria Sanchez, Rigo thinks, staring out at the courtyard. He's avoided telling Anthea how he lost his virginity. It was a long time ago. He was young. Doesn't want to have to keep living it down for the rest of his life. Once was enough.

"Could be she wasn't lying just to you," his mother goes on. "Could be she was also lying to herself, trying to forget what had happened to her."

Rigo shifts his attention from the courtyard to his mother. "I don't see why you're defending her. Taking her side."

His mother reaches out stiff armed, crimps his fingers in hers. "Because I've been in her shoes, *mijo*. I know what it's like to get dumped by some *pajero* who's too stupid to know a good thing when he's got it."

"I wasn't sure you'd ever want to see me again," Anthea says when she opens the door, lets him into her ap.

"Some stuff's come up," he says. Her face is puffy, her eyes red. It's obvious that she hasn't been celebrating her potential availability for dating these last couple of hours.

"What kind of stuff?" She goes to the kitchen table, pulls out two chairs and sits down in one.

"After I left the hospital," Rigo says, settling into the chair next to her, "I went to visit Beto."

"And?"

Rigo shrugs. "He's pretty much how you'd expect. Trying to put a good face on things, keep his spirits up."

"How do things look?"

"Not good. He plans to defend himself." Rigo shakes his head. He doesn't want to get sidetracked—doesn't want to dwell on the misfortune of others. "Anyway, we started talking. About the night I visited my moms and called to tell you that I'd be late."

Anthea gives a tentative nod. "You called me back a little later to say you had to stop by work."

"Right." He's encouraged. She seems willing to listen, hear his side of the story. "Except what I was really doing was running an errand for Beto. I went to Salmon Ella's to meet with someone. A client of his."

Her eyes narrow. "The woman."

"A *vieja*," he says quickly. "An old gerontocrat, confined to an exoskeleton, who was dying and needed help. The thing is, it was bullshit. She didn't need help. She just wanted to meet me."

An uneasy look creeps into Anthea's eyes . . . like a wild animal trying to decide if it's in danger. The gnawed, ragged edge of her left thumbnail bites into the end of her index finger. "Why?"

"She was part of the Tiresias project, one of the

colonists. I didn't know that at the time. This was be-fore I learned I was going to be a part of the imple-mentation team."

"But she knew."

"Yeah." Rigo runs the tip of his tongue along the inside of his teeth. "I met her again on the comet. Turns out she wanted to give me a gift that I was sup-posed to pass on to you."

Anthea presses the knuckle of her thumb to her lips. "Why would an old woman—a gerontocrat—give you a gift for me?"

"Her name was Dorit," he says. "According to Beto she asked about you before the meeting with me."

Anthea's hand starts to tremble. She gets up fast. Makes a beeline for the bedroom, where she sits on the floor in front of the dresser and yanks open the bottom drawer.

Rigo follows at a safe distance. Watches from two meters away as she takes out the black-lacquered cof-fin box, puts it on the carpet, then picks up the binder and rests it on the crossed legs of her lap.

"What's with the skeleton?" he says. Might as well get the story while they're coming clean.

Anthea glances from the binder to the box. Opens the lid to expose the plaster figure with the black grin and red saxophone. "It's a Day of the Dead doll that my father brought home for my birthday one year. I named it Jobina."

"That's a pretty name," he says, moving next to her, hoping that now is the time for reconciliation.

Anthea nods. "It means 'sought-after.' For a long time a part of me kept hoping that he would show up one day. I don't know why. After all the trouble with my mother, I guess I wanted someone to care about me. Anyone."

"What happened to him?" Rigo says. "Where is he?"

"Good question. He was an old military-industrial-complex warrior. He took off when I was only four. That's all my mother ever said."

"Do you still hope he'll come back?"

"No. Not anymore. I'm not sure why I kept the doll. I should have gotten rid of it a long time ago."

"Maybe you're not ready to bury him yet, *mami*." Or whatever part of herself the skeleton embodies.

Anthea nods. "It's hard to let go. It was the only thing he ever gave me." She returns her attention to the binder, flips to the first page and traces the fragile stem of a flower with her fingertip. "I stole this from my mother, took it with me on the LOHop out of Hong Kong."

Rigo joins her on the carpet. "What is it?"

"Favorite plants from her private garden. She collected them during the ecocaust, before they died out."

"Shit must have meant a lot to her," Rigo notes. "She rapped nonstop about the past while we were together."

Anthea fans through several stiff pages, lots of them blank, containing only bits and pieces of the plants that used to be there. Stops when she gets to a faded plumeria flower close to the end.

"What was my mother like?" she says.

It takes a second for Rigo to find the word he's looking for. "Sad."

"How?"

"Full of regret about the past. Things she'd done.

Hadn't done. Shit that was extinct, gone forever. At the same time she seemed pathetic. Rundown, like she'd given up and was wasting away."

Anthea's mouth crimps tight at the corners. "Did she say anything about me?"

"No."

"I'm not surprised." Anthea flips the page to a dried sliver of bamboo leaf. "I got a delayed-delivery message from her this afternoon. After the hospital. It was sent a couple of days ago."

"Just after Tiresias blew up," Rigo says.

"I guess."

"What did she say?"

"That she was sorry. That she still loved me. That she met you and thought that I could do worse."

"Really? She said that?" Rigo can't believe it; no one's ever said that about him before.

Some of the brittleness in Anthea's lips relaxes, like wax softening under a candle flame. "I think she was trying to make amends. Give us her blessing. Not that it matters anymore."

"It might. If not to you, then to her."

"Maybe." Anthea closes the binder, as if shutting a book on that chapter of her life. "So . . . What are you supposed to give me?"

Rigo hesitates, tries to read her expression. "Are you still pissed at me?" he says, unable to gauge her mood.

"Does that make a difference?"

"I don't want to make things worse, *mami*." Any worse, and he'll have no one to dance merengue with except Varda.

"Do you have to give it to me?" Anthea gnaws her lower lip. "Can't you just tell me what it is?"

He shakes his head. "It's better if I don't. Trust me. It wouldn't be the same." Besides, there's no telling who might be listening in.

"Rigo?" Varda interrupts in a soft cochlear whisper. "I know this isn't the best of times, but I thought you should know. I've pinpricked Ibrahim."

TWENTY-NINE

Where is he?" Anthea asks, one hand on Rigo's arm.
"Costa Rica. The RiboGen reclade clinic in Puntarenas."

"The same place you were?"

Rigo nods, staring at the closed binder resting on the floor next to them. "They must be planning to reclade him. Either back to the Tiresias ecotecture or a completely different project."

"So what happens now?" Her fingers gouge his arm. "There must be something we can do."

"Varda?" Rigo says.

"I can remote-link you," Varda tells him over the conference connection his IA and Doug have set up so they can all infoshare. "Direct stream."

"I'm going, too," Anthea says.

"All you'll get are visuals," Varda says. "You won't be softwired the same way Rigo is."

"I don't care. It's better than nothing."

" 'Nothing is / But what is not,' " Doug says.

"Go to the sugar skull in the living room," Varda tells them.

"My *calavera*?" Anthea says. "What for?"

"It has a softwire link."

Anthea leads Rigo into the living room, over to the wooden crucifix tacked to the wall and next to it, on a small shelf, the brightly colored sugar skull she picked up in LA during a Days of the Dead celebration. The life-size skull is bone white, the sugar tinted red and green around the eye and nose sockets and embellished with frilly yellow and blue ribbons. It peers at them with tarnished tinfoil eyes.

"Softwired?" Anthea says. "I'm not sure I know what that means in the present situation."

"The skull contains molectronics to convert biochemical information into digital signals and vice versa," the IA says.

Rigo turns from the sugar skull to Anthea. "Ribo-Gen or BEAN must have set up the remote link to monitor you after Ibrahim disappeared from the clinic."

"In case he showed up here?" she says.

"Right. Through the skull, they could bombard your ap with sniffers. Or remote dose it with pherions or antiphers. That way, they wouldn't have to set foot in the place. Could take action as soon as they located him."

" 'Alack, there lies more peril in thine eye,' " Doug quotes, "Than twenty of their swords.' "

Rigo steps up to the skull. Lays both hands on the petrified lump of sugar. Sharp eyebrows and cheekbones, grainy under his fingertips. "Okay, whenever you're ready," he tells Varda.

Anthea's hand squeezes his upper arm, a tourniquet of urgency and fear as they link from the room into—

—a birdcage of vines. Lush jungle topiary, every leaf and blossom swarming with bees and clouds of variegated butterflies. Rigo salivates at the touch of lemon and cloves tainted with tannin. He tastes eucalyptus in the brackish air, peppermint, mildew, and fresh pine resin.

"What am I looking at?" Anthea asks.

"The ribozone," Rigo says. "Biomorph representations of ecotectural structures and data flow."

"Where's Ibrahim?"

"Over there," Varda says. A pink-and-chartreuse butterfly teeters in the direction of a tropical, spindly-limbed cactus that's twisted into the shape of a small boy pockmarked with flowers the way Maria Sanchez had acne. Under the petals the skin is shriveled and dry, starving for moisture.

Anthea walks over to the stunted figure. "This is him?"

"His clade-profile and iDNA pattern," Varda says.

"The various types of flowers represent different pherions," Rigo adds. "The bees and butterflies are information exchange."

"They don't look too healthy," Anthea says.

It's true. Compared to a much larger topiary figure—meticulously pruned and bursting with petunias, lilacs, goosefoot violets, and pansies—the flowers, butterflies, and bees on Ibrahim's poorly sculpted avatar look sickly. Lethargic.

"He's been sanitized," Varda says. "All unregistered pherions have been purged from his system."

"What about the slave pherion?" Anthea says.

"Officially, the unlicensed subpherion he got from Rigo has been removed. But the other three subpherions, which are legally registered, are still present and accounted for."

"So he's in the same situation he was when I first got him," Anthea says, hollow. "If he doesn't get dosed with the missing pherion soon, he'll start to get sick again and could die."

"Yes. It's back to one-squared all over again."

"Any idea what they plan to do with him?" Rigo says.

"He's being transferred to a RiboGen research station in Nepal that is gengineering humans for low-pressure and low-oxygen environments. It uses the same warm-blooded ecotecture as Tiresias."

"When does he leave?" Anthea asks.

If it's not for a few days, Rigo thinks, there might be a way to save him. Petition for his release through legal channels.

"As soon as he checkmarks out," the IA tells them, "and is given a clean invoice of health."

Anthea sags. "So it's over. We've lost him." Her voice is dead, blunt and dull-edged with defeat. "If we help him escape and can't get to him in time, we run the risk of killing him."

"Maybe not," Rigo says. "Can we spec what's happening to him? Realtime?"

" 'O, woe is me,' " Doug says. " 'To have seen what I have seen, see what I see!' "

A translucent, rectangular window, superimposed on the ribozone construct, opens up in front of Rigo. The nested picture-in-a-picture shows Ibrahim. He's lying on a bed in an examination room like the one where the cauc poked and prodded Rigo. His eyes are closed; he's sleeping or unconscious. Under the intense biolums his skin is sallow, the same tarnished ivory as Anthea's puppet.

Next to Rigo, Anthea tenses. Her breath catches, snags on a stifled cry. She reaches out with her free hand. A man appears, the same bald-headed cauc who prepped Rigo. Anthea's hand recoils, knots into a fist as the cauc picks up Ibrahim's right arm and adjusts a sensor pad pasted to the bony wrist.

"What about the remote link?" Rigo says. "Is there any way to stream Ibrahim the pherion he needs to survive away from the slave ecotecture? The pherion I gave him the night we were together?"

"He's not set up for a softwire connection," Varda says. "It's not possible for you to remote-link with him directly."

"What about indirectly?"

"Through the surrounding environment?" Varda says, skeptically. "A nearby plant or sensor?"

"I have something a little different in mind," Rigo says.

The arrangement of flowers on the rosebush topiary changes as Varda uploads the clade-profile of the cauc.

"It looks lots different from Rigo's," Anthea says. "Are you sure this is going to work—that you can do a cross-clade transfer?"

"Guess we'll find out," Rigo says. Until now, the data exchange over his softwire connection has been same-clade, between him and Tiresias.

"The molectric circuitry is ecotecture-independent," Varda tells them. "So is the digital information."

"No problem," Rigo says. He's feeling optimistic.

" 'Lord, what fools these mortals be!' " Doug says.

A third persona forms in the clump of rose-bushes . . . sprouts the familiar bouquet that identifies Rigo's clade-profile.

"Harness yourself," Varda tells Rigo.

He tenses, uncertain what to expect when the connection is established. A red butterfly detaches from one of his pansies, flutters in the direction of the old cauc. At the same time, a green butterfly clinging to the cauc takes off from a big tiger lily, drifts over to the pansy. Makes contact.

A faint tickle needles Rigo in the spine. Worms its way into his nerves, wriggles along myelin and leaps across receptors, riding a surge of adrenaline.

"How are you, *papi*?" Anthea says.

He can feel her gaze on him, the warm breath of her attention. "Pretty good," he says. "No big deal."

A wave of fatigue undercuts the rush. Body slams him. Turns his muscles into mush. All he wants to do is lie out on a beach, take a nap. He yawns, strains to keep his eyes not just open but alert. Focused.

The first butterfly is followed by a second, then a third, until there's a steady stream of them moving back and forth. A nonstop parade. All that's missing is confetti and music. Several of the flowers on his to-piary have changed color. Ditto those on the cauc as the two of them sync up, exchange digital body fluid. A few blossoms trade places while others change shape, reveal hieroglyphic configurations of line code as they reassemble and repixelate.

On the realtime window, the white lab-coated cauc leaves the room. Shuts the door behind him.

"Shit," Anthea says.

"He'll come back," Rigo says.

"What if he doesn't?"

"Then we'll find someone else who's remote-linkable." At some point, Ibrahim has to come into close physical contact with a person who can trans-mit the pherion to him *mano y mano.*

The door opens and the cauc reenters, coffee cup in hand. No wonder Rigo feels dead tired. He's run-ning on fumes.

"See," Rigo says. "He just needed a pick-me-up. A lit-tle something to jump-start his gentrified metabolism."

The cauc takes a swig, sets the cup on a desk, ad-justs his eyescreens, brushes a piece of lint from one cuff, and then walks over to Ibrahim. Touches his fore-head, peels back one eyelid to peer into dilated pupils.

Anthea eases her death grip on Rigo's biceps, ex-hales some of the tension she's been holding.

"Uh-oh," Varda says.

"What?" Rigo looks around. Doesn't see shit, but isn't exactly sure what he's looking for, either.

" 'One woe doth tread upon another's heel,' " Doug intones over the conference link, " 'So fast they follow.' "

"That's really helpful," Rigo says, "tells me a lot. Maybe you could repeat it for me in English."

Outside the frame of the realtime window, a butterfly the size of a bat emerges from the leaves of an
overhanging tree, lands on a branch of his avatar, and
morphs into a black-anodized beetle with scimitar
pincers.

"What the fuck is that?" Rigo says.

Neither IA responds. Meanwhile, the beetle is
promptly making its way up the limbs of his avatar
with Götterdämmerung certainty. Seems to know exactly where it's going and what it intends to do when
it gets there.

"Security pherion," Varda says, after its time-delay
hiccup.

Shit. Rigo rests his forehead against the front edge
of the shelf. "How come you didn't warn me there
was security?"

"What did you expect? A walk in the cake?"

Several more gargantuan butterflies appear out of
the surrounding foliage . . . change into beetles as
soon as they attach to him. Rigo groans. If this keeps
up, it won't be long before he finds himself in a disaster of Homeric proportions.

"You want to tell me what the hell these things—?"

The first beetle bites him, sinks its mandibles into
the stem of a violet and starts to grind away, like a
dog gnawing a bone. An acid rash blooms under
Rigo's skin. A slow, formic burn that stirs up the
smell of ammonia and the poisonous taste of lead.
His stomach clenches. He swallows at the queasiness.
Grits his teeth. His pulse races. He's got heart palpitations the way Lady Chatterly had orgasms.

"Don't worry," Varda says. "You're doped with
antiphers."

These turn out to be Lilliputian ants that swarm to his rescue. What they lack in size, they try to make up for in numbers. Problem is, the Puntarenas ecotecture boasts first-rate security. It's armed to the teeth. It doesn't take a genius to figure out that Rigo is fighting a losing battle. It's only a matter of time before he's overwhelmed. History.

"Download status?" he asks.

"Almost complete," Varda says.

Rigo grimaces. "Can't you speed up the transfer rate? I'm getting eaten alive here." The feeling in his extremities is gone, and a frigid paralysis is creeping toward his chest and lungs.

"It won't be long now," Varda says.

"You can say that again."

The carnage intensifies. Dead bees join the snipped flowers littering the ground at his feet. Rigo breathes deep, can't seem to get any air. The palpitations have slowed to a lethargic pace. Long time between beats, and getting longer. He can't feel Anthea's grip anymore. He opens his mouth. No words come out. His lips and tongue are elephantine. All he can manage is a slurred grunt.

"End of the line," Varda announces. Cochlear attenuation stretches the IA's voice into taffy. Elastic, fiber-thin words.

Rigo blinks. His vision remains blurred. Singed black from macular degeneration and retinal decay. The cloud of butterflies around his avatar looks amorphous, in chaotic disarray just before they disintegrate, turn to ash and settle to the ground in a funeral veil of black that darkens the inside of his wraparounds.

* * *

"Rigo? Can you hear me?"

The words detonate at the base of his skull. A big-bang flare that expands from a singularity, spreads into the darkness like a newborn universe. Rigo swallows, chokes on vomit, coughs.

"Get it up," the voice says. "Anthea needs you."

Varda. The IA's exhortation Dopplers in, siren urgent, high-pitched.

Face pressed hard to the floor, carpet smashed against his cheek and the crumpled foil of his wraparounds, Rigo flails for consciousness. Light seeps in around one edge of the collapsible frame, a knife-edge sliver. Scalpel sharp, it slices open his eyelids. Hurts like a motherfucker as it cuts his eyeballs.

"Hurry," Varda says.

" 'To unpathed waters, undreamed shores,' " another voice says, chorusing in.

"Anthea?" Rigo struggles to lift his head. Lets it fall back down.

" 'When sorrows come,' " the second voice says, " 'they come not single spies, / But in battalions.' "

Not Anthea. Doug.

Rigo reaches out a hand. Encounters braided strands of hair, spread out across the carpet.

Panic gores him. The hair is trembling. He follows one strand to cold skin caught in the grip of a spasm. His hand shakes in response, the seizure looping back with closed-circuit amplification. His spine shudders, his teeth rattle.

"Rise and sign," Varda says. "Up and atom. Vibrate a leg."

Rigo winces. Opens his eyes. Blinks away tears.

Anthea is collapsed on the floor next to him. Splayed arms and legs. Mouth open, eyes closed. Blue-tinged skin. Except for the twitching, she's not moving.

"What"—it comes out Wud—"happened?" Abend.

"You bled through," Varda says. "Transferred the Puntarenas security pherions to her."

While she was holding his arm.

"Ow lung ugh-o?"

"Three minutes, fifteen seconds" Varda says.

Rigo pulls his legs to his chest, rolls onto his knees, then inches forward at what feels like a worm's pace. His head throbs, ripe as a sun-distended melon. He licks copper and salt from his lips. Rubs at his nose. His fingers come away red, bright with blood.

" 'Hit."

"Anthea's not breathing," Varda says. "You're dashing out of time."

" 'Uck."

" 'Golden lads and girls all must,' " Doug says, " 'As chimney-sweepers, come to dust.' "

Rigo bends over Anthea. Brushes hair from her face, revealing cyanosis-pale lips. He eases her onto her back, tilts her head back, exposing the perfect skin of her neck and the accordion ribs of her trachea.

" 'Let Hercules himself do what he may,' " Doug says to him, " 'The cat will mew and dog will have his day.' "

With a thumb, Rigo opens Anthea's mouth. Then he inhales deeply, presses his lips to hers, and exhales, emptying himself.

THIRTY

The pod drops them off at the narrow footpath that leads into the Angel Tree park. It's late, well past midnight. In the dark, it takes several minutes for Anthea and Rigo to wrestle his mother out of the pod. It's hard work. With all the bone she's put on in the last few months, she weighs about twice what she would if she wasn't carrying two skeletons around inside her.

They prop her against the trunk of an umbrella palm, where she leans rigid as a cigar store Indian hauled out of museum storage and dusted off. Rigo fastens a biolum band around his head, hands another one to Anthea. With both of them lit up, the darkness retreats on both sides.

"I must be suicidal," Rigo's mother says, peering nervously down the trail. "Or maybe I have a death wish I don't know about."

"You're not going to die, Mama," Anthea says, chiding her. "I promise, we'll be careful."

"In your condition, you'd better be. If you slip and fall, you could be looking at a miscarriage."

"I'll take it slow." Anthea pats her stomach. "A little exercise is healthy—never hurt anyone. Our little Ibrahim will be just fine."

"I can't believe it." The old woman shakes her head. "*Que milagro!* I'm going to be a grandmother. *Imagínate.*"

"See," Rigo says. "If one miracle can happen, then why not another?"

His mother frowns, dubious. "About the only sickness that's going to be cured tonight is my constipation."

Rigo pulls the tab on the inflatable foam boogie board he picked up at a Boardwalk souvenir shop earlier in the day, watches it inflate at her feet. "What was it you said about having faith?"

His mother rolls her eyes, lifts an imploring gaze to heaven. "Now he's using my own words against me."

Rigo flashes a grin. "And all this time you thought I was ignoring you. Turning a deaf ear."

"Just because you're in business for yourself," she says, "doesn't give you free license to be a smart mouth. AD Ventures. What is that, anyway? Sounds like a travel agency."

"Architextural Design Ventures," Rigo says. He just filed the paperwork creating the company. "Varda came up with it."

"I just pray you don't end up like Beto. Spend the next ten years of your life in prison."

"Don't worry, Mama. It's legit." And it is. Mostly.

They have Dorit's collection of binders, filled with extinct plants and even a few insects. Preserved genetic material that can be used to create new ecotectural systems independent of RiboGen and the other big gengineering corps. As long as RiboGen, or BEAN, doesn't find out about the new company's softwire capability, Anthea's remote link to Tiresias, they'll be fine.

Rigo keeps replaying his final conversation with Dorit, thinks he finally understands what she was trying to tell him. After the ecocaust, it was the perfect time to create a better world. Instead, the surviving corps and governments chose to resurrect all of the old comfortable institutions. Rebuild the status quo on the ruins of the entrenched cultural and social edifices they were used to living in. Tiresias is the antithesis of that. That's why Whipplebaum wanted to control it. He knew the dangers posed by a totally new paradigm . . . the havoc it could wreak if it ever found its way into the world.

Too bad he didn't live to see his worst fears realized.

Still, Rigo plans to take it slow. A few test cases here and there, starting with his mother.

When the board is fully inflated he positions it on the ground. It's a little shorter than advertised, but should work.

They load her onto the boogie board. Feet at the front, pointing forward. Head at the back where it won't ram into anything.

"The last thing you need is a cracked skull," Rigo jokes. "You don't want to end up a bonehead like me."

She gives him a look. Ha ha. Very funny.

was here," she says, full of repressed

Not exactly the vote of confidence that Rigo, brother to the prodigal son, was hoping for. "Me, too, Mama. We could use some professional help with all this hard labor."

Anthea admonishes him with a sharp jab to the ribs.

"I didn't think I'd miss him so soon," the old woman continues. "But I do. It's only been five months. I can't imagine what it will be like after another nine and a half years."

"It won't be that long, Mama," Anthea says. "I'm sure he'll get an early release for good behavior."

"I just wish I could visit him, is all."

As part of his rehab, Beto's been assigned to a work clade that travels the dust belt, performing community service on assorted construction, farm, and bioremediation projects. No contact allowed.

"It's for the best, Mama. You said so yourself."

The old woman sighs. "I know. I wouldn't want it any other way. But it's not just the convicted who suffer. The family and friends they leave behind end up doing time, too. No one ever thinks of them."

"We're thinking of you now," Anthea says.

They secure her firmly in place with carbyne-fiber straps. Don't want her to slip off. "Okay" Rigo says, picking up her feet by the ankles, rickshaw-style, while Anthea takes up position in back. "Here we go."

And they're off, through the copse of umbrella palms, bouncing over rocks and exposed roots. The bacterial glow of their headbands is halo-bright under UV-reflective canopy. Elbows aside the blackness.

They cruise by the children's play area—with its swing,
slides, and jungle gyms—then the baseball diamonds
and soccer fields. The scent of grass clings to the air, a
permanent stain. It takes longer than Rigo remembered
to get to the shrine, the low fence plastered with photos
and the park-bench-style pews. A couple of tired votive
candles still sputter on the tables. The vases and bou-
quets of artificial flowers flicker in the light, wobble in
and out of existence under the vaulted ceiling of leaves.

Drenched with sweat, Rigo pulls up to the rough-
hewn altar, lowers his mother's legs gently to the barren ground.

"This is it?" she asks as they untie her from the
boogie board, tilt her to her feet so she can see the
Rorschach splotch of the Angel.

"Do you see her?" Anthea asks.

"Maybe the light is wrong," his mother says,
squinting.

"It doesn't matter," Rigo says. "You know how it
is with apparitions. You never can tell when they're
going to show up."

"Josué saw her," Anthea says. "Could be you just
have to be in the right frame of mind."

His mother nods. She's holding her rosary, has it
clutched in her good hand like a lifeline. "Now
what?" she says.

Together—Anthea taking her feet, Rigo her armpits—
they pick her up and ease her onto the table.

"Feel anything?" Rigo says after he catches his
breath.

"Just the bone spurs in my neck."

"Give it some time," Rigo says. "Close your eyes,
relax. We're going to sit down for a few minutes."

They go to one of the pews, take a seat. Rigo puts a hand on Anthea's leg and she takes it, twines her fingers in his. It's a nice night. Perfect. Things have been back to normal between them since RiboGen forced his reclade back to San Jose. A trade-off he doesn't regret for a moment, even though he's no longer soft-wired and has lost all contact with Tiresias.

After a moment, Anthea reaches into a pocket in her light sweater and takes out the box with the Day of the Dead doll. "Time to lay some old bones to rest." She stands, goes over to one of the altar tables and sets the box among the flowers, candles, and pictures memorializing the dead.

Rigo comes up beside her. "Are you sure, *mami?*"

Anthea nods. "I don't need her anymore. And I'm pretty sure she doesn't need me."

When Anthea opens the lid for one last look at the doll, Rigo swears he can hear music coming from the saxophone. Not sad but happy. He returns the up-tempo grin of the skeleton, then follows Anthea back to the pew.

"What's the status of the remote link?" Anthea asks when they're seated again.

"Thumbs up and running," Varda says.

In other words, all systems go. Rigo turns to Anthea. "How does it feel to be an angel, *mami?*"

"Fine, *papi.* I just hope your mom can say the same."

At first Rigo worried that the molectric circuitry he doped Anthea with prior to his retroclade might cause unforeseen friction between them. But the soft-wire connection is just like Varda said—clade-independent. After three months, there have been no adverse effects. Thanks to the antidote Dorit gave Rigo on Tiresias for the Hong Kong slave-pherion, Anthea has even started putting on weight. Filling out nice. Some of that's the pregnancy, but not all.

"Any word on Ibrahim?" he says.

"Nothing yet."

A week ago, the ICLU raided all known RiboGen research facilities around the world. A coordinated assault that freed thousands of indentured test subjects. Ibrahim hasn't turned up yet, but they keep hoping.

"You want me to online Doug?" Anthea asks. "See if it's mined anything new?"

"Maybe later," Rigo tells her. "Right now, I'm not really in the mood for Ogden Nash." The IA's latest fixation. "How are you feeling about Global Upreach?" he says. "You okay?"

Anthea sighs. "I'll miss it," she admits, "working one-on-one with kids." Word finally came down that the review board had decided against her reinstatement, despite positive testimony from Tissa and her co-workers. "I guess it was time to move on," she says philosophically. "Help people another way."

Rigo nods, lets it go at that. She's not bitter. Neither is he for the way RiboGen treated him. For a while, he was seriously pissed at Dorit. Blamed her for what happened to Rana, Antonio, Luis, TomE, and Naguib, until he found out through Varda that she wasn't the only one involved in the breakup of Tiresias. Did her best to delay the explosive moment long enough so he and his team could get clear. Thanks to Whipplebaum, shit happened faster than planned. It wasn't Dorit's fault. The colonists couldn't wait any longer. They had to make their break when they did or risk losing any shot at freedom.

"How's little Ibrahim?" he says.

Anthea moves his hand to the swell of her belly. "You tell me, *papi*."

"Feels good." Content, Rigo lets his hand rest there, rising and falling with each breath she takes.

"There's something you should know," Anthea says, turning her attention to the Angel Tree table.

"Another confession?" It's become a joke between them, a game. Something to laugh about.

"This is the last one," she promises.

"Right." Rigo doesn't believe it, but at least she's coming clean. For a while, she was spilling her guts every few minutes. Confessions have let up in the last month. Now she only gets the urge to unburden herself every couple of days. "Let's hear it."

"I was never here as a kid. The old woman I told you about, who was paralyzed and cured. That never happened."

Rigo looks around. "Then what's with all the candles and flowers? The pictures of people?"

"Everything else was true. There really was a guy who claimed he saw an angel and was supposedly cured of cancer. I guess I just wanted to make the story more real for Josué. Possible. Not something that had happened light-years in the past, to people who haven't been alive for ages."

Like in the Bible, Rigo thinks. "Maybe you wanted to make it more real for you, too," he says. "Something you could believe in. That was within reach."

"Maybe."

A snore rumbles through the air. Loud as thunder.

Rigo gets up and, Anthea at his side, goes to check on his mother. She's dozed off, fallen asleep under the dome of stars visible between leafy gaps in the umbrella palms.

"Maybe there was another remote link back then that no one knows about or can explain," Rigo says. "Like the Tiresias link."

Anthea smiles, traces the lines of grain in the wood with a fingertip. "Anything's possible, *papi*. All you have to do is believe."

And trust, he thinks. Even if it's only in himself.

ACKNOWLEDGMENTS

Special thanks to:

Matt Bialer, agent extraordinaire, for his longtime patience and support. Juliet Ulman, for her enthusiasm, attention to detail, and keen editorial insight. Charles N. Brown, for good company, good advice, and abundant food for thought. Gary Shockley, literary debugger. Tom Rogers, ad hoc philosopher and critic at large. Scott Whitfield, physicist and explorer. And finally, all of the attendees of the Nadacon and Rockaway workshops whose early comments proved invaluable.

ABOUT THE AUTHOR

MARK BUDZ lives with his wife in the Santa Cruz Mountains of northern California. *Clade* is his first novel.

Don't miss the next exciting

book from Mark Budz set in

this same universe

CRACHE

Coming from Bantam Spectra

in fall 2004